SHE SLID HER HAND BENEATH HIS SHIRT.

The warmth of his skin against hers was delightful. She could feel the heavy beat of his heart, the rigid muscles of his chest against her hands. She felt nearly undone when Rolfe pulled her closer into his arms, his mouth moving hungrily over hers.

This, she thought as his mouth possessed hers, was what all those stories about the brave knight-errant who carried the distressed maiden off on his white horse were all about. But when she felt Rolfe's hand brush against the side of her breast, a shock wave filled her very soul, ending all thoughts. Cassia threw back her head, unaware that Rolfe had unfastened the tiny buttons of her shirt. And as his hand closed over her bare breast, Cassia reached a wonderful peak of excitement she never knew was possible. . . .

D0880441

☆ TOPAZ

SEARING ROMANCES

☐ **TEMPTING FATE by Jaclyn Reding.** Beautiful, flame-haired Mara Despenser hated the English under Oliver Cromwell, and she vowed to avenge Ireland and become mistress of Kulhaven Castle again. She would lure the castle's new master, the infamous Hadrian Ross, the bastard Earl of St. Aubyn, into marriage. But even with her lies and lust, Mara was not prepared to find herself wed to a man whose iron will was matched by his irresistible good looks.   (405587—$4.99)

☐ **SPRING'S FURY by Denise Domning.** Nicola of Ashby swore to kill Gilliam Fitz-Henry—murderer of her father, destroyer of her home—the man who would wed her in a forced match. Amid treachery and tragedy, rival knights and the pain of past wounds, Gilliam knew he must win Nicola's respect. Then, with kisses and hot caresses, he intended to win her heart.   (405218—$4.99)

☐ **PIRATE'S ROSE by Janet Lynnford.** The Rozalinde Cavendish, independent daughter of England's richest merchant, was taking an impetuous moonlit walk along the turbulent shore when she encountered Lord Christopher Howard, a legendary pirate. Carried aboard his ship, she entered his storm-tossed world and became intimate with his troubled soul. Could their passion burn away the veil shrouding Christopher's secret past and hidden agenda?   (405978—$4.99)

☐ **DIAMOND IN DISGUISE by Elizabeth Hewitt.** Isobel Leyland knew better than to fall in love with the handsome stranger from America, Adrian Renville. Despite his rugged good looks and his powerful animal magnetism, he was socially inept compared to the polished dandies of English aristocratic society—and a citizen of England's enemy in the War of 1812. How could she trust this man whom she suspected of playing the boor in a mocking masquerade?   (405641—$4.99)

*Prices slightly higher in Canada

Buy them at your local bookstore or use this convenient coupon for ordering.

PENGUIN USA
P.O. Box 999 — Dept. #17109
Bergenfield, New Jersey 07621

Please send me the books I have checked above.
I am enclosing $_____ (please add $2.00 to cover postage and handling). Send check or money order (no cash or C.O.D.'s) or charge by Mastercard or VISA (with a $15.00 minimum). Prices and numbers are subject to change without notice.

Card #_____ Exp. Date _____
Signature_____
Name_____
Address_____
City _____ State _____ Zip Code _____

For faster service when ordering by credit card call **1-800-253-6476**

Allow a minimum of 4-6 weeks for delivery. This offer is subject to change without notice.

Chasing Dreams

by

Jaclyn Reding

We are such stuff as dreams are made on,
and our little life is rounded with a sleep.
—WILLIAM SHAKESPEARE

A TOPAZ BOOK

TOPAZ
Published by the Penguin Group
Penguin Books USA Inc., 375 Hudson Street,
New York, New York 10014, U.S.A.
Penguin Books Ltd, 27 Wrights Lane,
London W8 5TZ, England
Penguin Books Australia Ltd, Ringwood,
Victoria, Australia
Penguin Books Canada Ltd, 10 Alcorn Avenue,
Toronto, Ontario, Canada M4V 3B2
Penguin Books (N.Z.) Ltd, 182–190 Wairau Road,
Auckland 10, New Zealand

Penguin Books Ltd, Registered Offices:
Harmondsworth, Middlesex, England

First published by Topaz, an imprint of Dutton Signet,
a division of Penguin Books USA Inc.

First Printing, October, 1995
10 9 8 7 6 5 4 3 2 1

Copyright © Jaclyn Reding, 1995
All rights reserved
Topaz Man photo © Charles William Bush

 REGISTERED TRADEMARK—MARCA REGISTRADA

Printed in the United States of America

Without limiting the rights under copyright reserved above, no part of this
publication may be reproduced, stored in or introduced into a retrieval sys-
tem, or transmitted, in any form, or by any means (electronic, mechanical,
photocopying, recording, or otherwise), without the prior written permission
of both the copyright owner and the above publisher of this book.

BOOKS ARE AVAILABLE AT QUANTITY DISCOUNTS WHEN USED TO PROMOTE
PRODUCTS OR SERVICES. FOR INFORMATION PLEASE WRITE TO PREMIUM MAR-
KETING DIVISION, PENGUIN BOOKS USA INC., 375 HUDSON STREET, NEW YORK,
NEW YORK 10014.

If you purchased this book without a cover you should be aware that this
book is stolen property. It was reported as "unsold and destroyed" to the
publisher and neither the author nor the publisher has received any payment
for this "stripped book."

There are those special people in this world who give and give without taking, who offer without asking for much in return.

I dedicate this book to the best of them.

She is always there when I need her, willing to listen to my troubles, and always ready with her support. She's my biggest fan, my staunchest defender, the best babysitter and Grandma my son, Joshua, will ever have. She's my friend, my Friday night bingo partner, but most of all, she's my mother; Patricia Adamowicz, woman extraordinare.

This one is for you, Mom, with love.

Prologue

Cassia's eyes slowly fluttered open.

The room was dark and shadowed, lit only by a faint fire burning in the blackened stone hearth. Tiny bits of shattered glass littered the area around her. A chair lay on its side at her feet, one of its slender, spiral-turned legs snapped and splintered. The flickering flames had set eerie shapes dancing across the paneled walls that surrounded her, adding to the already hellish atmosphere of the room.

Cassia did not move, at least not at first, for her uncertainty at finding herself here, and not in her bedchamber where she'd expected, kept her still. She lay on her side along the floor, the heavy legs of a large standing cabinet stiff against her backbone. It took several moments for her eyes to properly adjust and she thought she must be dreaming, for she could not immediately remember where she was or how she'd even gotten here.

She was in her father's study, his private domain, where he spent most every waking hour of most every day poring over the piles of documents he brought home from his offices at Westminster. His cluttered burr-walnut desk, decorated with pear drop handles he'd had specially made, stood across the room from her. The chair behind it was thankfully empty.

Cassia's gaze moved about the room, scanning the

walls, paneled in dark gleaming walnut, displaying his personal memorabilia and various trophies gathered through the years. The wall behind his desk was lined floor-to-ceiling with burr-walnut cases, which were filled with his books, hundreds dated as far back as the previous century, for acquiring old and rare books was a hobby to which he devoted a great deal of time.

And then, suddenly, she saw him.

He was sprawled on his back about ten feet from her, arms splayed widely at his sides. His legs were hidden behind a large iron-banded chest he used for storing his correspondence—he never threw anything away—and she wouldn't have seen him at all if not for the carved silver-and-bone knife handle that jutted out at an odd angle from the side of his neck.

The knife was the first thing Cassia noticed when she saw him, and the sight of it set her heart to frightened pounding. She did not move. She lay there for several silent moments, her cheek resting on the thick pile of the Turkish carpet. She watched as the fire played upon the knife, the aged silver glimmering in the low firelight, as her thoughts began drifting back to earlier that evening.

He had brought her to the study not long after they'd returned home from the Mantons' ball, dragging her by her arm along the upstairs corridor as he had so many times before. Cassia remembered she had warned herself to remain calm, that it would be far worse if she tried to struggle. It was always worse when she struggled. She thought fleetingly, as he had pushed her into the room, slamming the door shut behind them, that perhaps he would just yell at her this time, tell her how ungrateful she was and be done with it.

She had been mistaken.

Cassia licked at the corner of her mouth where his

faceted onyx ring had sliced into her lower lip. She was surprised he'd struck her in the face this time, for he normally chose places that would be readily concealed from outside eyes, so no one would see, no one would question, no one would ever know the truth.

But this time had been different, this beating worse than most. She remembered seeing his face as he had raised his polished ebony walking stick with the ivory-knobbed top, ready to hit her. A look of madness had masked his features as he had brought that stick down on her, striking her in the ribs. She had felt so helpless as she'd stood there, buckled over, gasping for breath, and could but watch, frozen, as he had drawn back his fist, preparing to strike her again.

Her father hit her on the side of her face and the force of that blow had sent her reeling across the room. Cassia lay now where she had fallen after that last telling blow, before the welcome unconsciousness had come to claim her. She wasn't certain what she'd hit her head against—perhaps the tall burled fruit-wood case clock with its golden pointed finials, the one that her mother had brought back with them from France. Whatever it was, she had hit it hard, and whatever had happened afterward was lost to her, for her conscious mind had been instantly smothered by the blackness of oblivion.

Sweet oblivion.

Cassia could remember one other occasion when her father had beaten her so badly she'd lost consciousness. She remembered it well, as if it had been only yesterday, for it wasn't the sort of thing one was likely to forget.

It had been the first time he had brought her to his study, in the darkest hours of the night, months earlier, not long after her mother had died. He had come to her bedchamber that night the same as he always did, smelling of the brandy bottle and ranting at her like some sort of crazed lunatic from Bedlam. It had been Cassia's first inkling of what her mother's life had been like and she remembered, for a short time, actually being grateful that her mother was dead. She'd even wished she could join her.

How furious her father had been with her that night. Strangely, now, Cassia couldn't recall why. She could only remember him standing there, cataloging her shortcomings, calling her by her mother's name, and then, later, calling her by other names, vulgar names, the sort of names that had been whispered about her mother behind the decorated fans of the court gossips when she'd been alive.

After he had beaten her senseless that first time, he had left Cassia lying on the floor in his study, or so her maid, Winifred, had told her later. He'd locked himself away in his bedchamber and had passed the remainder of the night drinking himself into a similar unconscious state as if to make himself forget what he'd done to her, his only daughter.

Cassia had awakened some time later to find herself in her own bedchamber, lying on her bed, not knowing how she'd gotten there or even who had brought her. The coverlet had been pulled over her and soft pillows had cradled her head as if to say, except for the telltale bruises that colored her ribs and upper arms, that none of it had ever happened.

But not this time.

This time there was no bed, there were no soft pillows to cradle her head. There was only the hard floor beneath her and her father's body lying motionless across from her.

What had happened after she'd fallen? Who had taken that ancient heirloom quillon dagger, which usually hung among his other trophies on the wall, just beneath the stuffed and mounted stag's head with its glassy black eyes staring pitifully down at her? Who had plunged that knife into his body, leaving him lying there while his lifeblood spread across the carpet?

Had she snatched that knife from its place on the wall, sinking it into his body? Surely she would know if she had committed such an act. Surely some memory of it would remain. Shouldn't she recall the anger, the madness she must have felt to commit such violence? Shouldn't she remember the look of horror on his face as she came at him, ready to kill him, her own father?

Cassia suddenly wondered how much time had passed, how long she had been lying there on the floor beside his body. Had it been hours, or only minutes? Would there be some chance of saving his life? She hesitated. Did she really want to?

She started to turn her head, sucking in her breath at the pain that cut through the side of her face. She tried to move her jaw to see if it was broken, wincing against the soreness that came with the slightest movement. Remarkably, her bones still seemed intact, and after a short while, she finally managed to turn her head.

The case clock, which it was now obvious had been the object she'd fallen against, stood broken behind her. Its hands were frozen at ten minutes after ten, the precise moment she'd slammed into it, shattering the glass that covered its brass and silver face. Cassia tried to lever herself up from the floor, but every muscle in her body seemed to tighten in protest. She started to crawl on her forearms to where her father's body lay.

His eyes were staring blankly at the carved fretwork ceiling when Cassia finally reached him, frozen, it seemed, on the pattern cut there. Strange, she thought, how they looked so like the eyes in the stag's head hanging on the wall above him. It was then that Cassia felt her father's blood, the wet stickiness of it soaking the rug beneath her hands. She thought to herself that she should be screaming like a madwoman by now, shaking in fear of the grisly scene that lay before her eyes. Instead, she simply stared. She wondered at how even the sight of him lying there with that knife sticking out from the side of his neck, his blood covering her hands and soaking through her gown, did not seem to affect her as it should.

Cassia closed her eyes. Perhaps there was something truly wrong inside her, rendering her incapable of feeling anything for others. But there had been a time, so long ago, when she knew she had felt something. She had felt, she had laughed, she had even danced beneath the blossoming branches of the cherry trees in springtime, weaving chains of fragrant fuchsia flowers through her hair with her childhood friend Cordelia.

How long ago that had been, when they'd been away in France among the laughter and gaiety of the Sun King's court, gone from England and all the fighting, gone from her father, the Right Honorable Halifax Montefort, third Marquess of Seagrave.

As a child, Cassia had never known her father, in fact, had only heard of him through her mother, who had taken Cassia bag and baggage, leaving England and her husband on the eve of the bloody civil wars. That was nearly two decades before, when Cassia hadn't yet seen three summers.

Cassia hadn't seen her father during the years that followed. She'd rarely thought of him unless her mother had spoken of him, until the day she'd first set eyes upon him just four years ago in her eighteenth year.

It had been early summer, near the end of May, but the day had been ominously chilly. He had been waiting for them on the dock at Dover, arms crossed over his chest, when Cassia and her mother had come back to London with the newly crowned King Charles II. His only words had been "Good day, Judith," to his wife, and a nod in Cassia's direction before he'd turned and started for the coach, leaving them to follow behind him.

It was then that life had first changed for Cassia, when her mother had still been alive, before she'd died in childbed nearly six months ago. It was then Cassia had begun to learn who her father truly was.

Not that she hadn't already been told what a monster he was, this cruel and vicious man her mother had been forced as a young girl to marry. All the time they had been in France, far from England's shores, Cassia's mother had used the time to prepare her daughter for their inevitable return. She had filled Cassia's head with her hatred for the man she called her husband, telling her how he—"the Marquess," she would call him, never "Halifax" or "Seagrave" or even "My Lord"—had purchased her when she'd been sixteen, her head full of fairy tales and dreams. He had bought her outright for the amount of her dower, she had said, as if she had been some sort of finely blooded brood mare up for bid on the auction block.

Cassia could remember thinking how horrible her father must be for condemning her mother to a life sentence with him, this man she could barely tolerate looking at or speaking of without rancor in her voice. Their marriage had prevented her mother from wedding the man she truly loved, a man she called "dearest Edmund" with a smile in her eyes. It was the only time her mother had ever really smiled, for otherwise her eyes had been dark with the deep animosity, the fierce hatred she harbored for her husband, Cassia's father.

It was that same hatred that caused Cassia to resolve at the tender age of twelve never to allow herself to wed any man whom she did not already love, and never to wed a man like her father.

But as Cassia looked down at her father now, she could only think of how peaceful he looked, how the harsh lines that always made his face look so severe were gone. He must have been quite handsome as a young man, his full hair dark, his features classic and aristocratic. Suddenly he no longer looked like the monster she'd always believed him. He no longer inspired the fear in her he had by simply being in the same room. Now, lying there as he was, his body so still, his face frighteningly pale, he looked just like any other man.

Cassia lifted her hand and placed it gently atop his chest. The blood on her hand left a distinct mark on the starched white cambric of his shirt. She couldn't detect even the slightest rise, the smallest beating of his heart beneath her palm. It didn't surprise her; it was simply a confirmation of what she'd already known.

Cassia reached forward and carefully lowered the lids on his unseeing eyes. As she pulled her hand back, she felt the ever-present bulge of the gold-enameled watch he wore in the small pocket at the front of his waistcoat. She tugged at the red silk ribbon he'd taken to tying about it to keep from having it snatched by a footpad in the street. The watch slid slowly from inside. She lifted it up, running her fingertip over the design engraved upon it, a small sprig of an unknown flower. She turned it over. The curving hands upon it showed the hour at half past ten.

Twenty minutes. Twenty minutes had passed for

which she had no memory. Twenty minutes in which a man, her father, had been killed by someone—whom, she did not know, perhaps even herself. Cassia tried to think back, to remember what had happened in that short space of time, but all she found was emptiness. She started to push the watch back in its place, wanting it to appear as if nothing had been disturbed—which was silly, of course, for her hand had left a definite bloody print on his shirtfront—when she heard a key rattling in the lock.

The door burst open a moment later.

"I tell you, Mr. Clydesworthe, something is wrong. Very wrong. I heard him yelling, screaming at her, calling her such horrible names you'd never believe, and then there was a loud crashing noise, like glass shattering, and now nothing, no sound for so long and—"

Cassia looked up from her father's body.

The maid Lynette and the butler Clydesworthe froze the instant they saw her kneeling beside him, the knife sticking out from his neck, the room around them in disarray, her hands and gown stained red from his blood.

Lynette raised a hand to her mouth to stifle her frightened scream.

Clydesworthe made the sign of the cross before himself, saying softly, "Dear Lord above, she's finally killed him."

Chapter One

"Lord Ravenscroft has arrived, Your Majesty."

King Charles II turned from his chess game, immediately dismissing the overdressed courtier sitting across from him—who was still a bit flustered at having been given the honor of playing him—with a swift wave of his jeweled hand.

"Show him in," he said to the waiting footman, his voice deep. He watched silently while the man bowed and left the room.

The king was glad for the interruption for it was an interruption he'd been anticipating since waking, as he did each morning, at precisely 5 A.M. He'd long since grown tired of the chess game, his choice of an opponent having proved a bad one. The man lacked skill or even rudimentary knowledge of the game, it seemed, and had spent the better part of the past two hours complimenting the king on everything from his "fine and fashionable suit of clothes" to his "mastery of the game," all of which, Charles was well aware, had been uttered in a determined effort to gain a more favorable position at court. A determined, but failing effort it was.

How he hated such hypocrisy, the king thought, twisting the end of his mustache between his thumb and forefinger, a gesture he performed out of habit. Living amid such falseness as he did each day, Charles had begun to wonder if there existed a man within the whole of England besides himself who still had the backbone to simply speak his mind.

The king had his assurance of at least one other a moment later as the man he'd been waiting for strode into the room.

His well-practiced expression of ennui vanished the moment Charles stood and started toward the door. A wide grin, the one reserved more for his closest acquaintances, the one that caused the fair ladies of the court to swoon and flutter their fans the moment they saw it, lifted one corner of the king's mouth as his guest came forward and bowed before him.

"Rolfe, my dear friend, it is good to see you again. How long has it been? Six months? A year? Regardless, it has been too long between visits, much too long. I am pleased you were able to travel to London so swiftly."

"I am at your service, as always, Your Majesty."

Rolfe Brodrigan, Viscount Blackwood, and more recently titled Earl of Ravenscroft, rose to his full six feet and two inches, one of only a handful of men who could truly stare his markedly tall sovereign in his eyes without benefit of the fashionable elevated heel.

Here was a man uninterested in pretense, Charles thought assuredly as he shook Rolfe's hand. This man made no attempt at currying favor like the other members of the court did. He had no need to. Rolfe was a man who was sure of himself, a man who saw no need to dress himself up in fine satins and silks in order to give the impression of importance. His clothing was simple, his black hair wind-blown, jackboots spattered with mud from his ride, and he tucked his black, wide-brimmed hat under one arm, coming straight to the point.

"I left Sussex as soon as I was able, Your Majesty. Your summons indicated it was urgent."

"Yes, it is." Charles motioned toward a nearby pair of matching armchairs upholstered in royal blue cut-velvet which faced the windows.

Whitehall Palace was by far the largest of the numerous royal residences, situated on twenty-three acres along the northern banks of the muddy-watered River Thames. In truth, it was more a rambling village than a palace, made up of a multitude of wandering galleries, gates, and gardens all running into one another. The King's Drawing Room, to where Rolfe had been shown, was made cozy by an inviting hearth fire, giving a commanding view of the river through its wall of ceiling-high mullioned windows. Outside, the royal gardeners were at work on the Pall Mall court lawn along the river's edge.

The king took up one of his beloved brown and white spaniels, stroking it gently behind its furry ears. Three more of the creatures vied for attention at his feet, yapping and nipping at the wide velvet bows that decorated his shoes.

"Brandy?" Charles asked. He glanced at one of the uniformed menservants hovering nearby, who quickly bowed and went off to the drinks table when Rolfe nodded.

The king, Rolfe noticed, was dressed, as always, to the edge of extravagance, though not for any ostentatious reason. Where he'd spent the better years of his youth in impoverished exile, wearing threadbare coats and stiff woolen breeches, Charles now gloried in his restoration to the English throne. He reveled in rich velvets and golden gimp and galloon, curling his hair in the profuse French *peryke* style that covered his shoulders like a black bushy cape. It was a style most every man at court went through pains and a vast amount of guineas to imitate.

By contrast, Rolfe's hair was cut moderately to the collar, a simple style he'd assumed during the wars and had retained afterward. He took up the Venetian cut crystal goblet brought to him and quickly swallowed down the fine French brandy. The liquid burned along his throat to settle warm and deep in the pit of his stomach, but he welcomed the feeling, for he had ridden hard and fast across the wild English countryside soon after he'd received the king's summons the previous day. He returned the empty glass to the waiting silver salver and motioned for another, savoring this second glass a bit longer.

"How goes it in Sussex?" the king asked, settling back in his chair.

"Quite well, actually. The improvements are nearly finished on the eastern wing and I'm told the house should be fully habitable come spring."

"I was most sad when I returned to England and saw what had become of Ravenwood."

Rolfe nodded. "Wars do tend to leave destruction in their wake. The long period of time the house stood damaged and vacant wasn't much of a help, either. I actually found an oak tree growing in what used to be the ladies's morning parlor. I believe the renovations will be a decided improvement on the estate. We have stayed as close to the original design as was possible, adding modern conveniences, of course, wherever needed. By spring, I would say that Ravenwood should be well on its way back to its former glory."

Charles smiled. "It pleases me very much to hear that, Rolfe. As you know, Ravenwood was always one of my father's favorite places to visit. He used to love the seclusion of it, the quiet peace of the wood along the eastern fringes of the estate. He was an avid birder and he found some of the most interesting specimens there. He wrote about them, describing their every detail in a journal he kept. You can see the tiny creatures so clearly in your mind's eye when you read his record. Perhaps you would like to have his journal to keep at Ravenwood?"

"I would be most honored, Your Majesty."

Charles stared off, his voice softening. "My father used to say that Ravenwood was as close to heaven as was possible for a man to get on earth. It was for that reason I wanted you to have it when I gave you the Ravenscroft title. I knew you of all people would realize the estate's worth."

"That I do, Your Majesty."

"I miss him so very much, my father." Charles snapped out of his momentary melancholia then, sitting more upright in his chair. "But this is not the reason for my summoning you here today. There are other, pressing matters we must discuss. Matters of grave importance. As you may have already guessed, I have called you here because I wish for you to take on another assignment for me."

The statement came as no surprise to Rolfe. "Yes, Your Majesty."

"Rolfe, I have selected you for this particular assignment for several reasons. First of all, after risking your life to see me restored to the throne, you have served me faithfully and without error on every task I have called you to. You never question my requests and I have come to rely on you for certain things, as I know I can count on you to follow my wishes implicitly—and," he added, "discreetly."

Charles paused for a moment to take a sip of his brandy, the fine Brussels lace on his shirt cuff barely missing the glass as it caressed his jeweled knuckles.

"Second, since being bestowed with the Ravenscroft title nearly a year ago, you have been keeping to the estate, away from court, and thus are not privy to the recent goings-on here."

Rolfe noticed that Charles had tactfully neglected to elaborate on the events which had transpired nearly a year before that had brought on his self-imposed exile to Ravenwood, and that had caused him to be known thereafter as the Exiled Earl among White-hall's gossip-loving courtiers. He wondered, hopefully, if perhaps the whole episode had been forgotten, and then thought it more likely that it had instead been aggrandized to more provocative proportions. Such was the way of court society.

The king set the dog with the others on the floor and sat back in his chair, resting his chin on his fingers. He watched Rolfe carefully as he framed his next question. "Tell me, Rolfe, have you ever before heard of the Montefort family?"

Rolfe searched his memory over another sip of his brandy. "Halifax Montefort. A marquess, I believe."

Charles smiled. "Very good. The Marquess of Sea-grave, to be precise, although more recently he is known as the *late* Marquess of Seagrave. He was found murdered over a fortnight ago."

"Unfortunate. Has the murderer been found?"

"His daughter, a maid of honor in the queen's service, seems the primary suspect, and only through my intervention has she not been arrested and charged."

The king stood and walked over to the tall windows to peer out at the river traffic. The hour was yet early, not quite nine o'clock, and outside, the morning fog still clung tenaciously to the river's edge, giving only brief glimpses of the tiltboats and barges floating slowly downstream on their daily journeys to and from the city.

Rolfe remained silent while the king contemplated his next words.

"This leads me to the purpose for your sojourn here to the city." Charles turned. "I wish to place you as guard to the young lady until sufficient proof of her guilt or innocence of the crime can be discovered."

Rolfe looked at him. "I would guess, then, that you do not believe the girl responsible for the crime?"

Charles waved his hand through the air as if shooing away an imaginary fly. "Whether she is guilty or innocent is of no matter to me. I simply wish to make certain that the girl is not charged with a crime she did not truly commit. You know how things of this nature can be. The members of my court are bored. A noted nobleman is found murdered. Rumors begin to circulate through the galleries. They somehow hear that Lady Cassia was there when the crime was discovered and they have her deemed guilty before the body has yet grown cold. The possibility of her being innocent never crosses their minds, for, you see, that would not make for interesting parlor gossip."

Charles's disgust for that aspect of his court was evident, a feeling Rolfe, from personal experience, tended to share. Still, he remained curious. "If you don't mind my asking, Your Majesty, why has this case attracted your attention?"

"I do not wish to see the girl mistreated. Lady Cassia is . . ." Charles paused a moment, his expression softening, "most important to me."

Rolfe needed no further explanation. The king's amorous affiliations within the court were both numerous and well-known. This Lady Cassia Montefort was quite obviously just one of the great number of the king's mistresses, a constantly growing collection known laughingly around Whitehall as "the Cattle."

Thus the true and not-so-easily hidden purpose for his intervention on her behalf.

"So you wish for me to investigate and discover who is truly responsible for the murder?"

"Indirectly, yes. You see, I also want Cassia removed from court for a while. Without her here as a reminder of it all, the gossip will die down and this whole dirty episode will soon blow over. I am assigning you as guard to watch over her until such time as I feel it is safe for her to return to court. Make no mistake, though, the situation is quite serious. I am placing her life in your hands, Rolfe. The Montefort family seat is located in Cambridgeshire. I wish for you to take her there and keep her under your watchful eye until such time as I send word that it is safe for her to return to London. I realize this will prevent you from personally overseeing the work at Ravenwood, but I'm hoping it will not be for all that long. Several weeks at the most."

It wouldn't have mattered to Rolfe if the task would have taken a year. He had vowed himself in service to the king and when he was given an assignment, any assignment, it was his duty to see it through, no matter the inconveniences. "You believe Lady Cassia's life to be in danger, then, Your Majesty?"

"I have learned through experience never to discount anything. If there exists even the smallest possibility that Lady Cassia's life could be in danger, I wish to protect her. I know of no other man I would trust with the task. Your dedication to duty is unquestionable. Your honor is irrefutable. I have no doubt that you would risk your own life to save hers. I cannot say the same for others. In the meantime, I would also like you to make inquiries—discreet inquiries—through your acquaintanceship here in London to see if you can discover whether or not Cassia did, in fact, commit the crime."

Charles turned and stared at Rolfe, his eyes intent. "And if you find out that Lady Cassia is indeed guilty, I would that you bring your information to me, and me alone."

And there, in a tidy little package, lay his true intentions.

Rolfe suddenly realized that Charles did not particularly care if the crime was ever solved, nor did he care if this Lady Cassia Montefort had actually committed the murder. Indeed, it seemed as if he, as well as the other noble members of the court, already believed her guilty of the crime. Why else would he want this woman—a woman who was his mistress, no less—out of the city and thus out of his bed?

The king did not care if justice was served. He just wanted to make certain his mistress did not have to face it.

And it would be Rolfe's duty to see that he succeeded in that enterprise.

"Pray, where might I find the fair Lady Cassia?"

Chapter Two

Rolfe did not immediately go to where the king had told him he would find Lady Cassia, at Seagrave House, the Montefort family house in town situated near the elm-shaded walkways of Piccadilly. First he needed more information than he'd been able to glean from Charles through gentle prodding, more detail about who Lady Cassia Montefort, suspected murderess and mistress to the king, was.

Quite simply, he wanted to find out just what it was he was getting himself into.

It was not that he would refuse Charles's request should he find this assignment more than just a matter of simply transporting the lady from London to the country and keeping her secluded there while he set his contemporaries in search of the truth. Rolfe had long ago pledged himself in service to his king, and it was a pledge from which he would never remove himself. Without question. But being a man experienced as he was in years of the art of investigation during the recent civil wars, Rolfe also realized there was always more to any situation than first met the eyes.

Where had Lady Cassia come from? What sort of person was she? With whom—other than the king, obviously—did she associate? And why would it be so readily accepted within the court of Whitehall that she, a refined young lady of gentle breeding, could be capable of such a dastardly act?

Rolfe knew he would need all this and much more before he could even begin to search out the truth, and since his time in London was limited to finding the lady and removing her to the country, he knew precisely where and to whom to go in order to find it.

The morning sun was high over the steeply pitched rooftops in the eastern end of the city by the time the tiltboat he'd hired to take him down the Thames from Westminster to London glided toward the landing at Salisbury Stairs. Rolfe tossed a shilling to the boatman, a hunchbacked sort who muttered his thanks out of a toothless mouth, and started directly for the square and the town home of his friend Dante Tremaine.

Rolfe and Dante had known each other since their days at Oxford, and with their other friend, Hadrian Ross, they had been through many a scrape together. Through hardship and war, danger and fighting, they were as close as kin, as like as brothers. No matter the distance or length of time that managed to separate them, they remained connected. Rolfe trusted none more than those two.

And, with this assignment, he knew he would somehow need that trust.

Rolfe tipped his hat in greeting to a passerby as he approached the front door of the timber-framed house at the end of the narrow lane. He wondered, noting the shutters that were closed over a number of the small upstairs windows, if Dante was in residence. After several minutes of insistent pounding, he had nearly decided to leave when the butler, a tall and slender man named Chilton who reminded Rolfe of the strict schoolmaster they'd had as young men at

Oxford, finally answered the door. He looked startled to see Rolfe standing there.

"Lord Blackwood, good morning. I was not made aware that Lord Morgan would be expecting you at this hour."

Rolfe tossed him his hat, draping his cloak over the man's bony right shoulder as he pushed his way into the entrance hall. "Dante wasn't expecting me, and it has been Lord Ravenscroft for nearly a year now, Chilton. Didn't Dante tell you? His Majesty saw fit to make me an earl."

Before the butler could even begin to congratulate him, Rolfe had bounded up the stairs two at a time and was already on the second-floor landing.

"Wait! Lord Blackwood—I mean, Lord Ravenscroft, Lord Morgan is yet abed!"

His warning, though well meant, was too late in coming. Rolfe had already thrown open the door to the bedchamber at the end of the dark and overly furnished hall and was crossing through the room to the draped windows, nearly stumbling over something—a discarded boot?—in the process.

"Dante, you calf-lolly, it's daylight out. I know you keep city hours here, but it's long past time you got your sorry arse out of bed."

Rolfe whipped the heavy velvet drapery open wide and bright morning sunlight came pouring in from outside.

A scream immediately sounded from the vicinity of the high poster bed behind him, a very female scream, followed directly after by a muffled male curse.

"Damnation, Rolfe, what in perdition are you doing here?"

Dante Tremaine was lying quite naked atop the mattress on his carved poster bed, a heavy walnut concoction topped by oppressive-looking carved hawk's heads with beady yellow-jeweled eyes. The burgundy velvet bedcovering was rumpled and hanging over the edge of the mattress. A wide assortment of clothing was strewn about the floor, complete with one black silk stocking that had been draped around the neck of a tabletop statuette of Aphrodite. The room, Rolfe decided, taking in its every detail, exuded sex and its aftermath. He soon saw the reason why.

Beside Dante on the bed sat a very lovely and rumpled young woman. She was clutching the bedclothes to her chin and looking at Rolfe as if he were a vision of the devil himself.

Rolfe grinned. "Ah, good morning, Portia—or should I say, Lady Winchester? That is the name of the poor fellow you finally settled upon, isn't it? I always knew at the very least you'd hook yourself an earl. Anything smaller would have only resulted in your throwing the poor minnow back in and offering more bait for a bigger fish."

The striking young blonde narrowed her eyes at him fiercely. "Well, if it isn't the Exiled Earl finally come out from his rustic cave. Have you decided you'd kept yourself in hiding long enough, my lord?"

"That will do, Portia," Dante broke in, his tone low with warning.

Rolfe sallied back at her gibe. "Actually, Portia, I decided it was safe for me to come back out among the living. I mean, now that you are safely wed, I need no longer worry about finding myself caught in your silken web, do I? I dare say, though, my lady, isn't it a bit late for you to be out? I'm certain Lord Winchester is beginning to wonder just where his new bride went off to last night—unless, of course, he is hiding somewhere under that tangle of sheets as well?"

He lifted one corner of the bedsheet by her feet

as if to peer underneath. Portia slapped the covering back down.

"No doubt my husband is still abed himself at the home of his dog-faced washerwoman of a mistress. I believe she was to be performing on the stage last evening, a hideous rendition of Davenant's latest production, no doubt. Not that it would matter if she hadn't, for even without waking beside her, my husband never rises before noon, since, of course, he never retires until dawn. My absence, I'm certain, is far from heeded by the likes of him."

Rolfe laughed, dropping down on the mattress beside her. "What's this? Has the blushing bride's nuptial bed grown cold already?"

Portia glared at him, pulling the bedsheet tightly against her breasts. "The condition of my marriage is none of your concern, Lord Ravenscroft, nor is my presence here. Now, since I'm certain Dante would never think of asking you to leave, kindly turn your arrogant head so I may retrieve my clothing and be gone from here, and from the likes of you as well."

Rolfe bowed his head in a gallant gesture. "As you wish, my lady."

She was gone in a flash of white skin and blond mussed hair, along with any trace of her, slamming the door loudly behind her.

"Thanks, Rolfe," Dante muttered from beneath the pillow he'd placed over his head in an effort to ease the shrill sound of her voice. "You saved me the effort. I was just lying here trying to think of how the devil I was going to get her to leave without protest before breakfast."

"Glad to be of service, my friend." Rolfe said, standing. "Think nothing of it."

Dante yanked on his breeches and ran a hand over a chin darkened by the shadow of a night's growth of beard. The gesture reminded Rolfe that he, himself, was in dire need of a shave. Indeed, had the two of them been brothers, they could not have shared a closer resemblance. Both men stood tall, had hair blacker than sin, and skin that darkened easily in the sun. And both had spent a goodly part of their youths in pursuit of the ladies, though Rolfe—unlike Dante, who was known far and wide as a veritable rakehell— was not quite the wencher his friend was, having never acquired the ability to bed a woman at night then ask for her name in the morning.

"So, what number notch cut in your bedpost is our dear Portia?" Rolfe asked, tossing his friend a clean cambric shirt from the tall mahogany wardrobe at the foot of the bed.

Dante chuckled. "Who's counting? I'm a discreet man, Rolfe. Never bedded a woman who wasn't willing or already married."

"Good thing I've taken to living the bachelor life, else I'd spend every waking moment trying to make certain my wife didn't add to your collection."

"I am a gentleman, my friend, bound by honor, and there are some women even I won't touch, one of which would be your wife, should you ever decide to take one. But as for the others"—he grinned— "the ones I do touch, you'll not hear a single one of them complain. I've never ruined an innocent or wrecked a marriage. They come to me, remember? Their husbands take them for granted. Who am I to deny them? Love them well and leave them when their husbands start to suspect, I always say. Keeps me from making that bothersome jaunt to the dueling field, as well."

"Words to live by," Rolfe said dryly, "but you really should seek a mistress with a more pleasing disposition, Dante. That one is a viper."

"It's not Portia's disposition I am concerned with,

my friend. Old Winchester is a fool for seeking out the bed of another, even if she is an actress. For a girl of nineteen, Portia is quite inventive, but then again, what lady of our glorious king's court is not? It seems a prerequisite to being allowed within the hallowed halls of Whitehall. Can't for the life of me figure out what keeps you at that lonely, crumbling estate in the wilds of Sussex when there are all these fine young flowers here in the city to pluck."

"That is precisely what keeps me in Sussex, Dante. I've had more than my fill of 'plucking' from within Whitehall."

Dante grinned. "You know what they say, my friend. Once you fall from the saddle, it is best to climb back on it and ride hard and fast again."

"It's not the riding that sent me to Sussex in the first place, but the perfidious fences one is made to hurdle once astride."

"Perhaps it's simply time you sampled a different mount."

Rolfe muttered something that Dante wasn't able to hear. He chose not to pursue it.

"Now," he went on, "I'm sure you didn't come all this way just to banter with me, especially this early in the day. So, just what is important enough to bring you to my bedchamber at this wretched hour?"

Fifteen minutes later, seated in Dante's study with a fire crackling in the hearth and a steaming silver pot of coffee settled between them, Rolfe told Dante of his visit with King Charles at Whitehall earlier that morning, while Dante's valet, Penhurst, saw to the ritual shaving of his master's chin.

"So," Rolfe said finally, "what more can you tell me about Lady Cassia Montefort?"

"Ah, yes, Whitehall's own *Lady Winter*. She recently turned two and twenty, older than most of the unmarried ladies of the court, and far wiser than she should be at her age, as well. She knows full well what she is about, and with her maturity she seems to have acquired the skill of holding her own among the more challenging of Whitehall's personalities. She doesn't smile much, not that she has much to smile about, and tends to keep to herself. She seems fond of repairing to the gardens when no one else is around. Prefers solitude to the multitude, you might say. As I understand it, she stands to inherit somewhere around thirty thousand pounds on the death of the marquess. That is, of course, if she is not charged with the murder."

"An attractive sum," Rolfe said. "In and of itself, motive enough for ridding herself of her father. No doubt she has had many eager swains clamoring after her."

"Aye, that she has, but she doesn't show an interest in a single one of them. In fact, she has set each and every one down with the skill of a practiced tactician."

Rolfe's mouth thinned at that bit of information. "No doubt, like so many of the other ladies at court, refusing to lower herself to anyone lower than a duke."

"You refer, of course, to our dear Daphne. She's married now, you know."

Daphne. There had been a time when just hearing that name would set Rolfe's heart pounding. Now it only brought a bitter taste to his mouth. Funny how time and a change in scenery had a way of making things look vastly different.

"Why should it matter to me that she's married? Was there ever any doubt that Daphne would one day net the prize she wanted?"

The prize she thought I would never be.

The words went unspoken but were nonetheless clear.

Dante motioned Penhurst away at the anger—and the pain—he still heard so fresh in his friend's words. "Deuce take it, Rolfe, I'm sorry. I only meant—"

"I know what you meant, Dante. Forget it. That's history now. Ancient history. And I am all the better for her having not accepted my proposal. It would seem, though, that Lady Cassia is comparable to Daphne in one respect, in refusing to lower herself to the lesser ranks of society. Although, at her age, I should think she should follow Daphne's example and at least begin entertaining the thought of settling on one of them before her time on the marriageable shelf runs out."

"One would think so, but that is not the way of it with this one, Rolfe. Lady Cassia has had offers from as high up the social scale as a young woman could possibly hope for. And her advanced age is by no means a hindrance. It only seems to serve as more of an attraction. With age comes experience, or so they say. No, there is something else. It is as if she wants nothing to do with marriage at all. I believe she'd be thoroughly content passing her days in spinsterhood. I can't speak from experience, but I have heard it said that if ever it were possible for ice to flow through a woman's veins, it would be so in hers. Hence the nickname Lady Winter. One stare from her will freeze a man dead, but she is so damned beautiful, it hurts just to behold her. As untouchable and as blindingly cold as the winter sun."

Rolfe considered this a moment. "What do you know of the recent murder of her father?"

Dante stood, crossed the room to the washbowl, and doused the remaining shaving lather from his face. "As you might have already guessed, her father's killing has caused quite a stir in court circles," he said into his drying cloth. He tossed it aside. "Anything of this magnitude naturally would, especially murder. Seagrave was a man who held a modest amount of power and it seems scandal has never been far from the family's path. As I hear it, Seagrave married himself a young court beauty with a mind of her own, back in the reign of the previous King Charles. It was an arranged marriage, made for monetary reasons, of course. Nothing new among the aristocracy, but there were rumors that Seagrave was not the most indulgent of husbands. He is reported to have beaten his wife."

"So he was a bastard," Rolfe said. "But why does the Montefort name sound so familiar to me?"

"Most probably from our dealings during the wars. His holdings have been on the increase in recent years. Some say his fortune goes well beyond the figure I mentioned. It will be interesting to see just what the marquess left behind. I have heard that during the wars, Seagrave was one of those who set his flag in the field of whomever was ahead at the time. A turncoat when it best befitted him. Somehow he managed to avoid involvement with the Protectorate and was appointed to a position at court soon after the Restoration."

"So his wife, Lady Cassia's mother, is still at Whitehall?"

Dante shook his head, taking a sip from his coffee. "Seagrave's wife—Judith, I believe her name was—died earlier this year in childbed, and given the public knowledge of her lack of affection for her husband, it was a getting quite obviously not by the marquess. You see, the marchioness also made a name for herself among the members of the court, though not one that was spoken of in polite circles. 'The Whore of Whitehall,' she was called, and from what I hear, aptly so. Filled any bed that would help her to climb through the ranks of Whitehall's noted beauties."

"And you mean to tell me this lady never warmed your bed?"

Dante chuckled. "Hard to believe, isn't it? Truthfully, the lady was far too manipulative for my tastes. I watched her. She was like a leech bleeding many a man dry, and all the while making her actions a public spectacle. It was rather humiliating for poor Seagrave."

"I should say. And the child she died birthing," Rolfe went on, "I would guess it is now with the father?"

"No one knows for certain just who the father of the child was; there were so many possibilities. The unfortunate babe survived only hours after the birth and subsequent death of the mother. Lady Cassia was immediately removed from court by Lord Seagrave. Since she is unmarried, the marquess made it known he was searching for a husband for his daughter." He paused, then added, "For the right price, of course."

"Of course. Still, despite the scandal of the mother, Lady Cassia, being an heiress and comely as well, would have no doubt attracted many offers."

"Aye, that she did, but refused each one of them. I've watched her, Rolfe, and it is as if it is all some sort of game to her. Her dances are always taken by a number of men, any one of them a comparable match, but should any of the poor idiots show the slightest bit more than a passing interest, Lady Winter turns to ice before their eyes."

Rolfe considered the over his coffee. "If it is not because she seeks a better match, could it be because she is a mistress of the king?"

Dante grinned. "You have already done some fishing, I see."

"Like mother, like daughter?"

"I have heard the rumor that Lady Cassia is one of

the many who frequent the king's bed, but I cannot be certain of its veracity. Unlike her mother, King Charles is the only name Lady Cassia can in any way be tied to. But whenever she is near him, the king's attentions are more brotherly than anything else. Still, I've never heard of her denying the rumors and it is no secret that Lady Cassia will sometimes spend hours in privacy with the king. Odder still is that she remains outstandingly and publicly devoted to his wife, Queen Catherine. Lady Cassia is quite an enigma, which most probably explains why she is now being called a murderess as well. As you know, anyone whose behavior is the slightest bit uncommon is certainly cause for suspicion among the gossip-loving *ton*."

Rolfe sat back in his chair, wishing he had something stronger to drink as he reflected on his friend's words. To have had pluck enough to have survived the scandal of her mother was odd enough. Most—in fact, all—of the ladies he had ever encountered behind the walls of Whitehall would have melted into social oblivion if faced with a similar situation. But not this one. No, she mocked society and its standards, welcoming no less than the king himself to her bed while befriending his own wife!

This Lady Cassia Montefort certainly wasn't some witless miss, which, Rolfe had to admit, made it all the more likely that she would be guilty of the crime of which she was accused. Still, he was suddenly looking forward to meeting her.

"Now tell me your feelings about the murder, Dante. Do you believe she killed her father?"

Dante took a moment before responding. "The evidence does seem to support it. She was found with the marquess's body, a knife stuck in his neck, his blood on her hands, amid signs of a struggle. I have heard that the servants confirm this was not the first such struggle between them. It would seem Lady Cassia could be the only logical suspect, yet she remains free, due, no doubt, to the intervention of the king. Still, to look at her, Rolfe, you would never think her capable of such an act. She has this look about her. A vulnerability I cannot describe in words. There is something about her that stands out, and somehow, despite her parentage, she has managed to acquire the social graces to become the example of a properly bred young lady. A study in gentility. It is more than passing strange."

"This assignment should prove, at the least, interesting."

"Be careful, Rolfe. Something tells me the lady is dangerous."

Rolfe laughed. "I never thought the day would come that I would hear you, of all people, calling any woman dangerous."

"Just be careful." Dante swallowed down the rest of his coffee. "Am I to guess that you would like me to look into the matter further?"

"You always were perceptive, Dante, but you must tell no one, except me, what, if anything, you do find out."

"And where will I find you once I have the information for you?"

"You won't find me. I will find you." Rolfe stood. "Now, if you wouldn't mind, I am in sorry need of a washbowl and a change of clothing before I go to meet the intriguing Lady Cassia. I wasn't able to pack proper clothing before leaving for the city and my valet won't be arriving until tomorrow."

Dante grinned. "We wouldn't want the lady believing you always went about smelling like your horse, would we? She might take it to mind to run you through with her embroidery needle, faced with you looking as you do now, all hairy in the face and bucolic. Penhurst will be at your disposal, my friend, while I will begin making immediate inquiries for you."

Rolfe shook Dante's hand. "I am indebted to you for your information in this, Dante."

"I have only repeated that which is common knowledge at court."

"Still, had I asked about in court circles, I would have been told nothing but a prejudiced version of what you have just told me. I needed information, not gossip, and certainly not the opinions of those at court. It's good to know one can always count on one's friends."

Dante stood and started walking with Rolfe toward the door. "We've been through hell and back together, my friend, remember? From Oxford and on through the wars, it's been the three of us—you, Hadrian, and me—always there to watch over each other's backsides. Hadrian, being older, was always the leader. You were the fighter who saw wrong and had to right it, or risk life and limb trying. And me," he added, smiling devilishly, "I would simply charm the ladies left behind. Speaking of our absent third partner, I received a message yesterday informing me that Hadrian and Mara have just arrived in the city with the family for the season."

"The family?"

"Aye. Young Robert, their daughter, Edana—Dana, they call her—and a third who's on the way."

Rolfe shook his head. "Wasn't Hadrian the one who used to say he'd never make the mistake of procreating and continuing the doomed St. Aubyn line?" He smiled. "I'm happy for him. Actually, I'm amazed he and Mara managed to stay wed. But then, Hadrian's no idiot. He knows a good thing when he sees it, even if she did make him look the fool in the beginning. Give them my regards for me, won't you?"

"I take it you won't be staying in the city, then?"

Rolfe stopped just outside the door. "I would say it is a fair guess that as soon as I find Lady Cassia Montefort, I will be occupied as far away from court and the city as I possibly can be for some time."

Chapter Three

Rolfe doffed his hat, standing just inside the low doorway, when Dante's warning about Lady Cassia came to mind.

Dangerous.

She certainly didn't look dangerous, he thought, standing as she was on the other side of the cluttered room atop a small wooden ladder, removing books from a shelf that was crammed with aged leather-bound books, volumes of them, all of different widths and sizes. Other books were scattered around her on the floor and about the room, and a number of wooden crates, already filled with other various books, were neatly stacked atop one another near the doorway.

No, Lady Cassia Montefort didn't look dangerous at all. She simply looked busy, engrossed in her task of leafing through each book before determining in which designated pile to place it. In fact, for a suspected murderess, she appeared oddly content, humming a cheerful tune to herself as she worked. She had not heard him enter the room, and rather than announce himself, Rolfe decided to remain silent a moment to observe. People, he had learned, tended to reveal more about themselves when they were unaware of anyone else, so he crossed his arms over his chest and leaned his shoulder against the oaken doorjamb to watch her as she worked across the room.

Her back, slender and graceful, was to him but he could see that she wore an apron to protect her gown, a strict and undecorated style done in dour black. She had decided to adhere to society's rules, he noticed, wearing mourning regardless of the accusations against her in her father's death. In fact, the entire house had been appropriately amended, black crepe covering the mirrors and draping every window. Even her chestnut hair was tied back at the nape with a length of black ribbon. It fell in a soft cascade of waves down the length of her back, the ends of it curling loosely just above her narrow waist.

She must have sensed finally that there was someone standing behind her at the door, for she said without turning, "Lynette, would you please tell Quigman we will need additional crates for the rest of these? I've already filled the ones he brought earlier and I'm not yet halfway through the shelves. I will certainly be glad to see these dust-ridden things go. And when we are finished here, we'll move upstairs to begin packing away Lord Seagrave's clothing for delivery to the almshouse at Bridewell."

Her voice was dulcet and distinct, the voice of a woman who was not at all uncertain of herself. Rolfe remained silent.

"Lynette, did you not hear me?"

When Rolfe again did not respond, being that he wasn't this Lynette person and he didn't yet wish to relinquish his unobstructed study of her, Cassia turned and stared at him steadfastly, as if she were not at all surprised to see him, a man, and a stranger at that, standing there in her hallway.

"Excuse me, sir," she said, gripping the shelf to

keep herself steady atop the ladder, "but may I ask who allowed you in this house?"

Rolfe did not immediately respond, for her face, now turned fully toward him, gave him definite pause.

She was a vision, more lovely than should be humanly possible. Even in the low morning light with dust motes floating about the air around her, she was a sight to bring nations to war, the mythological Helen reincarnate. Words failed him, all sense of his reason for being there vanished, and in that moment, Rolfe immediately realized that he wanted her. He wanted her naked and in his arms, he wanted her silken hair loose and tangled in his fingers. He wanted to bury his face in her breasts. It was a feeling he hadn't known for a woman in some time, not since Daphne, but then, he'd not been standing before a woman like this one in quite some time, either. She was everything Dante had told him she'd be. Dangerous, yes, realizing his immediate reaction to her. Beautiful to the point of poetry. Impeccable in appearance. A study of elegance and social grace.

And, quite possibly, a murderess.

He mustn't allow himself to forget that.

Rolfe noticed her eyes, dark and expressive, set under brows that were defined and slanted elegantly upward. From where he stood, he couldn't tell their exact color, only that they were dark, taking hold of anything they met. She was fine-featured, with high cheekbones and a straight, delicate nose. And that mouth—yes, that mouth—now, that he could see clearly. Full rose-colored lips, the bottom one slightly fuller than the top, looking soft and moist and sensuous. It was a mouth made for kissing, the sort of mouth that made a man instantly want to cover it with his own and taste its promised sweetness.

One thing was for certain, Rolfe thought as he continued staring at her like a dumbstruck fool, Dante hadn't been mistaken. In fact, his description of this woman could only be called a sad understatement. If ever Rolfe had doubted this woman's association with the king, seeing her there, the lovely sight she presented before him, he was now certain of it.

Lady Cassia was most assuredly one of the king's mistresses, for a man with Charles's sexual and epicurean appetites would never be able to rest until he had this woman in his bed.

"Did you not hear me?" she asked again, sterner this time. "I asked who allowed you in here, sir."

Rolfe managed to take hold of his rattled senses long enough to respond. "Your front door was open. I called, but no one answered."

"And you are in the habit of entering people's homes without an invitation, Mr. . . . ?"

"Ravenscroft, Lord Ravenscroft, actually. I apologize for showing myself in unannounced, but I come with an urgent message. I have been sent here to you by the king."

The cross expression at his intrusion instantly vanished from her face. She smiled brilliantly. "His Majesty has sent you to me? Have you a message from him for me?"

The transformation in her at hearing of the king, the sudden new softness to her voice, irritated Rolfe, he didn't know why. Why should it matter to him if this woman, this lovely piece of female stuff, was just one of Charles's many mistresses?

"Actually, yes, I have a message for you from the king, though not in written form. You see, *I* am the message."

Cassia looked at him in obvious confusion. She stepped down from the ladder, wiping her hands on the front of her apron. "Pray continue, Lord Ravenscroft."

"I have been sent here by His Majesty, the King, to escort Lady Cassia Montefort to the Seagrave estate in Cambridgeshire and to remain there with her until such time that her guilt or innocence of the recent murder of her father, Lord Seagrave, can be proven."

"You mean to tell me that you are to guard Lady Cassia, Lord Ravenscroft? And is it customary for a nobleman such as yourself to be employed in the role of common guardsman?"

Rolfe quickly gathered that she was not at all pleased by his announcement. Her voice had turned sour, the sweetness gone. He tried to avoid her questions. "You are Lady Cassia, are you not?"

She came forward and he saw that she had blue eyes flecked with gray, the color of the lowering sky. They were the sort of eyes a man could easily find himself lost in. No doubt many already had. "You have not yet answered my question, my lord," she said in a voice that was low and challenging. "Are you here to act as a guard to Lady Cassia?"

Rolfe stared at her. "I have been sent as a means of protection for Lady Cassia, not as a guardsman, at the request of His Majesty King Charles."

"Protection, hah! I would say it is more likely you have been appointed as a sentry, my lord. The king must needs make certain a suspected murderess doesn't attempt to flee the country for French shores, isn't that it, Lord Ravenscroft? Well, I am sorry, but I will not stand for it."

She took his arm, her slender fingers gripping his coat sleeve. "I thank you for coming, my lord, but I have decided that your services will not be required. I would that you would convey my appreciation to His Majesty for his ..." she paused, "concern, but I assure you I am quite capable of taking care of myself. You see, I refuse to leave London and hide myself away in the country as if to say that I am guilty as everyone is wont to believe. Thus your presence here is not necessary, Lord Ravenscroft. I thank you for coming. I am sorry you went to the trouble for no reason. Good day."

Her dismissal had been done in a most polite manner, and somehow, in that short space of time, she had walked him to the door, had ushered him out and onto the streets without his even realizing it, and was now about to unceremoniously close the door in his face.

Before she could accomplish this final stroke, Rolfe quickly placed his booted foot in the doorway, stopping the door from closing. He then pushed the door inward and, in the process, forced the startled woman to allow him back inside.

"Just a moment, if you please, madam. For, you see, you have not yet answered my question, either. Are you Lady Cassia Montefort, or not?"

Rolfe knew very well that she was—who the devil else could she be?—but something made him ask regardless.

She frowned at him. "Pardon me, Lord Ravenscroft. I do apologize. Yes, I am Lady Cassia."

"Good." He walked past her and headed directly back into the study where he'd first found her, weaving his way through the stacks of crates and piles of books, taking the liberty of seating himself in an armchair beside the stone hearth that gave off a heavy cloud of dust when he dropped into it. He smiled at her. "At least now I know I am where I belong."

Cassia glared at him with an icy expression she'd no doubt used with success many times before. "No, Lord Ravenscroft, it is you who are mistaken, for you do not belong here. You do not belong anywhere near here. As I have already told you, your services are not needed—or, for that matter, wanted."

Lady Winter. It was the name Dante said the court had given her, and though Rolfe wasn't fond of society's practice of attaching such tags to any person who stood out from the throng, he was beginning to see how the lady had acquired her title.

"Yes, I am aware of that, Lady Cassia. You have made your feelings very clear—crystal clear, in fact— but you see, I take orders from the king very seriously. I have been sent here to protect you and to take you from London to your family seat in Cambridgeshire, and that, my lady, I intend to do, with or without your cooperation."

Cassia peered at him a moment, then cocked her head a little to the side. It was an action Rolfe found most appealing. "You say your name is Ravenscroft, my lord? Pray, why does the name sound familiar to me?"

Rolfe's jaw tensed. Time, it seemed, could not do away with the past. "I used to be a frequent visitor to the palace."

"As have I. Do you not think it odd that we have never crossed paths before now?"

"Bad timing, I guess. I am frequently sent on assignment by the Crown."

"No, that is not why your name sounds familiar to me. I do not believe it is for any recent reason, but there is something I remember ..." She thought for a moment. "Something about an exiled earl ..."

Rolfe frowned. She was certainly straightforward, cutting right to the heart of the matter. "I have been away from court for some time, occupied with other concerns. But as of now, my only concern is in escorting you to Cambridgeshire."

Cassia released an annoyed breath. "Again we return to the subject of Cambridgeshire. This is beginning to grow tiresome. Pray, tell me, why is this retreat to the country so necessary, my lord?"

"The king feels strongly that the city is no longer safe for you," Rolfe said. He had had enough of her evasiveness. "Now, I would dearly enjoy spending the rest of the day getting further acquainted, but we will have ample time for that once we are in Cambridgeshire, and I do not think it will serve to help matters now. It is only delaying the inevitable, Lady Cassia, so I would suggest that you find your maid—Lynette, I believe you said her name was—and set her to the task of packing your things, for we will be leaving first thing morning after next. I have taken the liberty of sending a missive to Cambridgeshire, alerting the staff at your family seat that we will be arriving within the week. A coach has been hired. Every detail has been seen to."

"You presume too much, Lord Ravenscroft. You have no authority to give my servants orders."

"On the contrary, Lady Cassia, I have been duly empowered by His Majesty King Charles."

Cassia stared at him. She did not attempt any further refusal. Her face was expressionless, but her jaw was set and her eyes gave slight indication of the anger she must have been so practiced at suppressing. She was obviously unaccustomed to having a man refuse her. And, judging from her irritation, she was also unaccustomed to being told what to do.

Well, she could just get used to it.

Cassia did not move, not an inch, to summon Lynette to set her to packing as Rolfe had asked. She remained standing for several moments, quietly allowing Rolfe time to reconsider, which he had no intention of doing. After several silent moments had passed, her voice grew oddly soft, and she said, "Do you not wish to know if I did it, if I am truly guilty of murdering my father?"

"Whether you are responsible for the death of your father or not is of no matter to me, Lady Cassia. I have not been sent here to judge you. I have only been sent here to take you to the country to protect you from those who have already passed judgment and who want to see you swinging from the gibbet."

Cassia's face paled at this last statement, her mouth pressing into a firm line. "I will not hie away to the country like some frightened fool. Can't you see that would only be proclaiming my guilt all the more?"

"Your conviction is commendable, my lady, but I am afraid you have little choice in the matter. I stand by my duty to take you to Cambridgeshire. His Majesty has deemed it so and I mean to see his orders through. So, you see, your constant attempts at changing the subject and skirting around my reasons for being here are futile."

"That, Lord Ravenscroft, remains to be seen."

Cassia turned, her silk skirts rustling on the carpeted floor.

"Lynette," she called once in the hallway.

"Yes, milady?"

Rolfe smiled, pleased she was finally beginning to see reason. His pleasure was short-lived, however, vanishing the moment he heard her next words.

"Please have Quigman call a hackney coach for me. I haven't the time for him to hitch up the team."

Rolfe moved to the doorway just as Cassia took up her cloak from the waiting hands of her maid. As he watched her fingers fasten its closure, he wondered if her skin felt as soft as it appeared and he felt a sudden longing to run his mouth along the slender line of her lovely white neck. Before he could further explore this line of thought, Cassia turned, picking up a small, cloth-covered object set on a side table there in the entrance hall before heading toward the door to leave.

"I shall be back shortly, Lord Ravenscroft," she called without looking back. "Since you take your orders so seriously, you may retire to the parlor to wait, if you wish. Lynette will bring you some refreshment. My father's wine cellar is reputed to be one of the finest in London, stocked with only the best burgundies and clarets. You may have your choice."

She was polite, he'd give her that, even when she was spitting mad.

"That won't be necessary."

"As you wish."

Cassia headed out the door. She had nearly made it to the open door of the coach now waiting for her at the front of the three-story timber-framed house when she noticed Rolfe following closely behind her. She stopped.

"What do you think you are doing?" she asked, irritated.

"I am going with you."

She held up one kid-gloved hand, placed it flat against his chest, and pushed, not overly forceful, but firmly enough to get her point across. "Excuse me, Lord Ravenscroft, but let me assure you that I have been traveling around this city by myself for quite some time. I did not have need of your protection before and I am not of the opinion that I am in need of it now. I am an adult, not a child, and I am quite capable of riding in a coach unescorted."

Rolfe returned a smile. "Orders, Lady Cassia."

"I do not care about your orders, Lord Ravenscroft. I have attempted to be polite, but like all men, you do not seem capable of taking a hint. So now I am forced to be blunt. Please take heed when I say that

I will not suffer your presence any longer. You are boorish and far too forward. I find it difficult to believe you can call yourself a gentleman. Quigman, kindly remove this man from the area at once, please."

The groom, who was of impressive size but still not quite large enough to give Rolfe pause, stepped forward.

"I'm sure you are quite used to heeding her ladyship's wishes, Quigman—as if you had a choice—but if you value anything in life, you will think twice before acting any further."

Rolfe lowered his hand to the hilt of the rapier that rested at his hip.

Quigman froze. He glanced at his mistress, confused as to what he should do next.

Rolfe turned to Cassia. "Quigman here seems a nice enough fellow. I should hate to have to run him through. And besides, you wouldn't want to be called responsible for the deaths of two people, now, would you, Lady Cassia?"

She ignored him. "Quigman, would you please summon Freddy from the house?"

"I assure you that calling another manservant to try and somehow prevent me from going with you will only serve to complicate matters all the more."

Cassia spun about. "*Winifred* is my abigail, Lord Ravenscroft, and though she does tend to be a bit overprotective of me, I do not think she could do you any serious damage, especially if you feel it necessary to threaten her with your sword as you just did poor Quigman. I don't know why it is men feel they can bend the world to their will whenever they get a weapon in their hands. I am not stupid, Lord Ravenscroft. Since you are obviously armed and are much larger than me, and since you will not remain here as I have asked you to, I have no other choice but to suffer your presence. But if it is all the same to you, my lord, Winifred will be riding with us in the coach. There is still a modicum of propriety that must be followed. Would you have me driving about town in the company of a gentleman unchaperoned?"

Rolfe fell dumb at her pronouncement, actually stunned beyond words. Here she stood, Lady Cassia Montefort, mistress to the king, as well as a publicly accused murderess, and she was concerned about the appearances of going about the city with a man unchaperoned. It was ludicrous. It defied common logic. It was, quite simply, insane.

Dante had been right on one account. This woman was certainly an enigma.

"By all means, my lady," Rolfe said, holding out his hand to assist her into the coach.

It came as no surprise to him when she ignored his hand and climbed inside unassisted.

Ten minutes later—with the maid, Winifred, a stout older woman of Austrian stock who glared at Rolfe from the corner of her eye, situated safely between them—they were finally ready to leave.

"Where ye be going?" the driver asked. Having been witness to the earlier exchange, he seemed not at all certain to whom he should address the question.

Rolfe looked to Cassia. "Well, my lady?"

She frowned at him before nodding to the driver. "To Whitehall Palace, and hurry, if you please."

Chapter Four

Cassia did not speak during their ride through the city, but sat silent, staring straight ahead, gloved hands folded neatly in her lap, Winifred's stout body shoved properly between them on the narrow coach seat. Rolfe thought to himself that it was a pity, and mildly curious, this sudden quietness from her, and wondered if Winifred's presence had anything to do with it. Somehow, he knew it did. He had enjoyed their verbal row and had found Cassia a challenge, one that he welcomed. It had been a long time since he'd matched words with one so skilled, and never with a woman. He couldn't help but wonder if she'd be just as spirited in bed and envied the king for having received that liberty from her. Still, he thought, if her behavior earlier was any indication, the weeks to come should prove interesting at the very least.

If there was one thing Rolfe had learned since making her acquaintance, it was that Cassia wasn't the sort of woman who was often refused. Having failed in her own efforts to remove him from his assignment, Rolfe would wager his favorite bay mare back at Ravenwood that she was now on her way to make an appeal to the king, her lover, for the same. She was seasoned at facing down the court fops, men whose cravat strings were starched stiffer than their backbones. And she was most probably accustomed to twisting the king around her finger like a pliant strand of thread, for that was one of King Charles's worst weaknesses, his inability to deny anyone anything. Charles hated to refuse any request and was known to waste an inordinate amount of time and energy trying to please the many who came to him. But, if she hadn't already, Lady Cassia Montefort would soon learn that Rolfe would not be that easily manipulated. He'd been led around and made fool of by the best of them, and once was enough for any man with even a limited amount of sensibility.

There being no prospect of conversation until they reached Whitehall, Cassia's chosen destination, Rolfe busied himself with attempting to watch the city through the cloudy coach window that looked as if it had never seen a cleaning. The city hadn't changed much in his absence. The streets seemed a little narrower than he remembered, the market at the Cross a bit more crowded, but he put that off as his being accustomed to the openness and solitude of the country. Life was simpler in Sussex, he thought, less hurried. A man could walk about without having to worry that his pocket might get picked, or worse, that he'd feel the sharp edge of a knife blade being pressed up under his chin should he chance to venture down a darkened alleyway. The vice that ran so rampant in the city, the intrigue and the scandal, rarely surfaced, excepting, of course, the occasional tea parlor twitter. And murder—that was a word that was never spoken, it never had need to, especially not in relation to a lady, even a lady with a tongue that cut sharp as a sword.

The coach finally arrived at Whitehall, circling around in order to leave them off at the Public Court Gate. Though only a short distance separated the palace from Lady Cassia's residence near Picadilly, it was now midday and it had seemed to take an especially long time for the hackney to navigate its way along the narrow streets and through the heavy traffic going to Westminster.

After the coach had rolled to a stop, Cassia didn't wait for the driver to open the door for her, but stepped out even before he'd alighted, with Winifred bearing the mysterious covered package. Rolfe was left alone behind them to pay the hack's fare.

By the time Rolfe managed to catch up with them, Cassia had managed to gain admittance, ahead of the lines of citizens waiting to get in the palace, from the squinty-eyed palace porter. She did not stop before the two sentries who stood guard at the palace entrance to request an audience with the king, as Rolfe had earlier that morning. Instead, she simply turned into the entrance of the cobblestoned pebble court, with its meticulously trimmed hedges and pink marble fountain of Poseidon holding his golden trident with water bubbling from his mouth, continuing on her way.

They came to the famed Stone Gallery, the palace's public promenade. The walls of the lengthy corridor were lined with the valuable collection of paintings once amassed by the king's father, Charles I, only recently recovered after having been sold off by the Protectorate during its brief, but nonetheless memorable rule.

The gallery was swarming with people, and courtiers loitering about turned to openly stare, whispering excitedly among themselves as the trio passed by. A suspected murderess made for immediate diversion. Cassia didn't seem to notice the stir her presence had created; if she had, she kept it well hidden. She held her head high, greeted no one they passed, and paused only when they reached the sash door leading to the outside Privy Garden to allow Rolfe to open it for her.

Propriety, as always.

"Thank you, Lord Ravenscroft."

Outside, in the garden, with its ivy-covered walls and exotic flowers from faraway lands, it took Cassia only a moment to spot the king out taking his midday promenade. His tall, dark presence stood out amid the vibrant blossoms and trimmed topiary bushes in the garden. He was throwing corn to the birds flocking around him, followed after by a cluster of yapping spaniels and a group of courtiers attempting to keep up with his swift gait while vying for a forward position.

Rather than attempt to weave her way through the throng, Cassia cleverly circled around near the center sundial, to where they met the small congregation head-on. She put on a brilliant smile as the king drew near, lowering into an elegant curtsy, acting as if it were any other day, and, Rolfe thought privately, as if she had no ulterior purpose for being there.

"Ah, good morning to you, Lady Cassia," the king said, drawing to a halt. "What a pleasant surprise. I had not expected to see you about Whitehall this morning."

Charles pushed a fat black curl from his shoulder and kissed the slender fingers of her outstretched hand. Rolfe wondered how he hadn't noticed Cassia removing her glove.

"And I see you have brought Lord Ravenscroft with you," Charles added.

Though veiled in politeness, Charles's meaning was not readily hidden. He'd sent Rolfe, his chosen man, to take her, his mistress, off and away, and that man had obviously failed in his duty. The sharp rise of his brow accentuated his words.

Cassia rose from her curtsy, her silk skirts rustling along the graveled walkway. "Good morning, Your Majesty. As you are aware, I have been away from my duties at court out of respect for my father's passing and"—she glanced quickly at Rolfe—"under normal circumstances I would not have come out as such but I have urgent need of a word with you, if I may?"

Charles smiled, motioning toward a nearby doorway that was nearly concealed by its canopy of ivy. "But of course. You know I am always available to speak with you, Lady Cassia, at any time. Come, let us retire to the Withdrawing Chamber." He glanced behind him at the group of courtiers, who were hanging on every word. "I find my walk has parched me somewhat and I am in need of some refreshment."

The king presented his arm to Cassia, which she took, sweeping her skirts outward as they turned. The action served to keep Rolfe behind them. Rolfe noticed she was smiling and quite satisfied with herself. He said nothing and followed the regal twosome, Winifred, still bearing the mysterious package, at his side.

Charles handed his plumed hat to a waiting footman, delivering the pouch full of corn to still another. "My wife, the queen, was just telling me this morning when I went to visit her how very much she misses having you at Whitehall, Lady Cassia."

"I, too, miss seeing Her Majesty. I so enjoy our chats together. I trust she is well?"

"In a matter of speaking, yes. She has been feeling a bit out of sorts, especially in the mornings, but we are hoping it is a result of our recent sojourn to the waters at Tunbridge Wells and we will finally be blessed with an heir."

Cassia smiled. "I do pray Your Majesty's suspicions prove correct."

"I shall convey your consideration after Her Majesty's welfare to her when next I see her."

Rolfe felt as if he were viewing a play, a parody put on solely for his benefit, and hoped the remainder of this visit did not continue along the same vein. Surely Lady Cassia had not come all this way to inquire after the health of the queen? Remembering her reaction to him earlier, her constant attempts at skirting him, he thought it more likely she was simply setting the mood before voicing her true intentions.

Once inside the withdrawing chamber, the door barred from anyone other than themselves, the king took a seat on an elegant gilt settee, motioning for Cassia to sit beside him. The spaniels that had been walking with him in the garden quickly deposited themselves around his feet. Cassia bent down and patted one gently on its head.

Charles waited until the servants had quit the room before speaking. "I see you have met Lord Ravenscroft."

"Yes, Your Majesty. We are acquainted," Cassia said, arranging herself on the settee. She folded her hands in her lap, and bowed her head demurely.

"Good. Now, what is it that brings you to grace this setting with your lovely presence today?"

Cassia eyed Rolfe who was standing beside an imposing, gray-marble hearth before continuing. "I was rather hoping for a more private audience with you, Your Majesty."

Charles smiled. "I would suspect Lord Ravenscroft may have something to add to the conversation, so, if it is not too much to ask, Lady Cassia, I would that he remain."

In that, Cassia gathered she should not press the removal of Rolfe any further. She wisely acquiesced. "Very well, Your Majesty. Firstly, I have been going through my father's effects and I came across something that I knew he would have wanted you to have."

She motioned to Winifred, who brought the cloth-covered object forward, setting it on the carved sycamore-on-walnut marquetry table in front of the king.

"What have we here?"

Charles's eyes lit up with the excitement of a child as he reached forward to remove the cloth covering. An instrument of sorts lay underneath, made up of a shiny flat brass plate and engraved with a strange-looking map inscribed in Latin. He took in an audible breath of delight.

"It is an astrolabe, Your Majesty," Cassia said, though Rolfe rather doubted the king even heard her, for he was thoroughly focused—nay, engrossed—as he peered at its many curious designs. "It is used for determining the altitude of celestial bodies, an ancient sort of timepiece, I am told."

"Yes, yes, I am well aware of its use," Charles said, taking the astrolabe up and inspecting it more closely.

Rolfe leaned back against the mantelpiece, smiling to himself, and shook his head in disbelief. Had he moments before thought Cassia was merely setting the mood? With this little item, she'd thoroughly stacked the deck in her favor.

Anyone who had ever been close to the king knew of his obsession with time-measuring and scientific devices. His famed clock collection had grown to such a size that he'd had to set aside an entire room in the palace just for their display. A servant had been employed for the sole purpose of winding them each day. Charles was fascinated with such items, and with this astrolabe being such a rare specimen, Cassia had most assuredly just bought her freedom with it.

She was a cunning wench, and knowing that one

thing alone made Rolfe's blood begin to boil with anger.

The king set the astrolabe back in its polished wooden stand, taking up Cassia's hand and kissing it earnestly. "Your kind gift is most pleasing to me, Lady Cassia. I will treasure it always."

Cassia beamed. "I am pleased Your Majesty is so pleased. I knew my father would have wanted it given to someone who would appreciate its intrinsic worth, and had he not come to such an untimely demise, I am certain you would have been his choice. Which brings to mind another matter I was hoping to discuss with you, Your Majesty."

Rolfe came forward then, awaiting his inevitable dismissal. He didn't know why it should displease him so, but it did. He hadn't particularly wanted this assignment at all, playing nursemaid to this lovely but conniving little package. In fact, he would have much preferred being left to his own in Sussex. Perhaps it was that he'd never been removed from a task once he'd undertaken it. Perhaps it was knowing that, having utterly beguiled the king, her lover, with the gift of the astrolabe, Cassia would have her way. Perhaps it was that he didn't particularly like being made to look the fool by a woman—a second time.

Whatever it was, he didn't like it.

"Your Majesty," Rolfe said, breaking through the small circle that had somehow woven these two people together as if the outside world ceased to exist, "I believe what Lady Cassia is about to request is that I be relieved of my duties of protecting her and taking her from the city to her family seat in Cambridgeshire as you had instructed me to do earlier this morning."

Charles looked at Cassia and raised one dark brow, feigning surprise at Rolfe's pronouncement. "Is this true, Lady Cassia?"

The king knew quite well it was true, but rascal that he was, he had decided to play along with her game.

Cassia gave Rolfe a stare that would have turned most men to jelly, before turning to face the king. "Yes, I'm afraid it is, Your Majesty. You see, I do not believe my leaving London would accomplish anything other than to create more scandal to run rampant through the galleries."

She stood and began pacing before them, the whisper of her silk skirts the only sound in the silent room. "Surely by sending me to the country, Your Majesty, you do not intend to somehow cause the members of the court to forget my father's killing, and," she added, her voice softening, "the supposition of my guilt thereof. 'Out of mind as soon as out of sight,' or so Lord Brooke is oft quoted as saying."

"Cassia, my only intention is to protect you."

Rolfe noticed that something in Charles had changed. The humor that had previously danced in his dark eyes had gone, and his voice had taken on a much softer tone. There was also something else that had changed. Up to that point, he had been addressing her as "Lady Cassia"; now he had given in to the familiarity of using her given name.

A familiarity one would employ more in the bedchamber.

Cassia stopped her pacing. "Were I to hie off to the country, would that not be affirming my guilt more than my innocence? I have already been judged guilty, not by a court of law, but by the people of this palace. Your people. In their eyes I have been deemed a murderess and thereby should be executed as one, a public spectacle for all to see, the last Montefort gone to ruin."

Charles stood and moved across the room, hands clasped behind his back. He seemed lost in thought as he stared out the window that faced onto the Pebble Court, the rooftop of the magnificent Inigo Jones Banqueting House rising in the distance. Sensing the king's need for time to think, neither Cassia nor Rolfe spoke while he stood there. They remained beside one another in the middle of the room, neither moving, waiting for his next words.

"I know well of what you speak, Cassia. My own father was judged unfairly. They severed his head from his body just outside that Banqueting House there. If you look carefully, you can see the second-floor window he was made to come out in order to stand upon the scaffold in disgrace before the people. His own people. They say the groan that rose from the crowd at the sight of the executioner holding up his head was louder than any cannon shot. To this day, the identity of that man, the blackguard who killed my father, is a mystery. I have vowed not to shed any more of the blood of those who were responsible for killing him, but were I to ever learn who it was who actually wielded the ax . . ."

The passion and the cold fury that colored Charles's words brought a heavy seriousness to the room. Rolfe felt the misery, the chilling grief of his sovereign in like fashion, for his own family—his parents and his two young sisters—had themselves been butchered by the marauding Cromwellians at the outbreak of the war while he'd been away in the Colonies. It had been that event which had prompted Rolfe to take action to risk his life in the fight for his country's renewal. It had been that event which had changed the course of his life.

Charles paused a moment, then went on. "Every day, I must walk by that spot, that damnable spot where injustice ruled over right, where evil reigned over good, knowing the blood of my father was spilled there by Puritan zealous greedy for power. And they called themselves 'servants of God.' "

He gazed out the window a moment longer before turning back toward the two of them. The wetness of tears shone in his dark eyes. "You make a solid argument, Cassia. You would have made a brilliant litigator had you been born a man."

"It is a misfortune of birth, Your Majesty."

"Nay, for had you been born a man, dear Cassia, our lives would not have been graced by your beauty."

"As I said, Your Majesty, a misfortune of birth."

Charles smiled. "Nonetheless, I have come to a decision in the matter. I will only allow you to remain in London on one condition. I do not wish to see you detained in the Tower. There are too many there I do not trust. I cannot guarantee your safety there. So should you not agree to my terms, then I am afraid I will have no other choice but to send you away to the country."

Cassia nodded. "Your Majesty?"

"I will only allow you to stay on in the city under the protection of Lord Ravenscroft. I assure you he is a most capable man, Cassia, and I am confident he will see to your safety. I would trust no one else to it. Until such time that the mystery surrounding your father's death can be uncovered, everywhere you go, Rolfe will escort you. He will at no time or for any reason leave your side. He will be your constant companion. I know you do not agree, nor do you understand, but I do this for your own protection."

Cassia looked at Rolfe. Her eyes were steady as she stared at him. He knew she wanted nothing more than to dismiss him outright, send him away and packing as she had so many others before him. This woman did not take kindly to be controlled by a man, any man. But Rolfe also knew that if Cassia placed any sort of value on her freedom, she could not in any manner refuse the king's offer. She had told Rolfe she was not stupid. He had seen enough to know that was true. She really had no other choice but to agree.

Rolfe did not move, did not say a word in addition to Charles's decree. He merely stood by, watching her as she came to her decision.

"Cassia," the king asked, awaiting her reply, "have I made myself clear?"

Cassia bowed her head, saying quietly. "Yes, Your Majesty. It is understood."

Chapter Five

Cassia and Rolfe left the king's Withdrawing Chamber a time later, having arrived at a truce and somewhat of an accord on the terms of what Cassia had come to call her "compulsory surrender."

It had been politely discussed, arranged over a tasty dinner of cockle soup and salted oyster patties. The meal had been splendid, the conversation enlivening, but even the sweet lemon cream pudding hadn't been able to remove the sour taste left in Cassia's mouth at having been sorely defeated in her efforts to get Ravenscroft removed from his accursed duty. Though she had succeeded in remaining in the city, she hadn't managed to get out of her head the image of Ravenscroft's smug grin when the king had told her she must tolerate his constant guardianship each day. Oh, he'd enjoyed himself quite thoroughly at her expense, lout that he was, even if, she was forced to admit, he was a handsome lout at that.

Cassia thought back to when she'd first turned to see Ravenscroft standing in the doorway of her father's study earlier that day. She should have been frightened at the sight of him, a man, a strange man suddenly there, inside her home, a home she now, for all intents and purposes, resided in alone. But there had been something, something about him that had assured her she wasn't in any danger. After considering it a moment longer, Cassia came to the conclusion that the something she'd seen had been in his eyes.

His were intense eyes, but not at all menacing, and were, Cassia had decided after studying them at intervals from the corners of her own, a shade of hazel sparked with green unlike any she'd seen before. They were a perfect complement to his dark hair and sharply chiseled features, his long, straight nose, the set of his clean-shaven jaw, even that cocksure grin that was accented by a small dimple that tended to appear at the corner of his mouth. They were also eyes that had the uncanny ability to see most everything without appearing to see anything at all.

Ravenscroft was unlike any man Cassia had ever encountered. He dressed differently, wore his hair differently, and he certainly acted differently than other men did. The men she was accustomed to fell over themselves in their efforts to stand out from each other, dressing more extravagantly than the next as a means to make a name for themselves. Ravenscroft stood out by natural means, for he was tall and solidly built, and somehow Cassia could not envision him wearing flounced shirtsleeves and curling lovelocks, pinching snuff from a decorated enamel box with the other dandies at court.

All in all, the image Ravenscroft presented was one of inherent and unyielding strength. And he was certainly the most stubborn man Cassia had ever met.

He refused to budge, even an inch, and was obviously accustomed to giving orders and having them followed without complaint, as evidenced by his persistent refusal to abandon his duty. The resonant tone in his voice spoke of his expectation to be listened to. The way he carried himself, the broad set of his shoulders, showed his confidence in his authority. A man to be reckoned with, if one was up to the challenge.

And Cassia was definitely up to that challenge.

At least, she thought with some small amount of satisfaction, she had succeeded in preventing his removing her to the country. And having cleared that bothersome hurdle, she could now get on with the next, one that was a bit higher and far more treacherous: the unpleasant, but necessary task of proving her innocence of her father's murder.

While Cassia was pleased at having managed to remain in London, she was disappointed to learn she could not fully return to her duties as maid of honor to Queen Catherine, though not overly surprised by His Majesty's decision. Ravenscroft couldn't very well follow her into Her Majesty's bedchamber while Cassia attended to her toilette and other matters which required the utmost privacy. And the king had given Cassia permission to return to Whitehall to visit the queen and to attend whatever court function she chose when it pleased her, as long as her appearances at Whitehall were not made with any regularity, for the very idea that a suspected murderess should be given free rein at the palace would not sit well with the courtiers.

So, it seemed, she was not to be made a complete prisoner in her own home, after all—but only by the barest of margins.

The dutiful Winifred immediately appeared at Cassia's side the moment she emerged from inside the king's Withdrawing Chamber. The uniformed guards who stood outside had no sooner closed the doors behind them than they were set upon by a small group of ladies taking air in the Privy Garden. That the small assembly seemed to have been waiting for them to emerge was more than suspect, especially since, Cassia quickly noted, the colorfully clad group was made up of a number of those whom she preferred to call "the

Malicious Ambitious." These ladies, who spent their every waking moment seeking ways to rise above the other ladies at court, were commanded by no less than the king's most prominent and long-standing mistress herself—Barbara Palmer, the Countess of Castlemaine.

"Ah, Lady Cassia, how very *unexpected* it is to see you at the palace today," Lady Castlemaine said, coming forward with all the regal bearing and arrogance to which she assumed she was entitled. "I really must speak to the porter about being more careful in his selection of who to allow inside. I wouldn't have thought that one of your . . ." she paused, her chin rising a degree, "obvious social caliber would be permitted within the walls of the palace these days."

Her gown was made of the finest sea-green watered silk. Jewels glittered at her ears and from around her throat in the sunlight. Her auburn hair was crimped in the latest style, side curls dangling over each shoulder. She looked as if she considered herself the uncrowned Queen of England and, indeed, one would discover that most everyone at court thought of her thus, for she used her position well to wield power.

Everyone, that is, except Cassia.

From the moment King Charles's new Portuguese wife had arrived in England nearly two years before, Cassia had stood fast in her loyalty to Queen Catherine, against every stab and social humiliation Lady Castlemaine and her entourage had gleefully delivered.

Cassia often thought it was fortunate that Queen Catherine's knowledge of the English language was limited, for it enabled her to shield the queen from the scandalous gossip surrounding the bedchamber antics of her husband and the woman who had such a mysterious hold on him. No two women could have been created more unalike. Where Barbara was considered exotic and wildly passionate by nature, Catherine was serene and calm, a convent-bred innocent sent over from the Continent to a foreign land filled with vice and debauchery.

From the moment she saw him, Queen Catherine had adored her husband much as a lovesick puppy would a child. In turn, Charles was drawn to Catherine's innate kindness and contentment, so very different from the demanding nature of his most famous paramour. Cassia herself did not try to understand this arrangement, with Charles running to one woman for physical satisfaction and back to the other for mental redemption; it was almost as if he believed Catherine too good, too pure for his sybaritic self. But, having been herself both witness to and victim of the damage of scandal and gossip through most of her years with her mother, Cassia refused to allow the innocent Catherine the same humiliation, preferring to take it on herself in her place.

And for that, it seemed, Cassia would now bear the sting of Lady Castlemaine's venom this day as well.

"Well," Barbara Palmer said, "what are you doing here, Lady Cassia?"

The question was direct, framed with just the right amount of contempt to draw attention. Everyone standing within earshot of the two ladies drew nearer, anxious to witness the brewing confrontation. Not a sound came except the faint trickling of water flowing through a marble fountain somewhere amid the trimmed garden hedges and the distant trill of a wood lark hidden in the treetops.

Everyone waited to see how Cassia would respond to Lady Castlemaine's jab. When the silence became nearly overwhelming, Rolfe started to step forward, to escort Cassia away and spare her any further humil-

iation. Cassia saw his intent and put out a hand to
stop him.

"And good day to you, Lady Castlemaine," she
said, never taking her eyes from the other woman.
She smiled politely. "I would say that it is also rather
unexpected to see you out taking a leisurely stroll in
the Privy Garden just now. Should you not be occupied in performing your duty in attending to the needs
of Her Majesty at this hour?"

The implication was clear to all. The scandal of
Lady Castlemaine's appointment as a lady to the
queen's bedchamber was still one that was whispered
about at late night soirees when every other subject
had been exhausted. It had been formally requested
by King Charles soon after his new wife's arrival in
England. It was obvious to everyone that the idea of
it had come about only at the insistence of Lady Castlemaine. It was meant as an open insult to the new
queen, an attempt to show her who really held power
by forcing Catherine to tolerate her husband's most
notorious mistress in her bedchamber, a bold move,
even for Barbara Palmer.

At first, Catherine had flatly refused it, having already been duly advised by her mother, Donna Luiza,
Queen Mother of Portugal, of Charles's flagrant paramour. The king, though fond of his pretty new wife,
did not much like her refusing his suggestion, an innocent one he assured her. He especially didn't like her
defying him before his subjects, making him look the
fool.

Despite the queen's objection, an objection coupled
with extreme dramatics, Charles stood fast in his insistence on Lady Castlemaine's appointment. Catherine
stood just as fast in her refusal of it. Edward Hyde,
the Earl of Clarendon, and Lord Chancellor of England, was even called upon to help persuade Her

Majesty to relent. Still Catherine refused. Wagers were placed as to who would prevail. Surprisingly the odds favored the spirited little queen. And then, after months of constant sparring between the two newly-weds that had even brought on rumors of an annulment, Queen Catherine quite suddenly and most mysteriously acquiesced and was now made to suffer Barbara Palmer each day.

"Her Majesty is feeling poorly today and has taken to her bed," Lady Castlemaine said, toying with a corkscrew ringlet just above her right ear. She looked far too pleased with herself. "She said she wished to be left alone. I was most happy to oblige her."

"I'm certain you were, your devotion to your position being what it is." Cassia gave her a chilling smile. "I understand the queen could very well be carrying the king's child, the next King of England, even. His Majesty told me of it only a short time ago during our dinner in the Withdrawing Chamber. He was very excited, fair gushing, I would say, saying he hoped he would finally be blessed with a legitimate heir."

Lady Castlemaine's eyes narrowed at the innuendo, for it was no secret that she had already borne the king three bastard children, with, rumor had it, a fourth on the way. Before she could even begin to frame a response, Cassia went on.

"I believe His Majesty is now on his way to convey the good news to Frances Stuart in her apartments, he said. What a pity you shall miss him, Lady Castlemaine, but I'm certain he said he would be occupied with her for quite some time and didn't wish to be disturbed."

Barbara Palmer's eyes widened at hearing that the king had gone off to visit his latest conquest—and her most threatening competition yet.

"Well, I—"

"I am sorry to say that I cannot stay and chat," Cassia broke in. "I, too, must go, for I wish to stop by and visit the queen to extend my congratulations before I leave. Do consider donning a bonnet, Lady Castlemaine. The sun seems to be bringing a most unbecoming redness to your complexion. And we mustn't forget to try and stave off those tiny lines that seem to come upon a lady with age. We wouldn't want the king seeking younger, greener pastures. Good day to you. Lord Ravenscroft, Winifred, pray shall we continue?"

By the time Cassia had finished this parting sally, she had skillfully removed herself from within earshot of Lady Castlemaine, thereby preventing the woman from any response without giving the appearance of pursuing her, a thing Barbara Palmer would never lower herself to do. Even so, Rolfe doubted the lady could have spoken above two words at the time had she wanted to. Her hands were clenched tightly at her sides, her teeth dangerously set, and if ever he'd seen murder in a person's eyes, it was now so in hers. He wondered if Cassia realized the dangerous position she had just placed herself in.

As soon as they were a safe distance away from the Privy Garden, Rolfe came up beside her. "That was well done, Lady Cassia. I daresay Lady Castlemaine will think twice before attempting to rout you a second time. I wouldn't think it is too often she is shown the sharp side of another's tongue."

Cassia continued on her way. "Please do not commend me for my actions, Lord Ravenscroft. It is not something of which I am proud, but comes about only out of necessity to survive within the walls of this palace."

As Cassia worked her way deeper into the rookery of Whitehall, Rolfe could see that she was shaken from the confrontation, leaving him further confused. Most of the women he knew of, especially those at court, would have taken great pleasure in setting down someone as infamous as Lady Castlemaine. Such occurrences brought notoriety, and notoriety helped to raise one's social footing. Oddly, though, Cassia was genuinely displeased by the exchange.

Noting her reaction and, likewise, the vehemence of Lady Castlemaine's words to her, Rolfe began to see that he was not the only one to think living at the glittering royal court was not as enviable as many would believe.

Cassia stopped before the guarded doors that led to Queen Catherine's private apartments along the riverside of the palace. She turned. "Lord Ravenscroft, I know it is your duty to remain by my side at all times, but I must ask that you refrain from attempting to follow me in to visit the queen. She is yet quite wary of strangers in this country—as you can see from Lady Castlemaine, rightfully so—and being that she is indisposed and perhaps with child, I should think she would appreciate her privacy right now."

Rolfe nodded. "I will take you on your word that you will not attempt to leave through any door other than this one. I will remain here until you are finished visiting the queen."

"Thank you, Lord Ravenscroft. I give you my word."

Once inside the queen's inner apartments, the door shut safely on the outside world, Cassia took in as deep a breath as her stays would afford her. She put a hand to her chest to calm her pounding heart, holding onto the back of a nearby chair to steady herself.

Since leaving the Privy Garden and the confrontation with Lady Castlemaine, she'd been on the very brink of collapsing. It had taken every ounce of strength within her to keep herself calm, especially when she wanted nothing more than to run, to flee the palace, the city, and the ugliness that seemed to have taken over her entire world. But even as she thought this, Cassia knew she would never run, she could never leave, not if she was to rise above the charges society had brought against her.

It seemed that all she'd ever wanted in life was her freedom. Every other necessity was seen to. She'd never wanted for anything, at least anything that she knew of, except the freedom to go and do as she pleased. Her mother had taken her away from her home and family at a very young age. She'd left Winifred in charge of Cassia's upbringing, a task the maid had taken firmly in hand. And after her return to England, her father had begun in his efforts to wed her off. No one had ever asked what Cassia had wanted, how she had felt about all their grand plans for her life. She'd just been left to the wayside, a spectator watching as her future world was shaped by others' hands.

Cassia would close her eyes and dream of a time when she could do something as simple as sit among the flowers in her garden, a garden that would be at her own home, a garden filled with bright, fragrant roses and delicate lilies. She was most fond of roses, but they had never decorated her home for her mother had been horribly allergic to them. The most Cassia could ever hope for was to smell their sweet perfume from the trellis that grew outside her bedchamber window. In her own home, the home she had fashioned in her mind, she would fill every room with their brilliant blossoms, and when they withered, she would dry their petals to make a fragrant potpourri so as to keep them with her throughout the winter months.

But Cassia knew she could not remain thus, with her eyes closed, dreaming of this imaginary world in her mind. And she could not run away as if to pretend none of the rest of her life existed. That was precisely why she objected to the king's original plan to send her to Cambridgeshire. While an escape to the country might have quelled society's belief in her guilt, it would never have exonerated her. If she was ever to truly have her freedom, the freedom she so desperately desired, she would have to remain in London, to prove that she hadn't killed her father. Only then could she begin to think of the future.

It seemed like only yesterday her life had begun to attain some sort of balance, having just settled back since the passing of her mother in childbed earlier that year. The scandal of her mother having borne a bastard child had faded. Society had quickly turned to the misfortune of others for their amusements. Her father had been less easily provoked, allowing her to travel with the court to Tunbridge Wells under the chaperonage of her mother's sister, Claudia. Everything had begun to hold promise.

Until that final night.

That night. Cassia could still see the rage that had burned in her father's eyes when he'd come to her chamber late that night, flinging the door wide and startling her out of her sleep. She could not remember ever having seen him so angry, not in any of the numerous other times he'd brought her to his study to "punish" her, as he'd call it. She remembered how he'd pushed her down to sit in a chair while he'd proceeded to rail at her, pacing in front of her while telling her how ungrateful she was, how very like her mother she was, his wife, the Whore of Whitehall. Cassia had just sat there, afraid to move or even breathe, knowing from experience it was far better for her to remain silent and tolerate his ugly words than to speak up against them.

Far better and far less injurious.

But, this time, her silence only seemed to enrage him all the more. And when he'd raised up his walking stick, she had thought he would just slam it on the floor or against the desk as a means to frighten her into submission. It was a gesture he'd often employed in the past. But, not this time. This time he struck her a blow to her side and Cassia hadn't had time to fend him off before she'd felt him yanking her up from the chair, his fist coming straight for her face.

Cassia had closed her eyes before the blow. She couldn't recall the contact that had followed. What she did recall, and what she could not forget, was the moment when she'd opened her eyes to find her father lying in a pool of blood, the ancient quillon knife sticking out from his neck.

Chapter Six

"Her Majesty will see you now, Lady Cassia."

The Countess da Penalvo, a matronly Portuguese lady-in-waiting, came out from behind the closed door to the queen's inner chambers. She stepped aside to allow Cassia by, eying her warily, which was nothing new, for she'd always been distrustful of Cassia and the close relationship she'd come to have with the queen. The only difference now was that the countess made her suspicion even more evident, the damning rumors of Cassia murdering her father having spread their way into the sanctity of the queen's private apartments.

Thankfully, the queen's opinion differed from that of her waiting woman.

The Countess da Penalvo was the only lady-in-waiting remaining from the large entourage of older, darkly clothed Portuguese women who had originally accompanied Catherine of Braganza nearly two years before on her voyage to her husband and the new life waiting for her. The lot of the Portuguese detachment—excepting the countess, of course, who had devoted her entire life to serving the young queen—had returned to Portugal soon after the queen's arrival in England. Their stay, though brief, had not by any means been marked by pleasantry.

Catherine, who had been most eager to conform

with her new countrymen, had immediately adopted the very different English fashion soon after her arrival. Her Portuguese women, however, known mockingly among the courtiers as "the Farthingales" for their outdated style of dress, behaved as if doing so was somehow beneath them, drawing them a goodly amount of contempt and ridicule among Whitehall's thoroughly proud English nobles. It was all the excuse the women needed for an immediate return to their families in Portugal, leaving the frightened Catherine behind, virtually alone in a land among strangers.

Cassia thanked the countess in Portuguese, smiled and walked slowly by. She found the young queen reclining on a wicker-backed daybed that was set before the tall, leaded windows facing onto the Thames. A soft woolen blanket covered her legs and a worn and often-read leather-bound Bible lay open, face-down upon her lap.

Every time she walked into that room, it struck Cassia as strange, but somehow appealing how Catherine, at hearing of the dismal monetary state of the country, refused to waste a single farthing on anything other than the necessities. While the king and Lady Castlemaine lived in large roomy chambers that reeked of opulence, Catherine's walls were pathetically bare, excepting the few religious symbols and personal belongings she had brought with her from Portugal. Where Charles wore clothing that would rival Midas in splendor, Catherine had not so much as bought herself a single new gown during the entire course of the first year of her marriage. What allowance she was entitled to as queen was constantly being transferred into the hands of her spendthrift husband, who, it seemed, was ever in need of funds.

Cassia paused for a moment at the threshold, watching the queen. Catherine's dark hair was undressed, hanging in loose, thick ringlets about her small child-like face. She wore her nightclothes, a white linen gown decorated with blond Brussels lace, looking rather pale. One hand rested lightly on her flat stomach as if to somehow give strength to the babe growing there as she stared thoughtfully out the windows at the river traffic floating by. She presented a picture not of a queen of one of the world's most powerful countries, but of a little girl, lost and frightened. Still, somehow, at the sight of her, all the troubles and the ugliness that existed outside the walls of that room for Cassia seemed to melt into the background.

Catherine smiled when she looked up and spotted Cassia standing there. She motioned for her to step forward from the shadows of the antechamber into the room. She extended her hand toward Cassia, a hand that was ornamented only by her plain gold wedding band.

"Cassia, dearest friend, I was beginning to wonder if I would ever see your face at court again. I have missed you so very much. Come, please, sit here beside me so we can visit together awhile."

Catherine patted the cushion of the chair set beside her. As Cassia took the seat, she thought to herself how fragile Catherine looked and wondered if it perhaps had always been so and she was just now recognizing it after having been away these past weeks.

Catherine spoke to Cassia in her native Portuguese, for she still spoke very little of the English language. When she had arrived on England's shores, King Charles had not known more than a few words in Portuguese. Cassia had already been schooled in the Spanish language during her childhood, and had begun instruction in the queen's comparable tongue as soon as the union had been agreed upon. She was often called upon to act as translator for the royal couple.

"I have missed being in your service as well, Your Majesty. How do you fare?"

Catherine glanced out the windows for a moment, her dark, soulful eyes turning suddenly sad. Cassia noticed that she took a slow, deep breath before responding.

"I am well enough, I suppose. The royal physician believes this pregnancy will succeed, but after losing the other, I still worry so. I cannot seem to keep a crumb of food in my stomach and I fear for the health of the child. The physician tells me this sickness is a good sign and that it only lasts through the first few months."

Cassia smiled. She knew how very much Catherine wanted a child. It was a topic they had discussed often in their private conversations over tea. In Catherine's eyes, giving England an heir was her only true obligation as queen and one in which she was now desperate to succeed since the frightening miscarriage of her first pregnancy in the first year of her marriage.

With that unfortunate miscarriage, brought on when a fox had slipped inside the palace, jumping on the queen's bed and scaring her fiercely, had come the renewed whispers, for rumors of the new queen's barrenness had begun to circulate among Whitehall's courtiers even months before she'd arrived in England. They had begun, in an effort to abort the union, brought on by those who were displeased with the match between King Charles and the Portuguese princess. The rumors had eventually died down after the marriage had taken place. But after having such trouble in conceiving, then losing one babe since to miscarriage, many were renewing the denunciation, some even having the temerity to suggest that the king seek a divorce from Catherine for it. It was a suggestion that thankfully fell on deaf ears.

Cassia leaned forward and took Catherine's hand. "What is it that troubles you, Your Majesty?"

Catherine smiled weakly. "You always could tell when something was troubling me." She closed her eyes against the tears that were already threatening to spill. "It is nothing really. I do not know why I let it bother me so. I have just heard that *she* is breeding as well."

Cassia did not need an explanation as to who the queen was referring to. Obviously Barbara Palmer had somehow managed to breech the language barrier enough to inform the queen of her own pregnancy. How miserable it must be for Catherine to want so badly to give Charles and England an heir, and to have such difficulty in doing so. And yet, unjustly, she was made to watch as the greatest rival for her husband's affections bore children with remarkable ease.

"What does it matter if she has fifteen children?" Cassia said. "No one ever knows for certain who the unfortunate father is. Her breasts sag more with the passing of each birth, and I hear tell that her maids have a difficult time trying to cinch her belly into her stays each morning. And," she added, "most importantly, none of her children, no matter how many she has, will ever be heir to the throne of England. Only your child will, the child you now carry."

Catherine released a frustrated breath, unconvinced. "If only I could be certain this child will survive."

"It will, Your Majesty, you just have to believe in it. You must have faith and all will be well. Now, tell me," she said, changing the subject, "how goes your English instruction in my absence?"

"Not very well, I must say, though His Majesty has taken to teaching me a few words when he comes to visit me in the mornings. Today he taught me the word 'ro—,'" she struggled with it for a moment, trying to form her lips correctly to make the proper sound, " 'roger.' "

Cassia managed to suppress her surprise at hearing the queen speak such an inappropriate word. "And did His Majesty perhaps tell you what that word means?"

"Not exactly, although I believe it has something to do with either a dance or a card game. He only told me that when he brings Lord Buckingham here to see me, I should tell him that—how did he put it?—he should 'cease practicing his skills at *rogering* with Lady Stedley lest Lord Stedley become jealous.' "

Catherine glanced at Cassia for a reaction. "From the look on your face now, I would guess I was incorrect in my assumption of its meaning."

Though Cassia knew that it had been meant purely for amusement and not in any way maliciously, this would not have been the first time the king had pulled such a prank, teaching his wife an impolite word merely for the fun of seeing her repeat it to his shocked courtiers. She smiled. "I am afraid His Majesty is practicing trickery again, for that is certainly not a word you should repeat."

"What does it mean?"

"Let me just say that should the royal physician prove correct in his diagnosis and you are indeed with child, it would seem His Majesty's skills at performing *that* word were to be highly commended."

It took Catherine a moment to fully understand Cassia's explanation of the new word, but when its meaning finally dawned on her, her eyes grew wide and her face turned a deeper shade of red than the velvet pillows that cushioned the bed she lay upon.

"Why would the king wish me to say such a thing?"

Cassia patted her hand, trying not to make too much of it. "You know how much His Majesty loves a good jest and you know he would never intentionally hurt you. He adores you. In fact, when I saw him earlier today, you were all he could talk of."

Catherine's dark eyes lit up. "Truly?"

Cassia nodded. "I'm certain he just wanted you to help him pull a prank on Lord Buckingham and meant no harm by it at all."

"But what am I to do? He is bringing Lord Buckingham here to visit me later today. I cannot repeat *that* phrase to him now, knowing what it truly means."

Cassia thought a moment. "Why don't you turn the tables on His Majesty?"

"How would I do that?"

"Instead of repeating the phrase he taught you, why don't you substitute one of your own? You could just say something like 'His Majesty is so skilled at *that word* that it would appear England is to be granted an heir come the summer.' "

Catherine considered it. "What if he should become angry with me?"

"How could he become angry with you? All you need do is remind His Majesty that it was he who taught you the word in the first place. Really, though, I don't think you have anything to fret over. I'm certain His Majesty will find it very amusing, will think you most clever for turning the tables on him, and you will have thoroughly delighted him in the process."

This was all it took to convince Catherine to alter her usage of the new word. Suffering as she did from a constant feeling of ineptitude amid the more worldly English ladies, Catherine would do just about anything to appear clever to her husband and cause him to regard her in a pleasant light. She nodded. "And I think I will be certain that *she* is standing nearby when I say that. It will serve her a deserving turn, don't you think?"

"Indeed, Your Majesty, a most deserving turn."

Catherine smiled. "Enough of me. Now, come, Cassia, tell me how you are doing. When will you be returning to court?"

Cassia's gaiety faded. "I'm afraid I will be away from the palace for a little while, at least until the circumstances surrounding my father's death can be determined. His Majesty thinks it best. I must follow his wishes. But he has consented to allow me to stay in the city and visit you whenever I wish."

Catherine squeezed her hand. "Charles always knows what is best. And I refuse to believe you were in any way involved. How could you be capable of murder, and of your own father? It is entirely unthinkable. Anyone who knows you would surely have to realize how ridiculous it all is."

Cassia nodded, but thought to herself that not many of those at Whitehall really knew her at all. They only knew the person she wanted them to see, the person she had so skillfully invented, the woman they called Lady Winter.

Cassia was a little surprised to find Rolfe still standing in the exact spot she had left him earlier, leaning casually against the Chinese wallpaper, a stone-faced Winifred filling the small chair beside him.

She realized she had secretly hoped he'd have grown tired and would have left by now, for having Ravenscroft constantly at her side only served to remind her of her father's murder, and of how most everyone in London believed her responsible for it. She'd purposely extended her visit with the queen, hoping he'd have grown bored and would have gone to other parts of the palace for more interesting amusements.

But it seemed she had underestimated his loyalty to duty.

"You are most certainly true to your word, Lord Ravenscroft. I've been in visiting with the queen for nearly three hours. I'd have thought you would have gone off to chase some pretty skirt through the palace hallways by now."

"Though the idea does have its appeal, Lady Cassia, if you think to dissuade me from my duty through tedium, I can assure you it would be a wasted effort. I have spent far longer periods of time in far less interesting places, waiting merely for a courier to arrive. I once passed the length of a day sitting in a henhouse at a farm not far from Versailles, hens and all. You will find, my lady, I do not abandon a task, any task, for any reason. So, I am afraid you are stuck with me for the duration."

"A most appropriate choice of words, Lord Ravenscroft—having you stuck with me for the duration—and how very noble of you to adhere to the task. But, please, do not allow me to keep you from your preferred pursuits. I assure you I have no intention of fleeing the city and becoming a wanted felon."

Rolfe stepped in place beside her as she started down the hallway. "I have no fear of that, Lady Cassia. I do not believe you would attempt to flee the city, for you see, that would be very foolish, and after watching the way you handled the king today, I can say with certainty that you, Lady Cassia Montefort, are no fool."

Chapter Seven

Cassia excused herself the moment the hackney coach arrived back at Seagrave House. She needed time to plan, time to think of how she was going to prove her innocence. She needed to gather her wits and restore her sense of being. Actually, she needed time to be alone.

Cassia kept trying to convince herself this new disquietude she felt had come about only after the confrontation with Lady Castlemaine. But no matter how often she told it to herself, she knew inside that wasn't the case. She had faced Barbara Palmer many times before. It had never unsettled her, filling her with this urgent need to escape. It was Ravenscroft, and his effect on her, that had set her stomach to twisting.

All of her adult life—from the age of sixteen, when an acquaintance of her mother's, and a blackguard at that, André le Singe, had first tried shoving his beefy hand down the front of her bodice—Cassia had been capable of taking care of herself when it came to the male species and its eccentricities. With Monsieur le Singe, it had been a swift kick in the shin, succeeded by one to his groin area that had left him buckled over and squealing like the pig he was. Since then, Cassia had subdued her tactics markedly, refining her defenses to where she now could prostrate a rude or uncivilized fellow with mere words.

Why, then, did just being in the same room with Ravenscroft manage to render her witless?

She told herself she just needed to get away from him for a spell, that was all. She needed time to collect herself, ready her defenses, and then she'd be prepared to face him again.

No sooner had her foot touched the first riser on the stairs leading up to her chamber than did Cassia hear Rolfe following her. She stopped and turned to face him, causing him nearly to collide with her. Rolfe remained standing on the step just below the one she stood on, face-to-face with her, bare inches between them. The nearness was disconcerting.

Cassia took a step back, pleased that she now stood several inches taller. "Lord Ravenscroft, I am going to my chamber to be alone. I would like privacy. I can assure you I have no plans of slipping out a window or climbing down the southern rose trellis to make a break for the coast, so I do not think it necessary for you to follow me upstairs. If you would prefer, I shall sign an affidavit—in blood, of course—vowing to report to you should I feel the sudden need to leave."

Rolfe didn't move, not an inch. Damn him.

"Have I done something to offend you, my lady?"

"You mean besides forcing your way into my life without my consent? Why on earth should I be offended at that?"

This woman was far too young to be so damned cynical, Rolfe thought as he faced her. Surely it hadn't just come about since his arrival in her life earlier that day. No, this habit of hers of using well-placed words to display her utter distrust of the world and her contempt for every person in it had come about from years of practice, for she was far too skilled at it now. Perhaps he should try more subtle tactics, attempt to put her at ease.

"Lady Cassia, a word, if I may?"

Rolfe stepped down to the bottom floor. He motioned toward the parlor door, indicating she should proceed him inside. Seeing him, the way he stood there, Cassia suddenly had the impression that Ravenscroft was the true owner of the house, and she was now the guest. It was an impression she didn't much care for. Still, she was curious as to what he had to say, so she stepped down and walked straight past him, seating herself on a small settee at the center of the room.

"Would you care for some refreshment?" Rolfe asked, again acting the host.

"No, I would not, but since this is my house, Lord Ravenscroft, were I to desire something, I would simply get it. I do not think it your responsibility, nor your right, to ask me if I would like to have something that is already mine. You are the stranger here, sir, not I, a thing you obviously need to be reminded of. I should be the one asking you if you would like any refreshment."

She stared at him. He noticed the offer of the drink never passed her lips.

Rolfe took the seat across from her. He fished inside his coat, removing a white handkerchief. He unfolded it and waved it slowly in front of her face. "I surrender, all right? You win."

When Cassia didn't respond to this mild attempt at humor, Rolfe set the handkerchief aside, parted his legs, and leaned his elbows on his knees. He steepled his fingers under his chin choosing his words carefully. "Lady Cassia, I understand your hostility at having me in your home against your wishes. I am certain it cannot be pleasant for you. But please allow me to remind you it is not as if I requested this assignment. I was ordered to, as you put it, force myself into your life without your consent. Neither one of us has much of a choice in the matter, so can we somehow try to set aside our differences and attempt to make the best of it?"

Cassia frowned. She knew Ravenscroft was right. She shouldn't be angry with him. He hadn't been the one to place himself in her life; he was just doing what he'd been ordered by the king to do. She couldn't in all honesty say that she wouldn't do the same, had she been placed in the same situation. It had just been convenient to lay the blame on Ravenscroft, as he was always at her side.

He must think her an ill-bred, ill-tempered virago. Thinking back on it, her behavior since their meeting had been less than civilized. Winifred would be aghast; she would say she had taught her better. Cassia was about to apologize to Rolfe for her inappropriate behavior, to offer a fresh beginning, but before she could, the butler, Clydesworthe, presented himself at the door.

"Milady's cousin, Geoffrey Montefort, and a Mr. Finchley are here requesting an audience."

Cassia nodded. "Thank you, Clydeswo—"

"You may show them in."

Cassia whirled about, ready to inform Rolfe that although he might be in her home to protect her, she still held the authority over the household. It seemed, despite their truce, he would need constant reminding of that fact. Unfortunately, she had to temper her tongue. Her guests were already coming into the room.

Mr. Silas Finchley was her father's solicitor and had been so since Cassia and her mother had returned from France four years earlier, and long before that, no doubt. He was nearing fifty, a short man with a squat build whose curled periwig was slightly crooked, his suit of brown woolen cloth outdated. His pinpoint eyes were made to appear even smaller by round gold-rimmed spectacles perched on a nose that was round and red as a new spring cherry, a nose that seemed constantly congested. Even now he was pulling a crumpled handkerchief from his pocket and blowing his nose with the blast of a trumpet, muttering his apologies as he stuffed the cloth back into his coat.

Still, Mr. Finchley had always been kind to Cassia, standing beside her at her father's burial and patting her hand comfortingly.

Following Mr. Finchley, and arriving with all the grandeur of the king, came Cassia's second guest into the room. Geoffrey Montefort was her cousin, though the connection was a dubious one, and one the proud Monteforts would have preferred to forget. Her father's younger brother, a whimsical buck named Harold, had gotten a pretty laundry maid with child. When the transgression became known, much to the horror of his father, the previous Marquess of Seagrave, Harold off and wed the girl, a secret marriage, the documentation of which having never come to light.

Faced with their disapproval, Harold left the family fold and set up house with his new bride somewhere in the North Country. The child was born the following spring, a boy.

Since the previous marquess had had seven sons, the oldest of which was Cassia's father, and since all of the brothers who preceded the capricious Harold had sons of their own—excepting Cassia's father, of course—no one had ever bothered to refute the relation. The fear that the son of the laundry-maid-presumed-wife would ever lay claim to the title was nearly nonexistent.

Except for that unexpected and unavoidable peril

called war, for besides being accomplished at begetting sons, the Montefort men—excepting Cassia's father, of course—were also proficient at one other thing. They were notoriously horrible shots. All of her father's brothers, and her father's brother's sons, were killed during the wars, all, excepting the laundry-maid-presumed-wife's son, Geoffrey, who now came into the room.

In contrast to Mr. Finchley's rather drab attire, Geoffrey wore what Cassia could only term a suit of utter magnificence. It was made up of rich red velvet, adorned on every seam with golden braid and shining buttons, epaulets topping both shoulders in an attempt to make them appear broader than they had been bestowed by nature. He wore a wig made up of a black profusion of curls, mimicking the king, for Geoffrey's natural hair was both short and a rather sandy shade of blond. It was the one attribute he'd inherited from his mother, the laundry-maid-presumed-wife.

Geoffrey's silk hose, the same red as his suit, encased his lower legs like a second skin, and slid into matching red shoes decorated with shining gold buckles. The cost of the entire ensemble would most probably keep the bread baker's family in cakes and ale for months, which was surprising to Cassia, since she didn't know how Geoffrey afforded such luxury.

With the exception of her mother's sister, her Aunt Claudia, who was currently abroad, Geoffrey was Cassia's only other living relative. Being that he was the sole Montefort male remaining, he would now be the fourth Marquess Seagrave as well.

Hence, the obvious reason for his flagrant attire and for the unscheduled visit this day.

"Good day, Cassia," Finchley said, taking the seat Rolfe had just vacated. He set the flat worn-leather case he used to hold his documents on his lap and untied its corded fastening. "It is so good to see you again. I hope we have not come at an inopportune time?"

Cassia shot Rolfe a quick look, then wondered why she had felt the need to. "No, Mr. Finchley, you know you are always welcome here."

Finchley smiled, his face flushing slightly. "You are looking quite well. How are you faring these days, my dear?"

"As well as can be expected, given the circumstances. Thank you for asking, Mr. Finchley."

Cassia glanced to the doorway where the diligent Clydesworthe awaited. "I believe tea would be in order, Clydesworthe, and some of the cook's buttered scones, if you please."

She returned her attentions to her guests. "Mr. Finchley, Geoffrey, please allow me to introduce Rolfe Brodrigan, the Earl of Ravenscroft."

She purposely didn't tell them why Rolfe was there.

Mr. Finchley shook Rolfe's hand, then settled back in his chair, ready to see to the business at hand. Geoffrey, sitting comfortably on a cushioned bench set near the tall windows, merely nodded, ignoring the social niceties. Perhaps, he thought, now that he was a marquess, he no longer needed to be polite.

"Cassia," Finchley began, "as I am sure you are already aware, I have come here to discuss the settlement of your father's estate. I would have come sooner, but there were some details that needed to be seen to, loose ends that needed to be tied off, if you will."

He paused then, glancing at Rolfe. "Ah, perhaps Lord Ravenscroft might prefer to leave us in privacy for a moment ... ?"

Cassia looked to Rolfe, fully expected him to quit

the room as had been suggested. He did not immediately move.

"I can assure you I have no interest in your business, Mr. Finchley," he said, "but I would ask to remain in the room, if you wouldn't mind?"

Finchley looked somewhat startled at Rolfe's response. When Cassia made no attempt to contradict him, he shrugged and went on. "As you wish. . . ."

Finchley started shuffling through the papers in his case. "I have asked Geoffrey to attend this meeting with us because, being that he is the last Montefort male, this will naturally concern him as well. Ah, here it is." He pulled a single document from the other papers, then looked up to regard Cassia directly. "Shortly after your mother's unfortunate passing earlier this year, your father came to me seeking my advice and assistance on a petition he wished to bring before the Crown. It concerned the distribution of his estate, you see—moreover, how certain aspects of this would be accomplished. I hold in my hand a copy of this petition. I would add that it was granted and stamped with the Seal of England not two weeks before his untimely demise."

Geoffrey, who had hereto remained in the background, suddenly leaned forward. "What sort of petition would this be, Mr. Finchley?"

Finchley cleared his throat and continued, speaking only to Cassia. "As you well know, Cassia, your father did not leave a son to continue the Seagrave line. Due to the war, neither did any of the brothers that followed, excepting the youngest one—Harold, I believe his name was."

"My father," Geoffrey piped in.

"Geoffrey, please," Cassia said, turning to Mr. Finchley. "Pray continue, Mr. Finchley."

Finchley nodded. "I am sorry to have brought up

the subject. I know it must only serve to remind you of the grief you must feel at the loss of so many family members—war is such a tragic thing—but I felt I must clarify a few things."

"It is quite all right, Mr. Finchley. Since I was raised in France by my mother, I did not know any of my father's relatives. From what I heard, there was quite a number of them. I only heard of them and of the tragedy of their deaths at my return, but I do thank you for your consideration."

Finchley smiled, taking his handkerchief out to blow once again. "Yes, well, this was a matter of great trouble to your father, the shortage of heirs. Citing the fact that your mother had served His Majesty King Charles during his years while in exile in France, thereby depriving your parents of the many opportunities in which to conceive a male heir, your father made a request of the king."

"What sort of request was this?" Geoffrey asked.

"Geoffrey, please," Cassia said. "I'm certain Mr. Finchley has every intention of telling us."

Finchley paused, glancing a moment to Geoffrey. He then handed the document he'd been reading to Cassia. "Cassia, it is my duty to inform you that your father sought and has succeeded in naming you sole heiress to his estate."

Chapter Eight

"What!"

Geoffrey nearly leaped across the room in his attempt to snatch the document from Cassia' hand.

Cassia pulled it back.

Mr. Finchley continued, reading now from his copy of Lord Seagrave's petition.

"At the passing of Halifax Montefort, third Marquess of Seagrave, it is hereby deemed that his only natural child, Lady Cassia Louise Montefort, shall be sole heiress to the Seagrave estate, and that, on the occasion of her marriage, her husband be made fourth Marquess of Seagrave in succession, a male son being made the heir. In addition, should Lady Cassia not contract such marriage and deliver a male heir, the rights of inheritance shall pass to the next presumptive male heir, Mister Geoffrey Montefort."

Cassia remained silent for several long moments, trying desperately to take this all in. "How can this be? How could I possibly inherit my father's entire fortune? Surely this cannot be legal. Surely there has been some mistake. Yes, that is it. It is all a misunderstanding, isn't that it, Mr. Finchley?"

"I agree, Cassia, this is unusual, most unusual, but it is most legal as well, I assure you. Should he choose to, the king could appoint most anyone he wished to the Seagrave title, even Lord Ravenscroft here."

He looked at Rolfe then and added, "I was only being hypothetical, of course."

"Of course," Rolfe replied.

"But a woman cannot acquire a title by birth," Cassia broke in. "Primogeniture forbids it."

"There are exceptions to every rule," Finchley went on. "Still, in this case you would not inherit the Seagrave title as would a male heir, Cassia. By your father's request and the king's order, the title would pass through you to your husband and any male children you should have. You would merely be a vessel for the title to pass through, if you pardon my choice of words. And, you must remember, that it has been stipulated that should no son come of your marriage who would by rights inherit, then Geoffrey would, of course, become the next in-line inheritor."

"That could take forty years!" Geoffrey said, throwing his arm outward in disgust. "I'll be wrinkled and decrepit! I could even be dead. What good would it do me then?"

"Geoffrey, please," Cassia said, trying to focus all her attentions on what Mr. Finchley was saying. "Surely this petition can somehow be reversed, Mr. Finchley. I never wanted this responsibility. I never could have dreamed my father would have done something so irregular and inappropriate as this."

Finchley took Cassia's hand. "It was his wish, Cassia. Your father felt very strongly that blood ties were more important to a legacy than a name. As Shakespeare says, 'That which we call a rose by any other name would smell as sweet.' "

"Perhaps, but Shakespeare had never met my father."

"You are his child, Cassia, his only child, of his blood, and it was his desire, his final wish that you would carry on the Seagrave line through your children."

"But I never wanted that responsibility, Mr. Finchley. My father well knew that. I refused every attempt he made at a marriage for me. Can you not simply forgo this whole terrible thing and allow me the portion that was originally intended, leaving all and sundry to Geoffrey?"

"Yes, Mr. Finchley," Geoffrey piped in, "can you not do that?"

"Geoffrey, please," Cassia said a final time.

Mr. Finchley shook his head. "I am afraid I cannot do that. It is too late. The petition has been decreed by royal writ and it has already passed the seal. It is virtually irreversible."

Cassia stared at the floor, seeing, but not really noticing the frayed edges of the carpet beneath the settee while she searched for some semblance of a solution to this ungodly mess. How could her father have done this to her? Why would he have?

And then it came to her. It came to her as if her father were suddenly standing there in the room before them speaking the words clearly himself. Though he'd tried countless times, through countless measures, he hadn't been able to force her into marriage while he'd been alive. This petition was simply his way of trying to force her to it in death.

Cassia would have sworn she could hear her father laughing, if not for the fact that he was lying beneath several feet of cold earth in the Montefort family cemetery in Cambridgeshire. That was one thing of which she was certain—perhaps the only thing anymore—for she'd stood right there and had watched as his coffin had been lowered into the ground, and she'd remained standing there, waiting while each shovelful of dirt had been tossed atop it, leaving only after it had been firmly packed down.

Cassia returned her attentions to Mr. Finchley. "Then the simplest remedy I can see to this debacle is for me not to marry. That way all will go to Geoffrey, will it not?"

"Not exactly." Finchley glanced at Geoffrey again, clearing his throat. "You see, your father thought you might respond in that fashion, Cassia, so he also attached a further condition to his will, an additional codicil, if you will."

Finchley removed another set of papers from his leather case. "Let's see. Here it is. Should you choose not to wed and continue the Seagrave line on through yourself as your father wished and as King Charles deemed, the title and its entail will indeed pass to Geoffrey. However, the remainder of his fortune and properties, totaling in excess, I believe,"—he glanced at his papers—"of eighty thousand pounds, will remain yours. Geoffrey would inherit the Seagrave title and that is all."

"Eighty thousand pounds!" Geoffrey exclaimed.

Finchley glanced at him. "Lord Seagrave was a wise investor."

Cassia was still trying to deal with the fact that her father had left virtually nothing for Geoffrey. "Am I to believe that my father made no further concession for Geoffrey? No allotment of funds? No allowance?"

"Of course not. Your father did stipulate an allowance for Geoffrey of, I believe ..." Finchley scanned the papers. "Ah, here it is. Geoffrey is to be allotted an annuity of fifty pounds, no more, to be given quarterly by you and to be overseen by me. The seat at Cambridgeshire, being that it is entailed, would be included as part of Geoffrey's inheritance. Of course, with only the fifty-pound annuity at his disposal, it would soon be financially ruined. The other properties—the estate in Lancashire, the holdings in Ireland, and Seagrave House here in London—being that they are not entailed, would be passed to you regardless."

"I was never aware my father had acquired these other properties."

Finchley sneezed and blew his nose. "He only came by them recently, in the past five years, I would say."

Cassia felt a strange and definite chill come into the room. It was almost as if her father's spirit were standing there, watching them and enjoying himself thoroughly as they attempted to sort through the messy predicament he had left them in. She had never realized, could never have guessed that her father held such ill will toward Geoffrey. If he had doubted the authenticity of his brother Harold's marriage to Geoffrey's laundry-maid mother, why then hadn't he made an attempt to investigate the matter further before?

"Why, Mr. Finchley? Why would my father have done such a terrible thing?"

Finchley looked at Geoffrey, frowning. "If you'll pardon my saying, given Geoffrey's past affection for the gaming tables, your father feared the total loss of the estate, which is why he has stipulated the amount of the annuity. He does this only to prevent that which he had worked for and amassed all these years from being lost through profligacy. And ..." Finchley opened his case a third time, removing a sealed letter from inside, "at our last meeting, your father gave me this letter to deliver to your hands in the event of his death."

Cassia took up the letter, but did not open it. She tucked it into the pocket of her gown and then stood. A letter from her father was too much to deal with now. No one said a word, leaving the room eerily silent.

Cassia looked at all the faces around her: at Mr.

Finchley, whose task it had been to bring her this most unexpected news; at Geoffrey, who looked as if he were preparing to explode into a riot of red velvet at any moment; at Ravenscroft—she'd somehow forgotten he'd even been in the room—looking at her now as if he actually pitied her.

Cassia felt inextricably trapped, caught between the insane urge to laugh and the immediate need to burst into tears. She fought to take hold of her troubled emotions. Finally she looked at Mr. Finchley, holding the damnable petition out to him. "Do you realize what this all means, Mr. Finchley? Do you know what will come of this? This makes it all the more likely that I did actually kill my father."

"But you did not even know of the existence of the petition before now," Rolfe said.

"Yes, you know that and I know that, and every person in this room knows that, but when word of this petition gets out at court—and it will, I can well assure you—it will all but seal my fate in the eyes of the law, and the world, for that matter. It will only be a matter of time before I will be charged and tried for the murder of my own father."

It had taken a half hour to calm Geoffrey down after the details of her father's petition had been disclosed. It had taken another half hour to get him to leave. Only after three glasses of her father's finest brandy and repeated assurances from Cassia that she'd had no knowledge of the petition before Mr. Finchley had brought it to them did he finally leave. Cassia worried over his state of mind, knowing how badly she would feel if she had just learned she'd been left with nearly nothing after expecting to get everything. Mr. Finchley kindly assured her that Geoffrey would be all right, once matters settled down.

In the quiet peacefulness of her bedchamber hours later now, Cassia's thoughts were no longer occupied with Geoffrey, or Mr. Finchley, or with her father's shocking petition. She was sitting, staring at the letter Mr. Finchley had been instructed to give her from her father. It was just where it had been since she'd left that upsetting meeting, atop her writing desk in her bedchamber, still unopened. His scratchy, almost illegible handwriting stood out boldly on the paper where he'd written her name, his unmistakable seal, the letter *S* surrounded by a thorny wreath, holding the letter closed on his last words to her.

Cassia wasn't certain she even wanted to read it. After the afternoon's events, she wondered what else her father could have done, what unexpected pitfalls awaited her inside that sealed letter. What else could her father have to tell her now, in his death, that he hadn't been able to tell her while he'd been alive? Was it an apology for his treatment of her, his heartfelt remorse for abusing her the way he had? Would he beg for her forgiveness so he could retreat to the afterlife with a clear conscience?

Something like that, an apology or even an explanation, if meant sincerely, could never be conveyed in writing, and somehow Cassia knew that had never been her father's intent in writing the letter to her.

It took nearly another quarter hour for Cassia to finally decide that she would open the letter. She could sit there speculating on it all night and into the next morning, too, and she would still never know what had been his purpose in writing the letter if she didn't at least open it and read what was written inside.

Before she could change her mind, Cassia took up the letter, sliding her finger beneath the edge, and broke the red wax seal.

To my dearest daughter, if you are reading this letter, then you have undoubtedly already been told by Mr. Finchley of my petition to the king and of your inheritance. Please know that I did this only for your protection. I have not always treated you as a father should a daughter and as I write this letter I cannot find any reasonable explanation for my actions. I will simply say that sometimes circumstances cause a man to do things he should not do, things he later regrets. Someday I hope you will understand. But that is not the purpose of this letter. Cassia, I feel I must warn you. There are things happening which you have no knowledge of, individuals who would seek to use you or take what you have been given. Your mother did not raise you to be a fool though, so I need not worry overmuch. But know this: if it should ever come to a matter of your life being in danger, there exists a means of protection for you. It is in the form of a document, and for caution's sake, I will not reveal here where it will be found. I cannot be certain these words will be read only by your eyes. If you think on it long enough, you will soon figure out where I have hidden it. I will tell you this— only you can know where it is. Your father, Seagrave.

As was his usual custom, her father had used a multitude of words to say very little.

Setting the letter aside, Cassia got up and went to lay on the bed. She took up one of her handkerchiefs, soaking it in a bowl of cool, scented water, and pressed it to her forehead in an effort to ease the ceaseless throbbing that had begun shortly after Mr. Finchley and Geoffrey had taken their leave. Having now read her father's cryptic letter, a letter that left her even more confused, the throbbing had grown to such proportion that she was certain anyone standing near her would be able to hear its pounding clearly.

Would it never end? Again, someone was telling her that her life was in danger. The king had stated it. Ravenscroft had repeated it. And now her father was sending her messages from the grave. What she wanted to know was, if it was so obvious to everyone else, why didn't she realize this danger herself? She did not feel at all threatened. Surely some keen, intuitive power would tell her if she was in some sort of peril. And what sort of document was her father talking about, this mysterious means of protection for her?

Cassia heard the door to her chamber open and looked as the maid, carrying a tray bearing a teapot and a small plate of biscuits, came in.

"Set the tray on the table by the windows, please, Lynette."

She'd asked down for a pot of the cook's special herbal tea. She didn't exactly know what it was the cook put into the flowery concoction, but it had always helped to calm her frazzled nerves in the past. It had done wonders for her after her father's murder. She was hoping now it would help to quell the incessant pounding in her head and allow her some inkling of relief.

"Will there be anything else, milady?"

"No, that will be all for now, Lynette. Thank you."

The maid bobbed a quick curtsy and turned to quit the room.

"Lynette, a moment, if you please," Cassia said. "I thought I heard someone knocking outside earlier. Was someone at the door?"

Actually, at the time, Cassia hadn't been certain if it had been the door or just the pounding in her head.

"Yes, milady, someone did come to the door. 'Twas

your cousin, Mr. Geoffrey. He asked to speak with you privately, but Lord Ravenscroft told him you were indisposed and asked him to return at another, more convenient time."

Cassia sat upright with an alacrity that startled even herself. "Lord Ravenscroft sent Geoffrey away, you say?"

"Yes, milady."

Cassia looked toward the door, wondering when exactly she had given Ravenscroft the right to decide which visitors she would see or not see. She knew he was committed to this task of guarding her, but he certainly seemed to be taking his duty a little beyond the proper parameters. Perhaps it was time someone apprise him of just who it was who ran the household.

Cassia started for the door, still clutching the handkerchief, completely forgetting that moments earlier, her head had been pounding so fiercely that even the slightest movement had left her feeling drained. "Where is he?"

The maid, Lynette, looked startled at her mistress's reaction. "Mi-mister Geoffrey is gone, milady, he—"

"No, not Geoffrey. Ravenscroft. Where is he? No doubt stretched out before the hearth fire, his feet propped upon the tea table, smoking a pipe?"

"Lord Ravenscroft is in the Green Chamber, milady, but—"

It was too late. Cassia was already through the door. She stopped when she saw that a makeshift truckle bed had been set up in the small antechamber outside her bedchamber.

"What is this?"

Lynette looked almost afraid to answer. "It is for Lord Ravenscroft, milady."

"I thought you said he was in the Green Chamber."

"He is, milady, right now, but he instructed Quigman to bring the bed up here for him to sleep on so he could keep watch over you at night and—"

Cassia spun about and started down the hallway, making her way directly for the Green Chamber.

Duty was one thing, she told herself, but this complete usurpation of her life was another. She didn't for one minute believe her life to be in danger. Wasn't it obvious? If whoever had killed her father had also wanted her dead, why wouldn't the murderer have just seen to it the same time her father had been killed?

Cassia was tired of taking orders from supposedly well-meaning men, tired of playing the proper and passive lady and doing what she was told to do. First the king with his having appointed Ravenscroft to act as her shadow, then her father with his damnable petition. And now Ravenscroft himself was directing her life and everything in it as well. What was it that made men think they had the God-given right to arrange the lives of others as if they were pawns in a chess game? Was this arrogance something they acquired in the womb?

Cassia halted before the closed door to the Green Chamber. She could hear nothing coming from inside. She prepared to knock, then stopped herself short of it, and grasped the door handle firmly to proceed inside.

Cassia froze not two steps into the room. The angry words she'd prepared to say faded into obscurity.

Rolfe was standing before the open windows that faced out onto the western side of the city, his back to her, the fading sunset casting a pink and orange aura of light around his entire body. His entire *naked* body.

He was in a copper tub that came only to his calves and was pouring water from a stoneware pitcher over his broad and soapy shoulders. His back was to her and he was obviously unaware of her standing there.

His body, Cassia thought with honesty, was simply magnificent. She stood there, unable to move, unable to even look away from him. She watched, fascinated, her mouth suddenly becoming dry as the clear water from the pitcher cascaded down over his back, his buttocks, the length of his long hairy legs.

He was as lean as if he had been carved from granite, like those lovely statues of the Roman gods that stood in the gardens of Whitehall, but even more fascinating, for, unlike the statues, Ravenscroft was alive and quite real.

Cassia would often visit the gardens when most of the court were occupied in other parts of the palace, and would spend hours just staring at those statutes, watching the way the sunlight would play across them. She would run her hands over their smooth lines, wondering at their craftsmanship, marveling at the remarkable men who were portrayed there.

These men, these heroic and courageous men looked so strong, larger than life, so very different from any man Cassia had ever seen before. She would tell herself that the sculptor who had made those magnificent creations had surely carved his work from a picture he held in his mind, for no man could ever be so finely crafted, so ultimately male.

Standing there now, faced with Ravenscroft's naked body, real and human before her, Cassia realized just how mistaken she had been in that assumption. She understood now why so many sculptors chose the male body—certain male bodies—as their subjects. Ravenscroft would have made a fine one.

An interesting warmth began to rise up inside of her, slowly, like the fanning of a newly sparked fire spreading through every limb as she stood there, watching Rolfe at his bath. She did not even realize that her heart was pounding against her chest, for all she was aware of was the sight of him bathed in the glow of the setting sun, water droplets glistening on his sun-darkened skin.

It was the first time Cassia had ever seen the male body unclothed. She thought him beautiful, each muscle defined, tightening, flexing as he lathered himself along his arms and the back of his neck. Cassia wondered how it would feel to run her fingers over his slick soapy arms, if he would feel as solid beneath her hands as he appeared. She was aware of a sudden sensation of wanting, a need deep inside, and she was clenching that handkerchief in her hands so tightly, twisting it in her fingers as she—

Rolfe started to turn.

Cassia spun about, rushing down the hallway, back toward her bedchamber.

"Clydesworthe, is that you, man? I need a drying cloth. Could you . . ."

Rolfe looked toward the door, certain he had heard someone come into the room. No one was there now, but he could see that the door was standing slightly ajar in the fading light.

He started to step from the tub and spotted something lying on the floor, something small and white and wadded into a ball. He walked across the carpet, leaving a dripping trail of water as he bent down to retrieve it.

It was a handkerchief, a very delicate and feminine handkerchief, edged with blond Venetian lace and embroidered in golden thread with the letter *C*.

A smile came to Rolfe's mouth as he lifted the handkerchief to his face and breathed in its heady scent, immediately recognizing the same scent that followed Cassia wherever she went.

Chapter Nine

Rolfe did not see Cassia again the rest of that evening. When she neglected to come down for the evening meal, he was quickly informed upon his questioning the maid, Lynette, that "milady had requested a tray brought up from the kitchens to her chamber, pleading off with a headache and extending her apologies to his lordship for her unexpected, but necessary absence."

Quigman, the groom and the unfortunate man to whom Cassia had assigned the unpleasant task of removing Rolfe from the premises earlier that day—a task that had gone off undone, Rolfe recalled—had left for a short time after supper, indicating to Clydesworthe that he had a letter to deliver for his mistress posthaste.

By ten o'clock that evening, Rolfe was beginning to wonder if Cassia had perhaps left the house without his knowing, using Quigman having gone off on his errand as some sort of decoy to keep him from suspecting anything might be afoot. Rolfe was beginning to realize that Cassia was not at all like the typical gently bred female. She may look like one, sound like one, even smell like one, he thought with a slight grin, but there was yet a decided difference to her. Cassia did not simply accept what others set down to her; she had a mind of her own, a characteristic not often seen in noble young ladies. It was a distinction Rolfe greatly admired, a distinction that only added to her innate originality. Knowing this, her having stolen away in the darkness of night was a distinct possibility.

At half past ten Rolfe went to Cassia's bedchamber and found that she had not, in fact, run off without his knowing, but was asleep on her bed, wearing the clothes she'd been in earlier that day, the dark mourning gown tight to her neck, curled up in a ball atop the pale blue damask coverlet.

She looked so vulnerable, lying there. Her supper plate was sitting, untouched, on a table beside her, a cup of tea, half filled, beside it. Her abigail, the stout and indifferent Winifred, lay on a truckle bed in a corner at the far side of the room, but even with the distance that separated them, her rumbling snore filled the chamber.

Rolfe turned to leave, his mind set at ease as to Cassia's whereabouts, but stopped himself short of it when he noticed a draft wafting its chilling way through the room. He turned and, seeing that the window near Cassia's bed had been propped open slightly, he started over to shut it.

He wondered at why the window should be open, especially since it was nearly winter and the night air had a definite bite to it. Could the window be thus because Cassia had, indeed, thought to flee and had gotten so far as the open window for her escape? It would explain her lying there still wearing her day clothes, but Rolfe couldn't see traveling bag, nor did it appear as if she'd packed up her toiletries. He thought for a moment. Cassia was no fool. She would know she would need at least a change of clothing and a hairbrush, perhaps. But there her hairbrush lay, at the edge of her dressing table, amid her hairpins and ribbons. He pulled the window shut, latched it, and turned to go.

It was then he saw a small stack of papers spread out across the writing table. Something about the way they were strewn so haphazardly across the table when everything else in the chamber was so orderly and neat, caught his attention. He didn't know why, but he picked up the topmost sheet and peered at it in the moonlight.

It was a sketch, depicting a small bird, a Dartford warbler, if memory served, judging from its short, pointed beak and large, inquisitive eyes. Its small gray and orange body was perched on an elm branch, its head cocked slightly as if it were curious about what it was seeing. Though drawn with only a simple charcoal pencil, the artist's eye for balance and shading seemed to give the viewer the impression that at any moment the tiny creature would hop from its perch and take flight from the page.

Rolfe set the drawing aside and started to glance through the others in the pile. There were a number of them, made up of various objects that were set around the room or that could be seen from the window's vantage. A gown draped carefully across a chair, a pair of slippers sitting beside it. The sign hanging crookedly outside the glove maker's shop at the street corner. Each drawing, while showing certainly ordinary things, had been made in such a way as to evoke a certain mood or feeling in the viewer. Not many artists whose work Rolfe had seen had that same ability.

There were several more sketches, these turned curiously facedown on the desk. Rolfe took them up and studied the first one. The unmistakably foppish form of Cassia's cousin, Geoffrey, was poised upon the page, sitting as he had been earlier that day, when he'd come with Mr. Finchley, before he'd learned of Seagrave's petition, when he still expected to be named the heir. Slouched in his chair, he looked as if he had the world on a gilded platter set before him. From his frilly shirt cuffs to his beribboned shoes, every detail had been taken into account. Except for one. Oddly, in the space where he should have had a face, there was nothing, just black shading, as if only that part of him were obscured by some sort of shadow.

The second facedown sketch was of a maid. She was standing, looking at herself in a mirror, and holding a gown up against herself as if to imagine what it might look like on. The gown was far too ornate to have been the maid's, and had the picture suddenly come to life, Rolfe knew, from the way she was portrayed, one leg extended, head cocked to the side she would be pretending to dance. Again, every detail had been taken into account, except the maid's face which was strangely obscured.

Rolfe didn't need to be told who the artist of the drawings was; it was obvious just looking at them, for surely the indifferent Winifred would never be so artfully inclined. Cassia had drawn them, and as he gazed at each one, Rolfe thought to himself that she was really quite talented. It made him wonder all the more why she had neglected to draw in the face.

Setting the sketches aside, Rolfe walked over to the side of Cassia's bed. With her face illuminated in the moonlight spilling in through the windows beside her, he knew she was undoubtedly the most beautiful woman he had ever seen. In sleep, she was even more lovely than in the daylight, for her face had taken on a softer appearance, giving up that cautious, ever-watchful expression as if she expected something or someone to come after her.

He could recall, when he'd been standing behind Cassia at the palace earlier that day, that the top of her head came to just above his chin, making her taller than most women, yet not overly so. Still, the way she carried herself might make one think she stood even taller.

Her breasts, what he could make of them, hidden as they were beneath the modest neckline of her black mourning gown, were neither too big nor too small, but like the rest of her, perfectly proportioned to fit her frame. He wondered at how they would mold themselves to fit the shape of his palm and longed to feel their softness beneath his fingers. He could see the rise and fall of them as she slept and wanted to bury his face against them, to hear her heart beating wildly in his head as she called out his name . . .

How could this woman, who drew such vivid pictures as the ones he'd seen on the desk, and who looked so innocent and so damned vulnerable lying there now with the moonlight spilling over her, ever be thought of as a murderess? Rolfe simply could not envision Cassia clutching a knife and plunging it so savagely into her father's neck as to kill him. Was she truly innocent? Had someone carefully arranged the whole scene to incriminate Cassia in a murder she hadn't committed? Or was she simply a talented actress, well practiced at making men believe what she wanted?

Innocence was his initial impression, but Rolfe couldn't be certain. He hadn't been with Cassia long enough to read her clearly. A woman of her complexity would take years to unravel. Perhaps a lifetime. The one thing, perhaps the only thing, of which he was certain was every time he turned, the thread of mystery surrounding this woman seemed to twist yet another time around.

Rolfe didn't know how long he'd actually stood beside Cassia's bed, watching her while she slept, so unaware of him there. When he did finally turn to leave, he spotted a small bottle of laudanum sitting beside the teapot on her bedside table. Somehow he knew it wasn't just Winifred's snoring that necessitated the dosage.

The day had been troubling for Cassia—it hadn't taken much for Rolfe to realize that—and sleep had obviously been long in coming to her. What struck him as truly odd was that it should be so.

For a suspected murderess, Cassia wasn't behaving as one would expect. Being an heiress, bestowed now with in excess of eighty thousand pounds, one would think she would be ecstatic, not holing up in her room as if her very world were coming to an end. In fact, Rolfe could not think of anyone who would not be fair shouting from the rooftops at receiving such a boon.

But Cassia wasn't. She had a fortune at her disposal and still she'd said quite plainly that she hadn't wanted it, rather preferred her cousin, that popinjay Geoffrey, have it, as, no doubt, he thought he should.

Geoffrey. Now, there was someone who bore definite looking into. Rolfe recalled Mr. Finchley's explanation as to why Lord Seagrave hadn't left his fortune to his nephew, whom most would think the preferred heir. He wondered just how fond of gaming cousin Geoffrey was, how far in debt his habit might have brought him.

Perhaps far enough to have spurred him into taking the life of Cassia's father, setting her up to take the blame and bringing him the inheritance to which he'd been entitled—or rather, the inheritance he thought he'd be receiving? It seemed a possibility. It actually made the most sense, certainly more sense than the supposition that Cassia had committed cold-blooded murder. Rolfe made a mental note to have Dante make inquiries along that line.

Yet, one could argue, being as close to the king as she was, perhaps Cassia had somehow learned of her father's petition, knew she would be inheriting the entirety of the Seagrave fortune, and actually had committed the crime. She had been found with her father's body, his blood on her hands. And, Rolfe knew from experience that women were accomplished actresses and could make a man believe whatever they wanted. An artful woman, a woman who had the looks and wiles Cassia had displayed in so deftly manipulating the king earlier that day, could charm the very robes off a celibate monk, befuddle him with kisses and promises of bedtime rollick, then steal his heart, his pride, and his very soul for the mere sport of it.

Rolfe knew this and knew it well, for he'd been charmed of his pride, his soul, and his heart by the very best, a mistake he was not about to make a second time.

"Good morning, Lord Ravenscroft."

Rolfe set aside his copy of L'Estrange's *Publick Intelligencer* and stood as Cassia came into the room.

He noticed she wore mourning black again, though this time the cut of the gown was far less severe, and her hair was arranged in a soft coiffure. Owing to the laudanum, she also looked well rested.

"Good morning to you, Lady Cassia. Might I say you are looking much better this morning? I trust you slept well?"

Cassia took a seat, waiting until her tea had been poured, a plate bearing a biscuit and a small bowl of the cook's quince marmalade thoughtfully placed before her by the dutiful Clydesworthe, before responding. "Yes, thank you, my lord. I am feeling more myself today. I owe you an apology. I was less than hospitable to you yesterday. So many things were happening all at once, what with my father's death, and with you showing up on my doorstep, and then Mr.

Finchley making his most unexpected announcement, I was simply overcome. I hope you understand."

"Of course. As well, I hope you can understand why I could not, in all good faith, abandon the king's orders."

Cassia smiled sweetly. "Of course."

As she took up her biscuit and began spreading it with a thin layer of marmalade, Cassia's mind unwittingly drifted back to the previous evening, and when she thought of the previous evening, what came to mind was having seen Rolfe at his bath. It was a sight she would never forget. She was so busy picturing his body all wet and slick from the bathwater as she moved the knife blade slowly over the biscuit that she hadn't even heard him speaking to her.

"Lady Cassia?"

"Oh, excuse me. I am sorry, Lord Ravenscroft. I was just remembering something."

"From the look on your face, I would wager it must have been a pleasant memory."

Cassia felt herself go red and hoped he hadn't been able to read into her thoughts, which was silly, of course. Her thoughts were the one place where she truly had privacy, where she could have her most intimate dreams and wishes and never have to worry about someone ridiculing them. Still, she was not at all certain how she should respond. "You were saying, my lord?"

"I had asked if you had misplaced this."

He reached forward and set something on the table in front of her. It was a handkerchief, one Cassia instantly recognized. It was the same handkerchief she had soaked in scented water the previous day to help soothe her aching head, the same one she'd later been clenching in her fingers when she'd watched Rolfe at his bath.

Chapter Ten

Cassia felt her face now begin to burn. How had he gotten that? Had she dropped it in the Green Chamber when she'd turned to leave? Good God, did Ravenscroft realize she'd been there watching him bathe?

Cassia looked up at him, trying to keep an unassuming lightness to her voice. "Wherever did you find that, my lord?"

"Funniest thing, you know, I happened to notice it on the floor of the Green Chamber last night when I was taking my bath there. It is yours, isn't it?"

Ravenscroft knew. He had to know, for the laughter was fair dancing in his hazel-green eyes. Perhaps she'd been wrong. Perhaps a person's thoughts could be seen by others like the open pages of a book. Perhaps . . .

"Lynette must have dropped it there accidentally."
Oh, God, had she really said that?

Rolfe's mouth curved in a smile. "Of course."

A rescuing knock came to the door in the entrance hall. Moments later the butler Clydesworthe was standing at the door. "A visitor to see you, Lady Cassia."

Cassia released the breath she'd been holding. "Of course. Show her in, Clydesworthe. I am expecting her."

The next few minutes were nothing more than a blur for Rolfe when a young woman clothed from head to toe in a bright canary yellow came bustling into the room. Her arrival reminded Rolfe of the strange storms that were wont to blow in off the southern coast at Ravenwood, so tumultuous it was.

"Cassia, dear, how are you doing? I am so happy you asked me over for tea this morning. After receiving your message, I was so anxious to see you, I was up with the dawn, but of course I waited until a more acceptable hour before coming to call. I have been going out of my mind with worry over you. I haven't seen you since your father's funeral. How are you faring? Court just isn't the same without you, although I do hear tell through the galleries that you did make a sudden appearance at Whitehall yesterday. Set tongues to flapping you did. I also hear you delivered quite a blow to the hauteur of our dear Barbara Palmer, much to my enjoyment, I might add. I wish I had been there. Her Majesty's spirits were decidedly lifted after your visit to her yesterday, so you see, you mustn't stay away from court for very long. I'll simply grow blue with boredom without you and—"

The chattering woman suddenly caught sight of Rolfe from the corner of one of her twinkling brown eyes and extended one yellow-kid-gloved hand. "And who, might I ask, is this very handsome fellow sitting in your parlor having breakfast with you? 'Tis no wonder you've been keeping to home, you naughty girl."

Rolfe stood, wondering how this petite and utterly beguiling creature could have possibly said all that she had in so short a space of time and in one breath. He took up her hand and kissed it politely.

"Lord Ravenscroft at your service, madam."

Her hand still in his, the as-yet-unnamed woman shot Cassia a look off pure wonderment. "Well, there you have it. I finally have the answer to London's most perplexing question these days. Yes, there truly is still one last gentleman left in England and here he stands. I'd begun to think they'd all lost their minds, morals, and their manners at the return of the king."

She turned toward Rolfe then, smiling brightly. "Good day to you, my lord. Cordelia, Lady Haslit, and I am certainly at your service as well."

The next two hours were passed over tea and a lost number of the cook's fresh biscuits as they sat in the parlor listening to every scrap of gossip at Whitehall. Rolfe was amazed at how much of most everyone's personal life this entrancing creature was privy to and hoped she never took it to mind to delve into his private affairs.

Lady Haslit was married to one Percival Fanshaw, the tenth and current Earl of Haslit, who was at present away from court, much to his young wife's chagrin. Lord Haslit was engaged in commanding a company of His Majesty's soldiers—where, exactly, she did not know. Actually, her husband's current whereabouts seemed to be the only thing this woman did not know, a fact that was of great trouble to her. The poor Cordelia hadn't seen her husband in nearly a year.

Rolfe learned that Cassia had known Lady Haslit— please call her Cordelia—since they had been bobbing-curls young girls. Both had left England during the civil wars, crossing the Channel for France with their families to follow the displaced English royal court into exile. They had met at a soiree hosted by Cassia's mother and had been virtually inseparable since.

One thing Rolfe immediately noticed was that from the moment Cordelia had come into the room, she seemed to bring a peace to Cassia, a sort of ease in her demeanor that hadn't been there before. Rolfe had never seen two women so very unlike one another and yet who seemed so comfortable together. Their differences were probably what drew them together. Where Cassia was an example of propriety and grace, Cordelia seemed not to care a whit for social standards, going so far as to lift her skirts to her knees in order to display her matching canary yellow slippers with the wide yellow bows, seemingly unmindful of the fact that Rolfe was there and looking on with two healthy male eyes.

Lady Haslit, he soon concluded, was a thoroughly charming and witty package. She was personable, intelligent, and from what Rolfe could tell, was not sharing another man's bed in her husband's absence like so many of her contemporaries, for since she spoke of everyone else's bed partners so openly, he had little doubt she'd have qualms about mentioning her own.

Though theirs had been an arranged marriage, which commonly resulted in both members seeking their own lovers and leading separate lives, Lord and Lady Haslit seemed to have found some accord with one another. From the sad light of longing that came into her eyes when speaking of her long-absent husband—"Percy," she called him—one might say Cordelia had done the unspeakable: she'd broken society's trend and had actually fallen in love with the man.

"And then," Cordelia said, breaking into Rolfe's thoughts, "when the king asked Her Majesty to repeat the new word he'd taught her for Lord 'Bucks,' with our dear Barbara Palmer standing beside her for all to see, the queen announced to the entire assemblage that the king was truly most adept at *rogering* with her, as evidenced by her current breeding condition."

Cordelia shot a look at Rolfe, whose shock at hearing a lady speak thusly was obviously registered on his face. She smiled and added quickly, "Please forgive me, Lord Ravenscroft. I seem to forget we ladies are not alone."

Having dispensed with that social obligation, she turned back to Cassia, oblivious of him once again. "I hear that Her Majesty was given this little lesson in English by a visitor she'd had earlier that same day. An unnamed visitor. I say, Cassia, wasn't that the same day you came to Whitehall to visit her?"

Cassia smiled, neither confirming nor denying the implication. "What did His Majesty do?"

"Threw back his head and roared for a full five minutes. They had to clap him on the back and throw open the windows to allow him to catch his breath. Everyone found it most amusing—even old man Clarendon was seen to crack a smile—excepting, of course, our dear Lady Castlemaine, who herself was seen to melt into the background and disappear soon after, most probably to devise some sort of attempt at retribution."

"Good for Her Majesty. It is so seldom she manages to get back at that termagant."

Cassia peered at the doorway, where Winifred had suddenly presented herself. She stood and went over to her, returning after exchanging a private word.

"It seems I must speak with the cook about the menu for this week. I should only be gone a short while. Pray continue to visit together while I am away."

Rolfe stood and watched her go, caught between the urge to go after her and the social obligation of remaining with Lady Haslit. His decision was soon made for him.

"Come, Lord Ravenscroft, do sit back down and tell me about yourself. As I understand it, you were most instrumental in restoring His Majesty to the throne. It sounds vastly exciting. Was it dangerous? I would simply love to hear the details."

Good God, Rolfe thought, how much had this little inquisitress already delved into his past?

"I was really just a small part of the consortium that sought to restore His Majesty's crown . . ."

It took nearly an hour and a half of recounting long-dead tales from the wars for Rolfe to realize he'd been hoodwinked. Not just hoodwinked, but thoroughly trounced. When reality finally dawned on him and he realized just what he'd been subjected to, he stood while Lady Haslit was in midsentence and calmly walked from the room.

As expected, Cassia was not in the kitchen, nor was she to be found anywhere on the premises. None of the servants, tight-lipped and loyal to their mistress, would divulge her whereabouts, not even the groom Quigman. A fine lot they were. As Rolfe stalked through the corridors, throwing open every door, his anger began to mount until, by the time he had re-traced his steps back to the parlor, he was downright furious.

He halted directly in front of Cordelia, his words coming slowly. "Where is she?"

Lady Haslit took a quiet sip of her tea and raised her eyebrows innocently. "Excuse me, Lord Ravenscroft? Where is whom?"

"You know damned well who I mean. Where in perdition did Cassia take off to?"

"My lord, you really should attempt to curb your tongue in the presence of a lady. I—"

"Don't make the mistake of attempting to further play me for a fool, Lady Haslit. Believe me when I say I am much more pleasant when I am one's ally than when I am one's foe. Now, I will only ask you one more time. Where is she?"

Cordelia took a moment to weigh her options. Realizing Rolfe would be a little more difficult to handle than the men she and her scheming friend were accustomed to, she dropped her head and said softly, "At her father's offices in Westminster."

Rolfe didn't even pause to respond. He strode from the room, barking for the hackney coach that was parked at the street corner beneath the shade of a wide-branched elm.

The roads to Westminster were an impasse, and between shouting at the driver and clenching his hands into fists as the coach crawled along on its way toward Whitehall, Rolfe tried to think about what he would do with Cassia when he finally caught up with her. He'd devised an assortment of punishments by the time they reached their destination, the last of which was to leg-shackle her to a tree, but was still undecided as to what he would actually do. One thing was for certain, though: when he did find her, there would be hell for the lady to pay.

Cassia peered about the deserted hallway, as she closed the door to her father's offices quietly behind her.

She hoped Cordelia had been able to keep Ravenscroft from noticing her absence this long, but somehow she rather doubted it. Ravenscroft was not a stupid man. Cordelia may have been able to distract him long enough for Cassia to have taken her leave, and perhaps even for a short time after that, but sooner or later a man like Ravenscroft would realize just what she'd done. He would realize that there hadn't really been any menus that needed discussing, that the cook had never summoned her, but instead, that she'd done just what she'd promised she wouldn't do: she'd run off without his knowing.

If only she had been able to find the document her father had alluded to in his letter there at the offices. Perhaps then she wouldn't feel this empty sense of failure, a failure that was coupled with a nagging guilt for having sneaked away.

Why should she feel guilty at having come here she told herself. She owed Ravenscroft no loyalty. It hadn't been her decision to appoint him as her personal sentry. He should have expected it of her, and indeed, he'd been remiss in his duties by allowing her to get away at all. And he called himself dedicated.

But regardless of how many times she tried to convince herself of this, in the back of her mind, Cassia still heard that tiny voice that always seemed ready to remind her of her shortcomings. She had been wrong.

Perhaps it wasn't too late, she thought. Perhaps she could sneak back into the house without his seeing her. She would simply evade his questions as to where she had been all this time. He need never know what she'd really done. He need never find out she'd left the house at all. She just needed to get herself back to Seagrave House as quickly as she possibly could.

Cassia tucked the key to her father's office she'd gotten from Clydesworthe safely into the lining pocket of her cloak and headed out of the building. She tried to avoid crossing anyone's path, ducking into a darkened alcove when she heard someone approaching. She waited until the person was well away, and even a few minutes after that, before moving out again.

If anyone saw her, and chanced to recognize her, it could prove disastrous, especially when news of her father's petition to the king making her sole heiress to the Seagrave estate became public, which would be so very soon. Nothing of any consequence was left to secrecy for long in this city, for the grand and glorious people of the court reveled in discovering others' most hidden secrets, bringing them out and celebrating them as if they were some sort of demented holiday.

Realizing the rumors that would be flying about Whitehall, labeling her a murderess who had killed her own father for the fortune he so naively left to her, Cassia could not risk being seen so near to his offices now. Any activity that appeared remotely covert or unusual would be cause for suspicion, and she had more than she could manage of that already.

Pulling the hood of her cloak over her head, Cassia headed for the street. Outside, the courtyard in front of the Horse Guards was teeming with horses and coaches and people. It was just after the noon hour, and carriages were awaiting their noble passengers to take them back to their dwellings in the city. Coachmen were shouting crude obscenities to each other, some waving their horsewhips high as they fought for a forward position closest to the footpath so as to keep their masters and mistresses from having to walk among the muck that littered the area, thereby gaining them a greater gratuity.

Cassia struggled to see her driver through the crush, for she'd asked him kindly and had paid him well to wait for her to return. After some searching, she finally located him parked alongside the roadway near the Holbein Gate entrance on the other side of the courtyard.

He did not seem to notice her standing there; he made no effort to come forward. Rather than attempt to wave him down, thereby drawing unwanted attention, Cassia started toward him, weaving her way past the other coaches to make her way across the courtyard to him. In trying to keep her hood in place and watch where and into what she might be stepping, she was pushed and jostled by the prancing horses and the other people milling about the area.

When she was within a short distance of her coach, she noticed the driver starting to pull away, heading, it seemed, in the opposite direction as if he were planning on returning to the city.

Wait! Cassia tried to hurry to catch him, pushing at a fidgeting bay who had backed up against her, and in the process of trying to veer away and avoid stepping in an unsightly pile of horse muck, her hood fell back. By now, she was more concerned with stopping the quickly fleeing coach, thinking she was about to be left there at the palace. She started to call out to the driver when suddenly something or someone hit her squarely between the shoulder blades.

Cassia fell forward onto the cobbles, but managed to break her fall with her hands. She struggled to get to her feet.

It was then she saw another coach, this one gleaming black and pulled by a team of matching blacks, racing straight for her.

Cassia froze, her eyes locked on the pounding, flashing hooves. It was running right for her. She would be trampled in seconds.

Had it not been for the two strong hands that lifted her around her middle, pulling her to safety just as the coach came racing over where she had fallen, she'd have been crushed beneath it.

Cassia turned, her heart pounding, ready to thank the kind gentleman who had surely just saved her life, when a familiar voice sounded close to her ear.

"I was wrong, Lady Cassia, when I said earlier that you were not a foolish woman, for only a fool would have done something quite as stupid as what you just did."

Chapter Eleven

It was Ravenscroft, and he was clearly angry at having discovered her ruse. He was pulling her now by her arm through the milling people and the coaches and the horses in the courtyard. His fingers were locked around her wrist. Cassia didn't know what she was more frightened of; the coach that had nearly run her over, or Ravenscroft. Cassia didn't say a word as Rolfe kept on pulling her, even when she thought her arm would surely spring free from its socket. He had no trouble at all navigating his way through the crowd—damn him—and did not stop until they were safely away from the crowd, where he then slipped into a small alcove set beyond the sights of the courtyard.

Rolfe took Cassia by the shoulders and shook her.

"Do you realize you could have been killed just now, you little idiot? How could you have been so stupid? What could you possibly have been thinking when you hatched on this ridiculous scheme?"

Cassia's heart was pounding as she stared up at him. He hovered over her, reminding her of a dark storm cloud, his eyes burning with his anger, his face so close she could feel the heat of his breath on her cheek. Where were the words that always seemed to come instinctively to her, ready to set down any man who would dare to treat her so? Why was she suddenly incapable of any speech at all?

Inside Cassia knew Rolfe had every right to be angry with her, for she had gone back on her word and had done the very thing she'd promised him she wouldn't do. She tried to think of something to explain her stupidity. Finally she managed two small words. "I'm sorry."

"Is that all you have to say for yourself? You're sorry? I should think 'Thank you for saving my life,' would be more appropriate. In case you failed to notice, you nearly got yourself killed, and you would have been killed if I hadn't come along precisely at the moment I did. Did you happen to think of that when you and your delightful friend set out to cozen me this morning?"

Cassia could think of nothing to say that would sufficiently explain her actions. In fact, at that moment, with him standing before her, repeating it all to her, she had never felt more foolish.

"Why was it so damnably important for you to put on this elaborate ruse just so you could sneak away from me? I would have brought you here myself had you asked. Why didn't you just tell me you wanted to come?"

Cassia wondered if she should tell him, if she could trust him in a world where, she had learned through hard experience, even one's friends could be one's worst enemies.

But Rolfe hadn't needed to come racing after her like he had when he'd finally discovered her gone. He could very well have left her to her own folly. He could have stayed at Seagrave House, drinking tea and chatting with Cordelia all afternoon, while Cassia was trampled to death by that racing coach. But he hadn't. He had come after her, and he had saved her life. No one had done such a thing for her before. No one had cared enough to want to protect her. But Ravenscroft had. Even if it was his duty, he had come after her.

"I had to come here," she said, fishing inside her cloak pocket, "because of this."

Rolfe took the letter and shook it open with his free hand, the other still holding Cassia's forearm as if he feared she would try to break free and make a run for it. He read the letter quickly, then returned it to her.

"I take it this is the letter Mr. Finchley gave you yesterday, the letter your father left for you?"

Cassia nodded. "I came here to see if that document he wrote to me about, whatever it is, was here."

"And was it?"

"No. Had I thought about it, I would have realized it sooner. My father was an extremely private man and was uncommonly suspicious, sometimes to the point of distraction. If he truly had such a document of the magnitude to which he alludes, he never would have kept it here at the palace where anyone at any time could attempt to find it."

Rolfe released her, but didn't step away. "What about at Seagrave House? Could this document be there?"

"I thought about that, but I've looked through most of his things there, and Mr. Finchley went through all his personal papers. We found nothing like this document he writes of."

Rolfe thought a moment. "Perhaps this so-called document just doesn't exist."

Cassia shook her head. "Why would my father leave me a letter telling me that only I could know where the document would be? No, the document does exist. It is hidden somewhere, somewhere I should know about. I just need time to think, time to figure out what he is trying to tell me in this letter, before it is too late. The one thing I do know is that I must find this document, as soon as possible, because it might just be the one thing, the only thing, that will help prove my innocence."

It was not until hours later that Rolfe saw Cassia again, for as soon as they returned to the town house, she immediately and without so much as a by-your-leave rushed up the stairs to closet herself in her bedchamber.

She came down for supper, surprisingly, sitting alone at the other end of the dining room table that was so interminably long Rolfe knew he would need a footman to deliver handwritten notes in order to frame any attempt at conversation with her. He gave that up and merely exchanged a nod or two between taking bites of his roast pheasant in tangy orange sauce.

As soon as the meal ended, Cassia excused herself and returned to her bedchamber, most probably to spend the rest of the night trying to think of where the supposed document might be hidden.

Sitting in Seagrave's study now, the very room where the murder had taken place, he'd been told, Rolfe wondered at this woman who seemed to hide everything, especially her most heartfelt fears, from the world. He was nursing a goblet of brandy, staring at the flames snapping and popping in the hearth, while contemplating everything he'd witnessed since his arrival.

Cassia was frightened, Rolfe didn't doubt that. She was frightened of being clapped in irons, frightened of being thrown into the Tower and forgotten, or worse, of hanging before the populace of London for a crime he had no earthy idea if she had or had not committed.

She seemed so certain of her innocence when she'd

shown him the letter from her father earlier that day, so desperate to find the proof she needed. Still, she could have staged the entire episode starting with the visit from the talkative Lady Haslit for the sole purpose of making him think just that. But somehow that didn't seem likely.

Cassia hadn't needed to show him her father's letter, a letter she'd not known existed before yesterday, a letter that could indicate someone else wanted Seagrave dead. Something had made Cassia trust him enough to show him that letter, and even if it was only an inkling of trust, Rolfe knew that her trust was not given easily.

Rolfe crossed the room, parting the drapery on the window to look outside. Just who was Lady Cassia? What sort of upbringing could have produced such a puzzling, intriguing woman?

He gazed out at the full white moon that hung above the rooftops, pondering it further. Cassia seemed to want for nothing. Her gowns were of the finest cut, her home filled with every sort of convenience. She was well educated, always cordial. Still, somehow the image she presented to the world lacked something.

Rolfe glanced at the small brass lantern clock ticking softly on the mantelpiece beside him. The hour wasn't that late, at least not by society's standards. Perhaps, when he asked the proper person, he would find answers to these puzzling questions.

And he knew precisely to whom he should go.

Rolfe left the room, grabbing his cloak from the peg on the wall, and started directly for Whitehall.

As the tiltboat neared the landing just below the palace stairs, Rolfe wondered if he should have left Cassia alone at Seagrave House, but then he thought she'd surely not attempt to leave, especially not so soon after the events earlier that day. He didn't plan on being away for that long and he'd made certain to post Quigman at the foot of the stairs with strict instructions not to allow anyone excepting himself in or out of the house.

Strains of orchestra music came to him as Rolfe walked along the tree-lined pathway that led along the perimeter of the palace toward the Banqueting House. Smoking rush torches lit his way and the soft murmur of intimate voices and wicked laughter could be heard coming from the shadows around him, the carefully trimmed topiary no doubt giving many a clandestine meeting the needed camouflage.

Rolfe stopped just inside the double doors of the Banqueting House and surveyed the faces of the moderate crowd inside. This evening, Whitehall's scheduled entertainment was a masque being staged by some of the ladies of the court, a seemingly terrible rendition of one of the day's more popular plays that was eliciting laughter in places where other, deeper emotions should have been prompted.

It took him only a few minutes to find the face he was searching for; she had a tendency to stand out among others. Rolfe started immediately for her.

"Lady Haslit," he said as he drew up behind her, "it is a pleasure to see you again."

Cordelia nearly dropped her wineglass at the sight of him suddenly standing beside her. She wore a concoction of varying shades of blue, presenting a vision of eccentric loveliness while managing to carry a degree of the outrageous for which she was, no doubt, well known. As he looked at her, Rolfe thought that Cordelia was not what one would call a great court beauty. In fact, once you got past her flamboyant attire, her features were somewhat plain, which, was most probably the reason for her outlandish taste in dress, a way to stand out among the other, fairer flowers in Whitehall's gardens.

It took Cordelia a brief moment to recover. "Lord Ravenscroft, I certainly wasn't expecting to see you this evening. Surely it wasn't this dreadful masque that brought you all the way to the palace. And I don't see Cassia. Is she with you?"

"No. When last I left her, your friend was abed, safe in the arms of Morpheus and dreaming, I'm sure, of finding new and clever ways to outwit me and make me look the fool. Scheming does tend to tire one, I would think. I am curious, though, Lady Haslit. Pray tell me, why is it that you are not participating in this evening's masque? After seeing firsthand your innate acting skill, I would think your presence would definitely enhance this evening's performance."

Cordelia smiled at him, patting back a stray dark curl. "Thank you for noticing my talent, Lord Ravenscroft, but somehow I do not think you deserted your duty to the king in guarding Cassia to come here this evening and discuss my missed calling for the theater. Cassia informs me that your loyalty to duty is without question."

"You are correct in that, so I need not tell you it must have been a matter of great import for me to have come here, leaving Cassia at Seagrave House. To cut right to the point, I was hoping for a private exchange with you."

Cordelia didn't immediately respond, trying to decide whether he was being sincere. Rolfe waited silently until she then motioned for him to follow her.

They slipped from the Banqueting House through a small side door at the rear of the building employed more for the use of servants than for guests. Rolfe followed Cordelia along several hallways, past an inebriated courtier lying facedown in a puddle of his own vomit, to a small alcove set off from the main walkway in the Privy Garden.

"Lord Ravenscroft, I do hope you realize I am risking my reputation in being here with you. I am a married lady, you know."

Rolfe smiled. "Somehow I think you would prefer a little scandal to be attached to your name, Lady Haslit. Had you been so concerned for your reputation, I should think you very easily could have gone to a more public place for our discussion."

"Touché, my lord. Although somehow I don't believe you brought me here for the purpose of exchanging witty retorts."

"You are right. I was hoping you would answer some questions for me . . ." he paused, "about Cassia."

The instant he finished his sentence, Rolfe could see Cordelia's defenses come to the forefront. Her eyes narrowed distrustfully. "Why do you want to know about Cassia?"

"You do not believe she killed her father, do you?"

"Of course not, although, if she had, I certainly wouldn't blame her."

"Why is that?"

Cordelia looked at Rolfe a moment, as if trying to decide what, if anything, she should reveal to him. "I just don't know . . ."

"I only want to try to help her."

Cordelia hesitated a moment longer. "Before I tell you anything at all about Cassia, you must look me straight in the eyes and tell me why you want to know."

Rolfe stared at Cordelia, his gaze unwavering. "I do not believe Cassia is guilty of murdering her father. I plan to prove it, but in order to do that, I must know more about her, such as why she is so reluctant to trust."

Cordelia studied his face yet a moment longer. "All right, Lord Ravenscroft, I truly believe you are trying to help her, so I will tell you what I know." She took a seat on a small stone bench in the shadows, motioning for Rolfe to sit beside her.

"You must understand, Lord Ravenscroft, Cassia's way of withdrawing into herself is a means of protection she has perfected through most of the course of her life."

"Protection? From what?"

"From her life, of course. Cassia left England at a very early age with her mother to follow the English court into exile in France. Before the civil wars, her mother was a lady-in-waiting to King Charles's mother, Queen Henrietta."

"You do not seem to have been forced into this same behavior. Weren't you taken to France as well?"

"Yes, but my situation was entirely different. I come from parents who married because they had fallen in love with each other and were fortunate enough to be given the choice of their mates. Cassia's parents came together as an alliance of two families, a monetary transaction arranged and settled upon even before her mother had left the nursery. Unfortunately, when Cassia's parents did meet, they did not suit. Worse than that, I believe Cassia's mother actually hated Lord Seagrave."

"That is not uncommon."

"Normally, you are right. Marriages are arranged over tea in the country most every day—look at my marriage to Percival, for example—but this marriage was different. Cassia's mother had fallen in love with another man and she detested Lord Seagrave for ruining the chances of that match. I have heard that on their wedding night, she even tried to deny Lord Seagrave his marital rights and Lord Seagrave forced himself upon her. It has been remarked that at the bridal breakfast the following morning, she wore a gown cut purposefully low so as to show everyone the bruises given her by her bridegroom."

"I was already told of Seagrave's abuse of his wife. I was not aware that he had raped her."

Cordelia looked at Rolfe. "I'm surprised to hear you call it rape, Lord Ravenscroft. Most men wouldn't consider it so."

"Anytime a man forces himself on a woman, it is rape, Lady Haslit."

Cordelia nodded. "That was not the only occasion of it, either," she went on. "Lord Seagrave was determined to beget an heir to carry on the Seagrave line and his wife was just as determined that he should not. His assaults on his wife continued until she was well with child. He expected a boy; the Monteforts were quite adept at siring sons. Lord Seagrave did not hide his disappointment well when the child born to him was a daughter.

"After Cassia was born, as a means of punishing her husband, Cassia's mother embarked on a career of occupying whatever bed it took to help her rise at court. Had she been of Cassia's age now, she would no doubt far surpass Lady Castlemaine in King Charles's bed."

"And what did Seagrave do in the meantime?"

Cordelia shook her head. "Sadly, I believe that Lord Seagrave loved his wife, but somehow that love translated itself into abuse when he found he could not control her. During our years in France, Cassia's head was filled with her mother's hatred for her father so that when we returned to England with the new king, she honestly thought a horned demon with forked tail would be waiting on the shores to meet her. When her mother died, after making Lord Seagrave a laughingstock in the worst of all possible ways, it seemed as if Cassia's fears about her father proved true. Lord Seagrave took to the bottle, and when he did, he would rant at Cassia, talking to her as if she were her mother, even going so far as to call her by his wife's name. Her name wasn't the only thing Cassia had to bear. Cassia was made to suffer his abuse as well. I know this to be true, Lord Ravenscroft, for I have been witness to the bruises."

Chapter Twelve

Rolfe felt his entire body grow tense. "Why did no one attempt to stop him?"

"Most everyone suspected what he was doing to Cassia, but Lord Seagrave managed to inflict his abuse where it would not be seen. And Cassia is not her mother. While her mother was busy occupying whatever bed she could, Cassia's upbringing was left to her abigail, Winifred. Winifred did her job well. She raised Cassia to believe in propriety and morality, to be a proper young lady. Unlike her mother, who preferred to advertise Lord Seagrave's abuse of her, Cassia believed that what happened with her father was never to be revealed. She hid it well from the outside world, even from me. I never would have guessed the truth, until I happened to enter her bedchamber once while she was dressing. I was horrified at the sight of the bruises. Cassia was just as horrified that I had seen them. She made me promise never to tell anyone of what I had seen. If she knew I was telling you this now, she would most likely never speak to me again."

"You have my word I will not reveal anything you have told me."

Cordelia smiled. "I don't know why, but I feel I can trust you, and I pride myself on being a good judge of character. Now perhaps you can understand why Cassia's shield is her indifference. It is the only means she has found to survive what she has. Cassia locks her feelings away, along with all the other frightening things in the world, in a dark place somewhere deep inside of her. I shudder to think of what is truly contained in that place, things even I do not know about. People think her imperious for this image she presents to the rest of the world. No doubt you have heard what she is called here at court."

" 'Lady Winter.' "

Cordelia frowned. "Yes, a truly odious name and one she doesn't deserve, for it all comes about from the way she was raised. It was inevitable that Cassia would one day become a very wealthy heiress, even without Lord Seagrave's petition. It was no secret that Cassia's mother refused to give her husband an heir, to somehow punish him for ruining her chances at a happy life. So his wealth, at least part of it, would someday come down to his daughter. And every fortune-hunting scoundrel out there knew well of it. Do you have any idea what it is like to be thought of not for who you are, but for what amount of money or title you can bring?"

Rolfe frowned, his thoughts drifting back to another woman, a woman whom he'd once thought the sun rose and fell upon. A woman who'd ironically placed that same distinction on him. "I can imagine."

Cordelia must have seen the dark expression come over him for she placed her hand on his and said, "I am sorry. I had forgotten that you were faced with a similar situation not that long ago."

"You gather your information quickly."

"It's not every day a girl comes face-to-face with someone as infamous as the Exiled Earl." She hesitated, adding, "I'm sorry if my bringing up that name offended you. Sometimes I open my mouth without thinking."

Rolfe smiled. "No offense taken. But I didn't come here to discuss my past. I came to learn more about your friend, more about why she is so distrustful of the world and everyone in it."

"After Cassia's mother died birthing what everyone knew was an illegitimate child, Lord Seagrave literally put Cassia up on the marriage market to the highest bidder. I think that is why Cassia has found such a common bond with Queen Catherine, another sacrificial lamb on the marriage altar. Lord Seagrave nearly succeeded in selling Cassia to the Duke of Manton's son, Malcolm. It was all arranged until she did the only thing she could to avoid the match, something so out of character for Cassia, I know she must have been desperate."

"Which is?"

"She refused the proposal, publicly, at a well attended ball, much to her father's and the duke's utter humiliation. You see, Lord Seagrave knew his daughter. He knew Cassia's regard for propriety. He thought that by making a public announcement of it, Cassia would never dare refuse the proposal. Goodness, poor Malcolm proposed before half of London that night. Even I was shocked when she refused him. That was the same night Lord Seagrave was murdered, so you see, knowing what Cassia's father most likely did to her once he got her behind the doors of Seagrave House, I could not blame her if she did truly kill him."

Rolfe was staring off at the lights of the Banqueting House, trying to take this all in. If what Cordelia said was true, it certainly did explain why Cassia behaved the way she did. And what purpose would Cordelia have for making this all up?

"What I still don't understand is if her father was such a bloody bastard, why didn't Cassia just escape his abuse by marrying? One would think she would have jumped at the first offer that came for her hand just to get away from him."

Cordelia nodded. "One could look at it that way, I suppose, but that was not an option to Cassia. You must understand, she has seen things a woman of her age should never be subjected to and because of it she believes all men to be abusive. The examples we have here at Whitehall only serve to add to that opinion." She glanced at Rolfe. "Except you, of course."

"Of course."

"Even my marriage to Percy hasn't changed her feelings. In Cassia's mind, were she to wed, she would only be sentencing herself to a lifetime of abuse by another, far younger version of her father. Instead, she preferred to wait it out, knowing her father would never live as long as a husband would."

Rolfe looked into Cordelia's eyes. "Do you realize what it is you are saying?"

She nodded. "It certainly gives Cassia motive for killing her father, doesn't it, even if she didn't know about his petition or her inheritance. But Cassia did not kill her father, Lord Ravenscroft. I am certain of it." She added, "I would stake my life on it."

Rolfe stood. He bowed and kissed Cordelia's gloved hand. "I thank you for your candor and your honesty, Lady Haslit. Cassia is most fortunate to have a friend in you."

"And I in her." Cordelia stood beside him and took his hand, squeezing it. "Cassia means more to me than any sister ever could. We grew up together and it goes against everything I believe in to betray her trust to you as I just have. I only pray you will never make me regret telling you this."

The lights from the numerous and glittering chandeliers set the crowded ballroom ablaze, the colorful silk gowns of the ladies swirling against the polished Italian tile floor as they danced. Most of the faces were familiar to her, for nearly every person of noble birth in the city was in attendance that evening.

Standing beside her, her father looked foreign and out of place in the gay and lively setting. He did not attend social functions such as this soiree at the Duke of Manton's, wishing to avoid hearing the comments, both real and imagined, that were still whispered about his wife behind his back.

Scandal wasn't one to refrain from speaking ill of the dead.

He was bringing her forward now through the crowd, introducing her to their host, the duke, and his son and heir, Malcolm, the Marquess of Newbury. And, suddenly, her father was gone, leaving to go behind the doors of the duke's study for some sort of political meeting, he said.

She'd just finished dancing with someone whose face and name were oddly a blur when her father came up to her and led her out onto the dancing floor. He was talking to her between the light skipping steps of the dance. What was he saying? That his meeting with the duke had proved a success, the terms had been set, all that remained was for her to consent. Consent to what?

Cassia started to question him but the music ended. Suddenly standing beside her, next to her father, was the duke and his son, Malcolm, the marquess. They were all smiling and looking most proud, and the crowd was gathering expectantly around them as the duke prepared to make an announcement.

"I believe my son, Malcolm, would like to make a request of a certain young lady now," the duke said.

A murmur of excitement rippled through the crowd. Malcolm came forward. His features were hazy and *when he spoke, his voice sounded as if it were coming from far, far away.*

". . . and if she would have me, I would be most honored to make her the Marchioness of Newbury and the future Duchess of Manton."

Cassia turned toward the crowd, wondering who it was the marquess had just proposed marriage to, expecting to see the blushing bride-to-be come forward from the assemblage.

But everyone seemed to be staring at her. Why? Why were they all watching her? Suddenly Cassia realized they were waiting for her to respond.

Good God, he'd been proposing to her!

"Cassia, haven't you something to say?" her father said low into her ear.

Cassia felt like the rabbit standing before the sights of the hunter while his bevy of hounds stood panting, foaming at the mouth, ready to pounce should she attempt to flee.

"I . . ." She looked around at the faces surrounding her. Why did they suddenly look so like bloodthirsty hounds? "I am most honored, but I am afraid I must refuse. I cannot marry you, Lord Newbury."

A collective gasp rose from the crowd. The duke looked fit to kill, her father even more so. It was eerily silent. Would no one say anything? Anything?

"You've done it now, girl," her father said, grabbing her by the forearm and yanking her after him as he stormed from the room.

While the coach rolled along the empty streets toward home, her father didn't say a word. In the faint glimpses of moonlight, she could see his fingers clenching the ivory knob atop his walking stick. As soon as the coachman opened the door, Cassia rushed up the stairs, past Clydesworthe and Lynette, making straight for her bedchamber door.

Once that door was safely closed, Cassia released a heavy breath. And then she heard him coming, his familiar shuffling gait, his walking stick hitting the floorboards as he drew nearer to her room.

"Do you think we're finished, girl?" he said, throwing the door to her chamber wide. "Did you really think I'd let you get away with making a fool of me again, Judith?"

Cassia backed away from her father as he started to come after her, and he was transformed into a horrifying creature with long yellow fangs and eyes that glowed red in the darkness. She wanted to run but her feet were somehow rooted to the floor and she opened her mouth to scream but no sound would come out and she could feel his hands on her, clawing at her, shaking her. He had pulled back his fist. Dear God, he was going to kill her—

"Cassia, wake up. You're having a dream."

Two strong arms were closing around her.

"No! Let me go! Please don't hurt me!"

Instead of a hard fist, Cassia's face felt the softness of cambric as Rolfe pulled her tight against his chest. She buried her face against his warmth.

"It is all right now. You are safe. You were just dreaming."

Rolfe's voice gave her comfort as the nightmare began to fade. Her heartbeat began to slow. Cassia relaxed against him, taking in the scent of him, the strength of his arms around her. The soft touch of his hand running over her hair quickly soothed her back to sleep.

Rolfe buried his face in Cassia's hair, speaking softly to her, soothing her. He did not move until he was certain Cassia was asleep.

Where in perdition was Winifred? He'd just come

back from Whitehall, having relieved Quigman of his post at the bottom of the stairs, when he had heard Cassia crying out as if the very hounds of hell were nipping at her heels.

Rolfe knew the instant he'd flung open her bedchamber door that Cassia was locked in the grasp of a terrifying nightmare. She was sitting up, straight as a stick, her hands out as if to ward the demons of her sleep away. Her eyes, though wide with fear, were empty and blank.

Having just spent the better part of the evening learning the private hell Cassia had been living, Rolfe had no doubt as to what she'd been dreaming. He cradled her gently, laying her back on the bed. The instant his hands left her body, Cassia curled up into a tight ball, as if she unconsciously feared the return of the dream. The room was cold, deathly cold, so cold he could see the fog from his breath. It was then Rolfe noticed that the window was propped open again. He wondered if Cassia kept it open as a sense of security, a last escape route should she need it. He reached over to pull the window shut, turning when he heard someone enter the room behind him.

"What do you think you are doing?" a voice hissed. "You cannot come into my lady's bedchamber like this."

Winifred, holding a cup of tea in one hand and the bottle of laudanum in the other, stood framed in the doorway, her stout frame silhouetted against the candlelight behind her. She was glaring at him dangerously.

"Where the hell have you been?" Rolfe growled. "It's cold as ice in here."

"My lady likes to keep the window open at night. I'll stoke the fire to warm the room." She started across the room.

"It would take a blasted inferno to warm this room. Where have you been?"

"I went to fetch tea for Lady Cassia. She was having a bad dream. Tea sometimes helps her to sleep."

"Yes, I'm well aware that she was having a bad dream, for I could hear her crying out all the way down the hall. Don't ever leave her alone like that again." He grabbed the laudanum bottle and tossed it into the fire. The glass shattered against the hearth-stone. "And you'll not continue to numb her with that."

"The physician said it would help her to sleep."

"Cassia needs to face her nightmares, not spend the rest of her life dulling her mind against them. It is the only way she'll ever be truly released from them. Don't let me see you giving that to her again. And keep that damned window closed before she catches her death of cold. If I see any different, you'll have me to answer to."

With that, Rolfe turned and left the room, leaving a gaping-mouthed Winifred standing in the middle of Cassia's bedchamber behind him.

Chapter Thirteen

Cassia moved the charcoal pencil in a wide arch across the vellum page, lightening the pressure of her hand as she used the flatter edge of it for shading. She narrowed her eyes, scrutinizing the image that was taking shape on the page. She closed her eyes to summon up her subject. This was the first time she was attempting to draw something from memory. She was finding this new method of working difficult, for she was accustomed to having her subject in front of her eyes, not behind them, to refer to. Still, Cassia was determined to see this sketch through.

While she worked, her hand sweeping in quick precise strokes across the page, Cassia's thoughts wandered as they lately seemed to do, to the letter her father had written to her, the last words she would ever see from him in this lifetime. She found herself ruminating on it, desperately trying to find the solution he'd hidden so well behind those many enigmatic words.

It is in the form of a document ... only you can know where it is.

What was this document she was supposed to find? And where was she supposed to find it? Her father had written that if she thought about it long enough, she would be able to figure out where the document was hidden. She'd looked everywhere, searching through every chest and drawer and cabinet. She'd even looked beneath every rug, thinking perhaps he had stashed it there, but each place, each time, she came up empty-handed. Cassia tried to think back on the few pleasant conversations she'd had with her father in the months after her mother had died, when he'd not fallen so far into the brandy bottle that he'd been comprehensible, when he'd actually spoken to her with civility.

Nothing would come to mind, oddly, it was as if she had completely blocked those conversations and that part of her life from memory.

Setting the pencil aside, Cassia looked at the sketch she had drawn, ready to inspect it with her ever-critical eye. Her eyes fixed on the drawing. While her thoughts had been caught up in her father's letter, her sketching hand had taken on a life of its own, filling the sheet with unconscious strokes and shading.

She had started out intent on drawing a small child she had seen earlier that day playing with a puppy in the street below her bedchamber window. The child's laughter that had initially caught her attention had filled her with such quiet pleasure, she'd wanted to commit that feeling to paper, to keep with her and to remind her of it in troubled times. But what appeared before her now was not the image of that child. Instead, it was the image of Lord Ravenscroft's magnificent naked body now blatantly revealed on the page. Everything she'd seen—the clean and muscular lines of his thighs and back, the curve of his buttocks, his broad shoulders—her mind's eye had seen and had committed them to memory.

Cassia wondered what Winifred would say should she happen upon this drawing among her others. She wouldn't have to say anything. She would simply cluck her tongue in disapproval of her mistress making such crude sketches, and of naked men, no matter how beautiful their bodies might be. Perhaps it would be better that this drawing remain unseen.

Cassia took up the sketch, ready to crumple it into a ball and toss it into the fire, but she stopped herself. Something held her back and she looked at the drawing again. It was a fine drawing, she thought to herself, regardless of its subject, a creation of which she should be proud. No one else ever had to see it or know of its existence. No one, except for her. Opening the top drawer of her writing desk, Cassia placed the sketch far back at the very bottom, beneath her blank sketching papers and the box of spare drawing pencils. She then closed the drawer and turned to peer out the window beside her.

The hour was early, but the fog that usually wound its way through the narrow lanes had dissipated quickly, burning off with an uncommonly warm late-autumn sun. Cassia had propped the window open a bit while she'd sketched to allow in the clear morning air, enjoying its invigorating chill as a slight breeze swelled over her face.

As she sat there, she wondered again where the document might be. It had to be somewhere in the house, some place she hadn't yet thought to look. She'd gone through her father's bedchamber, checking it, thoroughly but had found nothing, nothing at all. She had thus far avoided returning to his study to sift through his effects a second time, even though she knew the document had to be there. There was just no other place it could be. Still she remained reluctant, for going into that room would also mean bringing back the memories of what had taken place there, memories that already came to her at night, invading her dreams with frightful clarity.

But without the document, she couldn't prove her

innocence. Cassia turned from the window, knowing what she must do.

Cassia stopped before the door to her father's study, and hesitated in proceeding. She knew she was being silly, but a small part of her still actually feared that when she opened that door, she would find her father sitting there behind his desk, walking stick in hand, waiting for her. She tried to tell herself she shouldn't feel this way. It really wasn't a room that should inspire the fear in her it did. It was a small room situated on the bottom floor at the end of a narrow hallway that led toward the back of the stairwell. It was the only room, excepting a small storage closet hidden under the stairs, that opened onto it. Why then did it feel as if she were standing before the gates of hell?

She had nothing to fear, she told herself and grasped the handle, taking a deep breath as she pushed the door inward.

"Hello, Cassia."

Cassia nearly jumped from the unexpected shock at hearing a voice coming from inside. It took her a moment to realize that it hadn't been her father back from the dead calling out to her; instead, it was Geoffrey sitting behind the desk, his suit of bright aqua sateen making him stand out and look markedly out of place amid the dark, rich interior of the room.

Cassia's first thought as she continued into the room was that Geoffrey certainly looked comfortable. He had his feet propped upon her father's desk, a goblet of what appeared to be her father's burgundy cupped in his palm, as if he had every right and reason to be there. Her fear began to lessen as she realized that it hadn't really been the room that had frightened her, just what had taken place inside it.

"Geoffrey, Clydesworthe did not tell me you had come to speak with me."

Geoffrey swallowed down the last of his wine, setting the goblet down hard. Cassia realized then that he'd begun imbibing long before his arrival.

"He didn't tell you most probably because old Clydesworthe doesn't know I'm here. He was nowhere about when I came to the door, so I showed myself in. I am still a member of this family, you know, the only Montefort left excepting you. I shouldn't need an invitation to come calling on family. You should get rid of that miserable old man Clydesworthe, Cassia. I know I would if I were—"

Geoffrey's words dropped off as he became suddenly lost to his thoughts, staring off at the carpet pattern before speaking again a short time later. "Always giving me that look of his, Clydesworthe does, as if he wants so badly to tell me what a worthless lout he really thinks I am. Sent me away and packing the last time I came to see you, looking down his nose at me like he owned the place, this place that should by all rights be mine."

Cassia frowned. Geoffrey's words were becoming slurred, his tone not at all pleasant. "I am sorry, Geoffrey. I was not feeling well that day and—"

"Yes, poor dear cousin Cassia, your head must have been splitting in two, trying to think of how you were going to spend all that money, all your father's money, now yours. Money you know by rights should be mine."

"Geoffrey I had no idea my father had done such a thing before you and Mr. Finchley came here the other day. It was as much a shock to me as it was to you. You know I never wanted it this way. Had I a choice, I would that you were the heir."

"Yes, well, I'm not the heir, damn your father and his moralistic forethought."

Geoffrey stood, circling the desk, twisting the end

of his thin mustache. "I was never good enough to be your father's heir, even though by rights I should be. 'Heir presumptive' is what he used to call me to all his friends, as if he always knew how he was going to steal my inheritance right out from under me. Perhaps he should have referred to me as the 'heir assumptive' instead, for your father knew even back then what he would do, how he would deliver me this one final humiliation."

"Geoffrey, I—"

"I am the one who stayed on here in this godforsaken country all those years during the wars, paying court to him, seeing to his every command, all while you and that whore of a mother of yours danced around the Continent after the king and his court. No, I was never good enough for your father, the honorable Marquess of Seagrave, so instead he chose you to be his heir, his daughter, the daughter he never knew, the daughter he never wanted. He couldn't even leave me his pocket watch as a pittance, even though he knew I always admired it."

"His watch? You were fond of his pocket watch? Of course, something like that should have been given to you—"

"No, he left me nothing, except to look the laughingstock while you, his daughter who most probably really did murder him, reaps all the rewards of my rightful inheritance."

Cassia was fast growing tired of Geoffrey. "You realize, of course, there is nothing I can do about the petition now. Even if I choose to remain unwed, which I have every intention of doing, the money cannot, will never, be yours. So if you have come here to try and find some way—"

"I'm here, dear cousin, because I am in need of funds."

Geoffrey stared at Cassia, waiting for her to respond.

"Of course, the fifty pounds." Cassia crossed the room to the desk. "I will write a letter to Mr. Finchley right now, instructing him to release your allowance to you posthaste—"

"Fifty pounds won't even begin to pay what I owe my glove maker!"

Cassia looked to the doorway, realizing that Geoffrey was fast becoming unmanageable and that she was, by all appearances, quite alone with him.

"Looking for your guardian angel, the mighty Lord Ravenscroft, are you? Tell me, cousin dear, how did you manage to get the Exiled Earl to play at being your own personal linkboy?"

Geoffrey was coming toward her, wavering on increasingly unsteady feet. "What a stupid question," he said laughing. "It really is quite obvious. I would wager you did inherit some of your mother's talents for persuasion. Her bedchamber persuasion. It's born in the blood. God knows you give your favors freely enough to the king, the only man you ever deemed worthy enough to dive between your chaste legs. Perhaps it is time you gave your cousin Geoffrey a small sample. . . ."

He started to reach for her.

"Take one more step, Montefort, and it's a sample of my rapier blade you'll receive instead."

Geoffrey froze, sobering as if he'd been doused with a shower of ice water. Behind him, Cassia watched Rolfe come into the room. His sword was drawn from his hip scabbard, the blade shining in the sunlight and pointing straight at Geoffrey's back.

No one moved.

Finally Rolfe came up beside Geoffrey, sheathing his sword at his hip. "Rest assured, should you make any sudden moves, I can have that sword back out of its scabbard and have you skewered like the pig you are before you have the chance to so much as blink an eye."

Geoffrey glared at Rolfe, but didn't say a word. He didn't so much as budge.

"Next time you wish to see Lady Cassia, I would suggest you request a visit with her through the customary channels. Should she deign to grant her time to you, you will remember to speak to her with the respect due a lady."

Rolfe stared at Geoffrey, the promise of death in his eyes. "You may show Mr. Montefort the door, Quigman."

The groom came forward and reached to take Geoffrey by the arm.

Geoffrey jerked away. "I am leaving."

He turned to Cassia, his mouth curling in a sneer. "Remember what I said, sweet cousin. Another time, perhaps?"

Cassia didn't respond, but watched as he turned and walked with purposeful slowness from the room. In fact, she did not move for several minutes after he'd gone. She couldn't. She was frozen by the image of Geoffrey's eyes, so dark, so cold, as he had started to reach for her, comparing her to her mother as her father so often had.

What would have happened if Ravenscroft hadn't appeared at precisely the moment he had? Would Geoffrey have seen his threat through? Would she have had the strength to fight him off?

Cassia managed to relax her fingers which had been clenching the back of the desk chair. Without a comment to Rolfe, who was still standing there beside her, she started from the room.

Cassia was nearly through the door when she heard Rolfe behind her.

"I am sorry."

She stopped, but didn't turn. "For what, Lord Ravenscroft? Geoffrey certainly isn't your responsibility."

"No, but you are my responsibility and I failed to protect you. I was lured away on a false pretense, something I had always prided myself on recognizing and avoiding. It was obviously a pretense brought about by Geoffrey so he could get inside the house undetected. Nonetheless, I was fooled and that does not sit well with me, not at all. You have my word, it will not happen again."

"Thank you, my lord."

Cassia continued toward the door.

"What happened that night?"

Cassia stopped but, again, did not turn around. She worded her response carefully. "I don't know what you mean."

"It was in this room, wasn't it? This is where your father was killed?"

A chill washed over Cassia at the question. She wondered if she should continue forward and leave the room, pretending that she hadn't heard him. She knew he would persist. He would continue asking, hounding her until she told him. Suddenly she wanted to tell it to anyone who would listen.

"It was late and we had just returned from a ball we had attended . . ."

"That would have been the Duke of Manton's ball?"

Cassia looked at Rolfe, wondering how he knew that much, wondering if he already knew it all, the version society had invented. Why had she thought he would be any different? Why had she thought he would believe the truth, and not the fiction everyone else did? She was a fool. "Yes. I had gone to my bedchamber to retire for the evening. I was tired. My father was killed later that evening."

"You seem to have left out a detail or two, Lady Cassia. Were you not in the room with him when his body was found?"

Cassia eyed him. "Yes, I was. My father had wanted to speak with me. He brought me here to talk."

"About your refusal to accept the proposal of the duke's son, Malcolm," Rolfe finished.

"Yes. He was angry. My father wanted the match very much and he ..."

Cassia's words trailed off and she looked down at the floor. How could she possibly have thought she could tell him the truth?

Rolfe came up before her, tilting her chin so that she faced him.

"You can say it, Lady Cassia. He beat you. Your father abused you, and this was not the first time he had done so. Do not hide your face from the truth. There is no reason for you to be ashamed."

Cassia moistened her suddenly dry lips. She couldn't bring herself to admit the truth, to say the words aloud, even though Rolfe already knew it. It was a part of her life she wished had never happened. Refusing to speak of it helped to keep it from hurting her more. "As best as I can tell, I was unconscious for nearly a half hour. When I came to, my father was already dead. What I haven't figured out is how someone else could have gotten into the room, for he had locked the door after he brought me here." Her voice dropped and she added, "He always locked the door."

"Is that why you keep your window open at night? So you will always have a way to escape?"

Cassia didn't answer him. She didn't need to. Tears

were pooling in her eyes, tears she was fighting so hard to suppress, tears that should have been shed long, long ago. She closed her eyes when they started unwittingly to trickle down her cheeks.

"I am sorry for the hell you must have lived," Rolfe said, brushing them away gently with his fingers.

The moment was gone. It was as if a dark cloud came over the room, so quickly did Cassia's demeanor change. "Hell? What hell would that be, Lord Ravenscroft? I am one of the privileged, remember, one of the fortunate who need not worry about having a roof over my head or food on my table. Every physical need is seen to, even more so now that I have inherited my father's eighty thousand pounds."

"What about your emotional needs, Lady Cassia? Who sees to them? Eighty thousand pounds can do nothing for that."

Cassia started to turn. "I don't know what you are talking about."

Rolfe took her arm. "Oh, I think you do. I think you know very well of what I am speaking. While you may have had most everything you could ever want or need materially, your emotional upbringing has been far from the ideal. You spent the better part of your youth with a mother who detested your father and who made a career out of climbing the social ladder through the bedchamber door of any number of men."

"That is quite enough, Lord Ravenscroft."

"On top of that humiliation, when you returned home to England to finally meet the man the world called your father, you were faced with a drunken beast who preferred to exercise brutality rather than rationality, a man whose life's goal was to sell his daughter off to the highest and most influential bidder.

It is no wonder you cannot tolerate being in the presence of a man for any longer than a few minutes." ·

"I said that is enough!"

"How long do you think you can continue to suppress all of that emotional flotsam you keep locked away inside of you?"

Cassia narrowed her eyes at him, suddenly angry. "We all have our own cross to bear, Lord Ravenscroft. For some of us it is just made up of heavier wood."

"The cynicism you constantly wear is truly unbecoming to you."

"So is mourning, but like my cynicism, it is something I am forced by society's strictures to wear, regardless of whether I grieve or celebrate the passing of my father."

Rolfe took Cassia firmly by the shoulders. "To perdition with society's strictures. You of all people shouldn't care a whit what society thinks of you. If it pleases you then throw away the mourning, my lady, and your accursed cynicism with it."

Cassia glared at Rolfe with the most chilling expression he'd ever before seen in a woman's eyes. "As I already told you, Lord Ravenscroft, I don't know what you are talking about."

Damn her! Why did she have to be so bloody evasive? Why did she refuse to allow herself to feel? Perhaps it was the closeness between them. Perhaps he wanted to force Cassia to feel something, anything other than anger and hurt and ugliness. Perhaps he wanted to confront her with something she could not avoid, something real and alive, something other than her father's ghost. Without really knowing his reasons why, Rolfe pulled Cassia forward and covered her mouth with his own.

He felt her stiffen immediately. He tightened his hold on her, refusing to let her turn away. Surely she had been kissed before, for she certainly hadn't attempted to deny Geoffrey's accusations that she had bedded with the king. Why then did he sense inexperience mingled with her resistance to his kiss now?

Rolfe brought one hand up and pressed his fingers against Cassia's tightly welded jaw. He felt a slight yielding and deepened the kiss, moving his tongue into her mouth. The action seemed to surprise Cassia, as if this were a new and completely foreign experience for her, further puzzling him. She started to ease a little and her body leaned against his, molding its curves to him, and Rolfe knew, for that brief moment, Cassia had finally and truly felt.

But the moment Rolfe pulled away, he could feel the stiffness return to her body, the dark emptiness filling her eyes once again.

Cassia stood there, staring up at him, her lips still wet from his kiss.

She didn't say a word.

"Tell me now that you don't know what I'm talking about," Rolfe said.

Before Cassia could respond, if she could have at all, there was the sound of someone clearing his throat at the door.

"Excuse me, my lord, my lady. Lord Ravenscroft, there is a visitor here to see you."

It was Clydesworthe, and from the look on his face, Rolfe would have bet that he'd come to the door several minutes before he'd announced his presence.

Cassia quickly collected her senses, and with it, her defenses, that stiff, unyielding set back to her shoulders. "I'll leave you to your guest."

She was out the door before Clydesworthe had returned with Rolfe's visitor, his friend Dante Tremaine.

Chapter Fourteen

Rolfe was still staring at the door where Cassia had gone, several moments after Dante came into the room.

"Rolfe, is something wrong, man?"

"Nothing I care to talk about. Thanks for coming so quickly, Dante. I'm sorry I couldn't come to you myself, but as I said in my message, I'm housebound these days."

Dante grinned. "Yes, where is the lovely Lady Winter hiding herself these days?"

Rolfe frowned. "Her name is Cassia, Dante. Lady Cassia to you."

"I see."

Dante took a seat, dropping unceremoniously in a cracked leather chair that sat facing Seagrave's desk, wisely dropping any further use of Cassia's court label. "I believe you were seeking some information, milord?" he said in heavily accented cockney.

Dante's attempt at levity did not succeed in banishing Rolfe's deep frown.

"What have you been able to find out so far?"

Rolfe handed Dante a glass of brandy before lowering himself into the chair behind the desk. He leaned forward on his elbows and waited for Dante to begin.

"Well, I'm sorry to report I haven't found out much

at all, really. It's funny, actually, it's really most odd, but for some reason the usually loose-lipped members of the court are being rather reticent these days. They are refusing to divulge much at this time, other than to say that they all believe the lady guilty of the crime."

He removed a piece of paper scratched with notes from his coat pocket. "Let's see. I was able to verify that the lady's cousin, Geoffrey Montefort, has been in arrears with his creditors for several months now. What strikes me as odd is that up until recently, he had been living sensibly, never spending beyond his means, steering clear of the higher-stakes games, and always paying his creditors on time. Around the time of the death of Cassia's mother, he suddenly began to spend like he had a tree that sprouted guineas in abundance. That is also the approximate time that his gambling debts began to grow to their current outlandish heights."

"How bad off is he?" Rolfe asked.

"I would say that unless Cousin Geoffrey lands himself an ignorant and rather myopic heiress, or unless he finds some other long-lost relative to leave him, say, thirty thousand pounds, he'll soon be vacating his stylish apartments near St. James Park and will be taking up residence in a small but cozy cell in the Fleet instead."

Rolfe digested this mass of information. So the desperation he'd heard in Geoffrey's voice just before he'd come into the room to find him ready to force himself on Cassia hadn't been imagined. He was in need of funds, dire need, and his fifty-pound annuity wouldn't even begin to pay his debtors. Geoffrey must have felt angry and powerless, making him want to punish someone for his misfortune. It certainly explained his behavior toward Cassia. It also verified all that Rolfe had already suspected.

"What about the night of Seagrave's murder? Have you been able to verify Geoffrey's whereabouts then?"

"Yes, that was one thing I was able to pin down. Geoffrey was seen at Manton's ball on the Strand that night, as were Seagrave and Lady Cassia, and very nearly every other person in the city who could lay claim to an ounce of noble blood. Hell, I was even there, though not for long, having engaged the company of a thoroughly delightful blonde with breasts like ripe melons and this tiny little . . ." Dante paused, noting the look of impatience on Rolfe's face. "But that is another story entirely. One we can go into some other time. As for Geoffrey, no one I spoke with can account for having seen him after Lady Cassia's public and rather unexpected refusal of Manton's son Malcolm's proposal to her, and her swift removal by her father thereafter. Geoffrey seems to have vanished suddenly afterward."

"So he could very well have followed Cassia and her father here to Seagrave House and committed the murder himself."

"A possibility. From the direction of your questions, I would take it you no longer believe the lady guilty of the crime?"

Rolfe fixed Dante a piercing stare. "I will only say this once and I will be quite clear in doing so. There is no possible way Cassia could have killed her father. I will no longer entertain any idea of it. I am concentrating all efforts on finding the real murderer. Now, what about Geoffrey?"

Dante nodded. "He could have killed Seagrave, I suppose, but honestly, Rolfe, do you really think he did? I mean, from what I've heard and seen of Geoffrey, I'm not at all certain he has the mental faculties to have brought it off, much less having managed to circumvent any suspicion of the crime to lay the entire villainous package at Lady Cassia's feet. He just doesn't strike me as being clever enough."

"Perhaps, but you also didn't see him standing in this room not minutes before your arrival threatening Cassia with rape."

Dante gave Rolfe a look of disbelief. "And the man still managed to walk out of here alive? You must be growing soft in your old age, Rolfe, for you'd never have let that sort of affront pass unpunished to any lady in the old days."

"Thirty years is not such an old age, Dante. Only a small number of months separate us, my friend. And believe me when I say that the man came within inches of sampling the sharp point of my rapier blade. Fortunately, common sense prevailed."

"How so?"

"Had I killed the swine, it would make my proving him guilty of Seagrave's murder a bit difficult, wouldn't you think?"

Dante nodded. "Good point."

"Now, back to Geoffrey's habits. With whom does he regularly associate?"

"Geoffrey seems to drift in whatever direction the wind of advantage will blow him these days. He appears to enjoy gambling with the sons of the higher aristocracy—the Duke of Manton's son, Malcolm; Dursley's boy; you know the sort. Curiously, our friend Geoffrey has lately been seen paying court to Lady Castlemaine as well, though the reasons seem to elude me. I had credited the lady with much better taste, but one never knows why a woman does the things she does. That is what makes them such fascinating creatures."

"Dante . . ."

"I will see what else I can find out for you along that line."

"And find out what you can about Seagrave's finances as well, especially since the wars. He amassed a rather tidy fortune in a relatively short period of time. I find myself exceedingly curious as to how."

"Consider it done."

The brass mantel clock suddenly chimed two o'clock. Dante stood.

"Well, Rolfe, that is all I have for you now. I will see what else I can find out before our next meeting, which, I take it, you will summon me for in much the same fashion as this one?"

Rolfe nodded.

"Then, if there isn't anything else you need now, I'll be off. I've an appointment with a lovely young thing back at Whitehall and I would hate to keep her waiting too long. Ladies get most offended at having to wait. It's a privilege they think only themselves worthy of."

Rolfe grinned. Was there ever a time Dante wasn't engaged in the pursuit of a woman? "Dare I ask the lady's name?"

"Certainly. None other than *La Belle Stuart* herself."

"Not King Charles's Frances Stuart?"

"One and the same, though when last I checked, she'd not been made one of his flock as of yet. Certainly not for lack of trying by our friend, the king. I hear tell he's been most diligent in his attempts to pick that stubborn little lock on her chastity belt. Frances has been called empty-headed and foolish for her fondness for making card houses and the like, but I think she's more clever than everyone thinks. She just wants her competition to believe she's got nothing more than blank space in her brain so they won't ac-

cuse her of being a manipulating harpy like
Castlemaine."

"I've heard it said that Miss Stuart thinks that by
putting the king off as she has these past months, she
will be rewarded all the more when she finally does
acquiesce and allow him her favors. Some have even
said she has her sights set on becoming queen."

"When last I checked, I believe that post was already filled. Besides, I have it on good authority that
the lady has her sights set on another gentleman."

Rolfe shook his head. "Whatever happened to your
personal code of conduct in bedding only married
ladies?"

"This little darling came to me, my friend. What
sort of gentleman would I be if I refused the request
of a lady?"

"You're playing a dangerous game with this one,
Dante. Be careful."

Dante began to laugh, unable to mislead his friend
any longer. "You needn't worry about me, Rolfe,
though I appreciate the sentiment. This time it is not
the lady's bedchamber I am frequenting. Call me Mer-
cury, for I am employed in the role of messenger this
time, nothing more. I am merely acting as a decoy for
the man who truly holds the young nymph's heart."

"A decoy, you say?"

"Aye. You see, our friend King Charles led by his
pernicious little paramour, Castlemaine, happened to
make an unannounced visit at Miss Stuart's apartments one morning when she had deliberately stayed
in late claiming an illness. You can imagine the good
king's shock at finding the young lady not at all ill,
but *en déshabillé,* and in the company of none other
than the Duke of Richmond, who was sitting at the
edge of the bed."

Rolfe rolled his eyes heavenward. "Good God. I'm

surprised the king's cry of rage wasn't heard all through the city. To have had Richmond win her favors over before him must have been quite a blow to Charles's reputation. He prides himself on winning over any wench he chooses."

"Suffice it to say Richmond won't be occupying his suites at Whitehall for some time. He's been banished from court and from the city while the little lady remains, though most unhappily. Which is where I figure in to this little drama. I, who could never see my way through to standing in the way of true love, have assumed the duty of delivering the lovesick Richmond's letters to the lady's fair hand each day."

He removed from his coat pocket a letter sealed on the back with a coin of red wax.

Rolfe shook his head, walking with his friend to the door. "And you wonder why I prefer the solitude of Sussex to all these court intrigues. I would lose my way just trying to keep up with your bed partners. I am glad to hear you are not planning on trying to add this particular lady to your collection. Still, I would repeat my warning, Dante. Be careful."

Dante grinned. "I vaguely remember giving you the same advice not too long ago about another young beauty. One who resides in this very house."

"Mine is an entirely different situation. Tread lightly, Dante."

"I will. Oh, before I forget, I've been asked to convey a message to you, from a beautiful woman with hair redder than fire, and a temper to match."

Rolfe smiled. "And the message is?"

"Mara says to tell you that you had better think twice before leaving the city without visiting her and Hadrian. Something about setting that maid of hers to placing a curse on you that will cause you to lose all your hair. Consider yourself duly warned, my friend."

Rolfe laughed. "Point taken."

After Dante had gone, Rolfe took the time to think about all he'd been told. Having now made Geoffrey the prime suspect in Seagrave's murder, he decided it was time to have a talk with Cassia, to apologize for his forward behavior, and to get her opinions of Geoffrey, the repudiated heir.

Rolfe found Cassia at a small table in the parlor, her eyes narrowed in concentration, her hand moving furiously over her sketching paper.

"I would like to apologize for my behavior earlier," he said, coming into the room without preamble.

Cassia's hand instantly stilled. She turned the drawing over to shield it from him before responding. "Behavior? What behavior would that be, Lord Ravenscroft?"

She obviously planned to pretend nothing had happened as if by doing so she could deny her response.

"Perhaps I should refresh your memory, Lady Cassia. I was referring to when I had kissed you in your father's study not a half hour ago."

"Oh, that." She shrugged. "Think nothing of it."

Rolfe didn't know whether to be offended or relieved.

He moved farther into the room. "I have been thinking, Lady Cassia, trying to find a way to prove your innocence."

Cassia looked at him. "I have been thinking as well, Lord Ravenscroft, and I have come to the conclusion that you really needn't concern yourself with my father's murder any longer. At the risk of sounding rude, it is my problem, and I will find a way to handle it myself, thank you."

A polite dismissal, he had to admit, but a dismissal nonetheless.

"Please, just hear me out a moment if you will.

From your father's letter to you, it would seem he had a notion someone might attempt to bring him to a swifter end."

Cassia shrugged. "I guess, if one wanted to interpret it that way. But I do not see what matter this has. Without the document he wrote about, we have no proof of anything."

"Humor me a moment, if you will." Rolfe sat down across from her. "Did your father have any enemies that you are aware of?"

Cassia set her pencil aside, her interest sparked. "Due to the nature of his duties in the office of the Lord Chancellor, being the closest assistant to Edward Hyde, Lord Clarendon, my father was not on the best of terms with any number of people at court. As I'm sure you are aware, Lord Clarendon is not a very popular figure."

"Yes, but what has that to do with your father?"

"A majority of my father's duties dealt with whether or not to bring petitions being made to the Crown before the king for his consideration."

Rolfe leaned forward. "Wouldn't that be a duty more befitting the king?"

"Not necessarily. Simply because one wishes to petition the king for approval on something or another doesn't necessarily mean it will ever be seen by his eyes."

"So, in essence, it was up to Lord Clarendon, and consequently your father, to approve these petitions first?"

"Yes, as a manner of weeding through and bringing only those petitions worthy of the king's consideration before him. Otherwise, if King Charles had to address every one of the petitions himself, being that they are so numerous, His Majesty would be spending every minute of his day seeing to them, and he would not have time for other things."

Such as visiting the beds of his many mistresses— yours included, Rolfe thought, then pushed that thought aside. "Did your father ever discuss any of his business with you?"

"No." And then she added firmly, "Never."

"So you would not be privy to any petitions that he may have rejected, thereby earning him an enemy."

Cassia cocked her head to the side, thinking. "Not necessarily. You see, in addition to those duties, Lord Clarendon also had final word on even those petitions His Majesty did see fit to grant. Should he deem it, Lord Clarendon could make certain that the parchment certain petitions were written on would yellow with age before they'd ever receive the stamp of the Great Seal of England for approval. Without the seal, even with the king's approval, the petition would be worthless. My position at court did give me the advantage of hearing most every bit of gossip. There were a few petitions set forth by certain individuals at court that it was publicly known would never see the seal pressed upon them. One person in particular stands out."

"And that person is?"

"Lady Castlemaine. You see, Lord Clarendon bears a great dislike for her. In plain terms, they despise one another. He has made it known that any patent bearing her name will never see the seal upon it. It is a game Lord Clarendon plays, and from what I hear, he enjoys it quite well. Lady Castlemaine puts forth a great deal of effort trying to convince the king to grant her requests, but when each one of them comes down for the seal, it is put to the wayside, so to speak, never to be seen again."

"I would imagine this is most displeasing to her."

"That's putting it mildly. She somehow managed to circumvent Lord Clarendon when her grant for the title of Castlemaine came through, but since then, every one of her petitions has been stopped at the seal. And as Lady Castlemaine is all too aware, a title will not pay the creditors. Only property and, subsequently, money will, but as long as Lord Clarendon continues with his policy against her, it would appear she will not be gaining too much more of either."

"Why wouldn't she just wait until Clarendon is no longer Lord Chancellor?"

"Lady Castlemaine would be a fool not to realize that her time as Whitehall's uncrowned queen is limited. Faith, with the arrival of Frances Stuart and the king's growing interest in her, Barbara's appeal in the king's bed has already begun to wane. One thing she cannot stop is time, and with time comes age, and unfortunately for ladies, with age goes beauty. Lady Castlemaine can be called many things, but one thing is for certain, she is no fool She has been pressing the king for some time for a grant on a piece of profitable property that will keep her long after she is inevitably succeeded in his affections."

Rolfe couldn't help but think it strange that Cassia was sitting here, discussing the king's assortment of bed partners with him so openly. "So, even were Lady Castlemaine to wheedle such property from the king, it would be useless unless Clarendon set the final seal. Quite simply put, the grant would not be granted."

Cassia nodded. "Precisely. Lady Castlemaine has been desperate of late to amass as much wealth and property as she can. Though the national coffers are fast growing thin, her jewel boxes, it seems, continue to grow heavier, far outweighing our own true queen's. King Charles gives in to her requests for property, but each time, her petitions are stopped at the seal. Lady Castlemaine has tried countless times to disguise her requests, seeking to keep Lord Clarendon from realizing they are hers. Lord Clarendon is a busy man, far too busy to waste his time examining every petition to assure it is not one of Lady Castlemaine's in disguise. So Lord Clarendon charged my father with the specific duty of singling out her petitions, regardless of what name they bore, and bringing them to his attention, or should I say, keeping them buried from the same."

Rolfe nodded. "Only Lord Clarendon could hold such an unenviable position to such success. Anyone else would be banished from court for such an effrontery to Lady Castlemaine. But Lord Clarendon has far more influence with the king than she. He was King Charles's tutor when he was a boy. It was Clarendon who helped him escape to France when the Cromwellians were calling for his head. He followed Charles into exile, managed his affairs and his policies; he even counseled him on his restoration to the throne. Charles would never think of punishing Lord Clarendon for refusing the seal. It would be like punishing his own father. Faith, I believe the king thinks of Lord Clarendon as a father, especially since his natural one was executed when Charles was at such a young and impressionable age."

"The king does seek out his advice often," Cassia said. "He listens to whatever Lord Clarendon tells him. That is the primary reason why Lord Clarendon is so disliked at court. It is also why Lady Castlemaine detests him as she does. He is the only person whom the king listens to more than her."

"And she would not risk an attempt on the life of so public an official as Lord Clarendon, but with your father—a lesser known thorn in her side, the very one whose duty it was to single out her petitions—gone and out of the way, the chances of her petitions passing the seal greatly increased."

"Precisely."

Rolfe sat back. "The intricacies of it all are exhausting, but fascinating, once one finally manages to figure them out. It certainly would seem to put Lady Castlemaine at the top of our list of suspects, though I doubt she would be so foolish as to leave any hint of evidence that could be traced back to her."

Cassia nodded. "And it very well could not have been her. One must remember never to lay false blame."

"You are right. It could have been any number of people. It could have even been your cousin, Geoffrey. In fact, excepting you, and now Lady Castlemaine, he would be the obvious choice."

Cassia frowned. "Since his visit here earlier today, that thought has crossed my mind several times, especially after his reaction to my father's petition, although he did not know of the existence of the petition before our meeting with Mr. Finchley."

"Which is even more reason to suspect him. He thought he would be inheriting everything at your father's demise except whatever portion you were to be allowed. At the risk of sounding presumptuous, Lady Cassia, I have done some checking since your meeting with Mr. Finchley and I have learned that your cousin Geoffrey has landed himself into a financial quandary. To a sum of nearly thirty thousand pounds. Unless you can think of anyone else who might have similar motive for killing your father, I would think Geoffrey the prime suspect."

Cassia sat in silence for a moment, thinking.

"I have considered an entirely different list of possibilities as well," Rolfe said. "Something even you may not have thought of." He paused a moment. "Do you have any enemies, Lady Cassia?"

It was something she'd obviously not considered.

"Why would that be of any consequence? I was not the one murdered. My father was."

"Yes, but let us not forget that excepting us, in the eyes of everyone else in this city, you are still the prime suspect. Should someone wish to damage your standing at court, or perhaps had someone been seeking revenge against you, this could be the way to do it. And we mustn't forget the near-miss you had with that carriage in front of the Horse Guards at Whitehall. I cannot be entirely certain that carriage was not intending to run you down."

Cassia looked down at her hands, suddenly feeling very vulnerable and very frightened. "So what am I to do? Run off to the country and hide for the rest of my life, leaving everyone to believe I am a murderess?"

"No. You are not to do anything of the sort, Lady Cassia. We are going to solve this thing—together. You see, you have won me over to your side on one issue. I see now that a sojourn to the country would not be at all beneficial to your proving your innocence. It could be that someone wanted you out of the city for some reason, perhaps even to find the mysterious document your father wrote to you about. In the country we could never find who that someone is."

"So what should I do?"

"You will need to remain here in London in order to find the true culprit and you will need to remain visible. But since our list of suspects seems to be growing and since I have been away from court for quite some time, I will need your assistance in reacquainting myself with some of Whitehall's more prominent inmates so I can begin paring down our list."

"How can I do that?"

"There is a costumed ball being held at the palace tomorrow evening. It would appear that most, if not all, of our suspects will be in attendance. I propose that we attend this ball and start ferreting out our man, or woman, whomever it may be."

Chapter Fifteen

Rolfe was on his way to the kitchen to request a pot of strong, hot coffee to drink while he went over the sheaf of papers just delivered from his steward, Penwiddy, back at Ravenwood in Sussex, when he noticed the door to the morning parlor was standing slightly open.

A delicately slippered foot dangled over the edge of a chaise just in his view, a hint of a stockinged leg barely revealed. The temptation was too much to pass. He came closer, pushing the door inward.

The morning parlor was suitably named, for it faced out onto the eastern side of the house with tall windows that caught the best sunlight, lighting up the interior of the room and making its pale yellow papered walls appear even brighter. The furnishing were fashioned from delicate fruitwood, suited more to feminine tastes, the perfect setting for Cassia to visit with friends over tea.

Coming into the room, Rolfe found Cassia reclined on the chaise, hence the foot dangling over the edge, her head falling charmingly to one side in sleep. Rolfe found it no surprise that she should have trouble keeping awake during the day, for he knew that she didn't sleep at all during the night. Since that first night when he'd come back from his visit with Cordelia at Whitehall to find Cassia crying out in fear of her dreams, he'd heard her every night since, either pacing the floorboards while Winifred snored, or sketching furiously through the wee hours, her charcoal pencil scratching across the vellum while the flickering light from her bedside candle sent a shaft of light beaming beneath the door that separated them.

Cassia had never questioned Rolfe's removal of the laudanum bottle, and her subsequent insomniac habits confirmed that Winifred had indeed heeded his orders not to bring another bottle of the stuff into the house. Even so, Rolfe knew that the maid would have continued to minister the laudanum to Cassia, regardless of his orders, had her mistress wished it. Obviously, thankfully, she hadn't.

Rather than dull her mind with the drug each night, and preferable to facing her nightmares clearheaded, Cassia filled the dark and silent hours of night with her pacing and sketching, until the first lights of the dawn were breaking on the eastern horizon. Somehow the security of daylight allowed Cassia a few peaceful hours in which to rest, and that, coupled now with an occasional midday snooze, seemed to provide her the respite she needed.

As he drew near to the side of the chaise, Rolfe spotted a book lying on the floor, a book Cassia had obviously been reading that had fallen from her sleepy fingers. He bent to retrieve it and noticed a sketch lying on the floor beside it. It was a drawing of a woman, her body draped all around with cloths, wearing a curious crown on her head. Rolfe immediately noticed that the woman depicted was as faceless as had been Cassia's other drawings.

Rolfe quickly tucked the drawing inside the book when he heard Cassia begin to stir.

"Excuse me, Lady Cassia. I didn't mean to wake

you. I was just retrieving your book from the floor where it had fallen."

He glanced at the red-leather spine, recently polished, as had been the other books she had decided to keep from her father's collection. This particular book told of the ancient myths and legends.

"Thank you, Lord Ravenscroft," Cassia said, rubbing at her eyes and smoothing back her hair as she sat up. "I was doing a bit of research. I guess I must have dozed off."

Rolfe allowed her a moment to fully awaken then asked the question that continually nagged at him.

"Why do they never have faces?"

Cassia stiffened immediately. It was a question she had not expected. "I am sorry but I don't know what you mean."

"I'm talking about your sketches. You create such lifelike, thought-provoking images, yet you never draw your subject's face. I was just curious as to why."

Cassia smoothed down the folds of her black mourning gown, trying to shake out the wrinkles. "I believe it was Guillaume de Salluste Du Bartas who is quoted as likening one's eyes to the window of his soul. I would tend to agree with Monsieur Du Bartas, although I would take it a bit further to say that one's entire face is more of a window to the soul, not just the eyes. And being that most people wear an assortment of faces in their efforts to hide their own true one, that one face that would reveal their innermost thoughts and dreams, I do not think it would be an accurate depiction to draw in the affected face a person chooses to masquerade behind."

Her view though filled with her usual cynicism, did tend toward the truth.

"And do you have dreams that you hide behind a false face, Lady Cassia?"

She looked at him. "Of course I have dreams. Doesn't everyone?"

"I would hope so. Without dreams we are nothing but flesh and bone. I had just wondered, since you've never talked about your own dreams."

"That is because some dreams are simply that—dreams, to be left in one's thoughts and never acted upon. I have found that acting upon one's dreams tends to leave a person sadly disappointed. And what about you, my lord? You are so interested in finding out my secrets, yet you never offer to reveal your own. don't you have dreams as well?"

"As you just said, doesn't everyone? But in speaking with you, I am beginning to wonder why anyone would wish to dream at all."

"Because one must always have hope," Cassia said lifting the book of myths. "Even poor Pandora knew that. Hope is what helps a person to survive in times of trial, often it is all they have, and sometimes they are surprised when their dream actually becomes reality. But I don't believe it is within one's power to make a dream come true. That is left to another higher being. If one is practical and honest, he can make that distinction and thereby prevent himself from spending his life chasing after a dream that will never be, and simply wait for those that the fates decide will."

Why had she just said all that? Cassia thought. Why had she bothered to respond to his questions at all? What was it about this man that made her suddenly so willing to speak her innermost thoughts, so free to confide things she would never have dared tell anyone else?

"I think that if everybody held the same pessimistic view you do," Rolfe said, "the world would be a much duller place in which to live. Surely men like Christopher Columbus and Sir Francis Drake had dreams, and had they not acted on those dreams, pursuing them as they did, we would not now know of the world that exists outside England and the Continent."

"What of your dreams?" Cassia asked, trying to pull his attention away from her. "I noticed you never revealed what they were."

Rolfe looked at the floor. "My dreams have always dealt with honor and setting the things that were wrong in this world to rights. There are some wrongs, though, that can never be reversed."

"I have heard that you were instrumental in restoring King Charles to the throne. Surely that is one wrong you did manage to set to rights."

"I, like so many others, had seen the evil that Cromwell had become."

"I'm told you bravely risked your life on more than one occasion."

"And I would do it again to help bring peace back to England. I never again wish to see her so nearly destroyed."

Cassia watched Rolfe closely when next he looked up at her. "Lord Ravenscroft, I am curious about something. If you worked so diligently to restore the king, why then did you leave London, forsaking the court as you did?"

Rolfe thought of Daphne, of the humiliation he'd felt when she had refused his proposal of marriage, the depths to which she had brought him, and decided not to voice those thoughts. Some memories were better left just that—memories—something to avoid, something to be forgotten. "When I was made an earl for my efforts in bringing King Charles back to the throne, I was also granted an estate in Sussex with the title. Ravenwood was badly damaged during the wars. For the past year, I have been overseeing the renovations on it."

"That is all?"

"That is all."

"And for this you are known as the Exiled Earl? Seems a rather silly reason to me."

"Society has a way of making too much of things." He looked at her. "As I'm sure you well know."

"Sometimes I wish I could do what you did, just up and leave, never to show my face again." She gathered up her sketching paper and pencils. "I guess that is one dream I was just not meant to live."

With that, Cassia stood and left the room.

So much cynicism for one so young, Rolfe thought, watching her go. And how sad for her that she would never consider pursuing her dreams. It was almost as if she were afraid of trying. But even as he thought that, Rolfe knew that Cassia's disenchantment came about from her being so at home with life's darker side, having lived there through most of her two and twenty years.

Staring at the vacant doorway, Rolfe suddenly wanted, needed to find out those dreams Cassia held so close but believed so little in, and somehow make them reality.

Rolfe didn't see Cassia the rest of that day, although thoughts of her filled his mind long after their conversation. Sitting at the desk in her father's study, he passed the hours wondering about her dreams, what they were, how he could make them come true. The sheaf of papers sent by Penwiddy went untouched.

It wasn't long before the clock was striking eight o'clock, signaling that they were in serious danger of arriving late to the palace masquerade. In fact, if they delayed much longer, they would be unable to blend in with the other arriving guests, and would be forced to make a singular appearance. Their presence might be noticed, deterring them from their investigations of the other guests. When yet another quarter hour passed, Rolfe decided he'd best see what was keeping Cassia.

He had just started up the stairs when his eyes caught a movement above him.

"I was just coming to see if you ..."

Cassia stood on the landing above him, her gown made of a shimmering white silk and cut in the style of the ancient Greeks and Romans. Her hair, which she'd powdered and had braided in coronet atop her head, was woven through with a strand of milky pearls. A mask made of white silk, covered her face from the nose up, her dark eyes barely discernible beneath it. She'd left her neck unadorned, powdering her skin with a sparkling, powdering substance that glittered beneath the light of the candles above them, giving her an otherworldly appearance.

She presented a vision of untouched and striking loveliness.

"I'm afraid my memory of mythology is not as clear as it once was, my lady, for I've no idea what character it is you are portraying."

"Isn't it obvious, my lord? I am Dice, one of the Horae, daughters of Zeus and Themis, and one of the three goddesses of the seasons whose task it is to guard the gates of Heaven, who along with my sisters, Eunómia and Eiréne, see to peace and order. My name stands for 'Justice,' and I am also known as the goddess of the season of winter. It is all rather fitting, don't you think?"

Rolfe could but smile at her ingenious creation. "I see you've decided the time is ripe to turn the tables on society." He bowed. "Well done, my lady."

Cassia came down the stairs and took Rolfe's outstretched hand. "At first I fancied going dressed as a sacrificial virgin, but then thought the better of it. So many of the young ladies who will be in attendance are such in reality, I do not think it proper to mock them in costume. I then considered going as Lady Macbeth or even Cleopatra, but their method of murder was more along the lines of poison, and, well, I could not find any notorious women in history who had wielded a knife. It took some time, and a little research, but I finally settled upon what I thought to be a most suitable character." She curtsied elegantly. "Lady Winter personified."

"Bravo, my lady."

Cassia rose and slanted him a glance. "And you, my lord, what is it you are portraying, dressed in black as you are and looking most sinister?"

"I guess you could say I was more inclined to hearsay than legend. It is said that during the civil wars, there was a secret alliance of those who worked closest to the enemy in their efforts to see King Charles restored to the throne. I believe they were known as the 'Nightmen,' for their dark attire and for their practice of passing about unseen in the night."

"Are you certain these Nightmen are merely rumor, Lord Ravenscroft? It would sound as if you speak from experience."

Rolfe merely grinned, neither confirming nor denying. "There is no proof of their existence and since nobody knows the true identities of the Nightmen, one can only guess if they really were at all."

Having come along the King Street entrance, the more popular venue, the coach carrying Rolfe and Cassia to the masquerade ball was made to wait in a long line of carriages when they arrived at the torchlit gates of Whitehall. They disembarked among the crowd of costumed guests making their way toward the brilliantly lit Banqueting House. Inside, the press was even more maddening, made all but intolerable as the musicians struck the first chord to signal a beginning to the dancing. At once, the colorfully clad and busily chattering bodies that had filled the dancing area pushed outward toward the outer fringes of the room like mice scattering from the cat; it made it nearly impossible to move.

Rolfe took Cassia's hand and started to lead her through the crowd.

"All right, my lady," he said quietly, having managed to secure them a spot off to the side of the orchestra that afforded them a decent overview of the ballroom, "you may start by acquainting me with some of the more prominent members at court."

Cassia narrowed her eyes beneath her mask, trying to discern the identities of the costumed crowd. "There, standing beneath the musicians' balcony dressed as the Roman war goddess, Bellona, is Barbara Palmer, Lady Castlemaine. But, I had forgotten, you've already met."

"If you will recall, we did not formally meet, for you were busy giving her a setting down the likes of which I'll not forget. You did not get down to the social niceties of a formal introduction, but I am familiar with the woman all the same."

Cassia looked on. "The oversized man standing beside her dressed as, I believe, a rather large rendition of Shakespeare's King Lear is Lord Talbot, one of her prominent underlings."

"Could he be our man?"

Cassia thought a moment, then shook her head. "It is a well-known fact that Lord Talbot cannot utter a coherent word unless he is three cups under. I shudder to think of how far into the bottle he'd need to be in order to accomplish something as serious as murder."

Rolfe began surveying the crowd himself. "I believe the golden-clad Adonis near the entryway making a path straight for us would be your cousin Geoffrey."

Cassia spotted him easily. It was impossible not to. Even among the other colorful costumes around them, the sparkling gold material of his certainly costly attire stood out. "Yes, it would seem you are correct."

"Who is the tall blond man walking so closely beside him?"

Cassia hesitated. "That would be the Marquess of Newbury."

"You mean Malcolm, the eldest son and heir of the Duke of Manton, the one your father wished for you to marry?"

Before Cassia could confirm this obvious distinction, the pair of them drew forward.

"Can it be? Has our dear Cassia decided it time—now that she has learned of the fortune her father left her—to come out of mourning?"

Cassia frowned at Geoffrey. "Good evening, Geoffrey." She allowed Malcolm, the marquess, to take her hand and press a polite kiss to it. "Good evening to you, Lord Newbury."

It was the first time she'd seen Malcolm since he'd proposed marriage to her the night of her father's murder. He had attended his burial, but on that day, Malcolm had preferred to remain on the outer fringes of the crowd. Cassia suddenly realized he had never come forward to offer his condolences that day. Perhaps it was due to the conversation she'd had with Rolfe when he'd brooked the question of her possibly having an enemy, but as Cassia stared at Malcolm now, she suddenly wondered if he could have murdered her father.

Malcolm smiled broadly. "Must we stand on such formality, Cassia? I mean, being that we were so nearly betrothed, I would think it proper and most acceptable for you to call me by my given name."

Cassia nodded. "As you wish, Malcolm. Now, if you gentlemen will excuse us—"

"Malcolm," came a voice from behind them, "I would like a word with you, please."

Cassia nodded to Rolfe, somehow knowing his raised brow was meant to communicate that he questioned if the newcomer was Malcolm's father, the Duke of Manton.

"Oh, excuse me, Lady Cassia," the duke said, suddenly recognizing the others standing with his son. "I hadn't meant to interrupt."

He eyed Rolfe with such open suspicion that propriety necessitated Cassia introduce them. "Your Grace, Malcolm, please allow me to introduce you to Rolfe Brodrigan, the Earl of Ravenscroft."

Rolfe shook first Malcolm's hand, then the duke's. "Gentlemen, a pleasure."

"Indeed," replied Malcolm.

"Quite," muttered the duke, still staring at Rolfe as if he were some sort of reprobate.

"If you gentlemen will kindly excuse us, I believe Lady Cassia has promised me the next dance."

Rolfe took Cassia's arm before they could respond and started moving with her through the crowd. He stopped at the end of the line of dancers now preparing to take to the dance floor. He bowed gallantly before her as the orchestra started to play.

"Now it is my turn to direct your attentions to a few of the people of the court with whom I am already acquainted."

Rolfe took her hand, lifting it upward in the motion of the dance. As he did, he gestured across the room. "Do you see the couple standing at the far end of the line of dancers?"

Cassia came around him in a circle, noticing a man of imposing stature holding the hand of a lovely, red-haired woman. "Do you mean the couple dressed as Samson and Delilah?"

"That would be they. Should you and I become separated for any reason and you find you cannot easily locate me, you may go to them. They are Lord and Lady Kulhaven from Ireland and they are close friends of mine. I trust them implicitly. You will be safe with them."

He turned and took Cassia's hand, bowing forward with the steps of the dance. He pointed to another figure, this one a tall man dressed, like Rolfe, entirely in black, standing at the edge of the dancing area. He was a little difficult to see, as he was surrounded by a small throng of ladies. "Likewise with Dante, if you can get through his vast crowd of admirers. Whatever you do, be certain to be near one of us at all times."

Cassia followed Rolfe's lead as he continued through the dance, and she took the opportunity to point out a few of the more prominent members of the court and her most recent suitors.

When the dance ended, Rolfe led Cassia off toward the far side of the ballroom.

"I must say," suddenly came a familiar voice from behind, "I do like your choice of costumes, oh Goddess of the Frost."

"Cordelia," Cassia exclaimed, embracing her friend. She stepped back to survey her costume. "And what is it you are portraying this evening?"

Cordelia's ensemble was a mixture of every possible color under the sun, complete with an array of different-colored feathers sticking out in a sort of fan from her stylish and extravagant coiffure.

"Why, I am a rainbow, silly, what else? And I've already had three thoroughly lecherous men, one even confined to a wheeled chair, ask me if they could see whether the pot of gold truly exists beneath my skirts."

"And did they find the answer to their question?" Rolfe asked with a grin.

Cordelia smiled, slapping him with the sticks of her fan. "You naughty boy. I told them that was one mystery that would remain so, at least during their lifetimes." She sighed then. "Or at least until the day my Percy returns—if he ever does."

Noting the melancholy direction of her friend's thoughts, Cassia quickly drew her attention elsewhere. "I have not seen the king or queen yet. Aren't they in attendance this evening?"

"The king is somewhere hereabouts. You know he would never miss the opportunity for a masquerade. He loves to disguise himself and come in with the crowd so as to enable himself to chase after whatever skirt he wishes without *La Castlemaine* finding out and throwing a fit of hysteria."

Cordelia surveyed the crowd. "I don't see him, but I have heard he is dressed as a wolf. Quite fitting, don't you think? Queen Catherine, I'm afraid, could not attend for she continues ill and is confined to her chambers."

Cassia's face grew dark with concern. "Her condition is growing worse? What of the babe?"

"The babe is still there and intact, as far as the physicians can tell, but truthfully, Cassia, she seems to grow frailer each day. I'm afraid they are not holding very much hope for her chances of a successful delivery."

Cassia turned to Rolfe. "I must go to her at once."

He nodded and followed her as she started for the door to leave.

It wasn't seconds later that he lost sight of her in the crowd.

Rolfe's heart began to hammer against his chest as he searched for Cassia among the many masked faces that surrounded him. Somewhere out there was the real murderer, and he was most likely watching Cassia. How could she have disappeared so quickly? Why hadn't he been watching her more closely? They hadn't been there a half of an hour and already he'd managed to lose her.

Rolfe was about to enlist the aid of his friends when he finally spotted her. She was on the dance floor, partnered by a tall dark figure—a figure, he noticed immediately, that was dressed as a wolf.

The king.

Rolfe came to the edge of the crowd and stood waiting for Cassia, watching the two as they moved together in time to the music. They made a striking couple, the king tall and regal, Cassia lovely and elegant, and they soon drew the attention of the crowd, for the king's costume seemed to be of no mystery to anyone. The other couples dancing beside them began taking themselves off to stand back and watch them as they circled and bowed with the steps of the dance.

Some of the courtiers standing beside Rolfe quickly guessed the identity of the king's dancing partner. Whispers of "Lady Winter" and "Murderess Montefort" wafted through the crowd like a gust of icy wind. He needed to get her away; the sooner he could manage it the better.

When the dance finally ended, Rolfe started forward. He stopped as he saw Charles leading Cassia away, off the floor, through a small side door, and out into the night with him beneath the very noses of the shocked courtiers.

Rage began to boil in Rolfe's stomach, a rage so

deep he could feel it to his soul. Everyone in that ballroom knew where the two were going to. With the queen convalescing in her bed, the king was at leisure to partake of his mistress's favors. He did not conceal, but instead advertised his infidelities, parading Cassia before the members of his court in a dance, before taking her off like the wolf luring away the innocent lamb.

And Cassia was already but one of the many in his flock.

Caught between the urge to go after them and the desire to smash his fist into something hard, Rolfe turned and started walking from the suddenly stifling ballroom. What a fool he'd been! What an utter ass! He could picture them clearly, Charles pushing away Cassia's gown, baring the white skin of her thighs as he laid her back, his dark wolf's head dipping down toward her. His mouth would suckle at her breast, moving down further, melting her icy reserve, replacing it with the heat of the passion she felt only for him. And Cassia would wrap her long, white legs around him while Charles drove into her with long, measured thrusts. She would cry out his name, the name of the one man she would not rebuke, the only man she allowed behind those icy impenetrable walls—Charles, the King of England.

Chapter Sixteen

Rolfe passed one full hour alone, standing among the gay and glittering crowd in Whitehall's Banqueting House. Not that he was watching as the tall case clocks that were set at intervals around the colorful and ablaze ballroom ticked the minutes away. He was far too occupied with swallowing down the glasses of brandy he'd whisked from the passing silver trays of the liveried servants milling about to pay much attention to the time.

When he'd tossed down the last from his fourth— or was it his fifth?—goblet, he knew he'd had enough. Quite enough. He'd had enough of thinking about what Cassia might be doing, enough of picturing her in the king's bed. He'd had enough of drinking to try to dispel that image from his head. And he'd had enough of standing around, looking like an utter fool, while waiting for Cassia to return from her lover's tryst with the king, his friend, the man he'd vowed to give his life for.

All of his adult life, since that fated day when he'd received the post informing him of the deaths of his family at the hands of the Parliamentarians, Rolfe had been bound by duty—duty to his country, and duty to his king. And, more recently, duty to his name. He'd been raised by his father to put right before wrong, that duty and honor came above all else, above personal desire, above monetary gain. Nothing was more sacred, nothing more just or honorable.

And Rolfe believed he had been doing the right and honorable thing by trying to help Cassia prove her innocence of her father's murder.

But there was also a limit as to how far he was willing to go in the line of duty, and standing around waiting while Cassia occupied the king's bed was beyond that limit. Far, far beyond it.

Rolfe set down the goblet with such force that those standing around him looked surprised the glass did not shatter in his hand. He turned, ready to leave the glittering ballroom, ready to leave London and return to Ravenwood—duty be damned—thinking to himself as he started through the crowd that the evening could not possibly get any worse.

He soon discovered he was wrong in that assumption.

"Good evening, Rolfe."

She was standing between him and the doorway, preventing his leaving and so near to him he could smell the fragrant scent of her lavender perfume.

She had always favored lavender, he remembered fleetingly.

He could not possibly feign that he hadn't heard her honeyed greeting, for the moment the words had left her Spanish red-colored lips, he'd rooted himself to the floor. Rolfe hated the fact that the instinct to do so remained even after all the months that had passed.

Hers was the last voice he had expected to hear calling to him there that night. It was not a voice he was particularly glad to have heard. In fact, it was a voice he'd have preferred never hearing again.

Rolfe looked over to her, assuming an expression of mild disinterest, and said, "Good evening, Lady Westcott."

She was dressed in the costume of a medieval dam-sel, her conical hennin cap draped with a pale blue wisp of a veil. A chain belt decorated by numerous small silver bells encircled her narrow waist, tinkling softly as she drew closer still. She had removed her mask, but even had her face been covered from chin to brow, Rolfe would have known it was her.

She was what was considered by most to be the purest vision of English beauty: petite, fragile, with hair that was a lovely shade of blond, and catlike eyes the color of the periwinkle flowers that filled the fields in the Sussex countryside.

In the months after his hasty departure from London society nearly a year before, Rolfe had come to hate those accursed periwinkles.

And now she stood here before him again, the woman, the one woman Rolfe once believed he had loved, the same who had left him standing a laughing-stock before all the court, on bended knee, begging for her hand in marriage.

Daphne Hudson, née Smithfield, wife to the wealthy Earl of Westcott, came forward—alone.

"You certainly are the last person I would have expected to see here tonight," she said, trying to break the awkward silence that had descended between them. "I hadn't heard you'd returned to London."

"Yes, well, I decided I'd been kept in exile in the country long enough," Rolfe said with heavy sarcasm. He raked his gaze swiftly over her. "You look well."

It was a lie. Marriage had not been kind to Daphne, not at all, Rolfe thought, noticing the hollow look to her face, the circles that shaded the fair white skin beneath her eyes. Even those eyes, those damned peri-winkle eyes that he'd found himself lost in so many times before, now looked lackluster and dull.

From the silence that immediately followed his comment, Rolfe realized that Daphne was not flattered by his tepid compliment. Knowing that pleased him.

"Thank you, Rolfe," Daphne finally said, "and you, too, are looking quite well. These months away from court have had their benefit for you. It would seem the country air agrees with you."

"Hard work and honest living do tend to bring out the best in most any person, I'm told. Perhaps you should give the same a try; but then, as I remember, honesty wasn't one of your stronger suits."

Rolfe was surprised he felt no regret at the hurt look that came into her eyes. Months earlier, had he ever dared to say such a thing to her, he'd have dropped to his knees to beg her forgiveness, claiming a momentary lapse in sanity. Now, instead, he went on.

"I was hoping to offer your husband my congratulations on your marriage. I apologize if I was remiss in not formally extending my felicitations to you sooner, but I only just learned of it. I haven't seen the good Edwin yet tonight. Is he here?"

Just then, as if answering his stage cue, Edwin Hudson came forward, stumbling slightly and nearly spilling his glass of burgundy on Daphne's pale blue damask skirts. He slipped his arm around his wife's waist, grabbing hold of the belt of silver bells to keep himself vertical. The very visible mark of another woman's lip paint was stamped on his neck just above his cravat.

"Now, Ravenscroft, don't you be forgetting Daphne's my wife. Hope there's no hard feelings, what with your losing her to me like you did."

The starkness of Daphne's face powder couldn't hide the embarrassed flush that spread over her cheeks at her husband's ill-placed comment. Had Edwin not been clutching at her skirts to keep himself from falling over, she'd no doubt have fled the conversation in an instant.

"No hard feelings at all, Westcott. Things have turned out very well for me, and I can see now that Daphne finally got what she was looking for. I wish you both all the best and many years of wedded bliss."

With that Rolfe took up a champagne glass from another of the numerous passing trays, lifted it upward in a mock toast, and tipped it to his lips.

It was at that precise moment that he spotted, over the rim of the glass, Cassia just returning to the ballroom.

It could have been the influence of the brandy he'd drunk early, but he would have sworn her gown was mussed.

Without taking his eyes from her, Rolfe handed the glass to Daphne, muttering, "If you'll excuse me, I just realized my attentions are needed elsewhere."

Rolfe did not wait for a response, but cut his way through the mob of people and headed straight for Cassia. When he was nearly at her, Cassia spotted him and smiled.

"Lord Ravenscroft, I was just—"

Rolfe grabbed Cassia by the upper arm and propelled her toward the door. "Outside, madam."

Cassia was so startled by the fierceness in Rolfe's voice, she did not say a word. She merely walked alongside him, trying to ignore the pain that was shooting down her arm from his fierce grip.

Once they were outside, away from the ballroom and the crowd, and secluded in the shaded alcoves of the Privy Garden, Cassia expected Rolfe would release her. She was stunned when his hand suddenly snaked around to the back of her neck and he yanked her forward, his touch none too gentle. His mouth covered hers in what was more an assault than a kiss.

Cassia wrenched herself away and slapped him hard on the cheek.

His eyes blazed down at her. "Did you enjoy your visit to the queen's bedchamber, my lady?"

Rolfe took a step toward her. Something in his angry gaze caused Cassia to retreat a step. She found herself backed against the ivy-covered wall and into the near darkness of the shadows.

"Yes, I did." Cassia eyed him warily. "I would ask that you please take a step backward, Lord Ravenscroft."

"Why, my lady? Is the distance between us too close for propriety's sake? Perhaps we should ask Winifred to join us. We certainly wouldn't want tongues to wag, would we?"

Instead of moving back, Rolfe came another step forward. Cassia could retreat no further. He placed each of his hands on her shoulders, his fingers tightening over her. The way he held her, Cassia felt sure he could snap her bones with the slightest increase in pressure. She began to taste the beginnings of fear, but tried to maintain her composure.

"You are acting strangely. Is something wrong?"

Rolfe smiled. "Wrong? What could possibly be wrong? I am curious, though, did you enjoy your visit to the king's bedchamber as much as you did the queen's?"

Cassia lifted her hands, placed them flat against Rolfe's chest and pushed at him with all her strength. She was a little surprised to see she'd managed to send him back a bit. "I would ask you again to please step back, my lord."

"Oh, I see. You are standing here ordering me to step away just after you've returned from allowing the king that and much more. Tell me, Lady Cassia, what was it the other day that caused you to turn to ice when I dared to steal a kiss from your lips? Wasn't I highborn enough to be given the honor of taking such liberties? Isn't my social ranking acceptable to you?"

"What are you talking about?"

It must have been the brandy talking, for suddenly, it wasn't Cassia Rolfe saw standing before him, confused and utterly lost at what he was saying. Instead it was Daphne, staring down her pert nose at him as if he were no better than a wharf rat. Without thinking, Rolfe went on. "No, I was not born to the heights of nobility. I earned my title in the field of honor defending what was right and just. Doesn't that account for anything? Surely it should qualify me for at least one night in your bed—that is, whenever I might chance to find it vacant."

Cassia gasped at Rolfe's crude accusations, even though she knew well of the rumors that placed her among King Charles's mistresses. In fact, she had done her very best to lend credence to them. Yes, she'd spent hours alone with the king, not occupying his bed as Rolfe and every other person at court believed, but passing hours over the chess board. Charles found Cassia a challenging opponent—she usually beat him—and they would play game after game, sometimes until the dark hours of the night.

Cassia hadn't really cared about the rumors and whispers that came as a result of these private times with the king. She'd never tried to deny them, nor had Charles, a request made of him by Cassia herself.

She had found that with the distinction of being thought of as one of the king's mistresses, came a certain amount of freedom, freedom to do as she pleased at court, freedom to avoid the attentions of unwanted swains. Not many of the men at court were eager to face King Charles as a rival for her favors.

Why then suddenly, did it bother Cassia so much that Rolfe believed her the king's mistress now?

"I will only say this once, Lord Ravenscroft, so listen to me well. I have never—"

Cassia never finished her sentence. Her body swayed unsteadily on her feet and her eyes rolled back into her head before she pitched forward and fell into Rolfe's arms.

"Damnation!" Rolfe slammed his fist against the desktop, sending a crystal inkwell skittering across it to drop to the floor. Ink dribbled in a black pool on the carpet, spreading fast. Rolfe didn't notice. "How could this happen, Dante? How did they, whoever the hell they are, get to Cassia so quickly?"

"I don't know for certain, but you had better take a seat and calm yourself before you explode. Wrecking the furniture won't do Cassia any good and it is sure to send Hadrian's lovely wife, Mara, flying in here to wring your neck. I happen to know she takes great store in that rug which you've now destroyed. I wouldn't want to be standing in your boots when she sees what's become of it as a result of your temper."

Hadrian Ross, the Marquess of Kulhaven and, along with Dante, Rolfe's friend and partner through most every trial of his life, came forward. "Dante's right about Cassia, you know. The physician assured you we won't know anything more, at least not until morning. There is no way of knowing at this point what manner or amount of poison Cassia was given, or even if it is poison and not some sort of sickness that has seized her. All we can do is wait it out and pray."

Rolfe dropped into the chair in front of the blazing hearth fire. He lowered his head on his hands and plowed his fingers through his hair in frustration, dreading his next words. "But what if Cassia dies?"

"You did everything you could to protect her, Rolfe, short of tying her to your side," Dante said. "Regardless of what you think, you, my friend, are not infallible. Nobody is. Like Hadrian said, it is in God's hands now."

His two friends needed no explanation as to what Rolfe's thoughts were at that moment. Seeing him sitting there, his fear of the worst so clear, they knew he was praying that history would not repeat itself.

"It's just like what happened with my family. I was supposed to be there to protect them, and I wasn't. They died, every one of them, because of me, because I was too busy traipsing around the world, filled with my own importance. And now the same thing has happened with Cassia."

"You must stop blaming yourself for the past, Rolfe," Hadrian said. "Had you been there when the Cromwellians came for your family, you wouldn't be sitting here with us now. How many lives did you save during the wars? You risked your own life too many times to count when no one else would dare. It's been nearly a decade. You've paid your debt several times over, if there ever really was a debt to pay. How long are you going to continue punishing yourself for what happened to your family?"

Rolfe looked at his friends. His face bore a strange, almost scary expression. "I had actually begun to feel as if I had paid my debt. I started thinking that my life was taking a new turn. I had a new title, an estate of which to be proud, everything my father had wanted for me. I even tried to find myself a wife, to do my duty by my name, but I failed miserably in that. All those months I was away at Ravenwood, I had been working to restore myself, to make myself worthy again. Until Cassia. All I had to do was protect her, this one woman. And now I've failed in that as well."

Rolfe leaned forward, elbows on his knees, staring at the flickering flames in the hearth.

Hadrian placed his hand on his shoulder. "Mara is with her, Rolfe. Between my wife and that eccentric maid of hers, Cyma, with their knowledge of herbs and the like, I would stake my two legs that Cassia is in the best of hands."

"I only hope you are right."

Dante spoke up then. "I don't know if this is the proper time, but my spies did bring me a bit of information tonight."

He had Rolfe's instant attention. "What have you found out?"

"You had asked me to do some checking into Seagrave's finances. What I found was most interesting. Seems Seagrave spent nearly every penny he had during the wars, financing both sides in his attempts to remain neutral. Not long after the Restoration, he started amassing his present fortune, the eighty thousand pounds he left to Cassia. He acquired an estate in Lancashire that was formerly owned by the Earl of Swindale, and other properties as well, but what strikes me as odd is that I can find no record of their having been any monies exchanged for any of them."

"A gambling debt, perhaps," Hadrian suggested.

"Not likely," Rolfe said, "given that Seagrave had admonished Cassia's cousin Geoffrey for the same failing."

"There were other monetary transactions," Dante went on. "Large amounts that came in sporadically from unknown sources."

Rolfe was silent a moment. "Blackmail?"

"It seems a possibility, and it would certainly seem

a good enough reason for someone having wanted to kill him."

"Which leads us away from Geoffrey as a suspect straight to a blank wall." Rolfe clenched his fist in frustration. "Sometimes I feel as if I am doing nothing more than going in circles. I'm supposed to be such a master at investigation, but I cannot even begin to solve this thing."

"Someone has covered his tracks quite nicely," Dante said.

"Give it time, Rolfe," added Hadrian. "It will all come out eventually."

"Yes, but will it be in time to save Cassia, that is if she manages to survive the poison?"

Neither man could answer him.

"No," Rolfe said, answering himself, "it has to be Geoffrey. He is as guilty as sin. I know he is somehow involved in this thing. Perhaps he found out that Seagrave was using blackmail to gain a fortune and decided the time was ripe to lay down his cards and stick his hands in the till."

"Either that," said Dante, "or someone is setting Geoffrey up to take a great fall."

"I just wish I could be certain." Rolfe slouched back in his chair. "At least then I would know what I should do."

"I'll see if I can find out what Seagrave would have had on Swindale to blackmail him with," Dante said placing a fresh glass of brandy on the table beside him. "In the meantime, drink this. It will help."

Rolfe pushed the glass away, the brandy spilling over the sides. "That is the last thing I need right now. It is precisely there where my troubles began tonight."

"What the devil happened?"

Rolfe sat up, hating himself, somehow wishing he could turn back the hands of time. "Cassia had told me she wanted to visit the queen. She was worried about Catherine's failing health. As we were leaving the Banqueting House to go to the queen's apartments in the palace, I lost sight of Cassia in the crowd. I was frantic to find her. After a short while, I spotted her again, dancing with the king. Before I could reach her, she left with him out a side entrance and didn't come back for some time. By the time she did return, I was well into several glasses of brandy and worse, had just come from running into Daphne. I was seeing nothing but red and I confronted Cassia about her bedding the king and—"

"You mean you actually accused Cassia of being his mistress?" Dante shook his head. "Rolfe, you ass, I told you that was rumor, not fact. The truth is Cassia did go with King Charles—not to his bedchamber, but to the queen's, as she'd said. That is the only place they went."

"How do you know?"

"I also saw Cassia dancing with the king and had my man follow them when they left. Charles took Cassia to see Catherine, remained there with her, and returned her directly to the ballroom afterward, running off in the direction of, I believe, Lady Castlemaine's private apartments as soon as he left her."

Rolfe shook his head. "My being an ass is the only thing I am certain of any longer."

"A lovesick ass, mind you, but an ass all the same."

Dante's statement brought Rolfe about.

"You don't know what you are talking about. How could I have feelings for a woman who is incapable of feeling anything?"

Hadrain came up beside Dante. "I'm afraid Dante does know what he is talking about, my friend. I see it in you as well. I know it's hard to admit. I, myself, refused to acknowledge it at first with Mara. Talk about being an ass. She made me look the paramount laughingstock. Me, a master spy known for my military stratagems, posing as one of Cromwell's closest advisers, and I was duped by a single woman who'd disguised herself as the woman I was supposed to marry so she could take revenge on me for crimes she believed me guilty of. She even had me believing I had taken her virginity against her will, in case you'd forgotten. All it took was a little hair dye and those ridiculous spectacles for Mara to completely fool me."

"And don't forget her little white cap. Her disguise wasn't complete without it."

"Don't try to change the subject, Rolfe. I know how you feel right now, how you refuse to believe it could be true. It's as if by verifying your feelings for this woman, you are somehow showing a weakness, a flaw in yourself. I know you vowed never to fall under the wiles of a female again after Daphne, but I see now there is no doubt. You are inextricably hooked."

"And you're one notch short of a sound mind, Hadrian. I was appointed to guard Cassia and discover whether she killed her father, that is all." And then he added, "There is nothing more."

"Whatever you say," Hadrian said, grinning. "The question is, what are you going to do now?"

Rolfe stood, turning his back on his friends once again to stare out the window at the black night sky.

What could he do? In all his other assignments, even when things hadn't gone off as planned, Rolfe had always managed to keep a clear head, accomplishing his goal regardless of the obstacles in his way. When he'd met adversity, he'd simply chosen a different course, oftentimes a more perilous course. It hadn't mattered to him that he'd been placing his life in danger, for Rolfe really hadn't cared if he lived or died.

But this time, it was different. This assignment was different. It was different because this time he did care. What would happen when this assignment was ended? Who would be there to assure that no one could attempt to harm Cassia again? She had no family to protect her. What if they never found out who had murdered her father? For the rest of her life, Cassia would be made to live in fear of every blind corner and dark turn. Who would be there to chase away the demons that hounded her in her sleep? Even while Rolfe wondered this, he knew what he must do. It was the only thing he could do. He turned to his friends once again.

"In answer to your question, Hadrian, I will do the only thing I can, to assure that, if by some grace of God Cassia lives, her life is never in danger again. I am going to marry Cassia in your house tonight, with you and Dante standing as my witnesses."

Voices.

Cassia could hear them, murmuring quietly nearby. There were several of them, some deep, some light, but she couldn't make out what it was they were saying. Her mind felt so very clouded, as if it were stuffed with goose feathers, and only sometimes did she manage a clear thought. For some reason, though, it seemed she'd forgotten how to speak.

Another voice, this one familiar, rising above the others and shutting them out. A deep voice, it brought calm and peace and security to that foreign place she'd woken to find herself.

"Cassia, can you hear me?"

Who was it? Why couldn't she see anyone?

The other voices returned, but she still could not understand what they were saying. Why couldn't she make out their words?

The deep voice, the familiar voice, came back to her again.

"Cassia, listen to me. Don't give up. You must fight. You cannot give up now. Show me if you can hear me. Scream. Holler. Squeeze my hand if you can. Show me that you want to live."

I do. I do. I do want to live.

Cassia fought to push the words out, but her body, her mouth somehow wouldn't respond. She tried to force her eyelids open, to see the face behind that voice that was calling to her, begging her to fight, filling her with the will to live, but even that was beyond her capabilities.

"Can you hear me, Cassia?"

Yes! I do! I hear you!

There were other voices coming from far away. She tried to hear what they were saying, but only bits and pieces came to her.

". . . to join this man and this woman . . ."

She felt someone take her hand. It was a large hand, a warm hand that covered her own.

". . . to have this woman as your wife . . ."

The deep voice spoke clearly. "I will."

The faraway voice returned.

". . . to have this man for your husband . . ."

There was silence in the room.

Rolfe looked at Cassia lying on the bed. Her eyes were still closed. She wasn't moving.

"She must respond, my lord," the priest he'd woken, dragging him here to wed them in the middle of the night, said. "This marriage is already most irregular. I cannot pronounce you wed unless she voices her consent."

Rolfe knelt down beside Cassia, his mouth close to her ear. "Cassia, can you hear me? It is Rolfe. You must listen to me. There is a man standing here beside me. He is going to marry us. You must tell him you will be my wife. I want to protect you, Cassia, and this is the only way I can see to do that. I will never allow anyone to hurt you again. You do want that, don't you, Cassia? Tell me you want that. Tell me you can hear me."

The room fell silent again. Rolfe felt Cassia's hand move slightly in his. He motioned for the priest to come closer to her.

"Tell me, Cassia. Please tell me."

He leaned his ear closer to her lips. The priest did the same.

"Yes."

Chapter Seventeen

"I do not love him and I will not marry him!"

Rolfe leaped from the chair where he'd fallen asleep and was at the side of the bed in a second.

Cassia, sitting upright, her body rigid as a poker, was staring at him, her eyes open wide.

"You cannot force me to wed him, Father."

Her voice was suddenly calm, the words slow, and Rolfe realized that she was locked in some sort of dream, not really seeing him, but instead seeing her father. A moment later she flinched as if she'd been struck.

"Please, no . . ."

Cassia began weeping then, holding up her arms in an effort to fend off the bastard's invisible blows. Her frightened cries tore straight through Rolfe as each blow struck her. He reached for Cassia, wanting to take her into his arms and protect her from her nightmare images, to somehow shield her from the hellish scene being played in her mind.

"It is all right, Cassia," Rolfe whispered to her, pulling her against his chest.

When she had quieted, he tucked her head beneath his chin. She huddled against him, clutching his shirt as if she wanted to crawl inside his skin. She started shivering violently. "He is angry with me. I'm so scared. I've never seen him so angry like this."

Rolfe stroked her hair. "Shhh. It is all right. He cannot hurt you any longer."

"No. You are wrong. He is coming back and he has the stick. He's raising it up . . ."

"Shhh," Rolfe whispered into her hair. He tightened his arms around her, "I will not let him hurt you again."

Cassia suddenly jerked in his arms. Her whole body went lax.

"Cassia?"

Silence.

"Cassia, can you hear me?"

Rolfe felt her move slightly, her voice quiet, muffled against his chest, sounding like a child's. He could barely hear her. "My head, it hurts so bad. It's dark. So dark. Please—please bring a light. I hate the dark. . . ."

Rolfe moved the candle burning on the bedside table nearer to them. "Where is your father, Cassia? Is he gone now?"

"No. I can still hear him. He is so very angry with me."

"What is he doing?"

"He is just standing there. He isn't saying anything. Wait. There is someone else in the room. They are arguing. Something about a note, a letter, I think. He wants it from my father."

"Who is it, Cassia? Who is there with your father? Can you see him?"

"No, it is too dark. I cannot see anything. it is a familiar voice. It sounds like . . ."

Her voice dropped off, her body falling limply against him.

Rolfe tilted her head back to look at her face. Her eyes were closed. "Cassia?"

Cassia did not answer him, but he could see that

she was breathing, her chest rising and falling softly. He laid her back on the bed, gently cradling her head until it reached the soft pillow. The moment his hands left her body, Cassia curled herself into a tight ball. She looked so damned vulnerable, so damned defenseless, and so damned frightened.

Rolfe didn't leave. He slid onto the bed and pulled Cassia against him. Closing his eyes, he tried to push aside what he'd just seen, tried to ignore the rage he felt imagining the horror Cassia must have gone through. It wasn't long before his entire body was shaking.

Bloody hell! What sort of bastard would have done what her father had done to her? Why would Seagrave have wanted to hurt her like that? There was no reason, no excuse for striking a woman. Ever. His father had taught him that, drilling it into his head when he'd been a boy. It was a piece of wisdom Rolfe had never forgotten.

Cassia was his daughter, for God's sake, flesh of his flesh, blood of his blood. Rolfe could find no reasonable answer to explain the madness Seagrave had shown in abusing Cassia like he had. The only thing Rolfe did know was that it was fortunate Seagrave was already dead, for had he still been alive, knowing what he now knew, Rolfe would have seen to it that it wasn't for very long.

He remembered Cassia's words. It was obvious she'd just been describing that night to him in her sleep, the night her father had been murdered. She said she had heard another voice in the room. A man's voice. Whose was it? Rolfe remembered Cassia telling him that she'd been unconscious and that she had woken to find her father dead when he had initially questioned her about that night. No one else had been there, she'd said. The door had still been locked. Cassia had told him she'd had no idea who could have come into the room. Still, just now, she'd been so certain of there being another man's voice.

Could it be that while she'd been lying there on the floor, unconscious from her father's beating, her mind been witness to what her eyes could not see? Had Cassia heard her father being murdered?

All through that night, Rolfe tried to think of how he could free that information from her. The more he remembered what she'd said, the more he began to believe that Cassia was the key. She knew the identity of the real murderer, whether she realized it or not. It was locked tightly inside her memory. He just had to find some way to release it.

Rolfe stayed with Cassia, holding her as she slept a deep and peaceful sleep, seemingly free of her demon dreams. Just a little before dawn, when the first inklings of sunlight were making their way through the windows across the room, the fever started to come upon her.

"So hot . . ."

Cassia rolled away from him and started pushing at the bedcovers that were tangled around her legs.

"Please . . . thirsty . . ."

Rolfe stood and pulled the coverlet back. He placed his hand against the side of Cassia's cheek. She felt warm, though not overly so. He thought that perhaps the room was just a little too confined, so he unlatched the window and pushed it open a bit. He went to fetch a cup of water from the stoneware pitcher by the door. By the time he'd returned, Cassia was moaning, her head thrashing back and forth on the pillow. Her hair was damp and sticking to her forehead. Rolfe felt her cheek again. Her skin was now burning hot.

Rolfe lifted Cassia's head from the pillow and touched the cup of water to her lips. He managed to dribble a small amount of it into her mouth before she began twisting away from him.

"No . . ."

A maid came into the room, carrying a stack of fresh linens. She stopped when she saw Rolfe bent over the bed, holding Cassia. "Milord?"

"I need a bowl of cool water and a cloth. Lady Cassia's burning up with fever. Hurry!"

It seemed to take the maid too long to return, when in fact it was only a few minutes. Mara, Hadrian's wife, came in with the maid, pulling on her night wrap. The maid had obviously just woken her, for her hair was hanging in a riot of red curls around her shoulders. "What is it, Rolfe?"

He was already wiping down Cassia's face with the wet cloth. "She's feverish and I can't get her to drink any water."

Mara placed the back of her hand on Cassia's forehead. Her eyes grew instantly concerned. "Keep soaking her skin. I'll be back shortly."

Rolfe barely heard her. He was completely focused on Cassia, trying desperately to bring her temperature down. He'd seen fever before and knew what it could do. How many men had he watched die in the battlefield before his very eyes once the fever had come to take them?

Mara reappeared at the other side of the bed, removing the cork on a small glass bottle. "Lift her head. We must try to get her to swallow this."

Rolfe did not question Mara's orders. With her knowledge of herbs and their healing powers, he trusted her to know what to do. He slid onto the bed behind Cassia and cradled her head against his legs. "Cassia, if you can hear me, try to swallow some of this."

Rolfe parted Cassia's lips with his finger to allow

Mara to give her the potion. As soon as the liquid entered her mouth, Cassia tried to turn away, but Rolfe held her still. "Just a little bit, Cassia. That's it."

Mara set the bottle on the table. "I think we managed to get enough of the potion into her mouth, but it will depend now on how far the fever has gone. Only time will tell." She looked at Rolfe. "I would wager you didn't get very much sleep last night. You look exhausted. Would you like me to send in Cyma to stay with Cassia while you rest?"

Rolfe didn't look up from Cassia's face. "No. I will call if I need anything else."

He didn't remember hearing Mara leave.

An hour later, Cassia was still burning up with the fever, her skin red and damp. When soaking her forehead with water did not seem to help, Rolfe went to the door, threw it open, and barked at the maid who'd been posted in the hallway there.

"A tub of water. Now."

The tub was brought in quickly and was filled with cool water fresh from the rain barrel outside. Rolfe ushered everyone out and returned to the bed. He lifted Cassia's limp body into his arms and carefully slid off her night rail. Then, gently, as if she were a newborn babe, he placed her into the tub, carefully tucking a folded-up cloth beneath her head to cushion it at the edge.

Rolfe took up a sponge and began soaking Cassia's hot skin with the cool water. As he ran the sponge across her shoulders and watched the water trickling down over her breasts, he tried not to think about how her nipples were growing taut, how he wondered what it would be like to take her into his arms and feel her around him as he moved inside of her. What sort of cad was he? Here she was, dangerously ill, and all he could think about was taking her. If it hadn't been for his insisting that they attend that accursed masquerade, Cassia would not be lying here now at death's door.

Finally, after soaking her skin for some time, Rolfe lifted Cassia up and out of the tub. He wrapped a thick drying cloth around her. He touched her forehead. She felt much cooler. He began to hold hope.

Rolfe laid Cassia back on the bed and drew up the coverlet to her shoulder. He climbed in beside her.

Cassia slept for several hours. Rolfe lay beside her, running his fingers back through the hair that had dried curling at her forehead. He filled the time by talking to her, even though he knew she could not hear him, telling her about his childhood, about his family, about the adventures of his youth. He made promises to her, assuring her no one would ever be able to hurt her again, vowing to help her prove her innocence.

And then, when he'd finally run out of things to say, he pleaded with her one last time to live, touched his lips softly to her forehead, and lay her back on the pillows, still cradled in his arms. Only then did he allow exhaustion to claim him.

Rolfe didn't know how long he'd slept with Cassia wrapped in his arms. The sky outside had grown dark with the passing of the day into night. When he did finally awaken, he did not immediately get up from the bed. He didn't want to leave just yet, reluctant to release Cassia from the circle of his arms. He lay there, staring at the ceiling and listening to her soft, even breathing in the silence of the room. Closing his eyes, he said a silent prayer, begging God to spare Cassia's life.

Cassia opened her eyes, only slightly, for the light on the other side seemed brighter than if she were staring straight into the sun. She tried to swallow, but her throat burned, her mouth scratchy, as if it were filled with sand.

Through squinting eyes, she could make out the canopy of a bed above her head hung with light blue and yellow damask. It wasn't her bed. As her eyes became accustomed to the light, and she was able to see more clearly, she saw that she was in a bedchamber—whose, she did not know. She licked at her cracked lips and glanced to the side of the bed. There, sitting on a bedside table, was an ewer of water with a glass, half filled, beside it. Cassia tried to reach for the glass, wanting it desperately, but her body refused to respond. Every muscle seemed incapable of movement. A tear of frustration slipped down her cheek as she stared at the glass, wanting it more than she'd ever wanted anything before, but knowing she was unable to reach it.

"Please . . ."

Somehow she'd managed to push that one word out. She didn't even know if there was anyone near to hear her.

"Cassia?"

Suddenly, he was there, that deep voice, the voice that she had heard so often in her dreams. It was the same voice that had begged her to fight her way back. He took her hand and came before her. She could not see his face clearly yet.

"Please," Cassia managed to say again, "water."

And then, mercifully, that glass was being touched to her lips and she could feel the wonderful cool liquid coming into her mouth, filling it, and she drank, gulping it down, savoring each drop until it trickled down her chin and neck. She didn't care. She closed her eyes and lay back on the bed, exhausted from that one simple exercise. "Thank you."

It was hen Cassia looked, truly looked at him. Before, she'd been so focused on the water that she hadn't really cared if Lucifer himself had brought it to her. But it wasn't Lucifer there beside her. It was Rolfe and he was looking down at her, his hazel eyes watching her, filled with concern.

Cassia wondered how she'd gotten here, wherever she was, whose bed she was lying in. She wondered why Rolfe looked so tired. She tried to think back on what could have happened to have brought her here. She remembered the masked ball at the palace. She'd been dancing with the king under the lights of the chandeliers in the Banqueting House. She'd gone to visit Catherine, who looked so very pale and weak lying in her bed all surrounded by pillows. And when she'd gone back to the ball, she'd found Rolfe waiting for her. But he'd been angry with her. Why?

Did you enjoy your visit to the king's bedchamber as much?

Cassia closed her eyes, remembering it all now, how Rolfe stood there, accusing her of being the king's mistress, of how she'd wanted to tell him the truth. She remembered that she had started to tell him, needing him to believe her. Had she been able to tell him? Had he listened?

"Cassia, how do you feel?"

She opened her eyes and stared up at him. She remembered everything about that night, the hateful words, the accusations, and then she remembered something else. She remembered other words, words that came later, telling her to fight, begging her to live. She remembered Rolfe stroking his fingers through her hair, over her eyebrows, down her nose. She had liked the way that had made her feel. She remembered feeling his strong arms around her, holding her. She remembered feeling safe, truly safe for the first time in her life.

"I'm tired," Cassia said, closing her eyes. "And hungry."

"I'll get you something."

By the time Rolfe returned from the kitchen with a bowl of thin broth and two thick slices of bread still warm from the oven, Cassia was asleep again.

"How is she?"

Mara came out of the room, setting the tray she'd brought with her on the hall table. They were standing outside Cassia's chamber where Rolfe had been waiting for the past hour, having been ordered out while Mara and her maid, Cyma, had changed the bed linen and had dressed Cassia in a clean night rail.

"She is still sleeping, Rolfe. She is very weak, but the color has finally begun to return to her cheeks. The decoction will need some time to fully take effect and do its good. Her body must rid itself of all the poison before it can even begin to heal. But I know in my heart she will be fine."

Rolfe prayed she was right. "Has she said anything?" He hesitated. "About that night?"

"She only awoke for a few moments, barely long enough for me to give her another dose of the Angelica treacle. She appears cautious and perhaps a little frightened. Wouldn't you be? She's woken up from a very difficult bout to find herself in a strange bed in a strange house and surrounded by strangers. And she doesn't yet realize that someone has tried to poison her. After all she's been through in the past few days, I would thank the heavens she hasn't attempted to run screaming from here by now. And she hadn't even been subjected to the children yet."

Rolfe smiled, knowing Mara was trying to ease his

worried mind. "I think a dose of those two imps of yours would do wonders for Cassia's recovery." He looked at her eyes. "I don't know how to thank you for all you have done. If it weren't for you and your potions, she would have ..."

Mara took his hand. "I have only done what I would have done for any stranger in the street. The treacle alone could not have saved her life. It was you who gave Cassia the will to live, Rolfe. It was you who spent every hour with her, stubbornly refusing to leave for a second, not even to relieve yourself. You must remember that."

Squeezing his hand, Mara turned, picked up the tray, and proceeded down the hall.

Rolfe stared at Cassia's door, remembering what Mara had just said. He wanted to believe her, to think that his words had somehow broken through the effects of the poison and the fever and had given Cassia the will to live. He wanted to think that he'd made a difference. But what had he given her the will to live for? What would she do when he told her what he'd done? What would Cassia say when she found out she was now his wife?

Chapter Eighteen

"Good morning," Mara said, coming into the room, "or should I say good afternoon? Goodness, I did not realize how late the hour was."

Cassia had a little difficulty levering herself up, her muscles still too weak to do the simplest of things. The red-haired woman, whom she recognized from the masquerade ball, and whom since she had learned was Mara Ross, the Marchioness of Kulhaven, came forward. She brought with her a tray that was filled with something—what, Cassia wasn't quite certain, but somehow she knew it must be delicious, for the aroma it gave off was simply delightful.

"What time is it?" Cassia asked as she took the cup of herbal tea Mara held out to her. She set the saucer in her lap and took a small sip of the fragrant brew.

"I believe it is just past noon. Goodness, it is dark in here."

Mara crossed the room to the heavy damask drapery and pushed it aside. Brilliant sunlight came pouring in, casting away the dark shadows and illuminating the whole of the cozy-looking chamber.

"I would have come to you sooner," Mara went on, now fluffing the pillows behind Cassia's back, "but I thought it better to allow you to get your rest. Have you been awake for very long?"

"I only just woke before you came in. Is it really

that late? I don't think I've ever slept this late, or this much, in my life."

Mara smiled. She handed Cassia a china plate heaped with buttered eggs, cheese wedges, and two thick slices of ham. Following this was a small basket holding a number of flaky biscuits. There was enough food there to feed a family. Cassia felt her stomach begin to rumble in anticipation.

"Sleep is good," Mara said, pushing back the coverlet so she could sit at the edge of the bed. "Sleep helps the ailing body to heal, and it does wonders for the mind, you know. There is no better medicine. And now you will need food to nourish the body as well. Don't think all six of those sweet biscuits are for you. I plan on eating at least two of them—one for me and one"—she patted her flat stomach—"for the babe."

Cassia quickly swallowed down the forkful of eggs she'd just taken. "You are expecting a child?"

Mara smiled. "Yes. It seems my husband need only look at me and my belly begins to swell outward."

"How many children do you have?"

"Two. Robert, who is going on three, and Dana, who is nearly a year now. I'm surprised you haven't heard them running about by now."

"But you are so thin. I remember my mother telling me if it hadn't been for birthing me, she'd still have a waistline small enough to be spanned by the width of a man's hands."

Mara laughed, a pleasant cheering sound. "What utter nonsense. It wasn't birthing you that caused her waistline to grow. It was more likely all the confectioneries she swallowed afterward during her lying-in. Don't let appearances fool you, either. I was nearly the size of a barn with Robert, and twice as big with Dana. They say girls are smaller babies and easier to birth, but don't you believe it. I would have sworn there were two of them in there. And as for my being thin now, have you ever spent your days chasing after a precocious two-year-old who it seems has inherited the stubborn determination of his father, and a toddling little girl who feels she must touch everything that exists on this earth at least once every day, all this with both of them running in the opposite direction at the same time?"

Cassia was mystified. Surely this woman sitting before her now was not of this lifetime, or of the same planet, for that matter. She had to be a figment. "You mean to say you care for the children yourself?"

"Yes. Well, not exactly by myself. You see, I have my husband, who loves to spoil them, and my maid, Cyma, but she was my maid when I was a child and though she hates to be told it, and would rather die before she would ever admit it herself, she is getting on now and she just cannot keep up like she used to. Robert has recently taken a great liking to playing Robin Hood, but Cyma isn't overly fond of bows and arrows and the like, even if they are only made of wood and cloth."

"You have no nursery maid to tend to them? I do not think I ever saw my mother for more than an hour each day until I was ready to come out into society, or after that for that matter."

"There is no one else I would trust them with. You know, I have always failed to see why so many people go through the effort of having children just to turn around the minute they are born and pawn their upbringing off on a servant. The children are learning someone else's morals, someone else's values, and the parents then wonder why their behavior is abominable. I love my time with my children and it goes by so fast. Too fast. I love to watch their faces when they are concentrating so hard on something so seemingly simple as the opening and closing of their own hand. You cannot buy that kind of joy, of watching their wonder at exploring a new world in their eyes. And all too soon that wonder is gone. So I enjoy it while I can. I have even been known to get down on all fours and go crawling after the baby as she giggles for me to catch her."

Cassia tried to summon up the image of this lovely woman with her silk skirts hiked up to her stocking garters, crawling underneath the furniture after a laughing infant. She just could not fathom such a thing. "I didn't know parents did such things with their children."

"Unfortunately, like your own mother, most parents do not, for fear of mussing their gowns or loosening a hairpin from their coiffures. Gowns can be pressed and hair can be redressed. But how can you possibly replace the closeness of spending that time with your children?"

It was a question Cassia found she could not answer. She'd never been around children, had rarely even seen them. She wouldn't know the first thing to do with them.

She finished eating her breakfast, surprised she'd nearly emptied the plate. "I should like to meet them someday."

"You mean you want to see the children? How about today? If you are feeling up to it, of course. Robert is just dying to know what it is I am hiding behind this door. I think he believes I've leashed a dragon in here complete with fire blowing through his nostrils or something like that."

Cassia smiled. "Actually, that is a fairly accurate description of how I have felt."

"I'm just glad you are doing better now." Mara stood. "Well, it looks as if I have eaten more than my two allotted biscuits. I do apologize. It seems whenever I am expecting, I just abandon my manners. In fact, my husband is fond of telling me I'd eat the house down around him if I had the chance. I'll leave the last biscuit to you and allow you to rest now. Perhaps later in the afternoon I'll bring in the children—that is, if you are still feeling up to it."

She started for the door, then stopped halfway there. "Oh, I nearly forgot. Rolfe brought something for me to give to you."

She moved to a tall fruitwood chest near the door and removed something from inside. She turned. "He said you might appreciate having these when you felt a little better."

Mara set Cassia's sketching paper and several of her charcoal pencils down atop the coverlet.

Cassia looked up at her. "Lord Ravenscroft brought these?"

"Yes. He apparently went to your house to fetch them for you late last night after I told him you were doing much better. He said you were fond of drawing and thought it might help to pass the time while you are convalescing."

She turned and started for the door. Cassia hardly noticed Mara leaving. She was too stunned by what she'd just been given. Rolfe had brought her sketching paper and pencils for her. He had gone to Seagrave House to fetch them himself. Such a small thing, seemingly insignificant, but to her, it was the finest gift she'd ever been given. She had never known anyone to do such a thoughtful thing for her and she really wasn't certain how she should feel about it. Part of her was delighted by the gesture, and yet another part of her was cautious. Her drawing had always been her private place, a hideaway where she could go and could lose herself and forget the world. And in the short time since he had come into her life, Rolfe had managed to uncover even that.

How was it that he seemed capable of seeing right through to her innermost thoughts and feelings? She'd been drawing for as long as she could remember. Many people had looked at her drawings: her mother, who had simply shaken her head; her father, who had told her she should devote as much time as she did to her scribblings to finding herself a husband; Winifred, who would have told her anything she had drawn was a masterpiece; even Cordelia, who had busied herself with needlepoint, a more feminine enterprise, while Cassia had concentrated on her sketching. Yet no one had ever noticed how deeply Cassia felt about her drawings.

But Rolfe had, and after having seen only a few of them.

"May I ask you a question?" Cassia asked just as Mara reached the door.

"Of course."

"You mentioned I would be convalescing here." Cassia hesitated, choosing her words carefully. "Did something happen to me?"

"What do you mean?"

"I mean I have been sleeping in this bed for what seems like days. I wake to find myself, if you'll excuse my saying, in a stranger's house, and I cannot for the life of me remember how I even got here."

Mara smiled. "I think your questions would be better answered by Lord Ravenscroft. I'll see if I can find him for you. In the meantime, I've had a daybed moved outside to the balcony for you if you would like some fresh air and sunshine. The weather is unseasonably warm for this time of year. I thought you might be growing tired of looking at the same four walls."

Cassia nodded, the fact that Mara had effectively skirted answering her question not at all lost on her. "Thank you, Lady Kulhaven, that sounds delightful."

"You're welcome, and please, my name is Mara. I like my friends to call me by my given name, and I do hope we can be just that—friends. Most of the time, Hadrian, the children, and I reside in Ireland at my family's castle there. It is rather a remote location and truthfully there aren't very many ladies around for me to talk and visit with. I have Cyma, but she tends to be rather rigid in her views and would prefer to bury her nose in her herb garden than exchange idle gossip over tea. The villagers nearby are so busy with their own lives, I hate to bother them, and I do miss female companionship. When I was a girl, my mother would sit with me and we would talk for hours about everything, which was nothing, actually, just small talk about things like fairy tales and boys. I'm sure you know what I mean."

Cassia didn't tell Mara that she would have had no clue about the scene she had painted so eloquently with her words. Somehow she could never envision herself sitting with her own mother, discussing the frivolities of life.

"I so miss my mother," Mara said, a wistful light coming into her eyes as she stared off at the sky outside the windows. Then, as if she had closed a mental door on an unpleasant memory, she turned her attention back to Cassia. "Not too many of Hadrian's friends are married, and the ones who are married have wives that I wouldn't want to take tea with, let alone tell my secrets to. You are different. I know we've only just become acquainted, but I feel as if I could tell you anything. I feel I could go shopping with you on Oxford Street, and I could trust that you wouldn't tell me that the very unattractive orange color of the bolt of silk the merchant was trying to convince me to purchase looked absolutely lovely with my red hair when I know very well that it doesn't."

She smiled. "But, well, I'm going on too much now—another thing my husband tells me I seem to do whenever I am expecting. He says my mouth runs faster than the Kilkenny Creek back home at Kulhaven on a rainy day, or something like that. I will leave you now. Ring when you would like to go out onto the balcony and I will come up to help you."

Cassia nodded, watching Mara go, knowing somehow that whatever it was, this mystery that had brought them together, the two of them would be friends for a long time to come.

Just what was it that had brought her here to this house? And why did it seem as if no one wanted to tell her? She hadn't expected Mara to answer her question, not really, and especially not when she'd already asked the maid who had brought her the freshly aired pillows the night before. The girl had just looked at Cassia as if she'd spoken to her in a foreign tongue, bobbing her head and quickly quitting the room. What was it everyone seemed so afraid of telling her?

Just after the door had closed behind Mara, Cassia heard the sound of shattering glass coming from somewhere down the hallway, followed soon after by a high-pitched child's squeal of laughter.

She then heard Mara calling out, "Robert Charles Ross, you naughty little boy, come back here this instant!"

It was just as the sun was setting that evening, its last red rays barely peeking over the western horizon, that Rolfe decided the time had come.

He'd been delaying going in to see Cassia all day, telling himself he was leaving her time to recover, but he knew his reluctance was purposeful. He didn't want to see the look in her eyes, the hurt, the betrayal he knew would be there the moment the words left his mouth.

Cassia would hate him, he knew, and regardless if his explanation was a reasonable one, she would never trust him again. It was her trust Rolfe wanted more than anything and even though he knew he had done the right thing in marrying her, the honorable thing to protect her, he also knew Cassia would never understand.

Rolfe also knew he could put it off no longer. Before long, someone would slip and Cassia would learn the truth. Mara had told him that Cassia had begun asking questions of her and the maids, wanting to know why she'd been brought here, what had happened that had caused her to be bedridden for so long. She needed to know that someone had made an attempt on her life, that somehow—Rolfe still questioned how—she had been given a rather large dose of poison, poison that Mara and her maid, Cyma, had mercifully managed to defuse. Cassia needed to know what he'd done afterward, the only action he could have taken to assure that he would always be there to prevent something else like this from happening to her. She needed to know the truth, that they were married. And this was one truth that she needed to hear from him.

Mara had told Rolfe earlier that night that Cassia was feeling much better now; in fact, she'd spent the better part of the afternoon visiting with the children in her chamber. She'd eaten nearly all of the roast mutton and baby potatoes on her supper plate, and had even asked if she could have a bath afterward.

So, it seemed, the time had come. There would be no more putting it off, no more excuses as to why he could wait yet another day. But how in perdition was he going to tell her?

When Rolfe reached the door to Cassia's chamber, it was slightly ajar and he could hear the sound of soft singing inside. He did not knock, but pushed the door inward and walked quietly in.

There were no candles to light the room, but the fading sunset cast a welcoming orange-red glow about the room from the open double doors that led to the outside balcony where the singing was coming from. Rolfe walked slowly across the room, making no sound. He stopped just inside the doorway.

Cassia was seated on a cushioned daybed, several thick pillows at her back. She was looking out toward the sunset and the slanted rooftops of the city. Sitting as she was, she would be unable to see him where he stood concealed in the shadows just inside the door. There with her, her soft red curly head resting on Cassia's shoulder, was Dana, Mara and Hadrian's young daughter, asleep, her tiny thumb stuck in her mouth. Cassia was stroking Dana's curls, singing softly to her, a French lullaby Rolfe had never heard before about princesses and knights and white castles.

Rolfe stood there for some time just watching them, listening to the lullaby, and it was then that he noticed the sketch sitting on the table beside her. It was a drawing of Dana lying just as she was now, her tiny fingers fisted so tightly as she slept. It wasn't the drawing itself that had caught Rolfe's attention, for he'd seen so many of Cassia's sketches before. But in this drawing of this beautiful child, she had finally included the face, full and clear features, and not the usual dark silhouette she'd favored before.

Watching Cassia softly singing with Dana curled against her breast, her fingers lightly stroking through the child's hair, Rolfe saw a part of her he had never known existed. She'd always been so adamant in her refusal of marriage; he assumed she would be just as adamant against children.

Something inside of him seemed to grow, pushing outward with a warmth that filled him to his soul. Perhaps it was the lullaby she was singing. Perhaps it was the way she looked so right sitting there with that child in her arms. Rolfe wasn't certain what it was that made him realize it, but suddenly he knew.

He knew that while he'd been trying to deny it, what Dante and Hadrian had said that night was true. He knew that this woman, whom he had only known a short time, had come to mean more to him than anyone else. Despite everything, the past, his conviction, Rolfe knew he had fallen in love with Cassia.

As he continued to stand there watching her, Rolfe pictured Cassia holding another child. Their own child. It would be a girl and she would have her mother's expressive eyes and that same stubborn tilt to her chin. And he would protect them both with his life, no matter what the cost.

Rolfe's mental picture was abruptly shattered at that final thought.

How could he be so damned stupid? After Daphne and her complete humiliation of him, he had vowed never to allow himself to care for another woman, never to leave himself open to the opportunity of being made the fool again. But he had come to care for another woman, this woman, somehow, without even realizing it.

And who had he chosen this time?

Like a fool, he'd chosen the one woman who would never return his love, for Rolfe knew if he were to tell Cassia, actually declare his feelings for her, she would look at him with ridicule and would laugh in his face. Hadn't Daphne done the same? And if by some miracle Cassia didn't, when he finally told her what he had come here to say—that in order to assure her safety, he'd wed himself to her while she'd been locked in a poison-induced unconsciousness, knowing full well that it would be the only way he'd ever get her to wed him—he knew she would damn him to hell for an eternity.

And that was something he just couldn't face.

Rolfe turned from the balcony, leaving Cassia as she was, softly singing the French lullaby.

Chapter Nineteen

"I understand you wanted to speak with me."

Cassia looked up from the sketch she was working on as Rolfe came into the room. It was good to see him, she thought, realizing that she had missed him, for it had been days since she'd awakened to find herself there, in that strange house, with strangers around her—friendly strangers, but strangers still the same. The only people she saw were Mara and the children—Cassia smiled; yes, the children—and the various servants who attended to her needs. She hadn't seen Rolfe since waking that first day. She'd missed him. Yes, it was good to see him again.

He was dressed in clothes that were well tailored to him, his coat of black camlet setting off his broad shoulders, his tan breeches snug. Regardless of whether they were fashionable or not, Cassia found she liked them, especially the manner in which they clung to his legs—muscular legs, she recalled, thinking of him at his bath.

Cassia set the drawing aside as Rolfe came more into the room. It was a sketch she'd made earlier that morning while sitting in the music room watching Mara with her son, Robert, on the floor. Her ice-blue silk skirts had been spread out around her like a crystalline pool as she taught him the proper method of plucking the strings of a mandola. With Robert sitting on her lap, Mara had intertwined his pudgy fingers with her own and was helping him to play a simple child's tune on the small lute set in front of them. Robert's head rested against his mother's cheek, and the look on his face as his fingers moved over the strings was most touching.

In watching them together, Cassia had seen that look, the look Mara had spoken of, the look of wonder a child's eyes saw in the world. It was precisely that wondrous expression she was hoping to portray in her drawing now. She'd completed most of the sketch that morning while in the music room and was just adding the finishing touches to it when Rolfe had come into the room.

"Good evening, Lord Ravenscroft," Cassia said. "I was beginning to wonder if you'd perhaps vanished from the face of the planet to reside on another, like one of those Galileo observed in his telescope."

Rolfe came forward. "I apologize for not having come to you sooner. I have been occupied of late." He glanced at the drawing. "I must say, Lady Cassia, you have quite an eye for finding the most emotion-filled subjects."

Cassia smiled at the compliment. "Thank you, my lord."

"But I had thought you said you preferred not to draw the faces."

Cassia glanced at him. "Yes, well, I have never before drawn a child. Children are innocent creatures. They know nothing of the evil of the world. Therefore, they have no reason to hide their true face behind one that is false."

Rolfe picked up the drawing, looking at it. "Yes, but you have also included Mara's face in the drawing."

Cassia took the drawing from him and placed it

facedown on her lap. "I have since learned, Lord Ravenscroft, that there are actually some people in this world who do not attempt to hide behind a false face."

Rolfe smiled. "Mara is a remarkable woman, isn't she? But as for her wearing a false face, you ought to ask her how she looked when she first met her husband, Hadrian. The black hair dye and spectacles made a world of difference from the lady you see before you today."

Cassia looked at him, completely lost to what he was saying. "I beg your pardon?"

"Never mind. That is a story you'll need to hear from her. But I am pleased you are beginning to see that not everyone is quite as deceptive as you had believed. Some people, my lady, are not out only to take advantage, although, living at Whitehall, I can surely understand why you would assume differently. That is precisely why I left London for the country. Country folk know nothing of the chicanery of their city-dwelling cousins. They prefer simpler, less harmful pursuits. Now, what was it you wished to speak with me about?"

"I wanted to ask you something."

Rolfe said nothing, waiting for her to go on.

Cassia sat more upright before posing her question. "What happened to me?"

Rolfe knew even before he'd come that this was what she had planned to ask him. He knew it and he'd tried to be ready with an explanation, a reasonable explanation. But there was nothing reasonable about what had taken place the night of the masquerade or afterward, and even as he'd begun climbing the stairs to her chamber, Rolfe hadn't yet come up with any satisfactory words.

"What do you remember about that night—I mean, before you woke to find yourself here?"

"I remember that we were at the masquerade at Whitehall. We were trying to investigate possible suspects in my father's murder. I had just returned from visiting the queen. She was so very ill. I'm frightened for her, my lord. Do you know her current condition?"

"It is much the same, I'm afraid. What else do you recall about that night?"

"I remember that you were angry with me."

Of everything that Cassia could have remembered about that night, his asinine outburst was the one thing Rolfe would have preferred she'd forgotten. "I am sorry for the way I behaved that night. I had no right to pass judgment on you as I did."

Cassia nodded, continuing. "The last thing I remember is that you had taken me to the Privy Garden."

"It wasn't long after that when you collapsed."

"I collapsed? Why? Had I taken ill?"

"Not exactly." Rolfe looked straight into Cassia's eyes. He could think of no delicate way to tell her, so he just said the words. "I'm afraid you were poisoned, Lady Cassia."

Cassia's face went white. It was a possibility she'd obviously not thought of. Even Rolfe still had trouble believing it. She stared at him, stunned, for several long moments. "Poisoned? Do you mean someone tried to kill me?"

"It would seem so. You collapsed while we were in the Privy Garden. I brought you directly here. Mara quickly determined that somehow, someone had given you a large dose of some sort of poison. She never quite arrived at its origin, but she and her maid, Cyma, were able to diffuse the effects with an herbal treacle they made. Whoever gave you the poison has no way of knowing they were unsuccessful. No one, with the exception of me, my friends, and your servants, knows of your current whereabouts. I have instructed Clydes-worthe to tell any callers that you simply aren't accepting visitors now."

Cassia closed her eyes. "Dear God . . ."

Rolfe came forward and knelt by the side of the bed. He took her hand. "Can you remember anything else about that night? Can you think of any time when you could have possibly been given the poison? Did you speak with anyone? Did someone give you something to eat or drink, perhaps?"

Cassia shook her head. "No, no, I didn't speak with anyone except you, the king, and . . ." She peered up at him. "The queen. When I was in visiting Catherine, I drank some of the tea that had been brought in to her."

"Who brought the tea?"

"I don't know. A maid, I guess. I do remember now that Catherine had been surprised by it. In fact, she said she hadn't remembered asking for it."

Of everything he'd thought of this scenario had never entered Rolfe's mind. He'd thought that perhaps someone had slipped something into Cassia's wineglass when she hadn't been looking. He hadn't even considered the time she'd been gone visiting the queen.

"And Catherine has been growing worse for some time," Rolfe said. "The physicians have been unable to attribute her illness to anything. They are increasingly dumbfounded."

"Dear God," Cassia said, closing her eyes, realizing the implication this news brought, "what if the poison hadn't been meant for me at all? What if someone wasn't attempting to murder me, but instead was planning to murder the queen?"

It had taken every ounce of persuasion Rolfe possessed to convince Cassia to stay with Hadrian and

Mara while he went to Whitehall to speak with the king. She was still weak from her own battle with the poison. She couldn't walk down the steps to the breakfast parlor without growing tired, let alone manage a carriage ride through the city and a long walk through the palace hallways.

Besides, Rolfe had told her, he could not completely rule out the possibility that the poison had been meant for her. There was still that near-miss with the carriage to consider. And Geoffrey's threats. He had to assure Cassia's safety at all costs, regardless of whether it appeared she hadn't been the prime target, at least not this time. Rolfe had learned through experience never to take anything for granted. Still, he must inform the king of their newfound suspicions.

Upon arriving Rolfe informed the guard posted at the palace entrance of his urgent need to speak with the king. No, he could not return in the morning, he'd told the guard who had tried his best to send Rolfe on his way. He had to see the king right then, that night.

The man eyed Rolfe cautiously, thoroughly caught between his fundamental desire to refuse him and the slight possibility that Rolfe could indeed have some urgent news for the king. The risk of losing his position was the deciding factor. A wise choice it was. The guard directed Rolfe to a small chamber just outside the palace entrance to wait, its only furnishing a chair Rolfe was too anxious to sit in. And there he waited.

An hour had passed, and Rolfe was ready to force his way inside and begin searching room after room when a footman suddenly appeared at the door.

"Lord Ravenscroft, His Majesty will see you now. If you would but follow me?"

The footman led Rolfe through a maze of twisting corridors, doorway after doorway, deeper and deeper into the palace belly, until Rolfe was certain he'd never be able to find his way out without benefit of an escort. He noticed that the hallways were deserted except for the occasional servant, indicating that most of the palace denizens had taken off for their own private amusements.

The footman finally stopped outside a closed door. A single candle sat in a gold sconce on the wall beside the door.

"His Majesty awaits you inside," said the footman before bowing and vanishing into the shadows.

Rolfe watched him go, confused that the footman hadn't shown him into the room, properly announcing his arrival. He knocked softly at the door.

"You may enter."

The room inside was lit by several branches of candles set apart from each other about the spacious chamber. Carved and gilded furnishings filled the room to excess. There were several chairs, covered in a rich cream-colored velvet, tall chests and elegant tables inlaid with mother-of-pearl topped by bronze and ivory statues crafted by the likes of Donatello and Riccio. Brilliant and colorful tapestries covered the whole of one wall, depicting various scenes from the Hundred Years' Wars. Rolfe stopped beside one that portrayed the Battle of Crécy, his eyes skimming the other walls that were decorated with gilt-framed paintings filling every available space.

Rolfe spotted the king across the room nearer to the tall windows whose drapery had been opened to reveal the starlit night sky. It was a striking view, set against the backdrop of the river, the moonlight rippling on the water's surface. Charles sat on the floor amid a number of tasseled pillows. Curled beside him like the proverbial satisfied cat, wearing an inappropriately modest amount of clothing, was none other than Barbara Palmer.

"Rolfe, my good man, welcome to the apartments of our dear Lady Castlemaine. Consider yourself privileged. Not too many men are allowed inside. Are they not the most resplendent you've ever seen?"

The king was in good humor, Rolfe quickly noticed. Pity it wouldn't be for long.

"They are fit for a queen," Rolfe said. *Or someone who fancies herself a queen, at the least,* he thought privately.

Lady Castlemaine's look of irritation at that statement was not lost on Rolfe.

"Babyface," Charles murmured to her, "Lord Ravenscroft is our guest. Have you nothing to offer him?"

"Babette," she said sternly, clapping her hands, "a brandy for Lord Ravenscroft."

"That is not necessary—"

The goblet was being shoved into Rolfe's hand by a meek-faced maid even before he had the chance to finish his refusal.

"Are you hungry?" Charles said. "I believe we have most anything you could desire: three kinds of wine, a number of cheeses, exotic fruits grown in the palace hothouse." He motioned toward an array of dishes and platters that were spread out picnic fashion on the carpeted floor.

"No, thank you, Your Majesty. I have already eaten."

"Well, then, I guess we'll have to eat yours for you," Charles said, laughing as Lady Castlemaine popped a sugared grape into his mouth.

He chewed slowly, and as he did, Rolfe took the opportunity to look around the room. He soon came to the conclusion that everything about the room—the decor, the furnishings, even the amount of food assembled for their private late-night supper—was obscene in its unrestrained excess.

"So tell me, Rolfe, what is so important as to bring you to the palace at so late an hour?"

Rolfe eyed Lady Castlemaine. Her attention, which had heretofore been focused on which morsel of food to select for the king, was suddenly riveted on him.

"It is a personal matter, Your Majesty. I was hoping for a more private audience."

Lady Castlemaine's lovely blue eyes narrowed.

Perhaps it was the seriousness in Rolfe's voice, coupled with the fact that the hour was so late and his reasons for coming there were obviously urgent. Rolfe didn't know what finally managed to divert Charles's attention away from his scantily clad paramour and her midnight feast, but he was thankful something had.

"My pet," Charles said tenderly to her, tracing his finger along the line of her chin, "would you please go and find me some of those delightful little cherries you had for me last night? I have never tasted any sweeter."

That she was teetering on the edge of refusal was obvious to both men. She took her time in deciding. When she finally stood and started from the room, Rolfe would have sworn he heard Charles release a breath of relief. Lady Castlemaine made it a point to look back several times before leaving.

Rolfe suddenly remembered Cassia telling him about rumors that had once circulated about court, accusing Lady Castlemaine of practicing witchcraft. She'd said they had begun in an effort to explain the extraordinary hold the woman seemed to have on the king. Queen Catherine had believed the charges so thoroughly, she had naively brooked her suspicions to the king, who had immediately quashed them, knowing the seriousness of such a charge. What Rolfe had just seen, the obvious influence Lady Castlemaine had over Charles, only lent credence to the rumors.

"Now, what is it you need of me, Rolfe?"

The transformation in Charles with his mistress gone was immediate. His voice regained its familiar baritone, discarding the mewling quality which had been painfully evident before. He rose to his feet and extended his hand, delivering Rolfe a strong handshake. It was the handshake of a king.

"How goes the queen?" Rolfe asked.

Charles looked startled at the question. "Surely you didn't come all this way at this time of night just to inquire about the health of my wife."

"Please, Your Majesty."

Charles stared at him a moment. "All right. To be quite honest, she does not fare well. In fact, she grows worse with each day that passes. I am most concerned."

The thought to ask him why he was here, in that room, with that woman, instead of at his ailing wife's bedside, crossed Rolfe's mind. It was a thought he would never dare voice. Instead he decided to cut right to the purpose for his intrusion.

"I thought you should know that several nights ago, the night of the masquerade, Cassia was poisoned."

Charles's alarm at the news was genuine. "What? Bloody hell, man, is she all right?"

"Yes, she is fine. At least now she is. It was questionable for a time whether she would live. If it hadn't been for Hadrian's wife, Mara, and the grace of God, Cassia might not have survived."

Charles stared down at the carpet. "I feared something like this would happen."

Rolfe looked at the king. "Your Majesty, is there

something more I should know? Something about the death of Cassia's father you haven't already told me?"

"What? No, nothing like that. I just never could believe Seagrave's murder was a random act. Nor did I believe Cassia guilty. I feared for Cassia's safety." Charles was silent for a moment. "Do you know who poisoned her?"

Rolfe took a quick sip of the brandy that had been forced on him, glad now for it. "I cannot say for certain. Whoever it is, he is adept at covering his tracks. I wasn't even certain how Cassia could have been poisoned in the first place, until I spoke with her about it earlier this evening."

"And," Charles broke in, "out with it, Rolfe. What have you come up with?"

"We have deduced that the only opportunity for Cassia to have been poisoned would have come when she drank some tea, the queen's tea, that evening when you took her to visit Queen Catherine."

Charles's face seemed to turn to stone. It hadn't taken him long to decipher the true meaning behind Rolfe's carefully phrased words. "Are you trying to say that you think someone is attempting to kill my wife?"

"It would explain the mysterious illness which grips her and that confounds the physicians and only seems to worsen every day."

Charles turned and stared out the windows. He did not speak.

"I cannot say with all certainty that the poison was indeed originally intended for the queen," Rolfe went on, talking to the king's back. "It is only a supposition right now. If it is, in fact, true, it would appear whoever is giving the poison to her is doing so in small doses so as not to bring about suspicion."

"Then why was Cassia so badly affected?"

"The only explanation I have come up with is the culprit had decided to increase the dosage that night—to lethal proportions."

"Why?"

"Well, being that most everyone would be occupied at the masquerade that night, and the queen would be left virtually alone—at least she would have been had you and Cassia not gone to see her—I can only conclude that whoever was giving her the poison decided the time had come to finish her off."

Rolfe could see Charles's hand tightening around the drapery cord.

"I am sorry to have to tell you this, Your Majesty. I merely thought you should be informed of the possibility of it. So precautionary measures could be taken."

There passed a long moment in which neither man spoke. Rolfe stood by and waited for the king to respond. When Charles finally turned back toward him, his eyes glistened dolefully in the candlelight.

"Dear God, what have I brought that innocent woman to? She has never done a thing to harm anyone. She has a kind soul, the kindest soul I've ever encountered. She only seeks peace, yet she is constantly falling under attack. They accuse her of heresy. They label her barren. And for what? Because she is my wife? The comments and whispers I can deal with, but this? This is an outrage. Who would do such a despicable thing? Who would want to kill the queen?"

Rolfe could think of several possible suspects, the most likely of which had just sauntered her way out of the room. He decided to keep the thought of Lady Castlemaine's involvement to himself. As Cassia had once told him, one should never lay false blame. At least not without proof.

"It may not be too late, Your Majesty. The queen still lives."

"Yes. You are right." Charles sprang to life. "I will go to Catherine at once and will dismiss all who attend her. I can trust no one. I will have her meals specially prepared and I will taste them myself, if necessary. If someone wants to kill my wife, they will have to do me in before her."

Charles made for the door, Rolfe with him.

"There is a treacle prepared by Mara that proved most effective with Cassia. I will have it sent over to you at once."

"Good," said Charles. "I cannot allow Catherine to die simply for the misfortune of having married me. I will not allow it. I will do whatever I must to see that she lives."

Charles left with Rolfe, never bothering to inform Lady Castlemaine of his departure.

Chapter Twenty

Mara set her teacup into its saucer with purposeful clatter in the formerly peaceful room. Her ploy, though obvious, proved successful, for seconds later, Rolfe was peering at her over the top of his news sheet, his attention definitely sparked.

"Was there something you wished, Lady Kulhaven, or have your fingers suddenly grown too feeble to hold your teacup aloft?"

Mara frowned at him. "You know what I want, Rolfe. Have you told Cassia yet?"

Rolfe set the news sheet aside. He had a feeling this was going to turn into a lengthy conversation. "No, I have not told her yet."

"Rolfe—"

"Before you begin to castigate me, as I'm sure is your intention, allow me to explain, dear lady. I simply need more time."

"More time? How long do you think you can avoid telling Cassia that she is now your wife? You already asked Cassia's friend Cordelia to make the marriage known to certain members of the court, individuals who will waste no time in relating the news to anyone with an ear to listen. It is only a matter of time before most everyone at Whitehall will know."

"I know, but I had to make my marriage to Cassia

public. How else am I to inform the person who killed her father?"

Mara furrowed her brow. "I still don't understand all that business. Precisely how does your marrying Cassia keep her from further danger?"

"By Seagrave's petition, Cassia is, in essence, his heir, unless, of course, she were to perish. Then her cousin Geoffrey becomes the heir, unless, of course, she were to wed. In that case, the title of the Marquess of Seagrave would pass to her husband—as it now stands, me."

"But didn't you mention a condition of children? If Cassia's cousin Geoffrey is the true culprit, I would think Cassia would still be in danger until she at least bears a son to you. Without a male child, the title would revert to Geoffrey, wouldn't it?"

"Yes, the title would, but not the eighty thousand pounds. Not a single farthing of it. Seagrave was most precise in saying that even should Cassia refuse to wed, the money would never go to Geoffrey. He is to be given his fifty-pound allowance, no more. I have seen enough of Geoffrey to know the title and its entail—which consists only of the family seat in Cambridgeshire, and which can never be supported by a fifty-pound allowance—mean nothing to him. It's the eighty thousand pounds he wants, or rather it's the eighty thousand pounds he needs in order to pay his hounding creditors and to set himself up to live in the style he wishes.

"I have consulted with Mr. Finchley, Seagrave's and now Cassia's solicitor, and have learned that since Cassia's father never stipulated that the money would go to Geoffrey in the event of Cassia's demise, it would follow the normal course of inheritance. The eighty thousand pounds would be left to her husband and any children first, before her cousin."

Mara contemplated this for a moment. "It's all rather complicated, don't you think? From what I've heard about Geoffrey in your conversations with Hadrian, I wouldn't think him clever enough to figure that all out."

"Which is precisely why Mr. Finchley has taken it upon himself, on the pretext of his position as solicitor, to explain it all, every last detail, to Geoffrey, at a meeting he has scheduled for tomorrow afternoon. By tomorrow evening, there will be no doubt in Geoffrey's mind of who now holds the purse strings on the Seagrave fortune. Instead of Cassia, he will need to direct his criminal attentions to me."

Mara nodded. "You still haven't told me what you plan to do about Cassia. Do you propose to keep her locked up here in my house, trusting that my servants can keep from revealing the truth when they were nearly all witness to your parading that priest in here in the middle of the night so he could perform your unconventional marriage ceremony? Even I was witness to it, although should Cassia ever learn the truth, and I find out it is not from your mouth, I will simply say you and Hadrian forced me to it."

Rolfe sat back in his chair, frowning. He steepled his fingers in front of him. "I know, Mara. You are right. I cannot delay telling Cassia for much longer. But I just need a little more time, time to show Cassia that I'm not the out-and-out cad she will no doubt think me once I do tell her the truth. The idea of marriage is not something she is fond of. In fact, she has fought against this one thing all her life. She feels it will take away her freedom, and freedom is the one thing Cassia values above all else. I need time to show her that being married isn't the prison she's envisioned it to be. I need time to show her that not all men are abusive cads like her father was. That's primarily why

I brought her here. Besides needing your knowledge of herbs to combat the poison, I wanted to show Cassia the closeness you and Hadrian have, the happiness you have found together. If the two of you—after your equally unconventional joining—can manage to make a life together, then surely Cassia must realize we can do the same."

"Need I remind you, Rolfe, that I did tell Hadrian the truth?"

"Eventually, but for how long did you parade about in disguise, playing at being Hadrian's betrothed, Arabella, wearing those silly spectacles, that ridiculous little cap, and dyeing your hair black?"

Mara frowned. She could not, in all honesty, refute the allegation.

"All I'm asking for is a little more time," Rolfe said. He leaned forward and took Mara's hands. "I will tell Cassia only after I feel I have done all I can to show her that marriage to me won't be as bad as she will believe it."

Mara stared at him. "What you are asking for is the time to make this girl fall in love with you."

Rolfe looked up at that statement. She certainly had a way of weeding through the rhetoric. "If that is what it will take, then so be it."

Mara stood, crossed the room to the side table and poured herself another cup of tea. "I fear you may be setting yourself up for another disappointment like Daphne, Rolfe. No matter how hard you tried, you could never get her to love you enough to see beyond a title to marry you. I would hate to see you hurt like that again. The only satisfaction I can take, after watching what that woman did to you, is that you were elevated to the earldom only days after she agreed to wed Westcott, and an awful marriage it is, from what I hear at court. Daphne never loved you, Rolfe. What if it is the same with Cassia? What if, despite all your trying and good intentions, she is just incapable of falling in love with you?"

Rolfe wouldn't consider it. He thought back to the kiss he'd shared with Cassia the day Geoffrey had come to Seagrave House to threaten her. Though she tried to deny it, he had sensed her response to him. He knew she had felt something, and it was that something he had to trust in now.

"I guess it is just a chance I have to take, Mara. I'm going to start by taking her out riding with me today. I know I can make Cassia fall in love with me. I just need a little more time and a little more of your assistance." He turned in his chair to look at her. "Will you help me just a little longer?"

Mara glanced at him, shaking her head. "I don't know why I am always so unable to refuse you."

"Because I am irresistible and charming and if you were not already married to Hadrian, you would be begging me to make you my wife." Rolfe grinned. "How could Cassia possibly say no to me?"

"Yes, how," replied Mara, taking a sip of her tea.

Just then, the door to the breakfast parlor flew open and Cassia came rushing inside. She made straight for Rolfe.

"You didn't come to my chamber last night after you'd returned from the palace." It was then she realized Rolfe wasn't alone. "Oh, excuse me. I didn't mean to interrupt your conversation."

"No need to apologize," Mara said, setting her teacup aside. "I was just leaving. I promised Robert I would take him and his sister to see the wild animals at the Tower today and I'm sure he's anxiously waiting to go. I fully expected it to be him just now bursting into the room when you did. Ever since Hadrian told him about the lions they have there, he says nothing but 'Bobert see lion, Bobert see lion' all day long. That is what he calls himself, you know, 'Bobert,' and well, if I ever expect him to utter anything else, I guess I had better take him there. Would you care to join us, Cassia?"

Cassia smiled, anxious for Mara to leave, so she could question Rolfe about what had happened when he went to the palace the night before. "No, thank you."

Mara shrugged. "Well, then, I'll be off. You two have a pleasant day." She slanted Rolfe a glance. "Whatever it is you decide to do."

When she'd gone, Cassia turned and noticed that Rolfe was dressed to go riding. He wore a navy riding coat and buff-colored breeches, his black leather jackboots, polished to an impeccable shine, stretched out at length beneath the carved baluster legs of the walnut dining table. "You are going somewhere, my lord?"

"And good morning to you, my lady."

"I'm sorry," Cassia said, lowering herself into the seat across from him. "Good morning, Lord Ravenscroft."

The Kulhaven footman brought Cassia a steaming cup of herb tea and was dismissed immediately afterward by Rolfe who had but to nod in the direction of the door.

"Did you speak with the king?" Cassia asked as soon as they were alone. "Did you tell him our suspicions about the queen, that we believe her life is in danger? Did he tell you what he plans to do?"

Rolfe grinned at her enthusiasm. It was so good to see she was feeling better. "Yes, and yes. I did speak with the king and I did relay our suspicions to him. He was most grateful to us for the information, was most concerned for the queen, and assured me he would take the matter in hand.''

"That is all? What if someone tries to poison the queen again? He cannot possibly be with her all the time. Perhaps I should go to Whitehall and see if he needs my help.''

Rolfe noticed that her excitement was bringing a healthy color to her cheeks. That was a good sign.

"No," he said, knowing if Cassia went to the palace, besides placing herself in further danger, she would most probably come across someone who had already heard of their marriage. Cordelia's networks were remarkable in passing information swiftly through the most advantageous channels. He could just imagine how Cassia would react to being congratulated on a marriage she didn't even know existed. Actually, he didn't want to think of that possibly happening. "You shouldn't go to the palace, not yet. It isn't safe. I'm quite confident in the king's abilities to take the situation in hand. We're not even certain that the queen was being poisoned, but just in case she was, I had a dosage of the treacle Mara gave to you sent over to the king this morning. So, all is well, and besides, I was hoping I might be able to persuade you to go riding with me in the park this morning.''

Cassia's eyes instantly lit up. Any thought of going to Whitehall was immediately forgotten. "You want me to go riding with you?''

"Yes. Unless, of course, you don't feel up to it yet.''

"No—I mean yes. I feel up to it. I feel more than up to it. I've been feeling restless, holed up here all this time. A ride in the fresh air will do me a world of good, I think. I feel like I haven't sat a horse in ages. If you would please but allow me a moment to change into more suitable clothing, I would be happy to join you.''

Rolfe watched Cassia turn and leave, pleased this was going so well. She had trusted and accepted his assurances about the queen. She'd agreed to go riding with him. If things continued along the same vein, he should be able to tell Cassia the truth in a few days.

Cassia was back within a quarter hour, dressed, surprisingly enough, in a moss-green velvet riding habit, complete with a white feathered plume in her black cocked hat. The cut of the riding habit mimicked a man's in style, flared coat buttoned over a white shirt and lacy cravat. Still, Rolfe thought, watching her as she skipped down the stairs, he had never seen a woman look more feminine. As he watched her tugging on her black kidskin gloves, he thought to himself, had Cassia been standing there attired in naught but a hempen sack, she'd still be a vision to behold.

"Did you happen to tell Mara I would be going out riding with you today?" she asked as he helped her with her cloak. Together they walked toward the entrance hall.

"No, I didn't. Why do you ask?"

"Well, I happened to think, as I was going back up to my chamber, that there most probably wouldn't be a riding habit among the clothing you had Winifred send over for me. But when I went into the room, I found this spread out on the bed." She swept her arm outward, gesturing to her attire.

Rolfe said a silent thank-you to his friend's forward-thinking wife. "Well, then, I guess there is nothing more to keep us from our ride."

The horses were saddled and waiting for them in front of the house, their breath fogging slightly in the chilly air. The morning had been dampened by an early rain, but the sun had since come out from behind the clouds and was now shining its brilliance down upon them, giving promise of a pleasant day.

After assisting Cassia into the saddle of what the Kulhaven groomsman had assured him was a sweet-natured, soft-mouthed bay mare, Rolfe vaulted onto his own horse, a dappled gray stallion he'd affectionately named for his friend Dante, after the horse had displayed a decided liking for following the mares.

"Are we off, then?" he asked Cassia.

"Yes, indeed, my lord."

With a kick and a swish of the horse's tails, they started off down the narrow cobblestone road in the direction of Hyde Park.

Despite the sunshine, there was still a decided bite in the air which Cassia found invigorating after having been confined indoors for days. She closed her eyes and deeply breathed in the icy air, letting it fill her lungs, losing herself in the excitement of having the world once again open before her.

It had been a while since she'd ridden, and she reveled in the feel of the horse's rolling gait beneath her, the thrill of finally being free. She clicked her tongue softly to the mare—named Clover for her fondness for the same, the Kulhaven groomsman had said—urging the horse into an easy canter.

Inside the park, they encountered no one, except for a small group of riders near the entrance gate who took no more notice of them than a slight tip of their hats and a polite "good day." Rolfe directed the horses away from the other riders and moved toward the northern fringes of the park, where the terrain was a little rougher and the woodland more dense. It was an area less frequented by the park visitors.

"Whoa, girl," Cassia said when Clover suddenly reared, jarring her in the saddle. She tightened her knees around the horse's middle.

"Is everything all right?" Rolfe said, coming to her side to steady the dancing mare. "I was told that mare had a gentle easy nature. Perhaps we should go back for a different mount."

"No," Cassia said, shifting slightly in the saddle. "Something just spooked her a little, I think. Everything is fine now."

They continued riding alongside each other for a good distance, past fields that had once been filled with lush green grass, now dried and awaiting winter's blanket of white. A short time later, they stopped the horses beside a small pond nearly hidden by a coppice of tall beech trees. The water rippled softly in the breeze, while two long-necked black swans floated elegantly on the surface.

Rolfe dismounted, then helped Cassia down from her mount. "Shall we walk a bit?" he said, offering her his arm.

She nodded and together they skirted the water's edge, listening to the birds hidden in the trees, watching as several red squirrels frolicked beneath the branches of a nearby oak, enjoying the peaceful solitude of the park. Cassia removed her hat and allowed her hair, which was tied back loosely with a ribbon, to trail down her back, a few stray tendrils loosened from the ride lifting in the gentle wind.

Rolfe looked over at her. Seeing Cassia there, he couldn't help but think of how close he'd come to losing her. His insides twisted as they did each time he thought of that night, of watching her fall unconscious into his arms. Never would he allow death that near to her again.

"You are looking much better today, my lady."

Cassia smiled. "Thank you. I am feeling much better today as well. It is such a lovely day." She stopped and turned to face him, her face a mask of seriousness. "You know, I don't think I ever properly thanked you for saving my life that night."

"And I don't think I ever properly thanked you for surviving it."

"You shouldn't belittle my gratitude with teasing."

Rolfe's face grew equally serious. "I'm not. If you hadn't had the strength to fight the poison, the world would most definitely be a sorrier place without you in it."

Cassia wasn't certain how she should reply. No one had ever told her that she mattered before, at least not in words that she believed. Somehow when Rolfe spoke the words to her, she heard his sincerity, and it gave her a feeling of true belonging. It was a feeling that was foreign to her, but it was a feeling she liked.

Rolfe stepped close to her and she knew he was going to kiss her. When he lowered his head and took her lips with his, she welcomed it.

Cassia leaned against Rolfe, her fingers clutching at the opening of his coat. She could feel him deepen the kiss, his tongue sliding into her mouth. Timidly she met it with her own. The intimacy between them filled her with wonder, curiosity, and eagerness for more. It was a heady feeling, this new boldness she felt and she placed her hands against his chest, moving them beneath his coat. The warmth of his skin against hers, separated only by a thin layer of cambric, was delightful. She could feel the heavy beating of his heart, the rigid muscles of his chest against her hands. She felt nearly undone when Rolfe pulled her closer into his arms, his mouth moving hungrily now over hers.

The feeling was intoxicating, like a strange wind blowing in, circling around them and drawing them closer. Time seemed suspended as they stood at the edge of that pond, the sunlight beaming down on them, birds chirping in the trees, excitement filling Cassia's every sense. She suddenly wanted more.

Much more. She wanted to feel Rolfe against her, their bodies touching. She wanted this strange feeling of expectation inside of her to grow. She wanted to be his.

When she felt Rolfe's hand brush against her breast, sending a shock wave through her that filled her to her soul, Cassia lost all sense of reason. She threw back her head as his mouth moved downward, kissing her neck and throat and ears. She didn't realize that he had unfastened her neckcloth and the tiny buttons of her shirt until she felt the cold air drifting over her bare skin. It added to the excitement, an excitement that reached a wonderful peak the moment she felt Rolfe's hand close over her breast.

Cassia instinctively arched her back against the seductive pressure of Rolfe's hand, wanting to feel him even closer. She gasped aloud, rocked when she felt his thumb rub softly against her nipple, teasing her sensitive flesh to hardness.

"Oh, Rolfe . . ."

Her words dropped off, speech beyond her now as the exquisite sensations rolled through her body. *Dear God,* she thought, her whole body trembling, *what is he doing to me? Why do I feel this intense wanting, this desperate need for more?* She pressed her hips against his, but that didn't seem to relieve the tension building inside of her. It only added to it all the more. The groan Rolfe released into her mouth told her he felt it as well.

"I want you, Cassia. I want you more than I've ever wanted before."

Cassia's heart was drumming, pounding in her ears. The world beyond the two of them, ceased to exist, until the sound of rustling leaves and boots crunching over the ground suddenly shattered the magical spell that wound them together.

"Oh, good heavens. A thousand pardons. I didn't know there was anyone this far north in the park. Normally people prefer the more public venues, the terrain up here being a little rough. I only come up here myself to view the wildlife." A pause. And then, "I say, my good man, is everything all right?"

Chapter Twenty-one

Rolfe instantly tensed. Over his shoulder, Cassia could see a man wearing a wide-brimmed hat and holding a walking staff had suddenly appeared through a break in the trees. He stood about fifty yards away. She took in a startled breath and she could have sworn she heard Rolfe curse under his breath.

"Is everything all right," the man repeated. He shaded his eyes against the sun to better see.

"Yes, sir," Rolfe answered back. "Everything is fine."

The man looked at them a moment longer then stepped back, eyes wide. "Quite," he said, appearing to have just then realized exactly what it was he had disturbed as he beat a hasty retreat back through the trees. It was, however, too late. The magic had gone, the wonder fading, leaving them locked in an intimate moment, facing an awkward silence.

"Cassia, I . . ."

Cassia bit her lip. "I—I don't know what to say. I've never done anything like that before. I'm usually only concerned with slapping the face of any man who would dare try to kiss me. It's something that comes by instinct. A reflex. Words are never necessary. But, this time, with you, it was different."

It was only then Cassia realized she'd been standing there talking to Rolfe so matter-of-factly while the cambric shirt of her riding habit was unbuttoned and hanging widely open. "Would you please turn around for a moment?" she asked, trying to keep a sense of calmness to her voice.

His back to her, Cassia was glad Rolfe couldn't see the hot flush that had crept into her cheeks. As her fingers fumbled with the buttons on her shirt, her mind kept repeating the same four words: *What had just happened?* It felt as if she'd been spun about in the vortex of a tidal wave, so awash and disoriented were her senses just then. In one moment, she was walking beside Rolfe, calmly discussing the scenery around them, and the next she was being taken into his arms and his mouth was on hers, evoking feelings and sensations she'd never before felt. She'd gotten lost in its heady wonderful confusion and for the first time in her life, Cassia hadn't thought about what was happening, hadn't worried about the consequences, but had just allowed herself to feel and experience what Rolfe had given.

It was like stepping through a door and facing a new world with wide, fresh eyes, and now that she'd seen what lay on the other side, she never wanted to go back.

When Cassia turned back to face him, her clothes properly arranged once again, Rolfe watched her face closely, trying to discern her thoughts. Had he gone too far too fast in his quest to make her feel something for him? In doing so, had he ended up losing whatever small amount of trust he'd managed to gain? He had never intended their being there together to progress so far, but when Cassia had looked up at him with those dark blue eyes so open and accepting while she thanked him for saving her life, kissing her had seemed the most natural response. But, from the moment their lips had touched and Rolfe had felt Cassia's immediate response to him, a response that was not at all wavering or uncertain, but that took what he'd offered and then gave back twofold, he'd been lost. His need for her overcame any sense of reason, and if not for the sudden interruption of the woodsman, he'd surely have taken her there on the forest floor. He only hoped that in doing so, he hadn't taken a step backward instead.

Rolfe hesitated, waiting for Cassia to speak, thereby giving him some insight into her feelings.

"Shall we return to the horses?" she said.

She smiled tentatively and Rolfe felt a flood of relief wash through him.

All was not lost.

Rolfe took Cassia's hand and started walking with her along the water's edge. "When I was a boy, there was a pond much like this at my family's home in Shropshire. I used to skip stones across it and count the number of times I could get one to jump on the surface. My father had a small stone belvedere built beside it. I remember how my mother would sit on this weathered stone bench there, reading from her poetry books for hours."

"Your mother's name was Abigail," Cassia said suddenly, then added, "I don't even know how I know that."

"You most probably remember me telling it to you when you were ill from the poison. I was just trying to pass the time while you slept. I didn't realize you were listening, and I certainly didn't expect you to remember anything I said."

Cassia stopped walking and turned to face him, her eyes lit with excitement. "Oh, but I do remember. Your father's name was George. George Brodrigan, and he was a viscount."

"Viscount Blackwood, to be precise."

"And you had two sisters, twins, named Sarah and Mary. They had blond hair. They took after your mother in that respect, where you inherited your dark hair and skin from your father's side."

Rolfe smiled. "You are right again. I'm certainly glad I didn't take it to mind to tell you anything that would threaten the country's security. Your memory is uncanny."

"I remember everything you told me about your family. I feel as if, should I pass them in the street, I would know them immediately. I should like to meet them someday. Where are they now? At your family's estate in Shropshire?"

Rolfe shook his head, his voice growing heavy as it always did when he spoke of the past. "My family is gone now. They were murdered by Cromwellian soldiers."

Cassia put her hand to her mouth, shocked at his words. He hadn't told her that when she'd been ill; she would have remembered it. "All of them?"

"Yes. The Blackwood estate was besieged and burned by Roundhead troops at the outbreak of the war."

"Dear God, why?"

Rolfe's eyes darkened and he looked away in the distance when he spoke. "That is a question that still plagues me in the dark hours of the night. From what little I managed to find out, the Parliamentarians had learned my father was staunchly Royalist in his views. Apparently he had been instrumental in helping a fugitive escape to France. That fugitive was the son from one of the neighboring estates. We had known their family for six generations. The soldiers who came to arrest my father decided to mete out justice—or what they called justice—directly rather than through a court of law."

"But your mother, your sisters . . ."

"Casualties of war," he said bitterly. It was a term that had been used in the letter informing him of the tragedy. It wasn't a term he would have ever wished to hear in relation to his family.

Cassia placed her hand consolingly on Rolfe's arm. "I am so sorry for you. However did you manage to escape?"

"I escaped because I was not there when it happened. You see, I had gone off to the American Colonies. I was considering settling there and very nearly did until my family was killed. I returned when I received the letter informing me of their deaths." He hesitated, contemplative. "My father hadn't wanted me to leave England. He told me I needed to stay, that it was my duty to carry on the Blackwood line. It was a title he was most proud to bear. I would that I could have been as proud of it myself. Perhaps then I would have been here, with my family where I belonged, instead of halfway around the world chasing after a selfish whim."

With his bitter words, Cassia could hear Rolfe's grief, a grief that was still so real and painful. She wished she could do something to ease the emptiness that burned in his eyes, but knew she could not. Nothing could change the past and bring his family back. Nothing would take away his terrible loss.

"England was a different place then," Rolfe said as he started walking again. "It was a place divided by dissension that was quickly turning to war. I saw whole families destroyed by it, brother pitted against brother, father against son. I grew tired of it, so tired of it. I wanted to find a place to live in the world where there wouldn't be this fighting, this constant struggle for power between Parliament and the Crown. My father could never understand this. Still, although he loved

England to his very soul, he did not begrudge me my feelings. But I was my father's only son, his heir. Continuity was most important to him. He feared if I went to the Colonies, I would be murdered by savages. He'd heard stories of other Englishmen losing their lives to the natives. He asked me not to go even as he knew I would. Ironically, going to the Colonies ended up saving my life. And it is something I will regret for the rest of my life."

"Surely you do not think that by going away, you were the cause of what happened to your family?"

"No, but I might have been able to prevent it, or at least I could have helped them to escape, had I been there where I belonged."

Cassia was looking at Rolfe's face as they came to the horses, trying to think of something to say. All her life, she'd lived with a family who didn't care for each other at all; in fact, they had tried everything they could to destroy one another. And here Rolfe stood, the only survivor from a family who had loved and cared for one another deeply, blaming himself for their tragic deaths. It didn't seem fair or reasonable in the least; it just seemed wrong.

"I'm sorry," Rolfe said, turning to face her, "I was hoping this ride would lift your spirits, not drag them down even further."

Cassia shook her head. "I'm sorry I caused you to recall such a painful memory."

Rolfe lifted Cassia up, placing her gently atop her horse's back. As soon as she settled herself into the saddle, Clover threw up her head and reared before breaking away into a gallop.

"Cassia!"

They were off before Rolfe could grab hold of the reins.

Vaulting onto Dante's back, Rolfe dug his heels into

his sides and started after them. It only took a few minutes to catch up to the slower-gaited mare. Rolfe saw the reins loose and flipping about dangerously close to Clover's pounding hooves. Cassia was hunched over, holding the horse's neck, trying desperately to keep from falling off.

"Hold on," he shouted over the thundering of the horses. "I am going to try and take hold of the reins."

Rolfe urged Dante forward, moving up alongside the panicked mare. Clover was foaming, eyes wide, nostrils flared. He reached out with his hand. The rein was jerking wildly about. Each time he thought he could take it, it twisted away. He looked in front of them. A feeling of cold fear twisted through his gut when he saw a wide, rocky ditch not more than a few hundred feet in front of them.

Rolfe dug his heels in harder against Dante's sides. "Come on, boy," he shouted, then he knotted his own reins and squeezed his knees around Dante's middle, reaching out with both hands. The ditch was drawing dangerously closer.

Rolfe stooped over, extending slowly toward the mare. The reins were just beyond his reach. He tried again, reaching with careful desperation and finally, just as they were about to reach the edge of the ditch, Rolfe managed to grasp the rein. He gave a sharp yank and as the mare jerked to an abrupt stop, he grabbed Cassia, pulling her over and across his legs. She trembled in his arms as he held her tightly against him. The edge of the ditch lay but two yards in front of them.

When her trembling had quieted, Rolfe set Cassia back from him to look at her, running his hands over her face, her shoulders, her arms. "Are you all right?"

"Yes, I think so. A little frightened, but fine."

"You are very brave."

Rolfe helped Cassia down from the saddle, then dropped to the ground beside her. Dante's sides were heaving, his nostrils blowing from the run. Rolfe followed Cassia as she walked over to stand at the edge of the ditch. It cut deeply into the ground, the sides of it jagged and rocky. Neither Rolfe nor Cassia spoke for the implication was clear: any further and the outcome would have been disastrous.

"I was assured that mare had a gentle nature," Rolfe said, walking over to her. "I don't see any injury to her leg. She seems fine now. . . ."

He patted the saddle seat. Clover tossed her head, dancing sideways.

"What the . . . ?"

Rolfe looked closely at the saddle. He started testing the fastenings, tugging on the straps, trying to see if something might be pinching the horse. He lifted the side leathers to peer underneath. It was then he noticed that one of the belly straps had been cut, a fresh cut, the leather clean along the edges. Only a small fragment of the strap remained intact, holding the saddle secure. He jerked sharply on the strap and it broke free. The saddle dropped limply to the side.

"Bloody hell," he muttered, "this strap was purposely cut. A few seconds more and you'd have been thrown off."

Cassia came up beside him, looking at the damaged strap. "But why would Clover have bolted like that?"

Rolfe pulled the saddle off Clover's back. A small, spiked object was embedded in the skin beneath it. Rolfe pulled it off, inspecting it closely. "It's a thornapple seed casing, all dried and hard and brittle. Those thorns are needle-sharp."

"No wonder she bolted like she did," Cassia said, rubbing her hand over Clover's sweaty neck. The mare nudged her gently with her nose as if trying to apologize for having frightened her. "How did it get there?"

"Obviously someone put it there."

"What if it was already stuck to her back somehow before the groomsman put the saddle on?"

Rolfe shook his head. "Even if it was, which I doubt, the saddle strap didn't come apart on its own. Someone cut it recently, someone who wanted you hurt." He glanced over to the ditch. "You could have been killed if that mare had reached the ditch. Her small legs never would have cleared it and you could have dashed your head on a rock as soon as that saddle came loose." His jaw tensed. "Someone planned for this to happen, someone who wanted you to fall."

Rolfe took the mare's reins and started back for Dante.

"What are you going to do?" Cassia asked behind him.

Rolfe tethered the mare to Dante's saddle. "I am going to find out who the bloody bastard is who is trying to hurt you, and when I do, I'm going to kill him."

Chapter Twenty-two

Cassia was sitting in the library, putting the finishing touches on a sketch she'd spent the past two hours drawing. It was a picture of Mara and Hadrian, sitting just as they were now, at a game of chess before the fire in the parlor. It was nearly midnight. The children were asleep, the house was quiet, only the sound of the fire crackling in the hearth was heard, setting a peaceful, comforting mood.

Mara, her hair loose and hanging in brilliant red curls around her shoulders, studied the position of the pieces on the chessboard. Her chin rested in the crook of her hand and her eyes were narrowed in concentration. Her husband, Hadrian, was sitting back comfortably in his chair across from her, a wineglass cupped in his left hand as he waited for his wife to make her next play. He wasn't watching the game, however. He was watching her. Silently. Intently. A look that spoke volumes of his feelings for her. It was that same look that had first prompted Cassia to sketch the intimate scene.

Rolfe had gone, leaving the house soon after supper, indicating he had a matter to look into. They hadn't spoken again about what had happened that morning in Hyde Park, of the horse bolting and the discovery of the cut-through saddle strap. Nearly everyone else in the household was talking about it.

Hadrian, upon hearing of the near tragedy, the third near-tragedy to touch Cassia in the past two weeks, had immediately summoned every servant in the household, including the groomsmen, before him. He was most intimidating, standing there, glaring down at them all as he asked—no, ordered—them to explain how such a thing could have happened.

No one had dared admit to placing the thornapple burr under the saddle, nor to cutting the belly strap, either. Nor had they seen anybody lurking about who could have done it. It was a mystery that only added to the already puzzling one of her father's murder.

Mara had been so beset that at hearing of it all, she'd had a great big wolfhound named Toirneach, a Gaelic name meaning "thunder," brought inside the house from his usual warm place in the stable to stand guard at the door. He had been Mara's dog as a child, Cassia had learned, raised from a pup, and having nearly lost him during the wars, she now took him with her wherever they traveled, much to Hadrian's disapproval. Cassia quickly gathered that both of them, Hadrian and Toirneach, bore a disaffection for one another, but tolerated the other out of love for their mistress. It was really quite amusing to see them, especially how they glared at each other when they thought Mara wasn't looking, like two rivals for her affections. The brindle-colored beast lay at Cassia's feet now, warming her toes quite nicely. Hadrian remained at the opposite side of the room.

Cassia looked up to check the last details for her sketch, the placement of the chess pieces, the small indentation at the corner of Hadrian's smiling mouth, so like Rolfe's, she realized. Her pencil stilled. Mara had glanced up from the chessboard, instantly catching her husband's intense stare. Her lips curved into a gentle smile, a knowing smile. Without his ever having to utter a word, she knew that it was time for them to retire. Hadrian set his wineglass down, stood, and held out his hand to his wife.

"Cassia, I believe my wife is in need of her rest now. It has been a tiring day what with her taking the children on the outing to the Tower and then with what happened in Hyde Park. She looks exhausted. Is there anything we can get for you before we retire upstairs?"

Cassia shook her head. "I will only be down a few minutes more myself. I just want to finish this sketch before I go off to bed."

Mara looked at her. "You are certain you will be all right?"

"Yes, quite certain. I've Toirneach here to look after me. No one would dare come near me now. You go on to bed. I will be going to my own chamber shortly."

They started to turn. "Good night, then," Mara said, looking back one last time, "and if you need anything—"

"I know," Cassia finished for her, "just ring. Thank you both for making me feel so comfortable here."

They walked from the room, Hadrian's arm possessively circling his wife's waist, her head resting softly against him.

After they had gone, Cassia wondered to herself, what it would be like to be so much a part of another human being as these two, so much so that words were not necessary between them. A look, a smile, and one knew precisely what the other was thinking. That love, that unconditional, unquestioning tie was something completely foreign to her.

Was it simply a rare and beautiful thing, meant only for those lucky enough to be given it, this love that Mara and Hadrian had found? Certainly it must be uncommon—extraordinary, even—for so many poets and writers chose to write about its wonder, its sheer seemingly unattainable bliss. How had Mara and Hadrian come to find it? Had they known the instant their eyes had met that they were meant to share their lives?

Perhaps, when one was born into the world, it was decided right then whether this person should be one of the fortunate few granted that all-too-precious gift. Certainly, if that were the case, then Cassia must herself be one of the unfortunate many who never found it, for none of the men she'd come across in her lifetime had ever made her feel that connection.

Except for one.

Cassia sat back in her chair, remembering the way she'd felt when Rolfe had kissed her in the park that morning, his mouth on hers, his hands touching her body, evoking wonderful and exciting sensations. It had been unlike anything she'd ever experienced. Could he be the one? Could Rolfe be the man she was meant to spend her life with, her life's partner, the one fated to be with her forever?

Cassia couldn't help but wonder what would have happened had the intruder not come upon them as he had, precisely when he had, interrupting them in their passionate and completely improper embrace. How much further would she have allowed their kiss, which was really more than a kiss, to progress before common sense would have come back to save her? And if it had, would she have wanted it to?

No man had ever affected her like this before, making her forget what she was about, making her abandon all propriety, all the standards she'd been taught since birth and had set herself to live by. What was even stranger was that she really didn't care. Cassia smiled. Winifred would be aghast were she to know what her young charge was now thinking. Still, she didn't care. Cassia had tasted pleasure, had liked it, and found that she wanted more. In fact, she wanted it all.

It had felt so right being held in Rolfe's arms. How she wished she could be certain, could know whether he felt the same for her. Rolfe had been sent by the king to guard her, a duty he had vowed to stand by until the end. But once his assignment was complete, once the mystery was solved, what would happen then?

No matter how she tried to ignore it, Cassia could not deny the possibility, the probability that Rolfe would leave her as quickly as he'd come, returning to his estate in Sussex to await his next assignment.

"Lord Ravenscroft, I was wondering if I might have a word?"

Rolfe looked up from the fresh stack of papers delivered him earlier that day by courier from his Ravenwood steward, Penwiddy. He was glad for the interruption for he'd spent the past few hours trying to make sense of the collection of thoroughly tedious explanations for the expenses on everything from the candles supplied by the local village to the charges for the retiling of the roof on the eastern wing. He was glad to note, however, that the renovations at Ravenwood were finally drawing to a close.

"Yes, Lady Cassia?"

After what they'd shared in the park the previous day, and knowing as he did that they were now husband and wife, Rolfe thought it strange, and a bit ridiculous, that they should address one another so formally. Still, he continued the practice.

Cassia came into the room, looking lovely. At Mara's suggestion, she had abandoned the strict mourning black, as a way, Mara had convinced her, of truly putting the events of the past behind her. The result was stunning, like the unveiling of a priceless artifact previously shielded by a dark covering. The gown Cassia wore was made up of pale Persian blue silk, full skirts caught up over a pearl-gray underskirt, the puffed sleeves slashed over a white muslin chemisette and tied off at intervals with darker blue bow knots. The deep rounded neckline showed off her white shoulders, and just a hint of the swell of her breasts, to advantage.

Watching her now, Rolfe found himself remembering how nicely her breast had fit into his palm, like she had been fashioned only for his touch. He remembered her whispering his name, arching her back against him. He felt himself growing hard at the memory, wishing he could take her, right there, right now, on the Turkish carpet in front of the fireplace. He wanted to see Cassia naked. He wanted to watch the firelight play across her soft skin. He wanted to take her into his mouth. He wanted . . .

"I was wondering, my lord, how long we would be staying at this house."

Cassia's question instantly brought Rolfe out of his thoughts. It wasn't what he had expected her to ask. "Is something wrong, Lady Cassia? Do you not like being here?"

Cassia sat in the chair across from him and folded her hands in her lap. "No, that is not at all why I asked. I find Mara to be most hospitable and the children are . . ." she hesitated, looking down at the carpet and smiling, "the children are a blessing, but I cannot delay the search for my father's murderer any longer. I have fully recovered from the poison. Judging from the saddle strap, my being here is no longer a secret. Obviously the person responsible for my father's death is still in London and the longer I go without finding him, the closer I come to being charged with the crime. I must find out who it is before it is too late."

"You needn't concern yourself with that. I have people working on it as we speak."

"At the risk of sounding rude, Lord Ravenscroft, do you not think this should be my problem to handle? I mean you were only sent here to protect me, not to try and set my world to rights. I never wanted to impose—"

"It is not an imposition."

"But it is my problem."

"It is my problem now as well."

"By what right, sir?"

"By the right that I am your husband—"

"Excuse me, Lord Ravenscroft, but what did you just say?"

Rolfe closed his eyes. He had dreaded this moment for so long. He'd tried to prepare for it, mentally rehearsing what he would say, waiting for the proper time to present itself. And now he'd just bungled it by simply blurting it all out. He was a fool. He looked at his hands and tried to calm himself. Finally he said, "I said that I am your husband. It is my right and my duty as such to find out who killed your father and who also attempted not once but thrice to kill you."

Cassia looked nonplussed. "Stop teasing me with such nonsense, my lord. I don't know what game you are playing here, but I must tell you it doesn't suit you, not at all. I never married you. I do not find your jest at all amusing."

"It is no game, Lady Cassia. We are married. While you were ill—the night of the masquerade, in fact—I secured a special license. We were wed right here, in this house, with Hadrian and Mara and several of their servants standing by as our witnesses." He reached inside his coat and removed a folded document from inside. "Here is the certificate of marriage, signed and sealed."

Cassia took the paper and read it over. In the space where the bride should have signed, someone had written in her name with a notation that she'd been unable to do so herself due to an incapacitating illness. Cassia set the document on the desk. She stared at Rolfe, not moving, not blinking, not saying a word.

There passed a long moment and Rolfe began to think she would deal with this little bit of news as she had everything else since the day he'd first met her— by putting up that damnable distant wall of hers and withdrawing behind it.

This time, though, he was sorely mistaken.

Chapter Twenty-three

"You bastard!"

Rolfe held up a hand to calm her. "If you would but allow me a moment to explain—"

"Explain! How dare you, my lord? How dare you marry me without my knowledge? This is not legal. I did not consent to this. Conscious or not, I never consented to this. No, this cannot at all be legal."

Rolfe leaned forward in his chair. "I feel I must inform you that you did indeed consent to this marriage. I assure you that you did. There was only one word required of you to indicate your consent to this marriage and, delirious or not, you did speak it. Before me, the priest, and several witnesses, you did give your consent to be my wife."

Cassia could remember nothing, nothing at all, except that voice, the voice that had spoken to her so softly, calling to her, begging her to fight, pleading with her to live, that voice that had given her the strength and the will to survive. It was a voice she had relied on. It was a voice she had come to trust.

It was Rolfe's voice.

Cassia dropped her head, slumping in her chair. She closed her eyes and wished she could just disappear.

"It must have been obvious to you when I regained consciousness that I had no recollection of this," Cassia said, standing, suddenly so furious with him she wondered if her eyes were crossed. "When did you plan to tell me the truth, my lord? On our anniversary, perhaps? When I became betrothed to another man? Would you have come forward only then to protest the banns and prevent me from committing the sin of bigamy?"

Rolfe stood before her. His voice was soft in an effort to calm her. "Cassia, listen to me. I wanted to wait to tell you all this until you had fully recovered, and then, when you had recovered, well, the time was never right. Believe me when I say I tried several times, but the words just never sounded proper. How do you tell someone that you are now her husband?"

"I imagine it would be difficult."

"You're bloody right it is. If it matters at all, I had every intention of telling you. I just never meant for you to hear it from me like this. I know you most probably hate the sight of me right now, but someday, perhaps, you will understand why I did this."

Cassia crossed her arms over her chest, her eyes sparked with anger. "And why precisely did you do this to me, Lord Ravenscroft?"

She made it sound as if he'd caused her a vile injury, an injury, Rolfe had to admit, he had in all likelihood given, for he had known even before he'd done it, that Cassia had never wanted to wed.

Rolfe was ready to tell Cassia his reasons, his truly honorable and just reasons for having married her without her knowledge, when the Kulhaven butler, Crandall, suddenly made an appearance at the door.

"Excuse me, my lord and my lady. A messenger from Whitehall Palace just brought this to the door. It is addressed to Lady Cassia. He said it was most urgent."

Cassia took the letter from him and quickly opened it.

My Dearest Cassia, I write to you with a despairing heart, knowing I must inform you of the ever-failing health of my wife, your dear friend, Catherine. You alone showed her the most kindness when she arrived in England to become my wife, you alone befriended her when others treated her with naught but contempt and disdain. I realize that by asking you what I am about to ask I may be putting you at considerable risk, having recently learned that your life has been placed in jeopardy, but I beseech you to please come and be at her side, for her time with us is growing shorter. I know she would want you to be with her to the end.

 Yours, Charles Rex.

Cassia's voice trembled as she handed the letter to Rolfe.

"I must go to Whitehall immediately. Queen Catherine is dying."

They were at the palace gates within the hour. Cassia wasted no time in rushing straight for the queen's private apartments. Two uniformed sentries were standing guard outside the closed double doors, rapiers drawn. When Cassia attempted to enter, they stepped in front of her, blocking her way past.

"Let me by, please. I must see the queen."

"The king gave us strict orders that no one save himself was to pass through these doors."

Beyond the point of annoyance, Cassia reached past one of the guards to grasp the door handle. "I do not care what your orders are. I have been summoned here by the king. You will let me inside."

Just then the door opened and the king himself stood framed in the shadowed doorway.

Charles was nearly unrecognizable. Gone were the splendid clothes and the air of majesty that usually surrounded him. His dark hair hung limp and lifeless around his haggard face. He wore only a plain cambric shirt, sleeves rolled to his elbows, and brown woollen breeches. The cheerful light that seemed ever to fill his dark eyes was now, instead, clouded with despair.

"Step aside," he said, his voice thick with misery. "You will allow Lady Cassia to come in."

The guards immediately stepped aside. Cassia rushed past Rolfe and the king and made for the queen.

Before she even reached the doorway to Catherine's apartments, Cassia was nearly overcome by the stench that filled the interior of every room. The windows had been tightly closed as if death had already come to take its innocent victim. The room was stiflingly hot, the smell of sickness overpowering.

Cassia pulled her handkerchief from her pocket and pressed it against her nose to fight the nausea from the terrible smell as she continued on toward the doorway that led to Catherine's inner bedchamber.

She nearly fainted at the sight that awaited her on the other side. Catherine lay on her back in the middle of her large bed, looking twice as small and weak as she ever had before. Her hair, the dark curls that had hung around her tiny childlike face and down her back, which had been the very essence of her innocent beauty, had been shorn to the scalp, a tight-fitting linen cap now covering her bald head.

Her face and arms, the only parts of her visible from beneath the heavy mound of bed coverings, were overspread with red, angry-looking blotches. The pale skin beneath had taken on the appearance of translucency. Only a few candles burned in the room, and the drapery was drawn closed over the windows. It was frighteningly dark, shadows from the candlelight lurking on the stark whitewashed walls. At the foot of the bed, near the queen's small feet, lay the fetid bodies of several dead pigeons, slain days before, a medieval practice that was believed to remove the evils of disease from the air. It only served to add to the noxious odor that filled the room.

Cassia slowly drew nearer. She could see that the sheets were stained with sweat and urine and bodily waste. She tried to swallow to keep herself from gagging. Her stomach lurched nauseously.

At the sound of soft weeping, Cassia looked up to see Catherine's faithful waiting woman, the Countess da Penalvo, sitting at the far side of the bed. Their eyes met and the countess immediately began wailing in broken Portuguese. Beside her, kneeling with his head bowed in prayer, was Catherine's priest, a short and heavily jowled man clothed entirely in black woolen. Near to the pigeon carcasses, at the foot of the bed, stood the court physician, preparing the leeches to bleed the queen.

"Stop!"

The countess ceased her wailing, her red-rimmed eyes peering curiously at Cassia. The priest lifted his head. The physician looked at her in surprise.

"You will not bleed her again," Cassia said. "The queen needs what little blood you seem to have left her in order to survive."

"But we must remove the sickly blood—"

"You will kill her if you continue to bleed her."

Cassia had to raise her voice to be heard, for, since the beginning of the confrontation, the countess had resumed her Portuguese chanting even louder than before. The priest added to the confusion when he began reciting a litany, making the sign of the cross over the bed. Catherine began to moan as if the din were crashing through her brain.

It was all too much for Cassia to bear.

"Get out, all of you!" she yelled.

The countess's wailing increased. The physician began to argue over her, holding out one of the slimy leeches with a pair of metal pincers that looked as if they had never been washed, as evidenced by the specks of dried blood that covered them, determined to set the creature on Catherine's pale skin.

Cassia moved in front of the physician, ready to do whatever it took to prevent any further bloodletting.

"Please step away, my lady," the physician said. "It is for the good of the queen."

"If you had half a mind, you would know what you are preparing to do will bring more harm to her than good."

The king came forward from the shadows, stepping into the chaotic scene.

"Your Majesty," sputtered the physician, "this crazed woman will not allow me to minister to Her Majesty!"

The countess's wailing rose to a crescendo. The priest began burning frankincense in a golden cup, sweeping it through the air in a wide splendid arc, sending a spiral of heavy smoke billowing throughout the room. He prayed aloud, trying to be heard above the noise of the others. "May the Lord have mercy . . ."

The physician stepped forward. "Your Majesty, I must bleed the queen . . ."

The countess broke into shuddering sobs.

Cassia stood fast, refusing to budge from Catherine's bedside.

"Enough!"

At the king's deafening shout, everyone in the room silenced. Charles looked over to Cassia. She just stared at him, beseeching him with her eyes. After a long moment, he turned to face the physician.

"You will take your accursed leeches and you will leave this room and the palace. I never want to see your face here again. And you"—he pointed to the praying priest and the countess, who, despite his outcry, had resumed her chant, albeit quieter now—"all of you—get out! And take that smoking contraption with you! Lady Cassia and I will tend to the queen now."

Charles followed the shocked and protesting group out of the room, making certain that the door was barred behind them. Cassia strode directly to the windows and yanked the drapery wide. Glorious sunlight came beaming in and she went on to unhitch the window latches, throwing the casements open to allow in the cool fresh air from outside in an effort to diffuse the sickly stench.

When she turned back to the bed, Cassia stopped, frozen. She then began to weep.

Without the veil of darkness, in the bright light of day, Catherine looked far worse than she'd at first appeared. Her eyes were sunken deep into her skull, her lips showing a pasty white. Even her fingernails had begun to yellow. If not for the slight rise and fall of her chest, one would think her already dead. Cassia returned to the window, grasping the ledge as she took in a long, steadying breath. Outside, on the lawn that bordered the river, several of the courtiers were playing at bowls, laughing as if they hadn't a care, as if their queen were not lying so near to death's door. It was all too much to bear.

"How in God's name did this happen?" Cassia asked, her voice cracking, as Charles entered the room.

"Catherine lost the babe early yesterday morning. The physician said it was inevitable, that her body just cannot sustain a pregnancy, but I suspect the poison is more likely responsible." He paused, and when he spoke again, his voice faltered. "As far as they could tell, the child was a boy." He closed his eyes and then continued. "Soon afterward, the fever struck. When the spots on her skin appeared late last night, they saw it as an omen that she did not have much longer to live. That is when I decided I should send for you. She has been given last rites. There is nothing more I can do."

Charles looked down at his wife lying there so still, so close to death, and his eyes began to fill with tears. "She cannot die, Cassia. I need her with me now more than ever. I cannot live without her by my side. Catherine must not be allowed to die."

Cassia stared at him, this man who was ruler over a nation, a man who'd not shown his wife more than brotherly affection during the course of their short marriage, but who'd obviously come to treasure her. She stood by as he fell to his knees and wept miserably into his hands.

Cassia spent the rest of that day and on into the night personally caring for Catherine. She would not allow anyone other than herself or the king to see to even the most trivial of tasks. While Charles held his wife's limp and unconscious body, Cassia herself stripped the bed of its soiled linen, ordering that it be burned far beyond the palace walls. The mattress was replaced, the room completely emptied of the pigeon carcasses and filth. Then Cassia got down on her hands and knees and scrubbed the bare floorboards with lye until her hands were red and raw and no evidence of the sickly stench remained.

Afterward, Charles helped Cassia to bathe Catherine in a tub of lavender-scented water, carefully sponging the sores left on her skin from the damaging leechings. Together they dressed her in a clean linen night rail and laid her back on the bed to rest.

Only then did Cassia allow herself the same.

The following morning, a cooking pot and supplies of fresh water and food were brought in, delivered by Rolfe, for Cassia refused to allow any food from the palace kitchens inside the room. Mara arrived later, offering her knowledge of herbs to help, but Cassia, not knowing if the queen's illness had been induced by some sort of contagion brought on by her miscarriage, or if it was due to poison, refused to allow her in for fear of putting her own health, and that of her babe, at risk.

She did accept Mara's herbal poultice for the leech sores and the pouch of tea leaves she had brought, and after steeping the leaves in fresh hot water, Cassia spooned small amounts of it between Catherine's cracked lips. Afterward, throughout the course of the day, she assiduously applied the poultices to every sore that marked her fair skin. When the queen finally succumbed to a deep, heavy sleep, Cassia sat down, her back aching from the scrubbing, her hands burning from the lye, and closed her eyes.

She thought only to take a few minutes respite.

In seconds she was sound asleep.

The morning sun was beaming its soft light through the windows when she first heard the queen's cry.

"The babies! Where are my babies? I want to see my babies!"

Cassia sat bolt upright. She saw Catherine sitting up in her bed, stiff as a poker, staring straight at her. Her eyes were wide, and her expression was frighteningly blank.

"Where are my babies?"

Charles had been summoned from the cot he'd had brought in to sleep on, and came forward. Neither he nor Cassia spoke. Something in Catherine's expression, the emptiness in her dark eyes, gave them curious pause.

Catherine turned to look at her husband, saying clearly, "Charles, where have they taken our babies?"

Charles glanced at Cassia a moment, then said, "They are sleeping, my love, in the nursery."

"They are well?"

Charles's voice broke only slightly. "Yes, my love, they are. Healthy little children, I am told."

Catherine turned to look at Cassia, who had not moved from her chair. "And the boy? Have you seen the boy, Cassia?"

"Yes, Your Majesty, I have."

"Is he very ugly?"

"Oh, no, not at all. He is a fine-looking son. A head full of dark hair. Quite the image of his father."

Catherine smiled and fell back against the pillows, her voice dropping off softly. "It pleases me to hear that. I so wanted to give Charles a son who would be as handsome as his father."

In the next moment, the queen returned to a deep state of sleep, leaving Cassia and the king to stare.

Cassia looked to Charles. "She does not know she lost the babe?"

"Apparently not. She was still unconscious from the poison when she began to bleed. She must not have realized what happened, that she miscarried the child with the flux. And we must not allow her to find out, either. Not now. Not yet. It may cause her to fall into a depression and lose the will to live."

Cassia nodded in agreement.

At odd times during the rest of the day, Catherine would speak out as she had that morning, asking about the children, requesting a drink of tea, telling her husband how much she truly loved him. Mostly, though, she slept, deeply and peacefully, giving Cassia the hope that she would soon recover.

Until the fever returned later that night.

It came upon the queen suddenly and with a fierceness that had Cassia working furiously to fight it. She soaked Catherine's burning skin with ice-cold water, trying to fight back her tears when the delirium took over and Catherine began to rave, thrashing about on the bed.

"The babe is dead! I saw him! They took him away all bloody!"

Cassia took Catherine's hand in hers and squeezed it hard. "No, Your Majesty, you are mistaken. Listen to me. The babe is alive. He is fine. He is sleeping peacefully now in his cradle in the nursery."

Catherine did not hear her. She began to weep, sobbing loudly, her head whipping violently back and forth on the pillow. Her hands reached out to invisible images. "Please, Charles, don't leave me. I will give you a son. I swear I will. Please give me another chance and I promise you I will not fail again."

Twice Cassia had to hold Catherine down, throwing her body over the queen's to keep her from flinging herself out of the bed. Catherine raved on and on, begging Charles to return her love, weeping about dead babies and her failure to deliver him an heir. Charles seemed to fall into a transfixed stupor, standing there watching while Cassia worked furiously to calm the wailing queen, staring at his wife as if he didn't know her.

Finally, just as dawn was breaking on the eastern horizon, the fever subsided. Catherine drifted back into a deep, restorative sleep.

Charles came to Cassia as she moved to fetch the fresh linens at the foot of the bed.

"Dear God, Cassia, what have I done to this poor woman? What will I do if I lose her?"

Cassia hugged Charles to her, this man, a king, so

helpless to do anything more than pray, and together they wept for Catherine.

It was thus Rolfe found them when he came into the room. He'd brought a fresh supply of water and the ingredients necessary to make a healing broth for the queen, having received Cassia's written request for it early that morning.

Seeing her standing there—his wife, the woman he loved—weeping and seeking comfort from the king, her lover, struck him a sharp and telling blow. Everything told him it should be him she was holding, clinging to for comfort, pouring out all of her grief and frustration. As her husband, he should be the one to soothe her heartfelt misery.

But then, even though he was her husband, he was still a complete stranger to her.

Caught between the urge to turn and leave, and the even stronger urge to break them apart, Rolfe remained in the doorway and watched until at last they separated. It wasn't long before they noticed him standing there.

"I have brought the water and things you asked for," he said, trying to mask the pain and the anger in his voice.

Despite his attempt, Cassia could see it in his eyes, and she knew the anger he fought at finding her there with the king, the man he believed to be her lover. She wished she could tell him the truth, that, despite the rumors, she had never been the king's mistress, but knew it was neither the time nor the place.

Instead she said simply, "Thank you, Lord Ravenscroft. You may set them on the table near the teapot."

And with that, Rolfe turned and left the palace.

Chapter Twenty-four

Nearly a week had passed since Cassia had gone to Whitehall. Though Rolfe had seen her when he'd brought fresh supplies, he had not spoken above a few short sentences to her since telling her they were married that seemingly long-ago morning. The days and the distance apart had been a good thing, he'd finally decided, giving Cassia the time she needed to come to terms with the fact that they were indeed wed. And with Cassia safely ensconced inside the palace walls, behind well-guarded doors, it had also afforded Rolfe the opportunity to continue the investigation into her father's murder.

The sickness had nearly taken the queen's life. Nearly. A new physician, one who applauded Cassia's conviction against the leechings and who sought other, more humane measures, diagnosed her condition as an infection brought on by her miscarriage. It had not been caused by any poison or contagion, easing Rolfe's mind, for he'd worried that Cassia might contract any disease it had been, coming into such close contact with Catherine as she had. He'd kept those concerns to himself, knowing, even had he voiced them, Cassia would have been deaf to them.

In so selflessly running to Catherine's side and working so diligently in helping her to recover, Cassia had shown a side of herself that Rolfe had not yet seen. A magnanimous side. A side that showed her true giving spirit. It only made the love Rolfe felt for her grow all the more. Despite having recently been victim to poison herself, Cassia had risked her own health and safety in order to save Catherine's life, and save it she had, for Rolfe had little doubt that, if not for Cassia's valiant efforts, England would now be mourning her queen.

Sitting alone at Seagrave House in her father's study, having spent the past days and nights relentlessly pursuing every lead he'd found in trying to unmask the identity of the murderer, Rolfe did not have much more information than what he'd started with. His frustration was mounting, for this was the only thing he saw he could do for Cassia, the one thing he could give her that she truly wanted.

And it was the only way he could see for himself to make amends for what he'd done to her.

Damn! Rolfe plowed his fingers back through his hair in utter exasperation. There had to be something more, something he was overlooking. No crime in history had ever been committed without leaving some evidence, however small, no matter how insignificant it might seem. He just had to have the wits to find it.

Geoffrey still stood out in Rolfe's mind as the most likely suspect. Every time he turned around, it seemed, Geoffrey was involved in some way. Rolfe just needed to find the proof that would uncover Geoffrey's guilt.

Rolfe had long ago discounted nearly all of Cassia's former suitors, either for being too inane to have hatched on something as serious as murder, or for having gone on since their pursuit of her to other conquests. A couple still bore looking into, one being Cassia's last and most serious suitor, the Duke of Manton's son, Malcolm. Rolfe was still waiting to receive his information from Dante on that one, but like the others, he would most probably show to have had nothing to do with the crime, thus crossing another name off the quickly diminishing list of suspects.

Rolfe had grown, however, increasingly suspicious of Lady Castlemaine, especially since the night of the masked ball. Someone at the ball had poisoned the tea Cassia had drunk, someone who, it would appear, had intended it for Catherine. With the queen's mysterious illness, so like Cassia's, and so close in time, the similarities alone were enough to mark her as a suspect. And with Cassia's father having been the main obstacle to Lady Castlemaine's attempts at monetary gain, Rolfe had come to look more closely at her, although he doubted she had committed the act herself.

And one question remained. How would Lady Castlemaine benefit by removing both Cassia and the queen? Court rumor had it that the lovely Barbara Palmer was growing more desperate each day to secure her position with the king. His growing attraction for Frances Stuart and his equally decreasing response to her own monetary demands were becoming all too evident. By poisoning the queen now, Lady Castlemaine could very well succeed in diverting Charles's attention away from his latest conquest. But did Castlemaine dare to believe she could become queen?

Why would she wish Cassia dead? Her dislike for Cassia was without question, particularly given Cassia's close relationship to the king. But was it enough to have caused Barbara Palmer to make an attempt on Cassia's life as well? And if Barbara was the true culprit, she had covered her tracks well. There wasn't a hint of evidence that could be traced back to her, at least none that Rolfe had found as yet. But, if she was involved, and had succeeded in hiding that involvement, it wouldn't be for long. Rolfe had dealt with enough strategists during the wars to know that sooner or later, and with enough persistence and determination, most every plot was uncovered.

Within the half hour, Rolfe had his assurance it wouldn't be very much longer before he found the proof he needed.

Clydesworthe, the Montefort butler, presented himself at the door to announce an unexpected visitor.

"The Countess of Castlemaine is here to see you, my lord."

She whisked through the door without waiting to be acknowledged, her wide silk skirts nearly knocking Clydesworthe aside as she strode into the room. She was dressed to extreme, her ivory and lace gown shimmering in the light of the candles. When she saw Rolfe sitting behind the desk, she managed a charming smile and extended her hand.

"Lord Ravenscroft, a pleasure to see you again."

Rolfe took her hand and pressed the obligatory kiss to it, noticing the many jeweled rings that decorated each of her slender fingers. Cassia's words came back to him then, ringing in his ears.

. . . her jewel boxes, it seems, continue to grow heavier, far outweighing our own true queen's.

"What is it I can do for you, Lady Castlemaine?" he asked, sitting back in the chair.

"Such formality. Please, call me Barbara. Especially since you have already paid a visit to my private apartments." She grinned. "First allow me to extend my congratulations to you on your recent marriage. However did you manage to gain Cassia's consent to it?"

If you only knew, Rolfe thought, then said, "I simply asked and she accepted."

"I, for one, thought she'd die before she'd ever marry. Caught us all by surprise, I must say, and so swift and secret a ceremony. It leaves one to wonder why the rush."

"I'm sure you understand, with the recent death of her father, how Cassia didn't think a display of pomp and ceremony appropriate."

"Of course. Poor Seagrave. He will be missed by us all." Her sorrowful expression changed in a second's time. "Nevertheless, I have come to extend an invitation to you."

Rolfe's interest grew. "An invitation, you say?"

"Yes, I am hosting an intimate little gathering at my apartments in the palace night after next. Only twenty or thirty of my closest friends, you understand. I was hoping I could count you among them."

Rolfe nodded, wondering how it was he had been elevated to the position of being considered one of Barbara Palmer's closest friends. His suspicion of her mounted.

"I see."

"Of course you will bring Cassia. I never for one moment believed that drivel about her murdering her father, you know. She just doesn't have the instincts necessary to kill."

Instincts like yours, Rolfe thought, and he decided to seize the opportunity she had so kindly presented. "Of course she doesn't. Cassia is innocent. In fact, I have found evidence that will prove it beyond a doubt."

Castlemaine's brilliant blue eyes lit up. "You have? Do tell me what it is."

"I'm afraid I cannot do that just yet, my lady. We wouldn't want the true culprit to learn of it and somehow get away, would we?"

Barbara smiled. Rolfe noticed it was a smile that

never quite reached her eyes. "Of course not. And where has Cassia been keeping herself these days?" She glanced out the door as if expecting Cassia to appear at the mere mention of her name. Obviously, thankfully, Cassia's presence at the palace had been kept secret even from the likes of Barbara Palmer. "I haven't seen her in some time and I wanted to congratulate her on her marriage. Who would have thought she'd finally meet the man to suit her?"

"Yes, who," Rolfe replied. "I'm afraid Cassia is indisposed at the moment, but I'm certain I can accept your invitation for us both. Night after next, you say? We would be honored to attend."

Mara looked up from the book she was reading as Cassia came into the parlor. "Are you feeling more refreshed after your bath?"

"Yes, much," Cassia replied, taking the seat across from her. "I didn't think I would ever get that sickly smell off my skin."

"The queen is on the mend?"

"Yes, and it appears, barring any further complications, she can expect a full recovery. She was looking much better when I left the palace. The color had returned to her cheeks and she'd eaten some of the broiled chicken and bread you had sent over for her."

"Splendid. I trust His Majesty will see her recovery continues along the same vein. And you, Cassia, how are you feeling?"

"A little tired, I guess. I had thought to rest a bit, but I wanted to talk with you first." She paused, then asked the question that had been on her mind since the day she'd left for the palace. "What can you tell me about Rolfe?"

Mara closed her book and set it aside. She thought for a moment, then said, "I have known Rolfe for the past five years, and from the moment I met him, I knew he was a very special man. It hasn't been easy. He has been touched by tragedy. Has he ever told you about his family?"

Cassia nodded. "He said they were all killed during the wars. Somehow I get the impression he believed himself responsible."

"Your impression is correct. I don't think Rolfe will ever forgive himself for having been away in the Colonies when his parents and sisters were murdered. What he fails to realize is that had he been there, he most probably would have been killed as well, and then the Brodrigan family would cease to exist altogether. I know this because the same tragedy befell my own family. I, too, am the only one left. During the wars, Rolfe accepted the most dangerous missions when no other man had the courage. He would never tell you this, but he even managed to be at Cromwell's bedside when he died—in disguise, of course."

"So he was one of the Nightmen."

Mara looked at her. "He is bound by duty never to reveal it."

Cassia nodded. "I am well acquainted with Rolfe's loyalty to duty."

Mara smiled. "I think Rolfe will spend the rest of his life trying to prove himself. That is why he is so loyal to duty. His family having been killed is like a shadow that follows him, and I do not believe he will ever feel he has paid his debt to them."

Mara's account explained a lot. But it did not explain it all. There was still something else, something more that pushed Rolfe beyond the line of duty. "Why did he leave London? I mean, he tells me it is because he was given an estate that had been damaged during the wars and he is seeing to its restoration, but I sense there is something more."

"You have good instincts, Cassia. Rolfe was a viscount when the king returned to the throne. His father had spent his life honoring that title, striving to see to its continuity. Rolfe decided he would honor his father by seeing to that wish. He decided to take a wife. Unfortunately, he chose a girl who was far too filled with her own self-importance. She dallied with him, making him think she really cared for him, but when Rolfe finally proposed, she refused him. You see, it wasn't Rolfe that mattered; it was his title. She had her sights set on marrying herself to an earl at the very least. Rolfe, being a viscount at the time, didn't qualify, and she made no secret of her reasons for denying him. Rolfe had cared for her very much. Her rejection of him was devastating."

Cassia fell silent.

"I gather from your questions he finally told you?" Mara said. "You now know that you are Rolfe's wife?"

Cassia nodded.

"And what was your response when he told you?"

"I was angry, of course—furious, actually. Wouldn't you be if you'd just found out you were married to someone who was, for all intents and purposes, a stranger to you?"

At this Mara had to smile. "I don't think I'm the one you should be asking this. My husband would more likely know the answer."

Cassia looked at her, confused. "Pardon me?"

"I myself deceived my husband into marriage. When I married Hadrian, he believed I was someone else entirely. Goodness, I never thought I would have to explain this again. You see, during the wars, my family's estate in Ireland was confiscated by the Protectorate. Many of the Irish landholders suffered the same fate. Kulhaven was given over to an English supporter of Cromwell, a man named James Ross. He was Hadrian's uncle. James Ross did not have any children of his own, so when he died, he left the estate to Hadrian. I learned that Hadrian was promised in marriage to a girl named Arabella Wentworth, a thoroughly plain child and the godchild of Cromwell, although he had never before seen her. I disguised myself as Arabella and traveled to Kulhaven to marry Hadrian, take my revenge on him, and regain my family's estate."

She looked at Cassia, who was staring at her with disbelieving eyes. "It's all rather difficult to believe, don't you think? But it is true all the same. So you see, I would not be the one to ask about marrying someone under false pretenses, for I am guilty of doing just that to my husband."

"But how can that be? You are so in love with each other now."

"Yes, now we are. Like you, Hadrian was furious when he learned of my duplicity, and if you knew anything about my husband, the one thing he insists upon in his wife is honesty. But, in time, he was able to forgive me for fooling him and we have built a wonderful life together. I had my reasons for what I did, and after he'd calmed down long enough to listen, which was, of course, after my maid Cyma had knocked him cold with a blow to the head and I had locked him away in my bedchamber, telling everyone he had the smallpox . . ."

Cassia was astounded.

". . . but that is another story entirely. After he had thought about it, really thought about it, Hadrian understood why I had done what I had. He even admired me for it."

Mara took Cassia's hand. "At least give Rolfe that consideration. Listen to his reasons for having wed you like he did, really listen to them. They are just and honorable, I assure you. And after you have had the time to think it all through, then you can decide whether you still want to string him up from the nearest tree."

She smiled then, trying to ease Cassia's very evident resistance.

"I will think about it," Cassia said. "That is all I can offer Rolfe right now."

"And that is all Rolfe would ever ask of you," came a voice from behind.

Cassia whipped about to see Rolfe standing in the open doorway. She wondered how long he'd been listening to their conversation. She'd never even heard him come in.

Still she couldn't deny the small thrill that had leaped inside of her at seeing him again. He looked so damned handsome, standing there in his buckskin breeches and polished jackboots, his hat tucked under his arm. She had missed him while she had been away ministering to Catherine, for even though she'd seen him on occasion, she had been so intent on the queen, she hadn't been able to give him much thought.

"How does the queen fare?" Rolfe asked as he strode into the room.

"She is still on the mend, but appears beyond danger, thank the Lord."

"Owing, I'm sure, entirely to you."

Cassia looked tired, Rolfe thought as he came around to face her. Actually, tired wasn't the half of it; she looked downright exhausted. Her eyes were shadowed and she looked as if she'd lost weight. In fact, she looked thin as a bloody twig. He spotted the small plate of cheese wedges and bread Mara had set on a plate before her, noting it had been left untouched. He started to remark on it, then held himself in check. This wasn't the time to carp on Cassia's eating habits. This was the time for long overdue explanations.

Rolfe wanted to speak with her, alone. He wanted to somehow weed through all the questions and mis-understanding that stood so solidly between them. He wanted to tell Cassia how he felt about her, that he loved her and wanted to spend the rest of his life with her. He still shocked himself at this thought. After Daphne, he'd vowed never to tell a woman how he felt, if he cared, for with that knowledge came power for a woman. But the thought of losing Cassia, of never having her in his life, was far too dear to risk.

He had decided the night before, lying in bed, staring at the ceiling, that he would tell Cassia everything, lay his heart on a platter before her and face the chance that she might destroy it. No mission he'd ever taken on had put him more at risk. Still, it was the only thing he could do.

Sensing his thoughts, Mara stood, ready to quit the room. "I'm sure you two have things you need to discuss privately and it is nearly time for Dana to wake from her afternoon nap, so I'll be off. Cassia, you know, if you have need of anything, all you need do is ask."

Cassia nodded, smiling.

Cassia didn't move from the chair she sat in; in fact, she did not so much as turn a degree in Rolfe's direction. She continued to stare at the space where Mara had been sitting, where now there was nothing.

"Lady Cassia, I—"

"Given that we are now husband and wife, do you not think it proper for you to address me by my Christian name?"

Rolfe paused. "Very well, Cassia, I think that would be a definite step in the right direction."

Cassia closed her eyes and exhaled a heavy breath. "I'm sorry. I did not mean to strike out at you as I did. I am just tired."

Rolfe came to sit across from her. "Perhaps we should postpone this discussion until after you have had time to rest."

"No, I think it has been postponed long enough. Let us just be done with it." She looked at him. "First, I think you should know I went to see Mr. Finchley this morning to find out about the possibility of an annulment."

Something inside of Rolfe tensed. "I see."

"I have learned that, given the rather irregular circumstances surrounding my consent to the marriage vows, an annulment would not be at all difficult to obtain. It would be merely a matter of signing a few papers and it would be done."

Rolfe was amazed at how calmly he answered. "By this little announcement, am I to assume you are determined to continue on this path of self-destruction?"

"I beg your pardon?"

"I cannot for the life of me understand what it is that causes you to seek the road filled with obstacles. I have spent hours pondering this, passed days wondering what it is that makes you act this way, and I have come up with only one conclusion. You would rather face the possibility of hanging for the murder of your father alone than accept the help of others and prove your innocence."

"I do not need your assistance to prove that which is true. I will find a way to prove my innocence myself."

Rolfe stood. "Why do you have to be so damned eternally stubborn? Why is it so difficult for you to accept my help?"

"Because the cost is too dear."

"What cost?"

"The cost of my freedom, which I have lost now by becoming your wife." She looked at him and added, "Unwillingly."

"Have I refused you anything, Cassia? Have I locked you away in a room and fed you only on bread and water? Pray, madam, what freedoms exactly have you given up?"

"None yet, but before long things will change. Things always change. A person never does anything without expecting something in return, my lord. There is always a price, always a condition. Your price was marriage to me."

"I did not marry you to hurt you, Cassia, nor did I marry you to gain anything from you. I told you once you were no fool, so stop acting like one. And stop looking at me like some sort of empty-headed cow. I married you for one reason. To protect you from whoever is trying to kill you. Need I remind you that someone killed your father, then attempted not once, but thrice, to kill you? That someone could very well be your cousin Geoffrey, next in line for the title. This has put you in a considerable amount of danger. You forget that your father left a condition that would make whomever you wed the next Marquess of Seagrave. By marrying you, I have transferred that danger to myself. He would now have to kill me to get his hands on the eighty thousand pounds. Even an idiot like Geoffrey can figure that out. And even an idiot like Geoffrey will see I'm much more difficult a target than you."

Cassia wanted to believe him, but something held her back. "And you expect me to believe that you did this thing out of honest concern for my well-being?"

Rolfe came down on one knee before her, taking her hand. "Is it really so difficult?"

Cassia looked at him, her eyes filled with doubt. "It is nearly impossible."

Rolfe dropped his head, resting it on her knees. Cassia felt the urge to put her hand on him, stroke her fingers through his hair, and, in fact, she actually lifted her hand, but dropped it back down when Rolfe looked up at her again. His face was filled with total frustration. "Cassia, answer me one question, if you would."

"Yes?"

"After you are proven innocent—and I promise you this, you will be proven innocent—what are your plans? How will you spend the rest of your life?"

Cassia took in a slow breath before responding. "I haven't really given it all that much thought. I've been so concerned with proving that I didn't kill my father, I haven't considered what I'd do if I finally did. I know I will leave the city for a while, probably to go to Cambridgeshire."

"Believe me when I say that running away does not make your troubles disappear. I speak from experience; they only follow you wherever you go. What about the future, Cassia? I've seen you with Robert and Dana; you are a natural mother. Do you plan to have children of your own someday?"

Cassia had thought of it. When she'd watched Robert playing the lute with his mother that day, she'd pictured herself doing the same. When she'd been singing to Dana as she slept, she realized she wanted her own child to hold, to rock to sleep. She wanted to give her children the love her mother had never given her. She wanted to spend the rest of her days watching them grow, teaching them about the world.

And whenever she pictured this in her mind, somehow Rolfe was always there with her.

But what about him? How could she trust him

again, after what he'd done? He had offered explanations, yes, but he hadn't offered her any declarations
of love. She had no idea how he felt about her except
that she knew he still believed her a mistress to the
king. That she had seen plain in his eyes the day he'd
walked in to find her embracing a grieving Charles. If
she decided to remain his wife, there would come a
time when he would learn the truth. He would learn
that she had never bedded with the king. He would
learn that she'd never bedded with any man. He would
learn that it had all been a sham, a disguise for her
to hide behind. What then?

"It is something I have considered, having children
someday. But I will only have children with someone
I love."

Rolfe felt something inside of him snap. *With someone I love.* Someone who obviously wasn't him.

But how could he expect Cassia to love him? She'd
just learned that he'd duped her into marriage. If only
she would give him time, time to show her that he
hadn't done it to hurt her, that he'd only wanted to
help her and protect her. But Rolfe knew he couldn't
force Cassia to love him. It hadn't succeeded with
Daphne. And it wouldn't succeed with Cassia now.

Rolfe stood. Mara was right. History was repeating
itself. And he was powerless to do anything but watch.

"If an annulment to this marriage is what you truly
want, then I will not make any attempt to stop you."

Cassia sat in her bedchamber alone, legs curled beneath her, resting her chin on her knees. Why did
everything have to be so difficult? Rolfe's explanation
of why he had married her seemed plausible—actually,
it sounded almost too good to be true. Selflessness
was not something to which she was accustomed. All
her life, everyone close to her had acted only for their

own benefit. Her mother had used her as a tool against her father. Her father had tried to use her as a means of gaining power through his attempts at marrying her off to the highest bidder.

Never had anyone done anything for her alone.

Except Rolfe.

Over and over he assured her that that was all he wanted. Rolfe was her protector, her savior, and now he was her husband. Yet she continued to fight him, to refuse his help at every turn.

Could she believe him? Dare she? Cassia closed her eyes and tried to find the answers. No matter how much she tried to tell herself differently, she needed Rolfe's help to find out who had killed her father, who was trying to kill her, and why. Her father's cryptic note hadn't been much help. All it had done was leave her racking her brains, trying to figure out where this mysterious document was. She could spend the rest of eternity trying to figure that out and still never find it.

Cassia stood and walked over to the bed, sliding beneath the thick coverlet. As she laid her head against the mound of pillows, she remembered how she'd listened to Rolfe's voice when she'd been ill, how she'd clung to it, fighting to live only on the strength of his words and the touch of his hand holding hers.

She thought of the day they'd gone riding in Hyde Park, of the need that had filled her when he'd kissed her, overpowering her. She'd wanted to be his that day, completely. She'd wanted Rolfe to take her there in the midst of that wood and forever mark her as his own. The touch of his hands, the feel of his mouth on her body had filled her with pleasure and excitement and joy. She wanted to feel that way again. She wanted to take him fully into herself, hold him against her, and never let go.

Cassia realized that she wanted all that and more. Much, much more. She wanted Rolfe to be there to share both happiness and tears. She wanted to know that he'd always be with her.

Cassia closed her eyes. She wanted to spend the rest of her life with him. That was her last thought as she drifted off to sleep.

Chapter Twenty-five

Rolfe sat in the shadows of his bedchamber. There was no candle or fire to light the room, just the moonlight that peeked in through the heavy damask curtain, half opened against the window. He was slumped in a chair with his legs stretched out their full length and crossed at the ankles in front of him. He was staring at the moon, contemplating the misery he felt at having once again fallen in love with a woman who would never return his affections.

Rolfe had just told himself what a fool he was for having been so monumentally stupid a second time when he first heard Cassia's scream. He was out the door in a second, running down the hallway, knowing even before he'd gotten there that it was another damned nightmare.

He could hear her inside as he came to her door, louder now, begging the demons of her sleep to leave her be.

Rolfe threw open the door. In the guttering candlelight, he could see Cassia sitting upright, her hands opened flat in front of her to wield off her unseen attacker.

"No ... please ..."

Rolfe strode across the room and took Cassia firmly by her shoulders, shaking her. "Cassia, wake up. It's only a dream. You are safe now."

Her sketching papers and pencils were lying on the bedside table beside the bed. An idea came to him and he grabbed them up as Cassia started to come out of her nightmare.

"He was there," she said, her voice sleep-slurred. "He killed my father."

"No," Rolfe said, shoving the papers and pencil toward her, "don't talk. Don't say another word. Draw. Draw what you saw in your dream."

Cassia looked at him, confused, still dazed from her sleep, then lifted up the pencil and began moving it across the vellum page. Soon her hand was flying over the sheet as if being directed by an invisible force, scratching lines and curves in a desperate race against time to record the images that were locked in her mind.

Rolfe sat and waited.

When Cassia finished a short time later, she set the pencil down and pushed the drawing toward him. She fell back on the bed, exhausted.

Rolfe lifted it up.

"What is it?" she asked, now fully awake. She brushed back a lock of hair that fell into her eyes. "Is there anything there?"

Rolfe was silent for some time as he stared at the drawing. He did not speak, just studied the drawing, his eyes narrowed intently. Finally he looked at her and there was a strange light in his eyes. "Cassia, do you know anything about your father's activities during the wars?"

"No, how could I possibly know that? I was in France with my mother. I was too young to know what was going on at all. If my parents communicated, which I would tend to doubt, I was never made aware of it. Why do you ask?"

Rolfe looked at the drawing. "What you have drawn

here is not simply a picture, but a series of images. This seems to be your father's walking stick. There is a gloved hand holding a knife which I assume was the knife used to murder your father. And," he added, now showing her the last image she'd drawn, "there is a picture of a sprig of the hemlock plant."

Cassia glanced at the drawing in the candlelight. "I do not understand the significance. What is so extraordinary about a picture of a hemlock plant? I didn't even know that was what that was; it is simply a design that is engraved on my father's watch casing."

Rolfe looked at her. "Where is this watch, Cassia?"

"It is at Seagrave House with his other belongings. Geoffrey had asked for it and I had planned to give it to him as a sort of peace offering after having learned from Mr. Finchley of my father's petition. I thought it was the least I could do, given the end result. That was before you told me your suspicions about him."

Rolfe sat forward. "You say Geoffrey wanted this watch? Was there anything else he asked for, or just the watch specifically?"

Cassia shook her head. "No nothing else. He was quite specific in his inquiry about the watch. It was that day he threatened me, when you came in the study. He was most agitated."

"Yes, he was." Rolfe glanced at the tall case clock that stood across the room. "It is too late to go to Seagrave House now to retrieve the watch. We will have to wait until morning."

He stood up from the bed.

"Rolfe, what is it? Why does this watch have any importance?"

"The watch doesn't, but the engraving on it does." He turned to face her. "Cassia, have you ever heard of the 'Regicides'?"

She thought for a moment. "They were the men who were responsible for bringing the charges against King Charles I. They signed their names to his death warrant and brought about his execution."

"Yes. But it has since been learned that some of the men who signed their names to that warrant were not really the Regicides, the men responsible for Charles I's death. These men were coerced, forced to sign their names to that warrant by Cromwell, so they would be the ones held accountable in place of the true Regicides. Cromwell knew, if ever the heir should return to the throne, the penalty for having signed that warrant would be death. King Charles II learned the truth, that the men whose names appeared on the warrant had been forced, set to look like they were the Regicides, when in fact they really weren't. But by that time, nine innocent men had lost their lives, executed for a crime they hadn't committed. The true Regicides, the ones who were too cowardly to sign their names to that damnable warrant, faded into obscurity, but remained bound together in a secret sort of society."

Rolfe paused a moment, watching Cassia. "The symbol of these men, the real Regicides, is the hemlock plant."

Cassia stared at the drawing. "My father was never without that watch. He even had it secured with a red ribbon to his clothing so it wouldn't be lost."

"And the red ribbon is said to signify the king's beheading."

Cassia couldn't believe what she was hearing. "You are saying my father was one of these men? My father was one of these terrible Regicides?"

"I will need to see the watch casing to be sure, but it would seem so. How this ties in with his death, I do not know. I am curious, though, as to why Geoffrey was so interested in the watch."

"Surely Geoffrey himself would have been too young to have been a member of the Regicides."

Rolfe nodded. "But he could have known of your father's involvement and thought to profit by it." He stood. "There's no use getting ourselves excited over something we don't even know is certain yet. And we won't know anything more until morning. There is no use staying up all night speculating on it, either, so why don't you try to get some sleep now. You must be exhausted. In the morning, you and I will go to Seagrave House and retrieve the watch."

He started for the door.

"Rolfe."

Cassia was staring a him when he turned back to face her.

"Please, don't go." She hesitated. "Stay with me."

Rolfe could see the fear shimmering in her dark eyes in the candlelight. He knew if he left her alone, she'd spend the rest of the night pacing the floorboards rather than chance the recurrence of her nightmare.

He walked slowly to the bed and sat down beside her. Silently he drew her into his arms. Cassia was asleep in minutes. With her head tucked under his chin, her cheek resting softly against his chest, Rolfe sat back against the pillows, staring into the darkness and waiting for morning to come.

When they arrived at Seagrave House the following day, they found the front door standing open. Inside, on their hands and knees among a litter of books, papers, and various small decorative objects in her father's study, were Clydesworthe and Lynette, employed in the task of cleaning up the mess.

"What happened here?"

Clydesworthe quickly got to his feet. "My lord, Lady Cassia. We found the room like this when we woke up this morning. It appears as if someone broke in here last night and did this damage. I was in my room sleeping, as were the others. No one heard a sound all night."

It looked as if a tempest had blown through the room, throwing everything into chaos. Pages had been torn from books. Drawers stood open, their contents strewn about. Even the rug had been pulled back, exposing the bare floor, as if someone had planned to begin ripping up the polished boards underneath.

"Is anything missing?" Rolfe said, taking Cassia by the hand to lead her away from the tiny shattered bits of what had once been a porcelain vase.

"We haven't yet been able to take an inventory, my lord," Clydesworthe said. "We decided it would be best to make some order of the room first."

"Good thinking." Rolfe looked at Cassia. "The watch. I would guess it was in this room?"

She nodded. "I had put it away until I could give it to Geoffrey, and then after you told me your suspicions of him, I just forgot about it."

She went to the hearth and removed a small decorated gilt box there. It stood untouched, odd, given the havoc that surrounded it.

It was no surprise to either Rolfe or Cassia when the box was found empty.

"What will we do now?" Cassia asked. She looked around blankly at the ruin.

"It is quite simple, my dear. We have been invited to attend an intimate gathering at the apartments of Lady Castlemaine tomorrow evening. No doubt, given their recent connection, Geoffrey will be there. You and I will attend this soiree and we will simply ask

Cousin Geoffrey if he knows where your father's watch is."

"Goodness," Mara said, looking up from her breakfast to see Cassia and Rolfe standing in the doorway across the room. She immediately noticed that they were dressed and had already been out. "You two must have been up with the sun. Wherever did you go at so early an hour?"

Rolfe removed his gloves, slapping them on the table. "We went to Seagrave House, where, it seems, someone decided to take advantage of our absence and break in."

"Good heavens, was anything taken?"

"My father's watch seems to be the only thing missing," Cassia said, lowering herself into the chair beside Mara. She smiled in thanks as the footman poured her a cup of tea.

"Cassia and I will be leaving today," Rolfe said abruptly.

"Leaving?" Hadrian replied. "For where?"

"We will be returning to Seagrave House."

"Didn't you just say that someone broke inside that same place? Isn't that putting you both in a bit of danger?"

Rolfe took a biscuit from the side table and ripped off a good-sized piece of it. "It is more dangerous leaving the house vacant. We still haven't located the document Seagrave wrote to Cassia about. Who is to say the thief wasn't looking for it as well?"

"Why don't you leave Cassia here with us, then?" Mara asked. "No one knows she is here. She will remain safe with us."

"If she would prefer—"

"Perhaps Cassia would prefer to return to her home now," Cassia said, to remind her husband and friends that she was indeed still in the room with them. She turned to Mara. "I am most grateful for your kind hospitality. You have made me feel more than welcome here. Please do not think I am being unappreciative."

Mara smiled, patting her hand. "It is all right. You need not explain. The time has come for you to go home. I have felt the same way myself on occasion. Just always know you have a place here should you wish it."

"Thank you."

"It is settled, then," Rolfe said. "We will leave today. I'll see about having our things packed so we can be back at Seagrave House by evening."

It was late that night when they finally had settled back in at Seagrave House. Cassia retired early, not more than an hour after supper, saying she was tired and anxious to be back in the familiarity of her own bed again. The study was once again neat and ordered, owing to the assiduous attention of Clydesworthe. A few miscellaneous objects had been destroyed in the thief's desperate search, but no one would miss them.

Rolfe had moved from his pallet outside Cassia's chamber to a spacious and elegant bedchamber with oak-paneled walls and a carved plaster ceiling. The room looked as if it had never been used, just dusted and aired periodically.

Cassia told him this particular room was reserved for guests, which they'd never had during the three years she'd been back in England. It was just two doors down from her own bedchamber and situated so that should anyone attempt to sneak up the stairs, the intruder would have to pass by Rolfe before ever reaching Cassia.

He lay on the bed atop a blue velvet coverlet, wearing only his breeches. It was quiet in the house, being so late an hour, and the servants had all retired for the night. As he lay there in the still silence, the fire in the hearth throwing shadows across the ceiling and walls, his mind played over his plans for the following evening.

Geoffrey had to be the one who had taken the watch. Who else would have known of its existence, and known where to find it? This made Rolfe wonder. Why had he been so desperate to get the watch, especially now that Seagrave was dead?

A floorboard in the hall outside his chamber suddenly creaked. In an instant Rolfe felt the familiar sense of danger, the same sense he'd relied on during the wars that had saved him more than once from filling an early grave. From where he sat on the bed, he had a plain view of the doorway. He sat very still as he heard the second creak, this time just outside the door.

Rolfe stood, grabbed the pistol Hadrian had pressed upon him earlier that day, and moved soundlessly to the side of the doorway. The door was ajar, though not far enough to allow anyone to slip inside. He stood off in the shadows, ready to spring.

He watched in the low firelight as the door moved slowly inward. His heart was pounding in his chest and he could make out the barest outline of the intruder as he came through the door. Rolfe waited until he was completely inside before lowering the barrel of the pistol on him to take aim.

"Do not move, you bloody bastard, or I will blow a hole straight through you."

The body stiffened.

"Rolfe, it's me."

Rolfe dropped his arm to his side. "Cassia? Bloody hell! What are you doing coming into my room like

that in the middle of the night? I nearly shot you."
Then, as his anger at her lessened, he added, "Is something wrong?"

He strode across the room and opened the draperies, allowing in the moonlight from outside. He moved to the fire and lit a branch of candles. He turned to see Cassia standing in the middle of the room, wearing her night rail, nothing more, her hair in waves down her back. She was looking down at her bare toes.

"I couldn't sleep. I . . ."

And suddenly he knew why she had come. Perhaps if she had come in with trumpets blaring he'd have figured it out sooner, idiot that he was. She was telling him she was ready to be his wife. Completely. In every sense. He came before her in two strides. She looked up at him and he could see that she was feeling awkward, unsure of what she should do, what she should say. She was teetering on the edge of her uncertainty, questioning whether she had done the right thing in coming to him.

Rolfe quickly gave her the answer to her question.

He swept Cassia up and into his arms and carried her across the room to the bed. Cassia did not speak, she barely moved an inch from where he'd laid her, but her eyes told of the emotions that were running rampant through her.

"It will be all right, Cassia. You were right in coming to me."

Rolfe came down beside her on the bed, staring down at her in the moonlight. He lowered his head, cupping the side of her face with his hand as he kissed her.

Rolfe could feel Cassia begin to ease, and it wasn't long before she relaxed, becoming used to him.

"I won't hurt you, Cassia," he said, pulling his mouth away and brushing his lips against her forehead. "I will never hurt you."

That was all the assurance Cassia needed. She lifted her hands and reached around his neck, pulling his mouth back down to hers. She met his kiss eagerly with her own, running her tongue tentatively against his, twisting her fingers through the hair at the nape of his neck when he groaned slightly into her mouth.

It was everything she'd ever dreamed it could be and more, Cassia thought as she released a breath. She threw back her head, marveling in the feel of his mouth as he kissed her on her neck, her throat, softly biting at the curve of her shoulder. She felt him pulling at her night rail, releasing the ribbon ties to expose her breasts beneath the soft fabric.

Rolfe cupped her breast with his hand and gently rubbed his thumb over her nipple, teasing it to pebble hardness. Cassia gasped as a shock of pure pleasure coursed through her. She arched her back upward, wanting more. She nearly cried out when Rolfe closed his mouth over her, suckling her nipple, pulling at her, teasing her sensitive flesh with his lips and tongue and teeth. She felt as if she were beginning to soar to the heavens and clutched at the velvet coverlet as tremor after tremor came through her body.

She never wanted it to end.

Rolfe moved his mouth lower, pushing aside the folds of her night rail as he kissed a path over her stomach and even lower still. In a whisk of white linen, he slid the garment off her. It was then Cassia realized she was naked before him.

While she would have thought she would have been embarrassed to be thus before a man's eyes, open and uncovered, and would feel the natural urge to cover herself with her hands, she couldn't help but admit to feeling excited by the fire she saw burning in Rolfe's eyes. He looked down at her in the moonlight. He stood, never taking his eyes from hers. He unfastened his breeches, pulling them off, and tossed them away. Only then did Cassia tear her eyes from his to look over the solid length of his body.

He was even more magnificent to behold than the night she'd seen him, looking like a statue, standing in the tub in the Green Chamber, pouring water over his body. His body was beautifully outlined in the firelight above her. His chest was covered with a thatch of black hair that tapered down in a line to the muscles of his belly, muscles that rippled in the firelight when he moved.

Cassia's eyes moved even lower, stopping at his erect sex. She took in a slow breath.

"There is nothing to be afraid of, Cassia. I promise you I will not hurt you."

She was still staring at him, the size of him, and her fear must have shown vividly in her eyes.

"Look at me, Cassia. Look at my eyes."

She glanced up at him.

"I want to be with you. I ache for you. I want you so badly, but if you are not ready for this yet—"

"No," she whispered, "I am ready."

Cassia held her arms out to him and closed her eyes as Rolfe lowered himself over her.

His mouth claimed hers again, hungrily this time, moving with measured desperation. His hand was on her breast, rolling her nipple between her thumb and forefinger, sending waves of pleasure through her. Cassia felt a sudden urgency that centered between her legs. The heat of it caused her to instinctively press her hips upward against his. The rock hardness of his sex nearly drove her to the edge of distraction and she was taken over by the desperate need to feel him inside her.

"Please, Rolfe . . ."

Rolfe ran his hand downward over her flat belly to

the nest of dark curls that lay between her legs. He pressed one finger against the sensitive flesh there, causing Cassia to buck upward. She was breathing heavily now and she cried out when she felt his finger move even lower, sliding along the slick, hot center of her.

He began to move his finger in a circular motion and the feelings inside of her seemed to mass together, ascending upward toward something she couldn't define, but somehow knew she must have.

The movements came faster, unrelenting, rhythmic, persistent, and Cassia was clenching her fingers into Rolfe's hair, tightening the muscles in her legs against the sensations pulsing through her. She was panting, gasping out his name as she came nearer and nearer to that unknown peak. She screamed as it came upon her in a burst of magnificent release.

"Oh, Rolfe . . ."

Cassia fell back on the bed. Every muscle that had been taut was now relaxed and weak. She was breathless, strengthless, filled with awe. She could only wonder at the all-consuming climax that was still rolling through her.

Rolfe raised himself over Cassia and moved slowly between her legs. He lifted her legs, bending them at the knees. Cassia placed her hands on his shoulders as he lowered himself over her.

In a single powerful thrust, Rolfe joined their bodies as one.

A sharp pain pierced through Cassia. Without thinking, she cried out.

"Bloody hell," Rolfe said, poised above her. He stared down at her in the moonlight. "Dear God, Cassia, why didn't you tell me?"

He began to shudder and pulled himself back, instantly thrusting into her again. He lost all control. Over and over he came into her. His arms were straight and stiff at his sides, his eyes clenched tightly shut. Cassia squeezed her fingers over his forearms, taking all he gave her, for after that first startling pain, she reveled in the feel of him, the size of him moving inside her, filling her completely, making them one. It was unlike anything she'd ever imagined.

He was pounding into her hard and fast, his breathing labored, and with one final thrust he buried himself completely within her.

"Cassia . . ."

His seed was spilling deep inside her, and Cassia knew a powerful sense of satisfaction.

Rolfe gathered Cassia into his arms and pulled her against him, crushing her to his chest. She wrapped her arms tightly around his neck.

They lay there, bound together for several long moments. Cassia was lost in wonder, breathless and in awe at the incredible sensations that had come upon her so unexpectedly, taking her higher than the stars and filling her with a feeling of utter completion.

Finally Rolfe released her. And Cassia lay back on the coverlet. When she looked at him beside her, she saw that his eyes were filled with concern—and regret.

"I am so sorry, Cassia."

"Whatever for?" she asked, touching her hand softly to the side of his face.

"I promised you I wouldn't hurt you and I did. I never thought . . . would never have imagined . . . damnation, Cassia, why didn't you tell me you were still a virgin?"

She refused to allow him to regret the wonderful thing they'd just shared together. "It no longer matters, Rolfe."

"But, why? The rumors. About you. About him. Why didn't you deny them—"

"That I was the king's mistress? Why would I do

something like that when I am the one who invented the tale?"

Rolfe's eyes were filled with disbelief. "Why would you do such a thing?"

"There is a certain advantage to being thought of as one of the king's kept women. A girl need not worry about unwanted attentions from certain men because most wouldn't dare attempt to seduce the king's mistress. Since I was an heiress and was thought of only for my monetary worth, being thought of as the king's whore was preferable to being pursued day and night by men who only wanted me for the dower I could bring them."

Rolfe could only stare at her. "But the king? Why would he play along with such a lie?"

"Because I had asked him to. He didn't want to—in fact, he nearly refused me at first—but I really gave him little choice. You see, he owed me a great favor and I simply delivered him his due notice."

"What could the king possibly owe you?"

Cassia smiled. "Do you remember when I told you about how, not long after Catherine's arrival in England, she and the king had a public disagreement over his request that she accept Barbara Palmer as a Lady of the Bedchamber?"

Rolfe nodded. "From what I understand, she was adamant in her stand against it, outraged at the mere suggestion of it. Oddly, though, soon after, she changed her mind."

"I was the one who convinced the queen to allow the appointment of Lady Castlemaine to pass."

"But I thought Catherine was your friend."

"She is. I care for her deeply, too deeply to sit idly by and watch her lose what she had rightfully earned. I did it to protect her, you see. You must understand, Their Majesties were well on their way to annulment over this one little thing. Catherine was most stubborn in refusing the appointment. Her mother is very overbearing and convinced her she must force Charles to mend his wandering ways."

"Not a likely possibility for a man like Charles."

"Exactly. In addition to this, the king was equally stubborn in insisting upon Lady Castlemaine's appointment. It came down to a matter of wills, and each of them, the king and the queen, were most determined to win. I simply explained to Catherine that she would be far better served if she would allow this one bitter appointment to pass, reminding her over and over again that no matter what Lady Castlemaine did, no matter how she tried to wheedle the king, she would never be the Queen of England, and therefore would never have the advantages of it."

Rolfe shook his head. "I have married myself to a remarkable woman."

Cassia smiled. "And don't ever forget it."

Rolfe moved beside her, pulling her against him. That was the one thing in his life he'd never forget, for it was the wisest thing he'd ever done.

As he watched Cassia slowly drift off to sleep, Rolfe thought about all the things she had been through in her life, all the terrible unpleasantness she had been forced to live through. All her life Cassia had spent her days running from something, and she'd overcome it all, the public scandal of her mother and the private abuse of her father, using her sharp wits and her inner strength.

Sitting there in the darkness, with her body soft and curved against his, Rolfe watched her as she slept. No one should have to live in such constant fear. He made a vow, a solemn promise to Cassia that she would never have to fear, never need to run from her life again.

And then Rolfe closed his eyes and fell asleep.

Chapter Twenty-six

Cassia opened her eyes, and immediately realized she was not in her bed, in her own chamber, but was lying beneath the warm thick coverlet on Rolfe's bed.

It hadn't been a dream.

She rolled over onto her back and stretched her arms high over her head, having just experienced the deepest, most peaceful sleep she could ever remember having without the assistance of a laudanum bottle.

And there had been no nightmares this time.

As Cassia thought back on it, she didn't know what had possessed her the previous evening, to walk all that way, two doorways down from her own, coming to Rolfe's chamber wearing only her night rail. It must have been madness. An inexplicable delerium. Whatever it had been, it was most definitely a headier dose than the laudanum she'd taken before he'd come into her life.

Cassia had known even before facing Rolfe why she had gone there. It was something she'd wanted, ever since that day in Hyde Park, but hadn't had the courage to do. All that time she'd wasted, trying to deny her feelings for him, adhering to her stand never to marry. It had almost made her lose him forever.

Cassia wasn't exactly certain when she realized she'd been a fool. It was after they'd talked the day she'd returned from Whitehall, after Rolfe had asked her point-blank what her plans for the future were. It had taken a little time afterward for her to come to the conclusion that whatever she did, whatever course her life would take, the one thing she knew was she wanted Rolfe to be in it.

Cassia slid her legs over the side of the bed. Sitting at the edge, she noticed the bloody splotches on the bedsheet beneath where she'd been lying. She remembered how startled Rolfe had been, how utterly disbelieving when he'd learned she'd still been a virgin.

And she remembered how he'd told her how sorry he was for having hurt her.

He hadn't hurt her, not really; she'd known that there would be pain the first time a man entered her body. For all her neglect and avoidance of parental responsibility, that was the one thing her mother had told her. Cassia just hadn't been prepared for the suddenness of it. It had startled her, that feeling of being completely filled by him, and she had cried out without thinking.

But Rolfe had cared enough to apologize for it, this one small bit of pain that all women were made to suffer—"the Punishment of Eve," her mother had called it—even though Rolfe had no power to make it any different.

What he did have control over, and what she'd never been told of, or prepared for at all, was the wonderful gift he'd given her that moment before he'd joined their bodies as one. She could still remember how it had felt, as if her body had been lifted upward and out of itself. She'd felt things, sensations she'd never had before, feelings only he could give her. It was unlike anything she could have imagined and Cassia now understood why so many writers and poets filled line after line with tribute to it, this wondrous thing called love.

Love. At the thought of that word, Cassia returned to the present. What exactly was love, besides a mere word? If what she had experienced, and what she still felt in the light of morning, could actually be labeled by a single word, surely it should be a more significant word than just those four letters.

Was love wanting to share things, intimate secrets and dreams and wishes with him, things you would never dare admit to anyone else? Was it the sense of safety, of utter peace and freedom you felt when you were held in that person's arms? For if it was, if this was what love consisted of, it was surely how she felt with Rolfe, and how she'd never felt with anyone else in her life.

Cassia thought of Mara and Hadrian, of the looks the two of them would exchange as if they were speaking volumes without having ever uttered a word. If all this and more went into that one little word, then, Cassia thought to herself, smiling widely . . . then she was most definitely in love with Rolfe.

It was thus that Rolfe found her when he came to the doorway: sitting there on the edge of the bed, feet dangling just above the floor, that whimsical smile reaching out to him and filling him with more warmth than he'd felt in a long, long time.

He never wanted it to end.

"Good morning, Cassia."

She looked over to him. She never lost that happy smile. "Good morning."

Rolfe came into the room. "Is everything all right? Are you ill—or hurt?"

"Do I look ill or at all in pain with this smile on my face? No, I was just sitting here thinking about things."

She stood, rose up on her toes, and kissed him gently on the cheek.

"What was that for?"

"For not shooting me last night." She slanted him a playful glance, adding, "Among other things."

Rolfe pulled Cassia into his arms and kissed her. He kissed her as a husband would kiss his wife. She was no longer stiff and cold in his arms. She was open to him, giving herself willingly, pressing against him, and returning his kiss with a passion that left him rock hard, taking heavy breaths, and wanting nothing more than to throw her back on the bed and make love to her again.

"If we continue along this vein, we won't see civilization until well after midday."

"I wouldn't mind. . . ." She nibbled at his ear.

It took every ounce of willpower Rolfe possessed to set Cassia back from him. "Believe me when I say, madam, that I would love nothing more than to return with you beneath the bedcovers and resume exploring this particular venue all day, but there is still the matter of proving your innocence. It is my duty to bring that matter to an end, a duty I cannot abandon."

"Always duty," Cassia said.

"Always duty," Rolfe replied.

When Cassia and Rolfe arrived at Whitehall that evening, they did not alight from the hackney coach before the palace gates. They went in through a side entrance near the Holbein Gate, one that would lead them more quickly to Lady Castelemaine's apartments.

A footman bearing a candle stood waiting for them inside.

"Good evening, my lord, my lady. Please follow me."

The footman opened one of the doors onto a room that was obscured by darkness. The faint sound of laughter and low discussion could be heard coming from another room that was farther inside. Rolfe and Cassia followed the footman as he led them through a series of dark rooms and hallways until they came to one final closed door. There awaited another footman, who at their arrival threw open the door and announced them to the assembly.

Their hostess was waiting for them at the door. "Good evening, my friends. I am so pleased you were able to come. Please, give the footman your cloaks and come in to join the others."

They followed Lady Castlemaine into a large and spacious dining room, at the center of which was a long table that, at first glance, looked as if it could have easily seated fifty. Most of the others were so engrossed in conversation, they hardly gave their arrival notice. A small orchestra was set up in the corner, playing softly. No one seemed to notice. Most were too busy eating and drinking, or losing their guineas at the gaming tables, to pay the musicians any mind. Lying on the floor, on a mound of pillows, was Barbara Palmer's underling, Lord Talbot, his round belly straining at the fastenings of his waistcoat as two young ladies on each side of him fed him morsels of fruit.

Lady Castlemaine led Rolfe and Cassia to the far side of the dining table where two seats across from one another sat empty, seemingly for them.

"Cassia, you sit here," Barbara said, directing her to the first chair, "And you," she continued to Rolfe, eyes twinkling in the candlelight, "come with me."

She took Rolfe around the end of the table and sat him across from Cassia, beside a stunning blond.

"I believe you are acquainted with Daphne, are you not, Lord Ravenscroft?" Barbara giggled, adding, "Excuse me, but it isn't Lord Ravenscroft any longer, is it? Having married Cassia, it is now the Marquess of Seagrave. My, how you have scaled the social ladder."

Cassia noticed Rolfe didn't respond to that final comment. "I am already acquainted with Lady Westcott."

Barbara smiled. "Of course you are."

For having made the lady's acquaintance, Rolfe seemed none too pleased at being placed beside her, but he really had no other choice. Cassia was displeased that the seating arrangements would give them little opportunity to discuss their reasons for being there.

The room was growing noisy, as some of the guests had left the table to pursue outside amusements. Cassia spotted the king's latest and most unyielding interest, Frances Stuart, sitting at a small side table, building a house of cards. She was surrounded by a trio of laughing men who were making wagers as to how high she could build the unsteady model before it came tumbling down. Their cheers rose to a rallying crescendo when she finally placed the last card of the deck successfully at the top.

The three men turned. Cassia recognized Geoffrey and Malcolm, the Duke of Manton's son, among them.

Geoffrey was the first to notice her.

"Cassia! Good God—you are the last person I would have expected to see here."

Rolfe was at her side in a second's time. "Why is that, Montefort?"

Geoffrey's gay expression vanished the moment he noticed Rolfe. "I see you are here as well."

"Being the lady's husband, one would expect that I would."

"Oh, yes, I had heard rumors to that effect, though, I must admit, at the time I believed them false. From your presence here tonight, I would say I had been wrong in my assumption."

"Quite."

There was a moment of awkward silence. Geoffrey extended his hand. "Well, then, allow me to offer my congratulations."

Rolfe shook his hand.

"And I, as well, would like to offer my congratulations," said Malcolm, coming forward to take Cassia's hand. He pressed a kiss to it—not on the back of her hand, but on her open palm—a kiss that most would have thought too familiar.

"I hope there aren't any feelings of ill will, Newbury," Rolfe said.

Malcolm smiled a rather treacherous smile. "Not at all. Cassia could have been my bride, but we just didn't suit. Nothing to spend the rest of my days brooding over. I wish her all the happiness she deserves."

Perhaps it was the way his eyes seemed to twitch when he'd spoken, but somehow, Cassia wasn't convinced.

"Cassia!"

Cordelia came forward, dressed in shades that ran from light peach to bright orange. "I was beginning to get worried about you. I had gone to Seagrave House to see you, but you weren't there and Clydesworthe wouldn't tell me where you'd gone. Stubborn sod, he is. He looked most agitated and told me that someone had broken into the house during the night. Is this true?"

Cassia nodded. "My father's study was ransacked."

"Oh, how terrible."

"Was anything taken?" Geoffrey asked, quickly entering the conversation.

"Yes," Rolfe broke in, "as a matter of fact, something was. It was Seagrave's pocket watch, the same one you had previously expressed a fondness for."

Geoffrey's face reddened. "If you're implying—"

"Oh, I never imply, Geoffrey. I was simply noticing how curious it is, the coincidence of you having asked after the watch and then it being stolen, especially when there were other items in that room far more valuable."

Geoffrey narrowed his eyes dangerously. "I ought to call you out for that insult, Ravenscroft."

"Have you forgotten, Geoffrey? By my marriage to Cassia, I am now the Marquess of Seagrave. And should you decide to make good on that threat, I'd be more than willing to name my seconds."

The two men stared at each other. Cassia held her breath. Dueling was serious business, and from the few occasions when she'd seen Rolfe brandish his rapier, she guessed he'd be more than formidable as an opponent.

Geoffrey quickly gathered the same.

"Some other time," he muttered, turning.

"I'll wait," said Rolfe.

They stood and watched as Geoffrey and Malcolm beat a swift retreat.

Cordelia poked Rolfe in the ribs. "You naughty boy, you frightened him so badly there was a white streak going all the way down his back. At least Geoffrey was smart enough not to issue the challenge. You'd have stuck him like a pig without blinking an eye." She turned to Cassia. "Now, what's this I hear about how you've gotten yourself married to this man? Here I thought the two of you couldn't stand the sight of each other, and suddenly Rolfe comes to tell me you've wed."

Cassia smiled, slanting Rolfe a glance. "His proposal was just too tempting to be refused."

Cordelia stared at them. "I knew there was something going on between you. It was like a flame, albeit a flashing one, that seemed to ignite whenever you were together. Just like me and Percy."

She stared off in the distance as if trying to mentally summon him forth.

"I should someday like to meet this incredible Percival," Rolfe whispered to Cassia.

"He is a man most definitely not to be believed," Cassia said.

Cordelia hugged Cassia first, then Rolfe. "Now, everything is just perfect, if only my husband could be here."

Cassia patted her friend's hand. "He will be coming home soon."

"Do you really think so?"

"I am certain of it. Somehow, the two of us will find a way to bring him home."

It was then Rolfe noticed Geoffrey making his way steadily toward the door. He was alone and seemed to be in a bit of a hurry.

"It appears your cousin has another engagement," he said. "If you will be all right here with Cordelia, I think I will follow him and see what he is about."

"Cassia will be fine," Cordelia said, all but pushing him away. "I won't take my eyes from her."

They waited until Rolfe was gone, then Cordelia took Cassia by the hand and led her across the room. They stopped at a table where an array of confectioneries had been set up. Cordelia popped a marzipan shaped like a lemon into her mouth. "I cannot abide Barbara Palmer, but she does entertain most splendidly, don't you think? She even has strawberries that were hothouse grown so they'd be at their sweetest during the off-season. Would you like me to get you some?"

"No, not really, but a glass of claret would be nice."

"I won't be but a moment."

Cordelia left Cassia and made her way for the drinks table. She was no sooner out of earshot than Cassia heard the distinctive swish of silk coming from behind, followed by a voice that dripped with sweetness.

"Now that I finally have you alone ..."

Chapter Twenty-seven

Cassia turned to see Lady Westcott, the woman Rolfe had been sitting beside, coming up behind her. She smiled. "It's Lady Westcott, isn't it?"

Daphne nodded. "Yes. And you are Cassia Montefort, Lady Seagrave. Actually, now it would be Cassia Brodrigan, wouldn't it—now that you have married Rolfe. I have heard much about you."

Cassia frowned. With Rolfe's unquestioning faith in her, it had become easy to forget that most still believed her a murderess. "Well, there is—"

"Please, there is no need to try to explain the rumors. I don't really care if you killed your father or not. From what I hear, he was quite a bastard. I simply wanted to meet the woman who Rolfe finally wed."

The woman's mocking tone and blunt words brought Cassia's defenses to the forefront. Cassia also noticed that for the second time in as many minutes, Lady Westcott had employed the use of her husband's given name.

"It would seem, Lady Westcott, that you are more than just recently acquainted with my husband. How is it that you know him?"

Husband. Cassia liked the way it sounded to say that word.

"I should say we are more than just acquainted with one another. Much more. Especially considering your husband had asked me to marry him just last year."

Of all the things this woman could have said to her, this was not one Cassia would have expected. In fact, she wasn't at all certain she'd heard her right. "Rolfe proposed to you?"

"Oh, yes, several times, actually. But, you see, I refused his proposal and married the man who is now my husband."

She looked across the room. Cassia followed her gaze to a man who was currently engaged in an intimate conversation with another young lady. It would appear Lord Westcott didn't hold much store by his marriage vows.

"Congratulations," Cassia replied.

"I might say the same for you, although it is Rolfe who must be congratulated on landing you for a wife, an heiress who brings him a title and a fortune, no less. It's really quite remarkable. I hear you've brought him eighty thousand pounds. He must be thinking his dreams have all come true."

Cassia was so busy trying to figure out why Rolfe would have ever wanted to wed a woman like Daphne, she barely heard her words. "Pardon me?"

"When Rolfe asked me to marry him, he was naught but a viscount with a shell of an estate in the north and not much in the way of monetary prospects. I brought a goodly dowry, a dowry that would have given him the money he needed, to elevate himself, you see. He was furious when I refused his proposal, for he had told everyone I would be his bride, his insurance. The king granted him the Ravenscroft title and his estate in Sussex not long after. That is when he left the court and the city. You have heard what he is called here at court, haven't you?"

"The Exiled Earl."

"Well, I was the one who sent him into exile."

Cassia could but wonder how this woman seemed proud of that distinction.

"Rolfe was devastated when I rejected his suit," Daphne went on. "He took himself off, rather than have to face everyone knowing I had refused him. In fact, I was surprised to see he had returned to London at all, but now I can see he had his reasons for doing so." She smiled at Cassia. "Rolfe managed to find himself an even bigger catch then I was."

Cassia simply stared, stone-faced. She didn't like this woman. Not at all.

Daphne took Cassia's silence as belief and fueled the fires of discord all the more. "Even after I refused his proposal, Rolfe told me that he would never love anyone as much as he did me. I see now that some things are more important to a man than love."

Cassia had finally had enough. "Well, I guess, then, it is I who should be thanking you, Lady Westcott. If you hadn't refused Rolfe's proposal, I would not be married to one of the most honorable men I've ever met. Some things, you see, are more important than money. I should think you would have learned that by now."

Daphne was too taken aback by Cassia's reaction to respond.

"Did you think I would believe you, Lady Westcott? I barely know you—in fact, I only just met you this evening." She threw a glance at Daphne's husband. "Appearances being what they are, I am more likely to believe that you are now regretting your decision to refuse Rolfe's suit."

Daphne's face turned red. She didn't respond. How could she?

"I thought as much," Cassia said, turning to leave.

She was three steps away when Daphne finally spoke up. "Has he ever told you he loved you?"

Cassia froze.

"Ah, I guess he hasn't. Rolfe used to recite poetry to me, you know, likening my eyes to periwinkle flowers. He vowed to die for me. He told me he could never love another woman more."

Cassia swallowed hard. She took a deep, measured breath. "It was interesting to make your acquaintance, Lady Westcott. I wish you well in your marriage."

Cassia started walking through the room, the faces around her becoming indistinct. Mara had said Rolfe had cared for Daphne deeply. Rolfe had told Daphne that he would never love another more. They were words Cassia had never heard him speak.

Cassia was nearly to the door when Rolfe came upon her. He took her arm.

"Cassia, where are you going?"

"I am tired. I am leaving to go home."

Rolfe knew instantly that there was something wrong. He'd seen her coming from the conversation with Daphne. He had no idea what could have transpired between them, but he was willing to wager it wasn't anything good.

The people standing nearby stopped talking and turned to stare at them, never bothering to disguise that they were attempting to listen to the conversation.

"What is wrong, Cassia?"

She forced a smile. "I told you. I am simply tired and I would like to go home."

Several of the people around them began to whisper.

"You are not going anywhere until you tell me what is bothering you."

Cassia stared at him. "Very well. I tried to avoid having this discussion out here in the open, but you, being a man and incapable of taking a hint, have forced me to go into this here and now. Why didn't you tell me that Lady Westcott was the first woman to whom you'd proposed marriage? I mean, you sat right next to her. I knew right away you knew her. I just never realized how well."

Rolfe didn't say another word. He wrapped his fingers around Cassia's upper arm and walked her slowly toward the door.

Once they were out of Lady Castlemaine's apartments, Rolfe finally spoke.

"I don't know what has suddenly caused you to take leave of your senses, madam, but I would like an explanation."

"You have not yet answered my question, my lord."

Rolfe suddenly thought of another conversation, a conversation very much like this one when he'd first met Cassia. He hadn't won that match, either.

"I will be happy to explain anything you wish to know. But we will not have this conversation here where the very walls have ears. We will talk, instead, in the coach."

Rolfe started through the palace hallways. When they were outside, Rolfe shouted to their coachman, who was waiting at the corner. He assisted Cassia inside, climbed in after her, and yanked the door shut.

"Drive!" he shouted to the driver, not caring where they went, only that they leave.

He turned toward Cassia. "Do you want to tell me what the bloody hell has gotten into you?"

"I just had a rather interesting conversation with Lady Westcott. She told me that you had once proposed marriage to her. I knew you had once asked another woman to marry you, but I didn't know who. Now I do."

"I did propose to Daphne, but that was a year ago. What does it matter now?"

"She also told me that you only wanted to marry her for her dowry."

"Is that so? Well, she was right about the wanting to marry for money, but she seems to have gotten the who of it mixed up. Daphne refused my proposal because she didn't think I was wealthy or titled highly enough for her. She could not see her way through to marrying a mere viscount without huge monetary resource and she was hoping Westcott would come to her with an offer, which he did."

Rolfe paused a moment, looking into her eyes. He continued. "Daphne had no way of knowing that just a few months later, the king was going to make me an earl and would give me a sizable estate. Whatever she said, I did not marry you for your inheritance, Cassia. I don't want it. Hell, I don't need it. If you like, I will be glad to take you to my solicitor and show you my financial records."

"That is not necessary. I told her it was ridiculous for her to tell me you married me for my inheritance. I know you are not interested in my money. I never questioned it."

"At least now you're talking sensibly."

"We've talked about so many things, Rolfe. I just can't help but wonder why you never told me about her, why I had to hear about her from someone else. I was unprepared when she came upon me like she just did."

Rolfe shook his head. "I am sorry, Cassia. I never set out to hide anything from you. That is a part of my life I prefer to forget ever happened. I should have expected you'd one day cross paths with her and that she would grab the opportunity to vent her spleen. Daphne has become a bitter woman because the man she thought would be the perfect catch for her has turned out to be no catch at all."

Cassia remembered seeing Daphne's husband with the other woman. She suddenly felt very much the fool. Still, something Daphne had said to her niggled at her brain.

Has he ever told you he loved you?

"Did you tell her that you would never love another woman as much as you loved her?"

"Yes, I did say that because, at the time, it was what I believed. That was before I saw Daphne with eyes that weren't clouded. That was before I saw beyond what she wanted me to see. You talked about people wearing many faces to hide their true one. Well, Daphne is the mistress at that sort of disguise. It wasn't until she laughed in my face when I'd gotten down on my knees to beg for her hand that her disguise became transparent."

He took Cassia's hand. "I told Daphne I loved her because I believed what I felt for her was love. That was before I knew what love truly was. That was before I found you."

Cassia was staring at him, silent.

"Did you hear what I said, Cassia? I said I love you. That is not an easy thing for me to admit. After Daphne, I vowed I would never allow a woman to have that much control over me again. I vowed I would keep a clear head, harden my heart, never to be so vulnerable again. But from the moment I saw you standing in the study atop the ladder that first day, I was lost. What I feel for you is something so much more than I ever felt for Daphne. I tried to deny it, even as I knew that every day I was with you, I came to love you more. Even as I knew that given your outspoken feelings for men and marriage, you would most probably never return my love."

When Cassia spoke again, it was so soft, Rolfe barely heard her. "One shouldn't assume what one does not really know."

Rolfe needed no further response. He pulled Cassia

onto his lap and took her mouth in a hungry, desperate kiss. He suddenly wanted to feel her in his arms, naked and open and willing. His fingers tugged at the strings at the back of her gown as he fought to loosen them.

"My lord," Cassia whispered into his ear, "can you not wait until we reach home?"

"No," he murmured, "I cannot wait another moment. I must have you. Now."

Rolfe loosened his breeches. He lifted Cassia over him. She knelt above him as he pushed away the layers of skirts, lowering her slowly over his erect sex.

Cassia's mouth fell open in a silent gasp, and she splayed her hands wide against Rolfe's chest as he filled her completely. She felt so tight around him, so delightfully ready and open. Rolfe held her against him for a long time, keeping her there, feeling her hold him. He reached up and pulled her mouth down to his, kissing her with abandon as his hand freed one breast from the bodice of her gown. He cupped the weight of it in his hand, teasing her nipple to hardness.

The rocking motion from the coach as it rolled over the cobblestone streets added a measure of excitement, setting the rhythm as Rolfe clutched Cassia's hips and lifted her upward before driving back into her. Cassia moved with Rolfe's thrusts, lifting her hips upward against him.

At first they moved slowly together, savoring each other, prolonging the magic. But soon their movements became faster, almost frantic, and when Rolfe finally grabbed Cassia and yanked her down, thrusting upward at the same time, Cassia cried out her release. Rolfe buried his face in her neck, groaning as his seed exploded deep inside her.

Rolfe trailed soft kisses along Cassia's neck and throat, holding her to him as if he never wanted to let her go. When he set her back from him, helping her onto the seat, he looked at her in the light of the coach lantern.

Her eyes were glazed with the passion they'd just shared. Her breasts were still bare beneath the folds of her cloak. Her lips were red and swollen from his kisses. She looked ravishing.

"It is amazing," he said.

"What is?"

"How much you affect me. I'm sitting here looking at you after what we've just shared, after just spilling my seed inside you, and I feel like I could take you again, right now."

Cassia smiled. "Well, unless you want to end up driving all over London, I would suggest you tell the coachman to take us to Seagrave House and quickly, where we can further pursue that line of thought."

Rolfe grinned at her, then yelled, "To Seagrave House, driver, and hurry!"

Their plans for that evening were not to be realized, for as soon as the coach pulled up before Seagrave House, another came around the corner, stopping just beside them.

"Rolfe, is that you?"

It was Dante.

"I've been waiting for nearly an hour. What the devil have you been doing?"

Cassia shot Rolfe a look that warned he'd better temper his tongue.

He smiled. "Our driver lost his way between here and the palace. We ended up driving through the countryside before we ever realized what was happening."

The fact that the Seagrave coachman had been directing them to and from Whitehall for quite some time never came to light.

"Dante, what happened after I asked you to follow Geoffrey?" Rolfe asked.

"He left Lady Castlemaine's apartments and went to Lord Seagrave's office. When I left to come here, he was in the process of trying to pick the lock on the door. If we hurry, we should still be able to catch him."

Rolfe threw open the coach door. "I think this would be the perfect time to question Geoffrey about his recent burgling habits."

"I want to go with you," Cassia said.

"No. You will be safer here. I will have Quigman stay inside until I return. We don't even know if Geoffrey is still at your father's office. And if he is, I cannot be certain of his state of mind. I don't want you placed in any further danger."

A small part of Cassia wanted to refuse, but she knew it would do her no good. She waited while Rolfe went to fetch Quigman, then stood there with him at the front of the house until the coach carrying Rolfe and Dante started down the street.

"Thank you, Quigman. I'm sorry his lordship had to take you from your bed."

The groom smiled. " 'Tis no trouble, my lady. Now let's get you into the house before you catch a chill. It's nasty out here."

There was only a single lit candle in the entrance hall when they went inside. Quigman locked the door and took his post on a chair just inside the entryway.

Knowing she would never be able to fall asleep until Rolfe returned, Cassia took up another candle, lit it, and went to the study to fetch a book.

"Aren't you going to bed now, my lady?"

"No, Quigman, I don't think I could sleep even if I wanted to. I want to wait for his lordship to return. I'm just going to get a book. It's all right."

She walked across the study to the shelf where she'd put the poetry books and novels. She placed the candle in an empty sconce and was just starting up the small ladder to fetch her favorite copy of one of Madame de Scudéry's novels when she heard the door to the study close behind her.

The next sound she heard was the key turning in the lock.

"Who is there?"

She could see the shape of someone standing near the door, but the light was too dim to make out who it was. Her heart instantly began to pound. Memories of the night her father had brought her here, locking the door in that very fashion, and standing in the shadows came rushing to her.

"If you attempt to scream, I will shoot you before the sound ever leaves your mouth."

It was a man's voice, oddly familiar.

"Who are you?" she asked.

The intruder walked out of the shadows, coming into the circle of light given off by Cassia's candle.

"Your Grace!"

The Duke of Manton stopped just before he reached her. The barrel of his pistol glimmered in the low light.

"Surprised to see me, Cassia?"

She was too stunned by his presence to answer.

"Ah, but you and I, we have been in this same room before, haven't we? Of course you wouldn't remember it very well, being that your bastard of a father had beaten you unconscious. Now come down off that ladder."

Cassia did as she was told, stopping when she had her feet back on the floor again. "You killed my father."

The duke put the pistol inside his coat. "You should

thank me after what he did to you that night. None of that would have happened, you know, if you would have just married Malcolm like we wanted. You wouldn't have been beaten. Your father would still be alive. And I wouldn't be forced to kill you now."

"Why?"

"Your father has something, something I want, which is why I haven't killed you—yet. He left you a letter telling you about it. I want that document, Cassia. You are going to give it to me."

How had he heard about her father's letter? Cassia tried to evade him. "I don't know what you mean."

The duke reached out and grabbed her, shaking her. "Don't play your little games with me, Cassia. I want the document your father left you, the one he told you about in that letter, and I want it now."

Cassia tried to pull away. "I don't have the document. I was never able to find it."

"Liar!"

The duke pulled his arm back, clenching his hand in a fist, readying to strike her. Cassia closed her eyes, preparing herself for the blow.

That blow never came.

"Release her, you bastard!"

Rolfe was suddenly there, springing from the shadows. He grabbed the duke by his arm and swung him around. He yanked him forward, smashing his fist into the duke's face. The duke fell back, then reached inside his coat.

"Rolfe, he has a gun!"

Rolfe grabbed something. She watched as Rolfe swung it at the duke's arm. There was a loud crack and the gun fell from the duke's fingers, skittering across the floor.

"I will kill you for that!" the duke yelled, and lowered his shoulders, running straight for Rolfe.

Despite his years, the duke was still a strong and solid man. He rushed at Rolfe, throwing him back, knocking his head against the wall. They wrestled each other and in the confusion and the darkness, the duke managed to knock Rolfe's weapon from his hands. It rolled across the floor, stopping nearly at Cassia's feet. It was her father's walking stick.

When Cassia looked up, the duke had grabbed his gun and was pushing it up against Rolfe's chin. A prickle of fear, real fear, ran down the length of her spine.

That fear spurred Cassia to action. She picked up the walking stick and lifted it high, bringing it down hard on the duke's head. The wood cracked from the force of her blow, snapping the stick in two. The duke crumpled unconscious to the floor.

Cassia rushed to Rolfe's side. "Rolfe, are you all right?"

"I'm fine, but I thought I was supposed to be the one saving you."

"You did. If you hadn't come in when you did, he would have hit me and then he would have killed me." She helped Rolfe to his feet. "He wanted the document. I told him I didn't have it. He didn't believe me when I said I didn't know where it was." She paused. "Why did you come back?"

Rolfe shook his head to clear it. "We were nearly to the corner of the street when I stopped the coach. I wanted to get the pistol Hadrian had given me, just in case I needed it. I told Dante to go on ahead and investigate what Geoffrey was up to. He was going to wait for me to arrive. When I came in the house, Quigman told me you had gone to the study. He had thought you closed the door because you wanted some privacy to read, but I knew you wouldn't do that. You never would have closed that door."

"I never told you that."

Rolfe looked at her. "Some things need not be told to be understood."

He glanced down at the duke's unconscious body lying on the floor. "It seems my suspicions about Geoffrey were unfounded. The true culprit was the duke all along."

Rolfe reached down and picked up the half of the walking stick that was lying near his feet, testing its weight in his hand. "Remind me never to get on the wrong side of you when you're wielding a stick."

As he lowered it, something small and white fluttered out from inside. "What the bloody hell?"

Cassia picked the object up. It was a piece of paper, yellow with age. She knew even before opening it what it was. It was the mysterious document. She remembered what her father had written, how, if she thought on it long enough, she would figure out where it was. She thought she had looked everywhere. She had forgotten one thing.

Her father never went anywhere without that walking stick.

Cassia unfolded the sheet carefully, holding it under the light of the candle.

"This is the document my father wrote to me about. It names all the original Regicides, including himself."

Rolfe peered inside the hollowed-out stick. "Clever how he had it hidden in his walking stick all along," he said. "I would guess the Duke of Manton's name is included on that list."

"Yes, it is, as well as a few other prominent court men. But why, Rolfe? Why would my father leave me something such as this?"

"He said it would protect you. I had my suspicions when you mentioned the engraving on his watch. I had Dante do a little checking. Cassia, your father amassed his fortune through blackmail. Is the Earl of Swindale's name on the list?"

Cassia scanned the list. "Yes, it is, right here. Why do you ask?"

"Your father used that document to blackmail many of the men on it. The estate in Lancashire he left to you was formerly owned by Swindale. When I could find no record of any monetary transaction for the exchange of the property, I started to grow suspicious. Most of your father's fortune was amassed that way.

"The last man he attempted to blackmail was the Duke of Manton. He tried to force him into having his son marry you. The duke is a powerful man. He could not risk being exposed as one of he Regicides. When you refused Malcolm's proposal, the duke most probably figured your father would continue to use the document in any way he could."

Rolfe glanced at the duke, still lying unmoving on the floor.

"I would wager the duke decided the only way to end it would be to kill your father and take the document so no one would ever know the true role he had played."

Cassia looked up at him. "What do we do now?"

Rolfe took the document from her. He refolded it and tucked it in his coat pocket. "We will give this to the person who has the right to the information it contains and let him decide what to do."

He took Cassia's hand, leading her from the room. "The king once said his one wish was to know who the men were who killed his father. We are going to grant that wish for him tonight."

Epilogue

"A toast!"

Dante stood from his chair at one end of the long dining table, raising his wineglass before him. The dining room at Seagrave House was ablaze with candlelight, the table covered with a feast for this, their last dinner together that season.

"To our host and hostess, Rolfe and Cassia. The social season draws to its end and you prepare to leave for your bucolic existence in Sussex. As you pass away the long lonely months ahead, may you always remember to keep a warm fire burning in your hearth by day, and," Dante added, winking, "a warmer fire yet burning in your bedchamber by night!"

"Here, here," chorused the others sitting around the table.

Cassia laughed, shaking her head. "I don't think that will be a problem."

"We obviously need not press the same advice upon you, my friend," Rolfe said to Dante. "I hear tell the fires in France burn even hotter than their English cousins."

Dante grinned. "Yes, well, I'll be sure to let you know whether there is any truth to that rumor upon my return—if I am ever permitted to return, that is."

"You'd best take care, else you'll take my place among the court as the Exiled Earl."

"When will you be returning, Dante?" asked Mara, setting down her wineglass.

"Whenever our good sovereign sees fit to allow me back in the country. He was none too pleased with me when he summoned me to Whitehall to inform me of my new position. A special envoy to France, he called it, but we really know what he means. When last I checked, I was to be occupied with this assignment well into the next century."

"I warned you to be careful," Rolfe said.

"I had only good intentions in this," Dante said in his own defense. "His Majesty will realize that once he has the chance to cool his anger and think on it with a sensible head. In the meantime, a journey abroad is just what I need right now."

"His Majesty must have been beside himself when he learned that Frances Stuart and the Duke of Richmond had eloped," Cassia said, "especially after she indicated that she would finally be willing to allow the king her favors. But what still puzzles me is how he ever learned of your involvement in it, Dante."

"I owe that bit of assistance to that harpy, Barbara Palmer. She came upon Frances and me at that little gathering of hers. We were in the midst of a discussion about the plans for Richmond to come and spirit her off. When Lady Castlemaine questioned me in that, eh, *subtle* way of hers, I managed to throw her off the scent, so to speak. When the elopement became known, she must have figured it all out and ran straight for the king to fill his ears."

He smiled then, a wicked sort of smile. "You needn't worry, though. I will find a way to pay her back in kind."

"And you'll have plenty of time to think of a fitting retribution while you're frittering away the months in

France," Hadrian said. "You're lucky you weren't thrown in the Tower."

"You're lucky you weren't castrated," added Rolfe.

"Good God, Rolfe, bite your tongue. His Majesty may have been angry at my involvement, but I don't think he is completely off the hooks. Castrate me? The Rakehell Earl? It speaks of insanity. Actually, I'm looking forward to my little journey. Exile in France at the court of the Sun King can hardly be called punishment for a man with my tastes in amusement."

He took another sip of his wine, turning to Rolfe. "That explains my hasty departure, but what of you, Rolfe? Why this sudden eagerness for the countryside?"

Rolfe looked at Cassia. "My work here is done. My assignment is concluded."

"With the Duke of Manton having confessed to killing my father," Cassia said, "my innocence has been proven and I am finally free."

"Yes," added Rolfe, "I promised my wife a quiet life in Sussex. Now that he has been publicly identified as one of the Regicides, the duke is occupying a cell in the Tower awaiting his execution."

"And to think Cassia was nearly wed to his son," Mara said. "Thank the Lord you managed to avoid that one. I shudder to think what would have happened had the match gone forward."

Cassia nodded. "Malcolm still states he had no knowledge of his father's involvement with the Regicides, and as there is no proof otherwise, he will remain free."

"And what of your cousin Geoffrey, Cassia? We were all so certain he was the real culprit."

"The only thing Geoffrey was guilty of was stupidity. Despite the fact that he seemed so suspect, he was never actually involved with any of it. His only vice was his greed and his liking for the gaming tables. When the duke offered to pay him for stealing my father's watch, Geoffrey had no suspicions. He was far too busy counting the promised coin. The night Dante's man saw him attempting to break into my father's office, he was working for the duke again. He was unknowingly acting as a decoy to lure Rolfe away from Seagrave House so the duke could get his hands on the document."

"Yes," Rolfe added, "and on Cassia as well. I don't know what saint in heaven made me stop and go back for the pistol that night, but whoever it was, he has my abject thanks. I don't want to think of what my life would have been like without Cassia in it."

Cassia smiled. "Geoffrey has since agreed to accept Rolfe's offer of financial support in occupying my family's seat in Cambridgeshire. His agreement is much owing, I'm sure, to his need to avoid the debt collectors who are now camping out on his doorstep."

"If I were you, I'd be sure to keep a sharp eye on any valuables," Dante said.

"That has already been arranged," replied Rolfe. "Seagrave's solicitor, Mr. Finchley, will be supervising everything. We're hoping the venture will keep Geoffrey occupied and far enough from the city to allow him to mend his ways."

"What about you, Hadrian?" Dante asked then. "When are you off for Ireland?"

"We'll be traveling to Dorset by way of Sussex with Rolfe and Cassia. Then, after a brief visit with my Aunt Hesteria at Rossingham, we will be off to return to Kulhaven. We hope to be back home by spring so Mara can ready herself for the birth."

"So, it seems," Rolfe said, "everyone is off to their own parts of the world."

"Not exactly."

Cordelia, who was sitting beside Cassia in an ensemble made—down to her silk stockings, entirely in red—and who had heretofore been listening silently to the conversation, suddenly spoke up. "With all of you leaving, I will be left here alone."

At that moment, a knock sounded on the door in the hall outside.

Rolfe stood.

"If you would be so kind as to hold that thought, Lady Haslit."

Everyone was silent with anticipation while Rolfe left the room. Everyone, that is, except Cordelia, who had no idea about what was going on. Rolfe returned a short time later, only to remain in the doorway.

"My dear Cordelia, Cassia and I discussed this very thing at length when we first decided to leave for Ravenwood. We came to the conclusion that it just wouldn't do for us to leave you here among the vice and debauchery of the city. I mean, there is your reputation to consider. So I have employed the services of a chaperon for you. . . ."

"A chaperon! But I am a married lady. I have no need of a chaperon. I . . ."

The door opened to reveal a very large man waiting in the entrance hall.

"Percy!"

Cordelia flew from her chair and ran straight into her husband's arms.

"This is Percival?" Dante said quietly.

"If I were you," Rolfe muttered in a low voice, "I wouldn't call him by that name. To anyone except his wife, he prefers to be called either Haslit or just plain 'Pierce' for his well-known ability with his sword."

"I'm much obliged for the warning."

"Everyone," Cordelia announced, beaming like a giddy schoolgirl, dragging her mammoth of a husband by the arm into the room, "this is my husband, Percival Fanshaw. Percy, dear, these are all my friends."

Percival had to stoop his head to make it through the doorway. "A pleasure to meet you all," he said, his voice a deep, rich baritone. "Thank you for taking such good care of my wife while I have been away."

"Why didn't you write and tell me you were coming?" Cordelia asked him, still smiling.

Percival motioned to Rolfe. "It was Rolfe who arranged it all. Even I didn't know of it. We were off the coast of northern France when I received a summons to return to the city for an extended leave of absence. I left immediately."

"But how did you ever manage it?" Cordelia asked Rolfe, looking at him as if he had just worked a miracle.

Rolfe smiled. "I had a long talk with His Majesty over a bottle of his favorite brandy. Being a man who is inclined to epicurean and passionate pursuits, he agreed with my thoughts on the matter. We both came to the conclusion that your husband had done more than his duty in his service to the Crown."

"I never would have dared to dream that you'd be coming home," she said, staring up at her husband as if she expected him to vanish at any moment.

Rolfe put his arm around Cassia's waist and pulled her closer to his side. He pressed a kiss to her forehead, saying more to her than to Cordelia, "Some dreams, my dear lady, are well worth the chase."

Author's Note

Mark Twain once said, "Truth is more of a stranger than fiction." Nowhere else have I seen this more than when I was researching *Chasing Dreams*.

King Charles II is known throughout history as the Merry Monarch. He was a cheerful sovereign at his restoration to the English throne; he had good reason to be. He'd just come through one of England's worst periods in history the victor, and though he may not have been the country's greatest king politically, he was certainly one of her most famous. It has been said of Charles that "he never said a foolish thing, and never did a wise one." He had great wit, was fascinated by all things scientific, and did amass quite a collection of clocks and timekeeping devices. But his youth had been filled with fear and loss, disappointment and deprivation, which made him seek the easy, pleasureful way of life. This, as well, made it all the more difficult for him to refuse the masses who brought their needs to him. He is known for his generosity and his humanity. He was never cruel and was ever forgiving. And he was, indeed, a lover of women, not in the selfish, avaricious sort of way, but in a way that showed his true appreciation for the indolent epicurean ways of life.

The love affair between King Charles and Barbara Palmer, Lady Castlemaine, is legendary and spanned more than a decade. He coddled her and saw to her every whim to such an extent that there were, indeed, rumors of her practicing witchcraft. This was a serious charge in the seventeenth century, one not to be spoken of lightly, but it was the only reasonable explanation at the time for this truly unreasonable hold she seemed to have over him.

The notion of King Charles's formal request to have Lady Castlemaine appointed to Queen Catherine's bedchamber was a true one. It came not long after Catherine's arrival in England and did, indeed, give the princess from Portugal quite a turn. Catherine did refuse it, and Charles did insist upon it. Her subsequent and most mysterious acquiescence to Lady Castlemaine's appointment has puzzled historians for centuries since.

Equally true is the occasion of Catherine's great illness in 1663. Charles was at his most attentive during this trial, hardly leaving her bedside, and was seen to weep when the chances for her recovery had seemed, at best, miraculous. Catherine did survive the ordeal, one that has not been positively explained, and came out of it with a husband who looked on her with new and more appreciative eyes. Sadly, this queen who wanted nothing more than to give her husband an heir would never be able to bear a child to him.

For the purposes of this novel, I have taken license to alter one event during this period—and that simply to bring it about sooner than it actually happened. Frances Stuart—"La Belle Stuart," as she was called among her Whitehall contemporaries— did prove one of King Charles's most perplexing conquests. She eluded him at every turn, toying with him with an innocence that only endeared her to him all the more. Her elopement with the Duke of Richmond (which occurred in late 1664, rather than a year earlier as portrayed in this novel) caused quite a scandal and did result in her husband being banished from the palace—for a time. But King Charles, being blessed with an uncommonly forgiving spirit, did allow the couple back, and was eventually rewarded with those favors which had been denied him while Frances Stuart had been a maid.

I found the period of the Restoration so fascinating that I will be continuing it in the third book of the trilogy that began with *Tempting Fate,* continued with *Chasing Dreams,* and will end with *Stealing Heaven.* In it, you will hear the story of Dante Tremaine, and of how this charming rakehell who, like King Charles, had a number of women but who finds himself faced with the one he finally loves—the one he may never be able to have. Join me again and reacquaint yourself with Hadrian and Mara, Rolfe and Cassia when they come together with Dante as he tries to steal away his own little bit of heaven. I offer you this: it promises to be a rollicking ride.

⬥ TOPAZ

WHEN THE HEART IS DARING

☐ **MOONSPUN DREAMS by Elizabeth Gregg.** When Dessa Fallon's parents died, she was left at the mercy of a man who would do anything for their money. The only person she could trust in this spider's web of greed, lust, and deceit was the tender Ben Poole. Now on a desperate quest for her missing brother on the lawless frontier, Dessa only had Ben, whose actions spoke louder than his words to teach her everything about being a woman. (405730—$4.99)

☐ **TARNISHED HEARTS by Raine Cantrell.** To Trevor Shelby, Leah Reese was a beauty forbidden to him by class barriers: he was a Southern aristocrat and she was an overseer's daughter. Trev's tormented past taught him nothing of tenderness, and he wasn't prepared for Leah's warmth and trust. His kisses taught her about passion, but she taught him about love. (404424—$4.99)

☐ **RAWHIDE AND LACE by Margaret Brownley.** Libby Summerhill couldn't wait to get out of Deadman's Gulch—a lawless mining town filled with gunfights, brawls, and uncivilized mountain men—men like Logan St. John. He knew his town was no place for a woman and the sooner Libby and her precious baby left for Boston, the better. But how could he bare to lose this spirited woman who melted his heart of stone forever? (404610—$4.99)

☐ **TOUCH OF NIGHT by Carin Rafferty.** Ariel Dantes was alone in the world and desperate to find her lost brother. Lucien Morgret was the only one who could help her, but he was a man of danger. As Ariel falls deeper and deeper into Lucien's spell, she is drawn toward desires she cannot resist, even if it means losing her heart and soul by surrendering to Lucien's touch . . . (404432—$4.99)

*Prices slightly higher in Canada

Buy them at your local bookstore or use this convenient coupon for ordering.

PENGUIN USA
P.O. Box 999 — Dept. #17109
Bergenfield, New Jersey 07621

Please send me the books I have checked above.
I am enclosing $_____ (please add $2.00 to cover postage and handling). Send check or money order (no cash or C.O.D.'s) or charge by Mastercard or VISA (with a $15.00 minimum). Prices and numbers are subject to change without notice.

Card #_____ Exp. Date _____
Signature_____
Name_____
Address_____
City _____ State _____ Zip Code _____

For faster service when ordering by credit card call **1-800-253-6476**
Allow a minimum of 4-6 weeks for delivery. This offer is subject to change without notice.

◆▼◆ TOPAZ

PASSION'S PROMISES

☐ **THE TOPAZ MAN FAVORITES: SECRETS OF THE HEART Five Stories by Madeline Baker, Jennifer Blake, Georgina Gentry, Shirl Henke, and Patricia Rice.** In this collection of romances, the Topaz Man has gathered together stories from five of his favorite authors—tales which he truly believes capture all the passion and promise of love.
(405528—$4.99)

☐ **DASHING AND DANGEROUS Five Sinfully Seductive Heroes by Mary Balogh, Edith Layton, Melinda McRae, Anita Mills, Mary Jo Putney.** They're shameless, seductive, and steal your heart with a smile. Now these irresistible rogues, rakes, rebels, and renegades are captured in five all new, deliciously sexy stories by America's favorite authors of romantic fiction.
(405315—$4.99)

☐ **BLOSSOMS Five Stories Mary Balogh, Patricia Rice, Margaret Evans Porter, Karen Harper, Patricia Oliver.** Celebrate the arrival of spring with a bouquet of exquisite stories by five acclaimed authors of romantic fiction. Full of passion and promise, scandal and heartache, and rekindled desire, these heartfelt tales prove that spring is a time for new beginnings as well as second chances.
(182499—$4.99)

☐ **THE TOPAZ MAN PRESENTS: A DREAM COME TRUE** Here is a collection of love stories from such authors as Jennifer Blake, Georgina Gentry, Shirl Henke, Anita Mills, and Becky Lee Weyrich. Each story is unique, and each author has a special way of making dreams come true.
(404513—$4.99)

*Prices slightly higher in Canada

Buy them at your local bookstore or use this convenient coupon for ordering.

PENGUIN USA
P.O. Box 999 — Dept. #17109
Bergenfield, New Jersey 07621

Please send me the books I have checked above.
I am enclosing $_____ (please add $2.00 to cover postage and handling). Send check or money order (no cash or C.O.D.'s) or charge by Mastercard or VISA (with a $15.00 minimum). Prices and numbers are subject to change without notice.

Card #_____ Exp. Date _____
Signature_____
Name_____
Address_____
City _____ State _____ Zip Code _____

For faster service when ordering by credit card call **1-800-253-6476**

Allow a minimum of 4-6 weeks for delivery. This offer is subject to change without notice.

ARE YOU HAVING TROUBLE FINDING YOUR FAVORITE AUTHORS?

NOW YOU CAN ORDER REGENCY AND TOPAZ ROMANCES BY PHONE!

1-800-253-6476
with Visa or Mastercard